Extraordinary Means

DONNA LEVIN

SIMON AND SCHUSTER

NEW YORK LONDON TORONTO
SYDNEY TOKYO SINGAPORE

CALIFORNIA STREET

Simon and Schuster
Simon & Schuster Building
Rockefeller Center
1230 Avenue of the Americas
New York, New York 10020

SIMON AND SCHUSTER and colophon are registered trademarks
of Simon & Schuster Inc.

Designed by Caroline Cunningham
Manufactured in the United States of America

10 9 8 7 6 5 4 3 2 1

Library of Congress Cataloging in Publication Data

Levin, Donna.
    California Street / Donna Levin.
        p.   cm.
    I. Title.
    PS3562.E88955C35   1990
    813'.54—dc20   90-34575
                                              CIP

ISBN 0–671–69300–X

For Gloria Loomis

ACKNOWLEDGMENTS

A lot of people have been better to me than I deserve. Among them are Eleni Benetatos, Joni Levin Erez, Rich Dyer, Bernard Frankel, M.D., Donna Gillespie, Suzanne Juergensen, Claire Levin, Helen Levin, Marvin Levin, Brad Newsham, Kevin Starr, John Winch, and Waimea Williams. Each of them generously made a unique contribution toward the writing of this book; they all know what it was, and I hope they also know how much I appreciate it.

Thanks to my editors, Nancy Nicholas, Trish Lande, and Cheryl Weinstein.

And to Michael Bernick, for a thousand daily kindnesses.

Now every normal person is only approximately normal: his ego resembles that of the psychotic in one point or another, in a greater or lesser degree, and its distance from one end of the scale and proximity to the other may provisionally serve as a measure of what we have indefinitely spoken of as 'modification of the ego.'

SIGMUND FREUD, Analysis Terminable and Interminable

Not only is there no God, but try getting a plumber on weekends.

WOODY ALLEN

CHAPTER I

THE SIRENS OF LA CIENEGA

On Tuesday afternoon, Joel's office phone rang, just after his last patient, and he recognized Margot's voice, husky and blue.

"Doctor," she said, "I need your help."

Anyone could have said that, and with anyone else—five billion people on this planet!—he would have known how to respond. But with Margot . . . She was the wife of Joel's oldest friend (though the word *friend* was generous), and as of five days ago, Joel had promised himself that he would never see either of them again as long as he lived. It was the rational way to behave; it was how a directive therapist would have advised him to handle it. Quit cold turkey. Dry out.

True, since he hadn't informed either Margot or her husband of this decision, and since he usually spoke to one or both of them several times a week, he could reasonably have expected Margot to call him at *some* point. Still, he had the odd feeling of surprise.

"What can I do for you?" he asked, in his best psychoanalyst baritone.

"Can you come over here?" Margot asked. "Right away?" She sounded calm enough, but now he knew it was something serious, because she usually began her phone calls with five minutes of did-you-hear-abouts and wait-till-I-tell-yous.

"To Playground?" In the background he could hear the squalls of children, and a high-pitched woman's voice parroting, *There, there. There, there.*

"Yes. And if you could hurry—"

"What's wrong? Is someone hurt?"

"N-no."

"Shall I call the police?"

"Oh, God, no." Joel distinguished another voice. *This is ridiculous, absolutely* . . . "I'd rather not involve the police. I know you can help us. Do hurry, if you can." Now she had the clipped, only slightly harried tone of an heiress in crisis. "You're so close." Then she clicked off.

Joel hopped into his car. He indulged himself in the metaphor of a fireman sliding down a pole into his truck, although he knew he didn't exactly have the dimensions of a hero: He was no more than average height, with the slim build of a runner. His curly black hair and his brown eyes, enlarged by stylishly outsized tortoiseshell glasses, didn't add to the image; and certainly his nose, just large enough to give his face "character," didn't, either.

But he *was* close, as Margot had said. His office was in "therapy row," nine square blocks in San Francisco which, because of its proximity to two hospitals, had attracted a number of his fellow practitioners. This quiet army of Ph.D.'s, M.F.C.C.'s, and L.C.S.W.'s had gradually taken over flats here in the quasi-commercial section of Pacific Heights, where the hills, stuffed with old money, descended into trendy shops along upper Fillmore, that same street which had once given its name to a famous concert hall.

Margot was all of twelve blocks away. But in San Francisco, you could travel through as many income levels, ethnic groups, and religious doctrines in the same distance. You could go from boutiques to dime stores, nouvelle cuisine to packaged sandwiches, BMWs to battered Buicks, and back again. Once you passed California Street, though, a subtle shift occurred: Even though gentrification was reaching down here, too, you were definitely in "the Fillmore."

California Street separated many neighborhoods like that— Chinatown and downtown, Presidio Heights and Jordan Park, Seacliff and the Richmond—but here, Joel thought, it was like crossing the river Styx, with souls from both sides washed up on the shore. As he waited for the light to change, Joel recognized the black woman in fuzzy yellow bedroom slippers who sat on the sidewalk with her back against the window of the croissanterie, laughing and then crying, with her head in her hands. Across the street, above the liquor store, hung a large banner: THE LOTTERY IS HERE.

The Playground Center occupied an old Victorian on Eddy, a couple of blocks from the projects. A private, nonprofit corporation, which had been formed "for the purpose of providing free day care for the children of qualified parents," it was Margot Harvey's creation, calling, and *raison d'être*. The house itself was blue-gray, and covered with little brown scabs, the mementos of this past year's rainfall; the maintenance budget had all gone into plumbing repairs.

Joel parked in the driveway.

Margot was standing on the porch. Like the old woman who lived in a shoe, she was surrounded by children: One little girl was rubbing her face with the hem of Margot's blue-and-white flowered dress, while another, who had wriggled between Margot's legs, appeared headless. Margot herself held a baby in her arms; there was a wet spot on the front of her dress where the baby had drooled. Margot wore a modern rendition of a cloche hat—white, with the whisper of a blue veil—but it was knocked askew, apparently by the same baby, who was now trying to clutch at her dark hair.

And this was how Joel knew that he was really in love: that she could have been standing there in a wrinkled flannel nightgown and argyle socks, and he still would have found her as sexy as when she had sprawled on his bed the week before, showing her thighs in rose-patterned white stockings.

Behind her, Joel could see Mrs. Tuttle—turtlenecked, too skinny, white-haired—and Rosa Avera, Margot's assistant. Rosa was a hard-eyed Filipina, who, although she did not resemble Margot otherwise, was of the same height and build. Her long black hair, when loose, reached to her waist, but it was braided today, and wrapped in a coronet around her head. When she smiled (which she did occasionally), she revealed a sparkling set of braces. She went everywhere she could with Margot, and had even adopted Margot's preference for lacy, drop-waisted dresses.

"I'm so glad you're here," Margot said, and her greeting was a limp version of her usual welcome: *There you are.* She handed the baby to Mrs. Tuttle, and gently pulled her hem from the little girl's fingers. "The children should be in the playroom, don't you think, Mrs. Tuttle? Rosa, perhaps you wouldn't mind giving Mrs. Tuttle a hand."

"What's wrong?" Joel asked quickly. He had never heard Margot use that tone of voice before: stiff, formal.

Mrs. Tuttle was muttering oh-dears as she shooed the children ahead of her, but Rosa did not move. "Why did you call him?" she demanded, indicating Joel with a sideways jerk of her head. "He'll get us in worse trouble."

Nice to see you, too, Rosa, Joel thought. But Rosa hated everyone who was close to Margot. He took Margot's arm. "Let's go inside."

"You'll be sorry," Rosa *humphed* behind them.

Margot seemed to revive at his touch. Once inside the foyer she hissed, "You know, I do think we should hurry. Come upstairs with me."

Upstairs? He didn't trust himself alone with her anymore. But he followed the switching blue of her skirt up to the second floor. She was wearing those white lace stockings again, too. . . . From the second floor, Margot led him up another flight of stairs—long and narrow—which dead-ended at a door. He counted as they climbed, one, two, four, six. . . . From the light shining underneath he knew that it opened onto the roof. Margot reached for the door with her long, square-tipped nails, then dropped back a step. "There's a woman up there," she whispered to Joel. "I didn't see what happened exactly. Mrs. Tuttle was alone with the kids for a while. She's so good with them, but . . . this woman came in and said she wanted to take her little boy home. Mrs. Tuttle almost let them leave before she realized that the woman wasn't Horatio's mother. Then she tried to stop her, and the woman ran up to the roof. I just happened to be on my way over, to check on some things."

"Horatio's one of the kids."

"That's right." Margot rubbed the back of her hand across her forehead, under the little veil. Her hat was still crooked; he had to resist an urge to straighten it. "He's up there, too."

"You've got to call the police."

"We—we can't," she said.

"If something happens—"

"Please. Trust me. I trust *you.* I know you can help us." Her eyes were big and blue, with thick dark lashes; she wasn't wearing makeup, and they were a child's confiding, unspoiled eyes. How could he say no to her, act like a wimp, when he could be a hero?

"Has she threatened anything? Said anything she wants?"

Margot shook her head. "I wasn't here. I didn't see."

He sucked in a breath. "All right. You'd better go downstairs."

She squeezed his arm. "Thank you."

He watched her descend, turn at the banister, and disappear. After a moment he cautiously opened the door and stepped onto the roof.

The light blinded him. Then gradually he saw the expanse of tar and gravel glittering in the afternoon sun; the line of chimneys stretching across the row of houses; and at the edge of the roof, looking over the facade to the street below, a middle-aged woman in a rumpled camel-hair suit stood holding the hand of a black child about two years old, who chewed on his free wrist. At the sound of Joel's arrival, the woman turned around.

"Hello," Joel said.

The woman held up one hand to shield her face from the sun, and stared at him. She was framed by a net of telephone wires.

"I'm Joel."

"Oh, terrific." The wind lifted her wispy, bleached yellow hair, and blew the jacket of her suit open; her large bosom was shaped into the twin points of ice cream cones. "Isn't *this* a pretty kettle of fish. You a cop?"

"No, a psychoanalyst." Joel smiled.

"I shoulda known. A shrink. I've met a lot of you guys. You all look the same." She added grudgingly, "You're cuter than most."

"I was hoping we could talk," he said casually. He didn't like how near the edge of the roof she was. And why didn't they keep the roof door locked?

"I don't have time. We'll be taking off soon."

"Where are you going?"

"There's a helicopter that's going to land here and take us home. I have a nice house in Pacific Heights. I've got lots of toys for him there. I know the mayor. My ex-husband might try to stop us, though. Al. He's a loser."

She pulled the little boy closer to her. Horatio wore red shorts and an undershirt; his skin was a creamy milk chocolate, except for a rash across his chest. "This is my little boy," the woman said.

Joel crouched. "Pleased to meet you," he said to Horatio. "What's your name?"

Horatio was gnawing on his arm now. Joel's eyesight—even

with his industrial-strength glasses—wasn't good enough to tell for sure, but he thought that there was a line of marks nearly up to Horatio's shoulder.

"His name's Robbie," the woman said, rubbing his hair. Horatio moved his head away. "You've scared him," she said.

Joel unbent his knees. The left one twinged. "I'm sorry."

"Huh," the woman grunted. "Shrinks. I've been to a million of 'em. None of 'em did me any good." She squinted at Joel. "The handsome ones are the worst, they always try to sleep with you. You're a real lady killer, too."

She wants to come down, Joel reassured himself. *She just needs an excuse. I bet she didn't want to come up here in the first place—Rosa probably cornered her.* "What's *your* name?" he asked. *Go slow*, he thought. *Get friendly with her.*

"So now you want to know my name," the woman replied coquettishly. "It's Betty, Betty Klass. With a *Y*, I don't go for this Bette Davis business, she always acted like such a tramp." She took a step forward, and Joel was glad—he wanted to get closer, gradually, so he could grab Horatio if necessary. "Are you married?" she demanded. "You're not wearing a ring. I bet you're married and don't wear a ring. I've met a lot of married guys like that, in bars."

Her last words were half-obscured by a wheezing bus. "It's hard to talk up here," Joel said above the noise. "Perhaps you'd like to come inside."

"That bitch downstairs will try to take my baby boy away. The little tramp." Betty tried to pick Horatio up, but he whined. Joel reflexively moved closer, held out his arms—but Betty stepped back, and her mouth twitched. A shudder ran through her body, starting at her waist and ending with the oscillation of her chin. "I couldn't remember where he was," she explained. "I thought he was lost. Then I was passing by on my way to the beauty shop and I realized that I left him here this morning."

The word *lost* struck Joel, like the first drop of rain on the sidewalk. *She lost a child. Robbie.* But this was hardly the time for confrontive tactics. He had to put a Band-Aid on *this* gunshot wound. He bit into his lower lip until his nerves relayed some measure of pain, wishing he had two years with her: time to let her remember, time to let her forget. Two years alone on the roof together: the sky so close, the web of wires, the toot, beep, *whoosh* of cars.

"Are you divorced?" Betty asked. "I bet you're a good ex-husband, not like my Al. I bet women love to run their fingers through those sexy black curls. You've got a great body, too, I can tell, even under that suit. Not like my Al, with that disgusting belly. And I like men who wear suits and ties, they look respectable. I bet you're a really good fuck." She held up her hand again. "I can't see you. The sun's in my eyes."

Joel moved into the shadow of the roof access. "Is that better?"

Horatio whimpered and Betty patted him on the shoulder. "I don't know how your wife let you get away. You have bedroom eyes, you know. Take off your glasses."

"I can't see very well without them." That was an understatement. Without his glasses, the world looked as if he were viewing it from the bottom of an unchlorinated swimming pool.

"Maybe you'll be my shrink. You're someone I can talk to. I feel like you understand."

Good, good, good. She had thrown herself a rope and not even known it; that was always the way it was. "I'd like to talk to you now," he said. "Won't you come inside?" He did not move any closer, but he offered one hand.

"I've been to a lot of shrinks," Betty reiterated. Coyly, "What can *you* promise me?"

"That there's hope." He said it without thinking.

Betty scrunched up her face in fury. "You're full of it!" she snapped. Then she picked up Horatio with a grunt. He wailed, and his tiny red sneakers kicked the air. "Shut up!" she barked. To Joel, "Go away. We're leaving now." She was moving backward, with her head tilted up to watch the sky. "I can hear the helicopter," she said. "Can't you? It's coming now."

Oh, God, Joel thought, taking in the distance toward the edge of the roof. She wasn't looking where she was going, and her balance was shaky with the squirming Horatio. But if he ran toward her she might run away, and then . . .

"Mrs. Klass," he said loudly, and with much more authority than he felt, "I can help you if you let me."

"You'll want to talk to me for ten minutes, then you'll never want to see me again. Every shrink I ever went to was like that, because they couldn't do anything for me."

"It could be different this time."

"That's what my ex-husband always used to say. Whenever he wanted me to take him back."

"It takes time. Sometimes it's scary. But I'll be there. We'll work together," he crooned. He was being seductive, but that hardly mattered now. "It can be an adventure."

"An adventure. Hah. My foot."

"What you feel now," Joel said, "you won't always feel."

She swayed back and forth, holding the boy, who struggled against her embrace. Someone started honking below, and a herd of cars took up the call, like a pack of hounds who have picked up the scent of a fox. When it subsided, Betty said, "You'll call the cops, or my ex-husband, which is worse, let me tell you." The wind blew her hair into her eyes and she tried to wriggle her hand around Horatio so she could brush it away.

"No." Joel took a step toward her; the gravel crunched. He stopped. He felt the wind on the back of his head, the perspiration on his neck, under his hair. "I won't let anyone call the police. I promise."

Horatio had finally squirmed out of Betty's arms. He was crying. He tried to run away from her, but she grabbed him by the collar of his undershirt. The elastic stretched out, holding him back. Betty raised her other arm. Her mouth was twitching again and Joel saw her arm start to come down hard, but in that moment, when she was concentrated on Horatio, Joel's legs seemed to know they had time to make the necessary sprint. He didn't make the decision; he only saw his own arms wrapping around the boy's chest. The collar of Horatio's undershirt slipped from Betty's hand. And then Joel felt the weight of the boy against his own chest, felt his small arms flailing his back, heard him scream in his ear. And Betty's shriek, "Give him back! Give him back!" Her nails clawed at Joel's interlocked arms.

But Joel held firm. "Sssh," he murmured, to both of them. "It's all right, everything's going to be all right."

Whimpering, Betty took a few steps backward. One of her spike heels twisted, and she plopped down on the roof, her skirt flaring out around her like a large beige flower. She rocked back and forth, hugging herself, sobbing.

Horatio looked down, fascinated, from the height of Joel's neck. He giggled, then stuck his wrist into his mouth.

Gripping Horatio with one arm, Joel held his other hand out. "Come with me now," he said to Betty. "We'll go inside and we'll talk for as long as you want."

Downstairs, Joel whispered to Margot, "We can't turn her in. I told her we wouldn't."

Margot nodded. They were standing in the foyer. Joel raked back his wind-blown hair—he hadn't realized how long it was getting—and took a deep breath. He felt the sweat on his forehead, then hoped that Margot would notice it.

"That's ridiculous," Rosa snapped. "She's a menace. We could sue her for trespassing at the very least."

"There'd be other questions," Joel said coolly. He still thought that Rosa had driven Betty up there.

Margot had almost grabbed Horatio from Joel's arms when he had come down the stairs, and she still held him, though he looked none too pleased at it. Margot, at least, was restored to her beloved histrionic self. "It's okay, Rosa," she laughed. "We don't need Betty's money." She winked at Joel. "We still have something cooking with the Ford Foundation."

"Get down," Horatio suggested.

"All right, cuddle bun."

In the parlor across from them, a dozen children were drawing with crayons on a single, room-length piece of paper. ("It will be such a perfectly lovely mural," Mrs. Tuttle had gushed.) Horatio toddled to join them, and promptly wrested a crayon from the nearest child, who howled. Margot patted Rosa's shoulder, and Rosa, grumbling, went to mediate.

Betty was in the kitchen, drinking tea that Mrs. Tuttle had made. What bits of their conversation Joel could hear was about wallpaper. Betty was now oriented, responsive, and apologetic about her "mistake" about Horatio. She had also said that she would come to see him on Thursday.

Joel thought that she had had a brief psychotic episode. He didn't believe that she was fundamentally dangerous, but certainly she was unpredictable, and perhaps she should be hospitalized. Not reporting this incident meant that he was crawling on an ethical ledge. But he felt the need, greater than those other risks, to keep his promises to her. Which he had made for Margot's sake.

"Doctor." Margot put her arms around him. She often hugged him, certainly more than a married friend should, but she was an affectionate woman . . . and when he felt her small body against his, felt her stray dark hairs tickling his nose, he didn't regret anything. If she knew how he felt, would she still be embracing him? He closed his eyes, just for a second, wanting to forget where they were. "I am *so* grateful," he heard her say.

And then he opened his eyes, and over Margot's head, he saw Rosa glaring at him, holding the disputed crayon like a knife.

Margot let go of him. "You *must*"—she pounded his chest, with the force of lightly thrown Ping-Pong balls—"*no* arguments now—you must have dinner with us tonight."

And for the second time in two hours, Joel broke his resolution to kick the Margot habit. Some day he was going to do a paper on the unconscious dynamics that made "resolutions" impossible to keep. Maybe he could link it to anal eroticism. "Of course," he agreed. "No arguments."

The Harveys had inherited their money; that is, Margot had inherited it. She was from one of the older San Francisco families: fourth generation on her father's side (her great-grandfather had founded the *San Francisco Courier*) and third generation on her mother's side (her maternal grandfather had built a small *schmatte* business into the eponymous department store, Jordan's). Although it had been sold to a conglomerate about twenty years before, Jordan's was still one of the more prestigious places to shop on Union Square.

But in just a generation, the dynamics of her family had changed. Margot still had the money, maybe even too much of it, but her cousin controlled the newspaper now. And Margot—only child of Francis Iddele, third publisher of the *Courier*—had further devalued her personal stock by marrying outside the endogamous tribe of San Francisco aristocrats: to Ted Harvey, an immigrant, like Joel, from Los Angeles.

Ted had been Joel's college roommate, and the two of them had been best friends for what was actually a short period of beer-guzzling contests and late-night breeze shooting, before they had found divergent interests and entered different social orbits at UCLA. They kept on sharing an apartment, though, because it was convenient, and they got along well enough. So Joel had always associated Ted with one of those brief eras in his own personal history that, like JFK's presidency and the Beatles mid-career, become so suffused with nostalgia that one cannot remember them with any clarity. He was living away from home for the first time, and he loved being able to watch TV as late as he pleased, ignore the phone, have a girl *spend the night*, and live on peanut butter.

He had kept in touch with Ted over the years, but it was by accident that they ended up in the same place again. Joel had wanted to return to California to do his internship after getting his doctorate at Columbia; he was tired of New York smells and weather. Still, his native and much-loved Los Angeles was far too small a place to share with his parents. San Francisco seemed the correct psychic distance. The psychoanalytic institute there had a growing reputation and Ted had just moved to the city, having followed his fiancée, Margot, back to her hometown.

Joel arrived just in time to be invited to Ted's wedding, a sprawling, formal event at Grace Cathedral. At the reception at the Stanford Court, Joel met a blond aerobics instructor he ended up dating for a few months, but he never did get a chance to meet Margot that night, other than to make out the silhouette of her face under her heavy veil, as she marched down the aisle on the arm of her then-ailing father.

That had been almost seven years before. What followed were several rather promiscuous years for Joel, but he was just out of a long-term relationship, and felt that he was making up for lost time. And now that the Sexual Revolution had put a totalitarian government in place, he wasn't sorry he'd taken advantage of his opportunities, some of whom Margot herself had indirectly thrown his way, by inviting him to the parties she gave so often.

That was his earliest real memory of Margot: opening the door to him and exclaiming, *"There* you are," as if he were the only guest who mattered and, with his arrival, the party could begin. But then she would disappear and he would only see her dashing around at a distance, trailing conversations like a long silk scarf. When he went to say good-bye, she would squeeze his hand and beg, "Please don't go yet! I wanted so badly to have a chance to talk to you!"

And such was his narcissism, or her acting ability (he could never decide which), that when he heard her gushing over other people that way, he diagnosed it as hysteria—but when she did it with him he believed her.

Gradually, Joel and Ted and Margot had struck that rarest of balances: They were a threesome, a dynamic which persisted even when he brought other women along. Joel hadn't ignored the obvious Oedipal implications of that, he'd just—well, ignored them. Ignored, for example, how he didn't mind going to the theater alone with Margot, if it was something Ted didn't want to see. After all, he went to games alone with Ted, didn't he? And sometimes a cigar was just a cigar. . . . Lately, perhaps, he'd worried about the situation a little, because he had noticed that he was seeing the Harveys more often, in spite of the fact that Ted had begun not only to drink more heavily but to become more contentious when he did.

And then there was that other matter he had noticed, which was that every time Margot touched him she unerringly placed her hand on a nerve ending connected both to his brain and to his genitals.

And then.

Five days before, Margot had buzzed his apartment. "No reason," she shrugged when he asked her why she'd come by. "I just realized that in all the years I've known you, you've never had me over."

"Now that you're here, you can see why," Joel had said. He had moved into his modest studio when he was doing his internship, planning for it to be temporary. "What can I get you to drink? I hope you like three-week-old orange juice or Calistoga water."

That was when she had sprawled on his bed. Granted, it was one of only three places to sit and the only one not littered with books. Joel was compulsive about making his bed, and keeping his clothes clean and pressed—and extremely sloppy about everything else.

"God, the definitive bachelor. Nothing." Then she giggled. "God *is* the definitive bachelor, isn't He?"

But Joel was distracted. Because in all these years, this was the first time he had been alone with her in such a private, *safe* place. And that was when he knew how he felt. He'd always liked her—but suddenly there was the new, ugly face of simple lust, rising out of his unconscious like the Loch Ness monster on steroids.

"Want to go for a walk?" he asked, hearing both how stupid that sounded and how his voice cracked.

"Oh no." She scrambled off the bed. "I just dropped by for a second. Rosa's waiting with the car outside."

Margot and Ted Harvey's house, on the last block of California Street, appeared rather small from the outside. But that was because only the peaks of the terra-cotta-shingled roof were visible above the hedge, giving the impression of a fairly narrow, one-story structure below. You had to go up the drive to see that the yard sloped downward, hiding the much larger ground floor of the white stucco Spanish Revival house.

Still, compared to what the Harveys could afford, it was quite modest. But Margot had shouldered, at least in some ways, a lifestyle that was relentlessly middle class.

Driving over, Joel had wondered whether perhaps he could wean himself slowly from his contact with them. But now, two hours after coaxing Betty off the roof, sitting in the yard behind the big house with Margot and Ted, Joel was wising up to his own scam: He would be like an alcoholic, promising to cut down to a drink a day. Joel sipped his Calistoga and watched Ted, who was grilling steaks on the barbecue. The analogy was appropriate, at least. How things change! When he'd first met Ted, at the age of eighteen, he'd admired him for being able to outdrink the average fraternity pledge party.

It was May, and at seven o'clock it still seemed like late afternoon. Ted wore a starched white chef's hat and a red-checked apron with black lettering that apologized, I MAY NOT BE EFFICIENT, BUT I'M CUTE.

Margot had just finished recounting the story of Horatio's abduction to Ted. "Good old Joey," Ted laughed. "He was always getting me out of the shitcan, too. I would have been expelled three times over if it hadn't been for him." He pointed at Joel with his long fork, and winked. "I copied his homework, too." Ted was tall, with a high forehead and a long nose with a slightly bulbous tip. He was Joel's age—thirty-three—and he now possessed a little less hair and a few more wrinkles than when he and Joel had shared the apartment with the triangular living room in Westwood.

"Lovebird, he *saved* us. *Saved* us. And you're making jokes." Margot was sitting at the foot of Joel's lounge chair, wearing a halter top (in spite of the fog rolling in over Seacliff), which exposed the smooth edges of her small white breasts. Her feet were bare, too, and her painted toes looked both exotic and familiar, somehow the most intimate part of her body.

"I'm serious," she insisted, as if sensing Joel's lusty gaze. She was still feigning a pout, which made her sound not serious at all. "Something like this could ruin us. I mean, it really was just a fluke, a woman like that walking in off the street. But this is what people will *remember*."

"A toast," Ted proclaimed. He poured another Scotch for himself. "To Joel Abramowitz, Ph.D., the hero of Playground. Ph.D.—that's 'piled high and deep.' Go easy with that Calistoga, Joey, you know how you get."

"How do I get?" Joel asked, holding tightly to his glass of mineral water. *Don't give him what he wants.* Margot was looking from one to the other of them with wide eyes and sucked-in cheeks. *For her sake.*

"Get down!" Ted flung out his arms and kicked one leg in the air, in a clumsy imitation of a break dancer. "Come on, Joey, take it light."

Maybe this had been going on for longer than Joel realized. Maybe he was only just allowing himself to see the hostility. Whatever. Joel was drawn to these psychoanalytic conundrums, but that didn't alter the fact that Ted had become a shit-faced drunk. It might not be so hard to relinquish the pleasure of his and Margot's company after all.

"I told you we're just about to expand the whole Playground program." Margot spoke quickly, and only then did Joel become aware of how long and awkward the pause had been. "You know, the job-training division for the mothers. It's called Women in Transition Here. WITH. Do you like that? It's positive, it's upbeat, like *with it*. Well, the press release went out this morning, this *morning*, that was the clincher." Her hands scalloped gracefully through the air as she talked. She always did that, quite unconsciously: drawing pictures, describing the peaks and valleys of her experience. "So the timing couldn't possibly have been worse, because we're funded through the next six months, but after that . . . Can you see it?" She puffed out her cheeks and held her arms out in front of her. "At the next fund-raiser, Mrs. Schlossberg: 'Zo, Margot, vat's zis about ze crazy vomen chomping from ze roov?' And Jody Daniels' column tomorrow." A Southern accent: "'Which formah debutante and phil*yan*thropist is pah-laying hostess to suicidal *may*niacs? Our little *spa* knows!'"

Joel chomped on an ice cube. He loved to watch Margot perform, but he felt a stirring of irritation as well. Was that the only reason she had had him risk Horatio's safety and his own career? Bad press?

"It's not the money," Ted insisted. "It's the image. You need the image in this rotten town." He thumped his chest.

"Ask me, I'm the image-maker." Ted had his own PR firm, Harvey & Fairfax, where his partner did any real work that was arguably accomplished. For his clients, Ted could thank Margot's family connections, her community involvement, and her effusive arm-linking at her elaborately catered parties.

Now Ted kept thumping his chest harder and harder, finally accompanying it with a Tarzan wail.

Margot rolled her eyes at Joel, while clapping her hands together slowly. "He's weird," she joked, "but he's mine." Joel felt her grasping for the comradery they used to have; the two of them indulging Ted while he played the clown. Acted out for them. Maybe Ted didn't want to do that anymore.

"So now you've got to take Looney Tunes on the Magical Mystery Tour." Ted jabbed a steak, twisting his mouth critically. "Isn't your schedule full, Big Man on Campus?"

"I'll manage." Now that Betty might be his patient, he couldn't discuss her with the Harveys. Nor did he particularly want to tell Margot that he would not have done what he did if he had known her reasons. Well, maybe the heiress of a newspaper fortune had the right to be phobic about the press.

Margot leaned close to Joel, putting her hand on his arm. Whammo! Right on those nerve endings again. He was aware of her faint, lemony scent, which always reminded him of the dolls in the play-therapy room at a clinic where he had once worked. Margot herself was undeniably doll-like, with the translucent, fragile appearance of a heroine from the days of silent films: her dark chestnut hair was short and surrounded her dimpled cheeks with curls; her small mouth had a deep cupid's bow; her skin was pale, and shadowed under her brows and cheekbones.

"I'm not going to let anything spoil tonight," she whispered. "After what you did." Louder: "I had Merlin make you fettucine. Vegetarian."

"I wish you wouldn't go to any extra trouble," Joel said.

"Don't mind me, I'll just sit in the dark," Ted mimicked him in falsetto.

"Merlin's *practicing* fettucine this week, lovey-birdey." Margot rose and gave Ted an elaborately smoochy kiss on the cheek, a sight which nauseated Joel much more than the smell of cooking flesh. Margot turned back to him, and put on her Yiddish accent, which she didn't do as well as she did some: "Believe me, dahlink, you're do-ink him a favuh."

Merlin was the twenty-year-old that the Harveys had rescued from unemployment. They had helped him to get his GED; now they overpaid him to be their houseboy while he studied hotel and restaurant management at City College.

"I *am* hungry," Joel said. "As a matter of fact."

"I'll go see if it's ready. Don't talk about me while I'm gone." Margot flitted across the yard. She was barely five foot one, with the figure of a girl just entering adolescence; even the way she ran, gawkily but with so much energy, had an anything's-possible rhythm that Joel associated with teenagers.

Ted watched her go. "Remember that old joke—grass doesn't grow on a playground?" He was on another Scotch and his voice was getting thicker. "That place is real important to her."

"What I wish is that she would take in every child in the world, and then in fifteen years I'd have no more patients." Joel's voice, too, sounded thick to him.

"It's that simple, huh? A little day care, they live happily ever after?"

"Well, no, of course not." Joel wished now for a quick, localized earthquake: Let the ground open and swallow Ted. "I hope you're proud of her, anyway." *You don't deserve her.*

"I am," Ted nodded. "You know I am. My life depends on her. I'd be dead without her."

"I think the steaks are ready," Joel said.

Ted sniffed. "We like them well done," he said, but dragged one of the charred hunks off the grill and onto a platter. Joel thought he should bestir himself to help, but an epithet that Ted had recently applied to him, *good old Joey*, kept rattling around in his brain.

Instead, he loosened his tie. He *was* tired after this afternoon, though he couldn't take any credit; Betty had chosen to come down. "Margot loves those kids so much." Then he spoke as if an idea had just occurred to him. "Hey, you guys ever gonna have one?"

Ted was staring at the underside of another steak. Joel noted with satisfaction that it had the texture of a boot sole. "I don't suppose you want to give me lessons on how to do it, O bachelor with straight dick."

Joel settled deeper against the nylon mesh of the chair. *I'm a*

real asshole. He knew perfectly well that Margot hadn't used any
birth control for a couple of years. Maybe she and Ted just
weren't sleeping together that much. *Dream on.* And what if
Margot did get pregnant? Maybe he'd displace feelings toward
his mother onto her; stop thinking of her as a sexual being and be
free of this obsession.

Or maybe he'd become "Unca" Joey, friend-of-the-family, included most holidays, bringing over toys. *Fuck that.* "Y'ever
thought about having tests?" He crunched the last of his ice. "I
mean, a hysterogram, a sperm count. . . ."

"I offered to go in with her, Joey. She said forget it, that she
doesn't want to know."

Joel sighed. His profession, and therefore his life, was based on
the premise that it was always better to know. But he didn't
really believe Ted anyway. He suspected that Ted wasn't too
eager to have his semen put on a slide to find out whether there
were enough of those little guys with the tails swimming around
in there.

"She says this way it could just happen, by magic. God, Joey,
I'd do anything to make her happy, *anything.* I mean, I get
scared sometimes."

"Scared?" Joel echoed ingenuously, actually prompting.

"Well, if Margot—you know. It's just that I need her so much,
and she's so—so wonderful. Too good for me." He glugged more
Scotch. "And you're the best buddy in the world. I'm so grateful
for what you did today. . . ."

Don't start with this. Joel preferred Ted's hostility to his
sentiment.

"So I don't want to lay our problems on you. I bet you hear
worst things most days, anyway."

"Most days," Joel agreed.

"I mean, we're so lucky, Margot and I—we have our health,
and each other, and a good friend like you." He raised his Scotch
to toast Joel; Joel, in Pavlovian response, raised his own empty
glass. He looked straight at Ted as he did, feeling at once
enraged, guilty—and afraid that Margot might ultimately agree
with Ted's assessment of their life together.

"You're the best there is, the best," Ted persisted. Then he
held up the platter. "Come and get it!" He called for Margot like
Tarzan summoning Jane; unmistakable possession. "Before it
grows a beard!"

Joel squinted, lining up his glass as the object of a possible free throw to the hoop that Ted had hung on the side of the garage. Well, if he couldn't have Margot, and he probably couldn't, at least he had his work. He was grateful for that. If you discounted the nights he came home exhausted, irritated, and wondering whether he was any good to anyone, then you could say that he loved it unequivocally.

As a boy, when he had lain in bed and heard sirens passing on La Cienega, he had wanted to follow them—put out the fire, revive the patient, arrest the bad guys. At seventeen, he had fantasized about delivering the world from hunger and protecting it from nuclear war.

Compromises are made. Now the first ring of his office phone was his equivalent of a siren. Now he tried to help one person at a time, and he survived on small daily victories: the slightest lift of someone's head, the report of a new lover or a new job. And once in a while, there was that spark, like the reflection of candlelight in someone's eyes: the look of a person about to see the world, and himself, in a new way. *If you save one person you save the world.* He lived for those times.

And he had had successes: Recently, there had been a man with severe agoraphobia that had gone into remission. And over the years, there had been narcissistic men who had married, dependent women who had started careers. Joel cultivated patience, an analytic trait which did not come naturally to him. Still, sometimes it was too much like building a pyramid with a pair of tweezers. Or sitting down to a jigsaw puzzle with ten thousand pieces—and each one of those pieces was the uniform blue of a cloudless sky.

Do I want to be God? he wondered. *Yes, I guess I do.* But therapy didn't work as it did in *Marnie* or *The Three Faces of Eve*—you measured changes through a microscope and were glad for them.

Margot opened the back door with her shoulder. Without looking at Ted, Joel knew that he was watching her, too. She bounded toward them, bearing a casserole large enough, Joel guessed, to feed him and a dozen of her own children for two weeks.

"Come upstairs for a sec."
The three of them had stayed outside until it got dark, around

nine. Ted kept drinking Scotch; he toasted Merlin's fettucine and Margot's new Playground program, and raised his glass several more times in honor of Joel's friendship and therapeutic skills. Then he tried to get Joel and Margot to join him in a chorus of "One million bottles of beer on the wall."

Now, with Ted snoring safely on the couch, Joel was about to leave. Margot had refused his chivalrous offer to carry Ted upstairs, explaining that he would awaken and come up within a few hours.

But instead of walking Joel to the door, Margot beckoned him to follow her. "I want to show you something."

"I've got—I really should—"

"Oh, come on."

He hesitated, then went upstairs with her. The master bedroom was huge: Margot had knocked out a wall to annex the smaller bedroom adjacent to it. She rearranged walls the way some rich women have plastic surgery. "What did you want to show me?"

"Nothing." She plunked down on the bed and patted the white brocade bedspread next to her. "I just wanted to get away from Rosa so we could talk."

"What's with Rosa these days?" Rosa had made a late appearance in the yard to accuse Merlin of smoking marijuana in the basement and complain that he had not brought her any dinner. Rosa and Merlin lived with the Harveys. It was the best of both egalitarianism and practicality: Rosa and Merlin got to live in a *premier* Seacliff home, while Margot and Ted had the convenience of live-in servants.

"Don't worry about her." Margot sculpted the air with one hand. "She's just upset tonight. Probably on the rag."

"Now if *I* said that . . ."

"But you didn't." Margot tilted back her head and laughed. There was not a single bit of metal in her teeth. "I really just wanted to thank you again for today. In private."

"You're welcome." *I shouldn't have done it.* But looking into those big blue eyes, he wished he had a chance to do it again.

"I'll never forget it," she said, putting her hand on his leg, just above the knee.

Her aim was better than usual. He felt himself starting to get an erection.

Margot smiled. Could she tell? She reached around his neck and stroked his curls. "You need a haircut," she said.

"Uh . . . yes." He wondered if the bulge was visible. Of course he should gently take her hand away, but it felt so good. . . . He'd always known that Margot was a flirt, but this was the first time he let himself think, *cocktease*. Because his cock was completely erect now, pressing against his jockey shorts. And he wanted her to put her hand down *there*, he wanted to kiss her, he wanted to take that halter top off . . . but Ted was sleeping—passed out—just a few feet below them, so she knew they couldn't. . . . *What are you thinking of, anyway? Ted's your friend!* But all that bare white flesh was more than any man should have to resist.

"I love your hair," she murmured.

"Is that a new photograph?" He stood abruptly, turning his back to her, hoping for an opportunity to sort of readjust himself.

"No," she replied. Sullenly, he thought. "It's been there for years."

"H'm."

"Are you still seeing Denise?" she asked. Her voice rose unnaturally at the end of the question. Denise was another therapist in Joel's office, an *aficionada* of performance art and street fairs.

"Uh huh. You know, we're friends." Joel stared out the window which overlooked the front yard. He concentrated on trying to identify the makes of parked cars.

"I'm jealous."

"Don't be."

"When a man says, 'we're friends,' in that tone of voice, it means that the fucking is awfully good."

He turned around, startled.

She laughed. "Oh, your face. Well, at least that got your attention."

She was lying back on her elbows. Damn those shorts! He could see all the way up to where the top of her thigh curved out just below her crotch. And his penis throbbed, screaming at him, *Get laid first, ask questions later*. This was much worse than that other time. This was like being back in high school. And maybe knowing that Ted was nearby made it even more exciting. . . . His ears were warm. He imagined the creaking of Margot's bed. Ted would never wake up. She wanted to, she'd been flirting with him, she'd wanted to all along. . . . That day at his apartment, she must have come for it—maybe she had lied when she said that Rosa was waiting. . . . He started to move toward her.

"Oh, God." Margot suddenly drew her knees up to her chin, rolling herself up into a ball. "Doctor, what am I going to do?"

He stopped. "About what?"

She pressed her hands against her temples, then managed a tight nod. "Ted. He's like this all the time now. He didn't used to be. You know that."

Joel tried to salvage some logical functioning capability from a brain stuck in the horny mode, wanting again to find some reference point, to remember how long it had been since Ted had joined the sloppy, fall-down school of drinking. Eight months? A year and a half? The change had taken place as gradually as one's parents age. Ted had always been an alcoholic, in the broader sense, but he had been of the discreet, fun-loving variety, a boisterous addition to Margot's fund-raisers and dinner parties, and the problem had been easier to ignore.

"I used to tell myself it was none of my business," Joel admitted. *Or maybe I just wanted him to stay that way. Maybe I knew this day would come.* When Margot would be down and out, and turn to him, and he could try . . . bastard! Women patients tried to seduce him, overtly and subtly, all the time; that was the nature of transference. He was immune to that, knowing as he did that it had little to do with "the charms of his own person"; knowing, too, that to breach the implicit trust a patient put in him was a crime little different from rape. Taking advantage of Margot's vulnerability might be more excusable— but was that what he wanted to do? Something *more excusable?*

Still, it was perfectly natural for him to sit on the bed again and put his arms around her. "He needs help. I should have said something a long time ago."

"What could you have done?" she asked flatly.

Of course I could have done something. "Intervention is the first step," he said pedantically.

"I've *tried* talking to him."

He patted the back of her hair. If she had been flirting with him, it was because of Ted—and he was so vain that he thought she wanted him. That was deflating, at least in the ego sense.

"I've tried so hard," she was whispering in his ear. "And I want to get pregnant! How can I do that now? I'd be afraid to have him around a baby."

Afraid to have him around a baby. Joel, who did not want children, grasped that as another wedge. Margot didn't really care who donated the sperm to make the child she wanted. . . . His nose brushed against the smooth surface of an earring.

"I'm not getting younger."

"What are you, twenty-nine? You've got forever, practically." He thought that he could feel her nipples through her halter top and his shirt. His penis was aching. *I have to get out of here.* But wasn't it cowardly to run? She was a friend who needed help. He thought of his snide exchanges with Ted before dinner and felt ashamed. "Have lunch with me tomorrow," he said. "We'll think of something."

She drew away and smiled at him sadly. He had expected—wanted?—to see tears, but her eyes were dry. "Tomorrow," she agreed.

She kissed him at the door. It was only on the cheek, nothing more than what was appropriate, but he hobbled slightly all the way out to his car.

CHAPTER 2

TEN THOUSAND PIECES OF SKY

At home that night, after he left Margot, Joel had a prizewinning bout of his recurrent insomnia. This gave him the leisure to analyze, then to intellectualize, and finally to obsess.

He'd considered marriage only once, and that seven years ago, to another student psychologist in the Columbia program. And even with her, Sonja, his recollection was mostly of their long clenched-jawed arguments about why living together wasn't good enough, and his own anger at being pressed.

Since he'd turned thirty, it seemed that every time he spoke to his parents his mother told him about another Fairfax High alumnus who had recently wed. So he might have reached an age when he should wonder what his own problem was.

But he hadn't. Instead, he'd been happy enough with the popularity that came to any single, heterosexual male in San Francisco under the age of ninety who didn't openly admire Charles Manson. And, when he'd grown tired (and wary) of slipping in and out of new beds, he'd gravitated toward Denise. Perhaps he'd unconsciously thought that she would protect him from falling in love with one of the have-it-all-yesterday superwomen he met at Margot's parties, or one of the idealistic, mooning twenty-four-year-olds who attended the graduate school classes he taught.

With Denise, he had broken his rule about not getting involved with another psychologist (a rule inspired, in fact, by his four-year relationship with Sonja), but somehow Denise didn't count. He thought of her as a friend more than anything else, even if they did have sex like rutting bunnies on a fairly regular basis. And what he supposed had happened was that, being with her, he had let some of his defenses down—and into this citadel had stormed Margot herself.

But he understood the dynamic. He and Margot were still two relatively mature adults who had come to a certain juncture in their lives and . . .

Maybe Ted would go to an alcoholic rehabilitation clinic, preferably in another state, and . . .

Maybe Ted would fall in love with the stewardess on the flight there, and . . .

Maybe Margot would need a good friend to stand by her through all of this, and . . .

So this was love! This was the feeling that had always been missing before—with Sonja, Denise, all of them—the feeling of wanting to possess and worship her very earlobes. The feeling that he would explode if he couldn't.

If this was love, he'd rather be schizoid.

Ah ha! But *was* it really love? Maybe it was just transference. But then, the distinction was so arbitrary. Some therapists claimed that *all* love was just transference. Joel actually agreed, but he thought it would be just as accurate to say that all transference was just love.

At nine the next morning Joel had an appointment with a new patient.

"I don't know why I'm here," Melanie said. "I don't think you can help me."

Joel sat in a Danish leather chair that was specially designed to prevent backache but didn't. To his left there stretched that wonderful anomaly, a couch. Unlike dental chairs and CAT scanners and iron lungs, couches of the requisite shape and style were not readily available from medical-supply companies. He and other analysts he knew improvised with modular furniture or daybeds. His own couch, repaired and reupholstered, had belonged to his grandmother.

Melanie Hardwicke sat across from Joel in a rust-colored armchair, having regarded the couch upon her entry with the suspicious, almost disbelieving, glance of most prospective patients. Then she had proceeded to give him a lot of information: occupation (model), hometown (Chagrin Falls, a suburb of Cleveland), current address (Nob Hill)—but was thus far hazy about anything which might bear on the issue of psychotherapy.

In spite of that, Joel was feeling mildly grateful to her. Once in his familiar surroundings and confronted with a new skein of secrets to unravel, he was *Dr. Abramowitz*, a man with work to do, a man who did not fantasize about adultery.

Melanie herself was just the kind of patient that therapists scrabble for: a YAVIS (Young, Attractive, Verbal, Intelligent, and Sensitive). She could be reasonably counted on to pay her bill, to confine her crises to weekdays, and not to develop a belief that he was the reincarnation of Elvis Presley.

"You haven't said how you came here," Joel said.

She flung her head back, in an affected motion which began with the oscillation of her shoulders. Her hair was thick and naturally blond, parted on the side, and constantly spilling into her long, slanted green eyes. Joel hadn't been surprised when she said she was a model: She was tall, bony, with high cheekbones and *retroussé* nose. She was as leggy as a newborn giraffe, her long limbs accentuated by a short denim skirt that could have been more accurately described as a wide belt. She wore high heels on bare feet; her legs were tanned enough for nylons to be unnecessary.

"I came here in my car," she said, and tilted her head, as if posing for an invisible camera.

"And why are you interested in therapy?" Congenial, but not responding to the joke. They were so good at getting you to do that—these patients who wanted you to help them without talking about themselves.

Melanie tugged on the hem of the skirt, then crossed her legs, exposing even more of her thigh. "Actually, a friend of mine said I should come. She said I'd feel better if I talked to someone. I was in therapy once before, I don't know if it did any good or not." She looked down at her high-heeled pumps, then said softly, "I want to be famous."

"Is that something I can help you with?" He guessed that she was throwing decoys at him.

"I don't know," she replied throatily. She leaned back. Her nipples were visible through the thin material of her blouse.

Her legs parted and he had an unobstructed view up to a white triangle where they met. He looked away, thinking that if she kept coming to see him he would be barraged with an entire wardrobe of postage-stamp-sized clothes. But here that would just be another puzzle piece to examine, rather than a source of arousal; somehow when he walked in that door he shed his sexual self—or maybe he buried it, under the weight of years of practice.

"You want to be famous." Back to the subject she had introduced. Wondering if she was conscious of what she was doing with her body. Too soon to point it out; she might see it as critical, rejecting.

"Yes—so badly!" She sighed. "Actually, my career is going great. I haven't done a cover yet, but everyone says I'm terrific, so I know it's just a matter of time." She pointed down at the Kleenex box. "Can I use this?"

Joel nodded, and she pulled out a single tissue and daintily dabbed at her nose. "So I don't know why I'm here, really. It's probably stuff I have to work out for myself." She lifted her chin. "At the agency, they say I'm *too* pretty. Don't get me wrong, I'm not vain. But they *do* say that—so how come they keep sticking me with these gruesome catalogues? I've got the height for ramp work. Not everyone does. But it's the cover I *want*."

She tilted her head and struck a pout. Her lower lip was full and the expression came naturally when she opened her mouth slightly. Or perhaps she was so used to modeling that she simply dispensed her emotions in snapshot doses. "It's just that there *isn't* a lot of time," she said, twisting the Kleenex. "I'm twenty-five." Pause. "How old did you think I was?"

He would have guessed older. Something about her skin, smooth as it was. Maybe she wore too much makeup. "Age is important to you."

"No, really, tell me how old you thought I was."

She was testing him early. He smiled. "I think what's more important than how old *I* think you are is your concern about it."

"Why *shouldn't* I be concerned? You get washed up in this business pretty fucking early. I have to be famous! I have to be famous soon!"

"Why?"

"Why?" she echoed. "What a stupid question. *Everyone* wants to be famous."

Joel didn't. Certainly not if being famous meant being on "The Donahue Show," promoting *The Inner Peace Cookbook*. "I'm interested, though, in why *you* want to be famous."

"Stupid." She spread out her fingers, then pointed with all ten of them to her face. "This won't last forever, you know. I need to use it now. Otherwise—" She flipped her hands upward, asking the ceiling to finish her thought, and Joel felt a thud in his stomach. Otherwise, he translated, something empty. Death.

"Someday, when I look really old and ugly, I want to have pictures so my grandchildren can see that I was beautiful once."

As if that would help. Joel thought of the seven gray hairs that occasionally glinted in the dull yellow light of his bathroom while he shaved.

"I have to do a cover. I've set that as a goal—if I don't do a cover by the end of the year I'll know I'm a failure."

"A sign from God?" He couldn't resist.

She scowled. "No—I'll just know, that's all. It's hard to get covers out here. I mean, what is there?" She counted on her fingers. "*San Francisco* magazine, *California* magazine, *Focus*, that awful *Here*—they don't even use cover girls for some issues, it really pisses me off. In the meantime I'm getting up at five A.M. because some fag photographer likes the light then. . . . It's much easier in New York. I went there when I left Cleveland. But I had a bad experience. A man—he was married."

Aha. He thought he'd picked up the scent. "Can you tell me more about that?"

She shook her head. "Another time. Anyway, I thought I'd try San Francisco for a while."

He nodded. That was it, then. He was glad that she was already thinking about coming back.

"So now I'm stuck here. It was a big mistake, a big mistake." Melanie hunched forward, hands between her knees. "Christie Brinkley did her first cover when she was seventeen. Brooke Shields when she was *twelve*. They're not any prettier than I am, and they don't have more presence, either." She sucked in on her lower lip, frowning. He was beginning to notice that she was not as perfectly beautiful as she appeared at first: her hands and feet were big and she had the suggestion of an underbite.

"I deserve it more than the other girls at the agency. They *all* have bulimia—they sit around and talk about the best ways to make themselves vomit. The winner so far is the one who uses a feather. She thinks it's refined because the Romans used to do it that way. Then there's another girl who chews food, then spits it out without swallowing. Really fun conversation, don't you think?" She leaned back again, stretching, thoughtfully passing her hand over her flat belly. This time the gesture did not seem meant to be seductive. Her body was just her means to a livelihood, like a farmer's tractor, and she had to get the plowing done before the motor gave out. "None of them have done covers yet, either. People don't realize how hard they are to get. But you know what really bugs me? I've done more work than most of them put together, and nobody knows who I am! Once I did the big Macy's ad in the *Courier*, and a couple of people recognized me from that—but after a week, it was all over. You—you didn't recognize me, did you?"

"No," he said simply, although his mind was whirring, planning strategy to find out *just what it was* that would make her so obsessed with this. What the obsession might cover over. What needs of her parents were wrapped up in it; what fears of her own. Chess with her unconscious.

"You see? People think that just because you're a model you're famous, but it's not true. The worst are the folks—my relatives— back home. I've just stopped calling them because they always ask me when I'm going to do *Vogue*. Shit, I make more money in a year than any of them will see in a lifetime."

"You want to be *very* famous, then."

Melanie scratched her leg under her gold ankle bracelet. This required leaning over, which exposed what there was to expose of her small breasts. The nipples were thick and brown.

"My mother's name is Shirley," she said. This being a rather loose association, Joel waited to hear more. "Do you know *why*?" she challenged.

"After Shirley Temple," he guessed.

"That's right. An entire generation of girls got that name. Just like—just like they used to name little girls Victoria, after the queen of England. That's how famous I want to be. I want there to be baby Melanies, after *me*. And maybe a Melanie doll." She pounded the arm of the chair, tossing her magnificent hair again, more spontaneously, and the motion was beautiful to watch, like the sprint of a well-bred horse. "Shirley Temple was famous when she was *five*. That's why I feel so—so washed-up."

Joel suppressed another smile, reflecting that when Percy Shelley was his age he'd been dead for three years.

"I'm running out of time," she insisted. "I should go back to New York."

"Are you considering that?" He wondered if she'd be surprised to learn how often, during a first session, a patient announced his intention to permanently leave town, usually for another time zone, sometimes for another continent.

"Yes." She massaged one knee, below the cap, where there was a small swelling. "It's just that there's a—a complication."

He had a guess, but waited for her to tell him.

"Another man." She stuck out her tongue. "Also married."

"How did you find out?" Joel asked, shifting a little in his chair. In graduate school, they used to say that you got the patient you deserved. The Great Therapist in the Sky was looking out for *him*, all right. Now he'd get to help Melanie analyze why she had this pattern of being attracted to married men.

"Well . . . I knew."

"From the beginning?"

"Yes. But I didn't think it was going to be anything at first, just one night." She snorted. "It wasn't even that special. But he was so sweet afterward. It was like he was starved for affection. Like a puppy."

"It didn't bother you then, that he was married."

"I just sort of put it out of my mind," she said, a bit shrilly. "And he kept telling me, you know, that he and his wife didn't sleep together and he wanted to leave her anyway. I sort of figured, if it wasn't me, it'd be someone else, so why not? Anyway"—she slouched lower in the chair—"I'm the one who's suffering for it now."

"Do you want to work on that relationship in here?"

Another head toss, another beaver shot. "I guess so," she said. "I mean, what I really want is for you to get him to leave his wife and marry me."

"I'm surprised," he said, "since it doesn't sound as though you think very highly of him."

"You're right, I don't." And then was quiet—a throbbing quiet that augured other things. "So I could just break up with him."

He hesitated. "That might be a good idea—if this man is the problem, rather than a symptom of the problem."

She sucked in on her lower lip. "I—I don't know what you mean."

"You mentioned another man in New York."

She bit down harder on her lip, then lowered her face into her hands. Her hair fell down like a thick yellow veil, and she sobbed.

Joel waited, feeling that at last they were getting somewhere.

After a few moments she lifted her head and snatched up several tissues, this time without asking permission. "Oh, God," she said. "What I must look like."

She looked better than before, when, whatever her complaint, her face had varied little from its natural expression of disdain. Now her eyes were greener, her nose only a little red. And most of all, there was the sheen of some honest emotion.

What Melanie looked like was the least of all her possible problems. But Joel knew better than to tell her, you're so beautiful, you're so young, you-have-everything-going-for-you. She'd probably heard that as often as Ted finished a bottle of Johnnie Walker Black. No: He was up against the tougher problem of reconstructing *why* a woman who was beautiful-with-everything-going-for-her might not be able to enjoy it all: sitting down to the jigsaw puzzle, to assemble ten thousand pieces of sky.

Melanie fluffed her hair. Then she folded her arms across her chest, and crossed her legs, making an extra tuck with her ankle around her calf. "This was different from the one in New York. This one—he *promised* he was going to leave her. He *swore*. How long can I wait? I'm getting so old."

"How long have you been involved with him?"

"About three months. Not quite."

Good. She might have said two years, three years. But this time, apparently, she had recognized the pattern early.

"The first few weeks were total heaven. We did all these *romantic* things, you know—like he took me to the touristy places I hadn't seen yet. He could just really make me laugh, too. And he spent money on me—he even took me shopping." She twirled a lock of hair around her finger. "Actually, I didn't like that as much, because I was afraid he was going to get into some weird Svengali thing, but it was still fun, because, you know, he was taking time off from work, during the day, for me."

Because that was when he didn't have to be with his wife. Joel felt a sudden anger at this unknown man who was becoming known to him; a signal, he realized, that what Melanie was saying was reaching into his own life. "Are you saying it's different now?"

"Hah! I'll say! Now he just wants to stay home and—have intercourse, and he can't even do that."

"So things have changed."

"I'll say." She bit her lip, about to cry again. "The good part never lasts, does it?"

Joel decided to let that one pass.

"He owes me," Melanie pouted.

Joel said nothing.

"What should I do?" she asked.

"I wish there was a short answer. But we could explore that if you decided to start therapy."

"God, are we out of time?"

"Almost."

"God." Her foot bobbed. "That went fast. Well—what happens now?"

"That's up to you. We could set regular appointments, if you like."

She tilted her head, posing. "It's not like I *need* therapy. I bear up pretty well under stress, and I'm very independent, but . . ." The pose drooped slightly. "You know, when I don't have a job to go to in the morning, it's hard to get out of bed. That's why my friend said I should come talk to you . . . to somebody."

"Was it your friend who gave you my name?"

"No—I"—she looked around the room—"I just found it."

Some mystery there; but she obviously didn't want to tell him yet, so he let it go.

Melanie leaned forward a little. "What I want to know is how long will it take? I mean, how long before I work things out?"

"That depends on you—on us."

"Huh." She studied him for a moment. "Well, okay."

She agreed to his usual fee before he could even tell her that it was negotiable. But she recoiled from his suggestion of twice-weekly sessions. "If I can't get my life together coming once a week, then I can't do it at all," she said.

"All right—then next week at the same time?"

"Unless I decide to just pack up and fly East." She laughed. "I'm only kidding, I won't do that."

As Joel wrote down her appointment, he saw the sessions

elbowing each other out of the narrow gray lines of his daily planner. And he had just taken Betty Klass on, too. Still, he was sorry that Melanie didn't want to come in more often. It was hard to get much done on a once-a-week basis, hard to get the feel of someone's daily life. And seven days would be plenty of time for her to patch up whatever chips he might make in her defenses. "Then I'll see you next week."

When she rose to leave she modestly tugged the hem of her skirt down, but halfway to the door (he was escorting her out as was his custom), she dropped her keys. Bending over precariously on her high heels, she showed him her panties stretched out against her buttocks, the curve of flesh at the top of her thigh, and the outline of the crack. Then, at the door, she said good-bye timidly, with lowered eyes.

But what he thought about later was his analytic attitude, which made him let her get away without agreeing to come in sooner, and he hated himself for it.

After Melanie, Joel saw Andrea Griswald.

When she entered his office ahead of him, Andrea plunked down on the couch with the *whumpf* she managed to get from its cushions at the beginning of most of her four weekly sessions.

A *zaftig* redhead, Andrea represented both the miracle of psychoanalysis and the tenacious constructs of character. She had been in analytic therapy with him since her first semester at Hastings College of the Law; now she was nearing the end of her second year of law school. Twenty-three, she still lived with her parents, who wanted her home by 9:00 P.M.; she ate compulsively; she sometimes had tantrums. She had scored in the ninetieth percentile on the law school boards, but had been on academic probation since her first exams.

She detested her red hair and freckled skin—sometimes referring to herself as "Raggedy Andrea"—but she went out of her way to dress sloppily, favoring sweatshirts and oversized sweatpants. "What's the point?" she would ask. "I'm fat anyway."

But things were better. A year and a half ago she had been dealing cocaine to support her own habit, a habit which kept her awake for days at a time. Late one night, driving in the rain, her vision had suddenly left her. For several minutes, completely blind, she tried to navigate herself off the street, expecting to die. Her recollection of what happened stopped there; that was the incident that had gotten her into treatment.

Now that she had given up drugs, Andrea complained that she was the only cocaine addict in history who hadn't lost weight, even though she was by no means the whale-sized creature she imagined herself to be.

Her parents, though ignorant of her drug use (and a lot of other things, in Joel's opinion), had wanted Andrea to start therapy, but when they realized that Joel would not act as surrogate disciplinarian, they had tried to get her to quit. Too late: Andrea's transference was swift and intense. She made a pagan cult out of Joel-worship. Though her preoccupation with relics, such as his coffee mug and the coat hanger on the door, sometimes embarrassed him, her devotion had its uses: Therapy was the one thing she would stand up to her parents about. She kept coming and she made them pay for it. Sometimes when she whined to Joel that she was afraid of them, he pointed out that they deferred to her on the one matter she had been firm about.

Andrea's father was a trial attorney whose field was personal injury; his specialty was class actions arising out of major disasters, such as hotel fires and midair collisions, which had earned him his daughter's private nickname, "Grisly Griswald."

Joel thought it was a bit of a joke on Mr. Griswald that his daughter had, over time, stolen more than three thousand dollars from Mrs. Griswald's purse and padded her school expenses to the tune of a slightly larger sum, exhibiting an impressive resourcefulness at forging receipts.

"I swear I'm going to drop dead over these finals," Andrea was saying now. She had been anxious about them for weeks. Yesterday she had taken her corporations exam; this afternoon she was to sit for antitrust. Mr. Griswald had sworn that he would throw her out of the house if she flunked another course. Considering her relationship with her father, Joel wasn't sure that would be a bad thing. "I know I should have studied harder," Andrea said. "But like last night, I was so depressed, I just kept eating."

She proceeded to enumerate the precise number of bites of each of the various flavors of Mrs. Field's cookies she had consumed (she kept a steady supply of them under her bed, trading for secrecy what they lacked in freshness). Andrea hit her Reeboks together as she lay on the couch, and Joel could see over the top of her pale red hair to where she counted off on her bitten-down nails. When she had first come to see him, she had been depressed about not having a boyfriend, but now she was in the throes of trying to get Joel to be her boyfriend. ("Since you see me as godlike," he had said to her once, "that would confer the same status on you.") Andrea had no deep-rooted illusions about the nature of their relationship, but she reveled in hopeless love. The men she had been drawn to were usually older, unresponsive. In high school she had been in love with a history teacher, had written him poems, letters, and suicide notes that she never mailed, and had driven past his Daly City house at night, trying to see in his windows.

"What am I going to do?" she whimpered now. "I know I'm going to flunk. My father will stop paying for therapy pretty soon. I'll have to quit and live on the streets, like all those people by the school." She chewed on her finger for a moment. "I always wonder if you'll see me for free."

"That would make you feel special."

"I was wondering if you would write a medical excuse for me so that I didn't have to take my exam today." This last was mumbled through the finger in her mouth. "If I had one more day to study for it . . . You won't do it, will you?"

From the beginning, Andrea's sessions had been peppered with such requests. "I think you know the answer to that."

"But *why*?" she whined.

"You want me to take care of you."

"But what's wrong with *that*?"

And so on. When, at the end of their session, Andrea shuffled toward the door, her shoulders were hunched forward, and her hands were stuck deeply into the pockets of her sweatshirt. The shoelace of one of her Reeboks was untied; the ends made a clicking sound against the carpet as she walked.

With her hand on the doorknob, she mumbled, "So I guess I'll see you tomorrow. Can I call you if things get bad?"

"I'll leave that up to you."

"Aren't you going to wish me luck on the exam?"

"It may involve more than luck."

"I wish you hadn't said that!" Andrea wailed on her way out.

Joel watched her for a moment as she slouched down the hall toward the stairs. He was about to close the outer door (there were actually two doors on each of the offices, for better soundproofing), when he saw Margot's head appear at the top of the stairs. She touched the banister, turned around, saw Joel, and smiled. She wore a pale blue ribbon in her hair.

She was early. At least five minutes! And Joel had managed not to think about her for most of the morning. When he had thought of her, it had been with a certain calm. He had resolved to subdue his feelings. When he saw her, those same feelings leapt up and started doing jumping jacks.

Andrea had just reached the top of the stairs. She peered at Margot (who seemed unaware of her), then glanced back at Joel; her shoulders straightened suddenly, and she stared at Margot's back as Margot glided toward him. Finally, Andrea clomped down the stairs. Joel, a little amused, thought, *I'm going to get it tomorrow.* Then he gave himself to seeing Margot, the small teeth of her smile and the bobbing of her curls.

"Hello, Doctor," she said. Her brows, as always, were plucked into thin, high arches. She did not look like the despairing wife of a man whose drinking had begun to get out of control. "How about that lunch you promised me?"

Margot could switch her voice to a certain mode which he knew was meant to be heard more than listened to: a soothing alto of anecdotes, gossip, chatter. Background music, like jazz on a car radio. Since he spent most of his day concentrating so hard on what people said, picking it apart for clues, he especially loved the melody of Margot's voice, with its bass clef of laughter. It was like a back rub for the brain.

So as they walked down the street—and Margot had a bouncy walk, almost a scamper—he heard the sketchy outlines of a story about a judge's son who was caught dealing drugs at his *posh* private high school, and how "they" were trying to hush it up, but—"Here's the funny part"—and she laughed her xylophone laugh—"the judge and one of the assistant DAs were talking about it at the Washbag, playing dice for drinks, and right behind them was Jody Daniels' secretary—you know, the woman who writes eighty percent of her column anyway?" More laughter. "So I do believe it is possible"—she danced in front of him, stopped him with a confiding hand on his arm, and whispered—"we will be reading the whole story tomorrow!"

They went to the Greek restaurant near the corner of Sacramento Street. The day was sunny and windless (a rare enough occurrence in San Francisco, even in May), so they sat at one of the two tables scrunched together on the sidewalk. The odors of dill and lentils wafted from inside.

"What wine shall we order?" Margot asked.

"None for me."

"No, of course not, heaven forbid." She leaned closer to him; he smelled her cologne—a floral scent—and edged away. Coward. Why not just kiss her here, now, as he wanted to? Plenty of reasons why. Because he would be acting out—just what he tried to get his patients to avoid. Watching her lowered eyes scan the menu, he realized that this hadn't been a good idea. He was supposed—no, he was *morally obligated*—to use his magic compass to point her back to the land of happy marriages, wherever that was, and here he was feeling like a little too much passion for one navy blue suit. "How's Horatio?" he asked.

"He seems fine. I was at the Center this morning." She peered over the top of her menu at him, like a veiled harem girl. "He's a tough little guy."

"Good." It was true that some children were more resilient than others, uprighting themselves like one of those clown punching bags, no matter how hard the blow was. Others cracked at a touch. Horatio hadn't struck him as one of the lucky, former type. If only you could put some of that bounce into the brittle ones; but you were grateful if you could glue them together at all.

Margot sighed, keeping her eyes on the menu. Joel guessed what she was thinking: *One of her own.* Her desire for a child was a little abstract to him; he understood it in the secondhand way he understood so many things—from hearing patients talk. Sometimes women spoke of how they started to weep at the sight of infants in strollers, or how, in private, they pushed their stomachs out and rubbed them like Aladdin's lamp. Some of those same women also talked of fear—of not being good enough mothers, of being sidelined in the careers they had to give up so much for. But whenever the desire or fear was particularly strong, there was almost always the opposite emotion, lurking like a U-boat underneath.

"Mrs. Tuttle is taking it harder than anyone." Margot roused herself, and then went on to describe how her assistant director was still dosing herself with herbs and vitamins in an attempt to recuperate from yesterday's upset. Margot's face grew longer,

assuming the contours of Mrs. Tuttle's; her hands shaped teaket-
tles, counted out invisible pills.

Joel laughed. *Imagine being able to watch her do that whenever
I wanted. . . .*

Margot moved her spoon sideways across the table in front of
her, and pressed the bowl down, sending the handle seesawing in
the air. Finally she said, "You know I did want to talk to you
about something *very* special."

"Ted," he sighed. Well, they'd better get it over with. He had
already made a mental list of marriage counselors he knew were
good who'd appreciate the work.

Rap-rap, went Margot's spoon. "Don't jump to any conclusions."

"Don't keep me in suspense, then." All right, so they wouldn't
talk about Ted. Good. He wanted to enjoy her teasing, her
flirting, for just one more day. *Tomorrow* he could start the
Margot Diet.

"Want to guess?"

"Is it bigger than a bread box?"

"Much."

"Let's see, this doesn't have to do with Ted?"

"I don't think so."

She had dropped the teasing. Like a pebble, his gaze skimmed
from the lake of her eyes to the safer shore of the blue ribbon she
wore in her hair. "What am I going to win if I get it right? I
already have a set of matched lightweight Samsonite luggage and
the Jeopardy home game."

Teasing again: "Well, there's nothing I can offer that will top
that. So I guess I'll have to tell you." But there was a long,
resistant pause before she went on. "I mean, well, I have an
idea." She gripped either end of the spoon, as if about to bend it
into a U. "When was the last time you took the afternoon off?"

Two young women passed close by his shoulder; they had
white-blond hair and wore luminescent blue tights. In the sun,
the colors almost blinded him. "Let's see. We're into the early
nineties already, aren't we?"

"Why don't we be wild and crazy and impulsive and drive down
to Carmel? We could go shopping."

"Shopping? For what?"

"For what, the man asks. Okay—I should have known that
shopping wouldn't be your idea of big thrills. We could go to the

beach. Or"—her husky voice was huskier than usual, and she
kept her eyes on the spoon—"there's a little bed-and-breakfast
there, very private."

A little bed-and-breakfast? Private? *Get your mind out of the
gutter, Joel.* She meant something else. "Yes? Do they have a
museum or something?"

She laughed, slightly off-key. "Wake up and smell the *latte*,
Doctor! The last woman who invited you to Carmel, did *she* want
to take you to a museum?"

Joel simply stared at her, unsure whether he was still on planet
Earth. Maybe something happened since last night, when she
curled up in a ball at his lascivious approach. Had she noticed his
arousal after all? *A little bed-and-breakfast.* He was in danger of
becoming aroused again.

"Would you like to hear our specials today?" The waitress,
looking harried, was suddenly between them, squinting to read a
blackboard inside the restaurant. Joel sensed that he and Margot
were looking up at her as if she had walked in on them naked in
the shower.

Margot ordered something, and he mumbled, "I'll have the
same," handing the menu back to the waitress, just so they could
be alone again. He needed clarification. He must have misunder-
stood. Maybe it *was* an innocent invitation to tour seaside resort
boutiques.

Margot was resting her cheek on her hand. The sun made her
dark chestnut hair auburn, and the downy hair on her arms
almost blond, so that she glowed around the edges. "That
invitation had an RSVP attached," she said. "I'm waiting."

"I can't think of anything I'd rather do. But I have patients."

"Cancel them."

He was surprised, even a little hurt. She knew how compulsive
he was about not missing appointments. "It's not like I'm a piano
tuner," he said lightly. Thank God, those commitments prevented
him from doing anything impulsive. Yes, he was rigid (hadn't his
own former analyst, Dr. Schneider, told him often enough?),
but only those beloved and crazy-making people could have kept
him out of Margot's bed this afternoon (if indeed that was what
she wanted). And he was glad they could, because it was a place
that he had no right to be.

She started seesawing her spoon again. "All right," she said. "I guess if I'm not going to get you away from the competition this afternoon we'll have to have our little heart-to-heart here."

He looked down at the spidery grain of the table, heard someone shouting at the corner. He wished they'd sat inside, where he might feel less like he was about to be part of a "Candid Camera" stunt.

"You know what I'm going to say, don't you?"

"No, I don't." But he thought he did. This was what he'd wanted, wasn't it? So why was he so terrified?

"God, you're really going to drag it out of me, aren't you?" She pantomimed a quick hara-kiri with the spoon handle. "You see, yesterday—well, when I needed you, you came. Do you know what that means? How rare that is? I knew you did what you did with Betty Klass for *me*. That's when I knew—how *you* felt. I'm not wrong, am I?"

Her tone was pleading, but he saw confidence in her eyes. Joel noticed that he had been rearranging his own silverware; fork, knife, and spoon lay horizontally in front of him. This was the moment when he could run or lie. She hadn't said anything about how she felt.

"No," he said. "You're not wrong."

"And then suddenly I looked back and it seemed that you were always there when I needed you. Isn't that what it's all about?"

"I—I guess so." He sounded like a developmentally disabled five-year-old, but somehow nothing else would come out.

"When I saw you coming down the stairs with Horatio"—her voice wavered—"I just knew that I wanted to be with you forever and ever."

"Margot." That was the only word he could manage. But when every point of reference you have changes so unexpectedly, you're entitled to a few minutes of catatonia.

"If only—" Margot began, then stopped. "If only I wasn't already married when I met you."

He shivered, in spite of his winter-weight suit. "But you are," he said. That was Ted for you. And it had always been like that: A course could be overenrolled, but Ted would get in. He could party all night and still ace a midterm the next day. And then a woman like Margot fell in love with him, just as easily as Ted popped open a beer can. No, beer cans were too working-class for Ted now. . . .

"I didn't *plan* it this way," Margot pleaded. "When I married

Ted, I wasn't thinking, Oh boy, I can't wait to get hitched so that when I really fall in love with someone I won't be able to be with him."

Joel raked his hair back impatiently. "But you *did* marry Ted."

Margot scraped her chair a little closer to the table. "I didn't know you then," she said. "Now, listen, because I want you to understand. Ted was so—vulnerable. He needed me." She stroked Joel's sleeve with one finger. "But it was more than that, I realize now. I was so young, and my father was sick. Nobody told me, but I knew he was going to die. Then there was Ted. I'd like to think I'd make a different choice now."

"I'm sure you would." Or would she? But oh, those big eyes, those thick lashes. She must be looking at him that way on purpose—she must enjoy knowing how it made him want to scoop up all that soft, soft white skin.

Margot had moved even closer; her eyes were even bigger. "And you wonder why I've stayed with him all these years, don't you?" she murmured. "Well, you're the doctor. You tell me."

"Don't get me started." Joel grinned. He wanted to tell Margot about all the gestures he'd noticed and appreciated for so long, the approval he'd come to need, the jokes he saved to tell her. But he suddenly felt shy, like a patient just starting therapy. He watched a barrel-chested man come out of the liquor store across the street, carrying a case of vodka. "Are you sure—it's not just that Ted's having problems now?"

"I know what I want," Margot said softly. "There's nobody like you in the whole world." She puckered as if to kiss him. Then her white hands flew up. "Besides, Ted's been having problems since I've known him."

But there was a new, parasitic doubt burrowing into Joel's mind. "Have you—have there—"

She drew herself up. "Have there what?"

"Nothing. I mean, it would be perfectly understandable—"

"As if it would be any of your business," she snapped.

"It would have been before," he reminded her softly. They had been friends before. And that reassured him: She would have told him if she had had lovers, just as she had demanded implicitly that he tell her whom he slept with.

"Not that I haven't been tempted." She flipped her hand in front of her face, as if brushing off the offense she had taken. "But

I'd just feel too guilty about cheating on Ted. He's so—*dependent* on me."

"Don't you feel guilty now—about this?"

"Of course I do! But this is different." She smiled and slid her hand toward his. "This is *you*."

Just what he wanted to hear. So why couldn't he just accept what she said, believe her? But now he was wondering, was she attracted to him *because* he and Ted had been friends? Or was she unconsciously thinking *baby*, and sick of Ted's functional impotence? One trip to Carmel and they could get into enough trouble to keep a crisis hotline busy for a month.

"You can talk to Ted, then," he said. "Tell him—well, I guess you don't have to tell him about *us* necessarily, but tell him what's going on with the two of you."

Margot clicked her tongue. "I told you, I've *tried* to talk to him. You saw him last night. He's like that *every* night by eight o'clock. In the mornings he's asleep, and in the afternoons he's hung over."

"I didn't realize things had gotten that bad."

"So you said"—she lowered her eyes—"last night."

"All the more reason you *do* need to talk to him." Joel was determined. To sneak off with Margot was just too sleazy. It wasn't really having her. And he was afraid, too—recalling Melanie sobbing in his office. *You get the patient you deserve.* "I don't want one glorious day that we have to pretend never happened. Do you?"

"Don't you know me better than that?"

"Maybe neither of us knows the other as well as we'd like." He had been rearranging the silverware again; now he pressed the blade of his knife against the edge of the table.

"I'm giving you a chance to correct that," she said huffily.

He couldn't help thinking that the best way to get to know someone was to let him or her lie on your couch for ten years and tell you little things at random, like what they think about when they masturbate. But that wasn't always practical. Or fun. "And it's the best offer I've ever had," he said. "You know that."

"There are alternative spots, you know," Margot said, "if you don't have time for Carmel." She twirled the saltshaker. "It's the most adorable little inn on Nob Hill, the quaintest thing you've ever seen. All the rooms have four-posters and fireplaces, but we have a favorite room we always stay in—it's one of the penthouse suites, actually. There's a grandfather clock in this one, it always makes me think of Grandfather Clock on 'Captain Kangaroo.' We spend the night there and just don't tell anyone where we're going, not even Merlin or Rosa."

He pressed his knife harder into the table; it was a dull knife but it was starting to make a dent in the wood. Go to a place where she and *Ted* had made love? "You have to do just this one thing first," he said. He could still think like a shrink, never mind that the imminence of possessing her would make him hard if he fantasized about it for all of one second. He knew how tenacious the roots of co-dependence were. Margot—if he thought of her objectively—was a woman who had married and stayed with a man with a drinking problem, prodromal or otherwise, for a long time. If she were unwilling to bring her troubles out in the open with Ted, then she wasn't serious enough about *him*.

"What is this, a test?" She scraped her chair back. "Do you know what I went through before I came here? I spent an hour in the bathroom at the Center doing deep-breathing exercises."

"I didn't mean it that way. It's just so, you know, he'll have some warning." He was afraid to be wholly honest, and he suspected that she felt the same way.

But Margot smiled suddenly. "I love you, you know. Even now, when you're analyzing the socks off something we should just *do*."

"I—I love you, too," he said, very softly. And suddenly saw a plate of food slipped in front of him: glistening dark greens and little doughy squares. "Is there meat in this?" he asked automatically.

Margot laughed.

"There's meat in the Chicken Cecilia, yes," the waitress said, tucking her hair behind her ear. "Enjoy your lunch."

"I love it that you don't eat meat," Margot said. "I love it that you don't drink. I love it that—oh, God, you're not just putting me off, are you?"

He pushed the plate to one side and leaned over to grip her hand. "We could go tomorrow. Tomorrow afternoon." He had a light afternoon scheduled, only student conferences after three o'clock; they were easy to change. "To Carmel, or to that place on Nob Hill or wherever you want to go. Talk to Ted tonight. Tell him—that you haven't been happy for a long time. Tell him that he needs help, and—whatever else you want to tell him." Forget the counseling. He didn't want to be a martyr. If the breakup of their marriage was inevitable, why prolong it?

She took her hand away and pulled on one pouffed shoulder of her dress. "You act as though I picked you up on the street."

"No, no—Margot. I want you, but I want you out in the open. I don't want to be stud service. I want to have a *right* to want you."

He wanted to protect himself, too. He already loved her—and if they made love he would only love her more. If he lost her then . . . And Ted might often be drunk, and hostile, and unreliable—but if those qualities weren't the actual attraction for Margot (and they might be), then he was still good-looking and funny, and he and Margot had a lot of history.

"I just don't want to *hurt* him," Margot said.

Exactly. That was just what he was afraid of. Margot loved Ted, and Ted loved Margot—there was no doubt about that. The problem was that word, *love*, which was just like "fingerprints." It was a general idea with a totally different connotation for each person, an individual blend of caring, sadism, competitiveness, self-sacrifice, possessiveness, and sex.

"It'll hurt him more if he finds out another way," Joel observed paternally, but testing, testing. "Then, tomorrow, you and I—"

"Tomorrow." She stabbed a dolma and twirled it. "All right," she promised. "I'll talk to him."

"Tonight."

"Tonight."

Suddenly he was disappointed. Had she pressured him a little longer, he would have given way, rationalizing that he had put up a good fight against the forces of libido. He would have asked Denise or fellow therapist Alex Forans to tell his patients that something had come up. That was the nice thing about pyscho-analysis: you didn't have to explain anything to your patients if you didn't want to. He looked down at his untouched food—the dough-entombed chicken was already getting cold and starting to smell like something dead—and comforted himself that he had done the Right Thing.

"Oh, God." Margot looked at her watch. "I haven't got time to finish this. Gotta dash."

For what—if we were going to— But he signaled for the check.

He walked her back to her car. Margot moved sluggishly now. She wore white lace stockings and there were tiny white bows on her shoes.

As for him, the emotions that had started with jumping jacks were just about ready for the Olympics now. Emotions he'd always thought he'd had, but obviously hadn't, because they'd never made him sweat or made his stomach churn until now. *I must have been one hell of a dull guy.*

But there was enough of that dull guy, the analyst, left to wonder, if Margot really wanted to be with him forever, the way she insisted, why was she acting as if it were today or never—as if this afternoon were their one and only chance?

Margot had parked her new white Jaguar Vanden Plas near Alta Plaza. Its smooth lines reminded Joel of a Persian cat with its paws tucked under it.

After she unlocked and opened the door he kissed her, on the mouth. (He hardly need feel guilty about a kiss when he had given up a chance to make love with her.) He closed his eyes, exploring that soft, dark space, feeling the crinkly material of her dress against him. Well, this was love, all right! But he was wrong to think of it as transference. It was more like the flu.

He hated to let her go. How was he supposed to go back to the office now? But then he had the brief fantasy that someone driving by would recognize *Mrs. Margot Harvey*, and see her kissing a stranger.

"Oh darn," Margot mumbled. Her body was half in the car, but she stretched to reach over the roof to wipe away a spattering of bird droppings with her handkerchief. "My mother always said don't park under trees."

Joel felt something like a breeze on his neck. Ted had told him that Margot's mother had committed suicide, locking herself in the garage and turning on the engine of her Corniche.

"Talk to him tonight," he said. "Do you promise?"

She nodded. He didn't feel reassured. Something was wrong. *You're projecting*, he told himself.

He wanted to kiss her again. "Then call me if you can. I have a class, but I'll be home by ten-thirty. I'll wait to hear from you." He would start clearing his calendar right away.

She folded herself onto her perfect tan leather seat and started the car without looking at him. "See you," she said.

Soon, he wanted to add, but resisted.

He watched her drive away. She had a personalized license plate: MAR GO. She didn't even slow down for the stop sign at the corner.

CHAPTER 3

![band of stippled texture]

EVENING FOG BLUES

At five to seven that evening (he remembered from the clock that was next to the Kleenex, on the table behind the couch) Joel was still at the office; he had just finished going over his notes for that evening's lecture. This semester he had been teaching a class in personality disorders at the Berkeley Institute for Psychological Studies, otherwise known as BIPS. The class started at seven-thirty, so he was running a bit late, although leaving at seven usually put him behind the rush-hour traffic that congested the Bay Bridge.

So when the phone rang he would probably have let his answering machine pick it up, except that he thought it might be Margot. He'd been jumpy since she'd left him that afternoon: putting her out of his thoughts, but never completely. "Hello?"

Silence.

"Hello?" Nothing. He was seized by the panic of the guilty. Margot—something had happened to her—and it was his fault, for wanting her. The generic images of disaster surfaced in his mind, grainy footage of troops landing, shacks blown away, palm trees uprooted, and Walter Cronkite's voice intoning, *You are there.* "Hello?" he demanded one last time, and was about to hang up when a slightly familiar voice spoke.

"Is that you, Dr. Abramowitz?"

It was Betty. "Yes, Mrs. Klass. Can I help you?"

"Is it safe to talk?" She was panting.

"Yes, Mrs. Klass." He looked at his watch, thinking about his class now. There probably wouldn't be any traffic—but his car was in his garage at home, a ten-minute walk away.

"Don't you record all your calls?"

"No, I don't."

"I'm in trouble." She spoke on an inhalation of breath; she sounded as though her larynx had been removed. "They're going to come after me."

"Did you—what did you do?" His mind made a third shift, and he pictured Betty on the top of the Bank of America Building, calling from a pay phone, holding on to another little boy. This was *really* his fault, they were going to take his license away, he was going to have to sell auto insurance for a living. . . .

Betty was humming loudly. "I'm not taping this call," he promised.

"*Ssshh.* I think my ex-husband has my phone tapped. The lousy louse." She hummed another moment. "Can I see you?"

"We have an appointment on Friday," he reminded her, just to gauge the level of her distress.

"Can I see you now?" She hesitated. "I have something to tell you about your friend."

"My friend?"

"Margot," Betty whispered.

For one paranoid second he reviewed the layout of the Greek restaurant, wondering if Betty had overheard their conversation. *Oh shit.* Betty didn't know that a little black boy wasn't her son, and he thought she knew about him and *Margot*? He'd better get it together and focus on her; it sounded as if she might be having another episode. Perhaps she should check herself into the hospital; he hoped he could convince her. "Can you come to the office right now? I'll wait for you here."

Betty, who had started humming again, paused long enough to say, "God bless you," before hanging up.

Joel trotted down the hall. Luckily, on Denise's doorknob, the "in session" sign was facing inward. He knocked.

"Hi, come in." Denise Walters—voluptuous, olive-skinned—held the head and body of a decapitated ceramic elf in one hand and a tube of Krazy Glue in the other. As Joel entered, she explained, "I had a little boy today who was pretending this elf was his father." She held up the torso. "He's just a *tad* hostile toward him."

Denise was a Jungian analyst who specialized in working with the sand tray. An entire wall of her office was lined with shelves; these were cluttered with the instruments of her work, which included small toys, figurines, and dollhouse furniture. Her clients chose from among these objects and arranged them in a small sandbox, then told her stories about the *tableaux* they created. On Denise's shelves, kings and queens reigned, brides and grooms were suspended eternally at their moment of union, dinosaurs and unicorns roamed, babies slept peacefully in their cradles. Nothing died there; nothing was lost or forgotten.

"Could have been worse." Joel glanced around, although he already knew that there was no comfortable place to sit. Denise had only two giant bean bags on the floor.

"Haven't seen you in a while," Denise observed, squirting glue on the elf's stump of a neck. "I was afraid the gallery was a bit much for you."

A week and a half before Denise had invited him to a South of Market photo exhibit: Women in Space.

"Not exactly too much," he said. "I'm just still trying to figure out what the point of the chewing-gum wrappers was."

"The point is that women get thrown away, like chewing gum."

"Oh." Joel and Denise had been seeing each other for almost a year, since Denise had moved her practice to San Francisco from Berkeley. What Joel really appreciated about their relationship was its looseness: Though he saw her most weekends, and they sometimes had dinner after work, there was no obligation on either side. In between, they usually ran into each other only when one or both had a patient. Psychological etiquette demanded that they ignore each other then, passing silently, with the air of monks on their way to mass.

"Listen, I hate to do this, especially after what you just told me about the chewing gum, but actually I've got a favor to ask."

"Sure. Whatever. Sit down." She indicated the bean bags with a movement of her shoulder; her hands were engaged in pressing the elf's head onto his glued neck. Denise was all in black: black beret over her black hair, which was cut like Prince Valiant's, a black leotard, and long black skirt. Her eyes, too, were black, almost plum-colored, and so dark that he couldn't tell the pupil from the iris. She had a beauty mark on one cheek that she called attention to by trying to hide, often covering that side of her face with her hand. Her clothes seemed a compromise between the urge to display and to hide her body: her breasts swayed in a loose bra, outlined by the leotard, while the voluminous skirt hid the rest. Still, he detected the outline of her hips: round, but not *too*.

"Can you take my class for me tonight? I've got an emergency."

"Sure."

Still standing, he looked at his watch. "It's at seven-thirty."

"That's okay. I had a big evening planned—there's a rerun of 'Cheers' on Channel Two that I've only seen four times." She grimaced but quickly salvaged a smile. He'd seen that grimace pass over her face before, the shadow of an unexpressed sadness.

"I've got some lecture notes. Just talk about bipolars and passive-aggressives. Let them do a little role-playing."

"No problem." Denise released the elf's head, held the body upside down, and dipped it in the air a couple of times. "There." She held it up proudly. "He's ready to go another round with the Shadow, don't you think?"

Denise was a come-through kind of person. If he had asked Alex Forans, who had the office between his and hers, Alex would have pretended he was busy rather than admit he had no plans for the evening. "Let me take you out to dinner this weekend." He made the offer without thinking.

She frowned. "What night?"

"Oh, I don't know . . . Saturday?"

"Sure." The grimace again, followed by the compensatory smile. "I guess I'd better get going if I'm going to teach your class."

"God, you're such a *mensch*." He squeezed her shoulders, then kissed her cheek. "I really do appreciate it."

"You'll owe me one." She put the repaired elf back on the shelf, between a fairy godmother and a winged horse.

Joel left her with a promise to call. He was lucky to have a friend like her. She was a natural therapist, stronger on empathy than technique, someone with the patience and compassion that should have been common to all therapists but was in fact not. It was a quality he liked and admired, for his passion to help people was more abstract, perhaps more related to his own self-aggrandizement, and sometimes, he feared, didn't extend to the very people he should have been the most concerned about: his family or, at this moment, Ted.

He shouldn't have made a date with her for the weekend, though. By Saturday, who could say what he and Margot might be up to? Oh well, it would work out somehow. Maybe at Saturday night's dinner he'd want to tell Denise what was happening between him and Margot, whatever that was. That might be awkward at first, but Denise would be happy for him, too, if he developed a serious relationship, since the two of *them* had already gone as far as they could go.

It was too bad, though, that Margot and Denise weren't friendlier. When the four of them were together, Margot made the occasional cruel-disguised-as-funny comment that Denise, fortunately, did not seem to notice. Once Margot had observed to Joel that much as she wanted to see him married, Denise would not be a good choice. Margot had explained, "She's just a bit, you know . . ." leaving him to choose among the implied adjectives: tacky, flaky, frumpy, shy. But Margot's hostility made sense now. Even then, he had written it off as jealousy. Margot aside, Denise was simply too Jungian for him, and by that he didn't mean the teachings of Carl Gustav so much as her entire *Weltanschauung*. She subscribed to a whole line of beliefs about life after death, ESP, even reincarnation. Sometimes at night, after they had made love, he found it comforting to hear her tales of patients or friends who felt the presence of dead loved ones, or who knew to avoid boarding a plane that later crashed. But he thought her need to believe in the stories was wish-fulfilling, and essentially immature.

Joel read while he waited for Betty. At least he tried; alone he felt more restless. He had explained to Betty how to use the combination lock downstairs, and when she hadn't arrived half an hour later, he wondered if she'd had trouble with it. He'd told her to use the doorbell if she did.

At eight-fifteen, when she still hadn't shown up, he went downstairs to see if the lock was working. It was. The sky was darkening, the sunset obscured by the fog which was rolling in from the west.

Back upstairs, he checked his machine for messages, in case she had called during the ninety seconds he had been absent. He was also hoping to have heard from Margot. It was too soon, he reminded himself. She would expect him to be at class.

Relax, for God's sake!

He decided to call Betty himself. He wouldn't have done that with most of his other patients, but Betty . . . There was a law in California which required therapists to report a patient's threat to the person threatened. The very existence of the law could jeopardize a relationship with someone almost incapable of trust; and Joel, who felt an almost mystical loyalty to the confidence between doctor and patient, would have obeyed that law only under extreme circumstances. Betty had never threatened anyone in particular, but he kept worrying that there might be other Horatios in her future.

After four rings, he got Betty's answering machine. "Hello, I'm so very delighted you called, but I can't talk to you personally just this moment, because I'm either working on a special project here at home, or I'm entertaining a group of friends. Please leave your name and number, the exact time and date of your call, and I'll be getting back to you just as soon as I can." A dog barked repeatedly in the background of the tape.

"Mrs. Klass, this is Dr. Abramowitz. Please call me."

Once again he sat in his leather chair with an unread book on his lap. There was a small fireplace to his right, which had been plugged up, but sometimes—like now—he could hear the wind trapped in the hidden passage, whistling a plea to escape.

He snapped his finger against a chunk of the book's pages, wondering if Margot had talked to Ted, wondering if there would be a message from her at home. . . . His heart beat faster at the thought. In twenty minutes—fifteen minutes—he'd call his machine to check.

But once she did talk to Ted—what then? For all he knew, Margot's confronting him would be the shock that Ted needed to stop drinking and get help. Shit! Joel slammed the book closed. He could imagine the scene then: Margot in tears (of course there would be tears) explaining that she had to give Ted one more chance. And how many more? What an idiot he was. He should have taken advantage of her offer that afternoon, staked out his territory. . . .

God, it was hard enough for a married couple to endure their own ups and downs—for the interested third party the same roller-coaster ride could produce terminal motion sickness. Joel loved melodrama—in *other* people's lives. Among his patients there was no shortage of it. But he didn't have the equilibrium for this kind of romance. He'd never had to wait for a woman to call *him*. And he'd never done anything he had to be ashamed of.

He tossed his book on the chair and paced. He was thinking of calling Margot to tell her he'd changed his mind about tomorrow. Tell her that they should forget they ever knew each other. Because in a logical world, Joel would have everything on Ted (or at least he liked to think so)—but in the real world, where people were often governed by the spoiled, mad dictator of the unconscious, Ted might be the winner. Even if Margot left Ted, Joel could imagine her running back to Seacliff to make sure that he was eating enough, or getting up in the middle of the night to bail him out of the drunk tank.

Then again, Margot wanted children. She wanted them badly, and she wanted them soon. Why else would she start a day-care center instead of, say, raising money for the homeless, or for AIDS research? She and Ted might have been unlucky; but it could also be that Ted was sterile. And Joel knew that *he* wasn't—because Sonja had had to have an abortion. He'd always regretted that—until tonight.

He paused in front of the window. The darkness was made gray by the fog, and the window became a mirror, reflecting back the yellow-lighted room and his own slightly distorted image.

Betty. He should be thinking about her. Once again he tried her number, and got her machine, but left no message. *Betty had said that she wanted to tell him something about Margot.* He hadn't given that much weight. Betty would know that Margot had gone to him for help yesterday. Betty had seen them talking together, maybe even hugging. She would know that Joel had some sort of special relationship with Margot, and sense that by involving her name she could draw Joel in, hold his interest. He mustn't let her manipulate him that way. On the other hand, he wished she were there so he could *confirm* that she was trying to manipulate him. . . .

At nine-thirty he walked home. The fog was thick enough to hide the end of the street, but its density was an illusion, for it dissolved as he approached. He walked quickly, thinking that Margot might be just about to call. . . .

That made him think of Melanie again, with more empathy than he would have liked; he could imagine her waiting to hear from her lover, surrounded by the silence of phones and walls.

· · ·

Although Joel's nervous system always came to attention at the sound of a ringing phone, this particular jangle, in the milky light just before dawn, almost gave him a coronary.

He had not yet heard from Margot. He had still been able to find a number of comforting explanations for that, at least; her silence was in some ways less troubling than Betty's, who by now, he imagined, might have boarded a Greyhound to Las Vegas with a little boy in tow.

He had called Denise at about ten-thirty, to see how class went. "I really *enjoyed* it," she said. "There's so much positive energy there."

"I'll bet they loved having you."

Denise replied with a tittering sound of pleasure.

He had made plans with her to go to a new Chinese restaurant that Saturday. And then he had finally fallen asleep, after watching Ted Koppel interview a terrorist by satellite and David Letterman display a replica of the Chrysler Building fashioned from toothpicks. He woke up two hours later to the carbonated nothingness of TV-off-the-air, turned off the set, and went to bed.

Now, without his glasses, the phone looked like a black frog crouching for a leap. Even when he squinted, the figures of the digital clock were no more than a red blur. He could only guess that it was about five in the morning.

"Joey?"

Oh, my God. Ted. And the scritchy sound, like scrabbling rodents, could only be weeping. This time the guilt fell down on Joel like a water balloon, bursting effortlessly on pavement. *Oh God just don't let him know please I'm sorry I didn't mean it it was a mistake.*

"It's my fault," Ted whimpered.

"Okay, calm down, keep breathing." Joel, who had finally found his glasses, took his own advice and inhaled deeply as he put them on. "Okay, tell me what's wrong." Margot might or might not have told Ted anything. *It's not up to me to tell him,* he thought, and then: *Right, you chickenshit!*

"It's Margot, Joel," Ted sniffled.

"Margot." Lying on his back, Joel nodded supportively.

"She's gone." Whimper.

"What do you mean, *gone?*"

Sniffle. Ted seemed puzzled by Joel's question. "I mean," he attempted to explain, "I don't know where she is."

During the night, sometime after Ted Koppel had finished his interview and David Letterman had put away the toothpick-skyscraper, someone had done a thorough job of ransacking the bedroom that Ted shared with Margot. At least that was what Joel concluded half an hour later, as he stood surrounded by the detritus of Margot's belongings. Drawers had been emptied, the contents almost neatly deposited in piles beneath them. Joel tried not to notice, but kept noticing, the bras and slips, the pantyhose stretched out like withered, amputated legs. The walk-in closet had been gutted. From where Joel stood he could see two bare, pink padded hangers on the rod. The silk pastels, the patent shoes, the bows and lace and frothy scarves had been dragged out and left in a huge heap, where they no longer looked like the pretty, frail things they were when Margot wore them, but rather like the eviscera of a dead beast, something that would soon begin to decay.

Ted, unshaven and with his burgundy satin bathrobe falling open, sat in the rocking chair, staring at the bedspread, which was pulled down to the foot of the bed like a white accordion. Slack-jawed, he cradled his head in a familiar gesture that was a veritable taste of *madeleine* for Joel. College hangovers. They used to rate them, like barbecue sauce or deli mustard: Mild, Hot, and Three-Alarm Blaze. This one looked as if it also had horseradish, salsa, and extra onions. . . . The sight brought back a clear sense memory of his own hangovers, the vows never to drink again (a vow that, one day, he kept), and it made his fingers curl with revulsion at the extent of Ted's reversion to a former life.

"When did this happen?" Joel was suddenly brusque. He picked his way through purses, beads, ribbons, and panties, over to the bed, aware of an urge both voyeuristic and scatological to examine all of Margot's things.

Ted stuck out his slippered feet. "That's what so weird," he said finally. "I don't know. I came in last night, and I guess I'd had a little too much to drink, and I just sort of fell asleep on the sofa downstairs." He touched his fingertips to his tongue and tried to flatten his uncombed thatch of hair.

"On the sofa?" Maybe Ted and Margot had fought, and Ted in

his rage had destroyed the room himself. Ted legitimately might not remember that this morning; Joel knew he sometimes had blackouts. "What time?"

"I don't remember," Ted moaned softly.

"Was Margot home then?"

"I don't *remember*."

"I was just wondering . . ." Joel picked up a small eelskin evening bag, absently looked inside, and tossed it on the bed. "Did you guys, um, talk about anything special last night? Or, I mean, since yesterday afternoon?"

Ted looked up. "No. Why would we?"

"Just wondering." Joel shrugged. *Tell him!* But quite apart from his admitted chickenshitedness, this didn't seem like the time to let Ted know that his wife was contemplating having an affair. Perhaps Margot had had an attack of cowardice herself and decided to let her absence communicate to Ted what she feared to say. "Tell me what you did last night," Joel suggested.

"I went out with Fred Mezzone after work." Fred was a county supervisor, well known as a heavy drinker who was slow to pick up a check; also a client of Ted's PR firm. "And then he wanted me to stop in with him at a party at the Hollenbecks'. Well, Margot hates the Mezzones and the Hollenbecks, and she had one of her board meetings to go to, so I just left a message that I'd be home later."

"How did you get home?"

"Joel, don't shout."

"I'm not shouting. I'm going to start in a minute, though."

"I guess I drove." He raised his head. "Isn't my car out front?"

"And Margot wasn't home?"

"Well, you see, I don't really know. I made it as far as the living room, and I thought that was doing pretty good." He smiled, ingratiatingly, then winced at the movement of facial muscles.

"When did you last see Margot, then?"

"The last time? Let me think." A ball inside Ted's skull rolled to one side, and his cheek fell into his hand. The motion made Joel feel Ted's nausea, and he sank down on the bed. There was Margot's husband, Joel's once-roommate, silhouetted against the drapes which were now illumined by the fully arrived morning. *I am an anarchist*, Joel thought. He had violated the law that enabled man to come down from the trees: I will not try to fuck the woman who belongs to you.

"I guess it was yesterday morning," Ted decided finally.

"Is anything missing?" Joel asked. The rest of the house, at least what he had seen of it on the way upstairs, was undisturbed.

"Oh, God, how can I tell in all this?"

"Why haven't you called the police?"

"Do you think I should? I mean, she's probably just staying at her cousin's place, or maybe—you know how many of those airhead girlfriends she has, maybe one of them is having a crisis and she's been too busy to call."

"Since you don't see any reason to be concerned," Joel said—molars, bicuspids, and incisors not breaking contact with each other—"why did you call me at five a.m.?"

Ted stared at Joel.

"Come on," Joel said, "let's call the police."

"No—not yet," Ted begged.

"Why not?" Joel folded his arms, Inquisition style, over his chest.

"It's nothing—she could be home in an hour—but Jody Daniels will have it in her column tomorrow, and she'll blow it up to sound like Margot and I are getting a divorce."

Don't I wish.

For a few moments, the creak of the rocking chair was the only sound. Then Joel got up and gripped Ted's upper arms, pulling him out of the chair. "Come on. We're going to find her."

Joel's father had owned a family-style drugstore for something over forty years, but it was no better stocked than the shelves of Ted's medicine cabinet. Joel found Tylenol among an array of common and obscure prescription drugs, some written to Ted and others to Margot. Then he went downstairs to make coffee. It was while he was performing this latter task that he discovered Rosa, Merlin, and the living-room stereo were all gone, disappearances which Ted had apparently been too preoccupied to notice. Disappearances, too, which Joel could not glibly explain to himself, although he tried.

Ted swallowed the pills with the coffee. "Start calling her friends," Joel instructed. "Try Mrs. Tuttle first. Does Margot have an address book?"

"She carries it with her."

Joel remembered now seeing a black leather notebook with

Margot's name on the cover, in gold. How had he forgotten that? "You must have something you keep here."

"Yes . . . we must. Where is it? . . ."

The *we* stung.

Ted finally dug up a battered address book in a room that Joel had never even been in. "It's a really, really old one." Ted stroked the cover of the cloth address book. It had blue flowers on it.

"Try it anyway. Call the people you know first."

"I've got to lie down."

The middle of the living room was sunken, so that the back of the sofa was flush with the floor behind it. Ted bypassed the steps which led down to this pit, preferring to descend from carpet onto sofa cushion. He shakily grasped the cordless phone; then he stopped with his index finger poised above the number three. "Isn't it too early to wake people up?" he asked timidly.

"Jesus Christ, *call.*"

By eight-forty Ted had made eighteen phone calls, none of which had led to any information. Joel had an appointment with Andrea Griswald at nine; he left Ted reclining on the sofa, in the pit of the living room, turning the pages of the address book as if it were a dull text he had been assigned to read.

Andrea trotted down the hall ahead of Joel, the hood of her oversized Hastings College of the Law sweatshirt flopping behind her.

As soon as she had flung herself on the couch, she declared, "I missed my antitrust exam. I just didn't go."

Joel slid lower in his chair, searching for a comfortable position. Back pain was endemic among therapists. Besides which, he hadn't had time to go running, or shave; the few swallows of hastily made coffee he had drunk were enough to form pools of acid in his stomach but not enough to wake him up. He hadn't been able to read the paper, either, to see whether there were any little boys reported missing, though at the moment, Betty seemed the least of his problems. What had Andrea just said? She didn't go to her exam? "Why not?"

"I didn't know any of it, so why should I bother?"

"By not going," he said gently, "you guaranteed the result you say you most feared."

"I know you don't care," Andrea said hollowly. Then she fidgeted. "They might let me take it over, if I had a good excuse.

Like a medical excuse. Maybe I could go to the doctor's and pretend that I was sick." Pause. "I don't suppose, I mean maybe, could you write me one, an excuse, I mean?"

"You asked me to do that yesterday." *Yesterday.* Wednesday. He wished he could go back and live it again.

"I know . . . but yesterday I didn't need it as much."

"And what would that excuse say?"

"That I was too fucked-up to take the exam." She cackled. "No, really, I sort of figured out what happened. I had an anxiety attack, so I was hyperventilating, or at least not breathing deep enough, and not getting enough oxygen. So I couldn't make very good decisions. Could you—would you do it this time?"

"I think, like yesterday, you already know the answer to that."

"You hate me."

"But if I lied to cover for you, that would mean I loved you."

"But you wouldn't be lying—I think that's what really happened to me."

"Then why not go to a medical doctor for an excuse?"

She cackled again, a sound bursting with self-disgust. "Because he wouldn't believe me, either."

Joel considered how he could use this marginal insight as a wedge. He could point out—again—that she used these requests as stalling tactics, postponing the "real stuff," or he could point out—again—that she wanted to make him responsible for her health, education, and welfare. Not going to the exam was fairly serious, regressive, and that worried him. In the midst of all this, Margot remained in his mind, but his preoccupation with her dimmed, like the single headlight of a motorcycle that he was outdistancing.

"I knew you wouldn't do it. You don't care. You know what it means, though? I'm going to flunk and they might even kick me out, because I've been on probation. That turd who claims to be my father is going to eviscerate me—" Andrea cut herself off. She was quiet for a while. "I wouldn't let you do it anyway. I just wanted to see if you would. The reason I wouldn't let you is I don't deserve it. Maybe if I take the punishment of flunking out nothing worse will happen to me."

Joel waited. The coffee was continuing to act out its resentment, percolating up his esophagus.

"I had an accident last night. I mean, I almost had an accident."

Joel would have been more disturbed by this announcement,

had Andrea not been lying there apparently uninjured. He watched her balance the heel of one shoe on the toe of the other. "So yesterday afternoon, I mean, instead of the exam, I . . . I went home. Then . . . then I had a big fight with my yucky father. He threw me out! He told me to leave the house!"

From where he sat, Joel could see Andrea's arms folded over her chest; she was hugging her elbows, as if trying to hold on to herself. "We fought about this summer again," she said. "I don't want to work in his yucky office. He's always got his latest jailbait girlfriend working there, you know, she's usually about twenty million years younger than I am. What's so funny is he doesn't even know that I'm probably going to flunk out this semester." Joel saw Andrea's elbows bob up and down. "So I just decided to split, you know, go over to Jennifer's house. She lives in Bolinas, I don't know if you remember me telling you that."

Joel did, but said nothing.

"So I took off, it was almost midnight, and I started driving up the coast, up Highway One. You know, that real curvy road right along the ocean, on the mountain, over the cliffs." She paused a long time. "You're not going to like this," she said. "You're going to hate me."

"You seem pretty convinced," Joel said. Oblique reassurance. He could hardly imagine (or maybe he just didn't *want* to imagine) how Andrea could give him a harder time than she already had: During her first year she had expressed a great deal of curiosity about his personal life, and when he hadn't provided her with the information she wanted, she had undertaken her own research, with an energy and resourcefulness she was unable to muster for her studies. On one occasion she had waited outside his office at the end of the day, and tried to follow him home, but had revealed her presence when, lagging a few yards behind him, she had crossed against the light, forcing a driver to brake suddenly and honk his horn at her. Though that had failed, she had eventually learned his home address by calling Alex Forans, whose name she got from the front of the building, and pretending to be a friend of Joel's from out of town. (Joel had never quite believed that Alex had *really* been fooled by her ploy.)

She had also asked him to come to a number of extra-therapeutic events, such as her father's office Christmas party. He politely declined that invitation, as well as the one to her moot court oral arguments. *Talk about why you want me there*, he had said. Finally she had revealed her fantasy that she would be able to pretend he was her date, that it would make her father jealous and cause him to respect her more.

Andrea had been known to call him collect from distant pay phones. Then there was the time she left her chewing gum under the couch.

She lived in constant expectation of his terminating her treatment. But instead he kept interpreting over and over why she did these things. Andrea wasn't a slow learner; it was just that the spoiled, mad dictator who lived in *her* unconscious was a little stubborn about some things. Still, Andrea kept coming back. So she and Joel were both doing their jobs.

"I think this is really it, this time. You're gonna kick me out, I mean." She sighed. "But I have to tell you anyway. I can't keep it secret. I'm going crazy."

For a moment she clapped her Reeboks together. Then she began slowly, "My dad threw me out, like I said, and I took off. I mean, what else was I supposed to do? So it was after midnight, and I was driving toward Stinson Beach. I was behind this car, I guess it was a Jag, and, you know, the license plate was M, A, R, space, G, O."

She paused, as if waiting for Joel to confirm that he understood the reference. He said nothing, while his stomach went another round with Mr. Coffee. M A R space G O was Margot's license plate, all right.

"I saw that same car yesterday afternoon"—Andrea sounded hoarse now—"parked down the street when I left here. I noticed the license plate then. I thought it was really dippy." She waited again, then went on, "I was so upset, you know, I was sort of pissed at you because when I asked you if I could call if things got bad, you didn't really say yes. I didn't think that being able to call you was a lot to ask. I mean, I've been coming here for a long time and I'm still into the same shit at home and the same shit at school, and I still don't have a boyfriend. And here's this MAR space GO woman who thinks she's so hot—I mean, when I saw the car yesterday I just had a feeling it belonged to the woman I saw who was coming up the stairs yesterday, she was really pretty, and *thin*, too, although I thought her nose was kind of funny-looking."

Joel , who had been resting his chin in his hand, moved his head and felt the stubble against his palm.

"I mean, it was obvious she was coming to see you, that she was a patient of yours, but you *like* her, I mean you never smile at *me* that way. I bet you'd go to a party with *her*, if she asked."

"You said you almost had an accident," Joel said.

Silence. "Maybe it wasn't her car," Andrea said finally. "I think I might have imagined the whole thing."

"Then why don't you tell me what you think you imagined." *Focus, Joel!* Margot had been traveling north on the coast highway Wednesday night. Why? At least he knew that she was all right.

"Okay." Joel couldn't see Andrea's face, but he could picture it: jaw clenched, eyes squeezed shut. "It was late and there were hardly any cars on the road. I was following pretty close behind her, that's how I saw the license plate, 'cause it was so dark. She was driving pretty slow. I was really upset, so I felt like I shouldn't be on the road anyway, like I was a menace, and I wanted to get to Jennifer's as fast as I could. So when we got to an even stretch of road, I honked twice, and I passed the Jaguar. That wasn't so terrible, was it?"

Joel did not reply. Now he was thinking how strange it was that Andrea would be behind Margot's car. It just wasn't possible; the coincidence was too great. *There are no coincidences.*

"Anyway, I just get back into the right lane and I'm driving along a little ways, and then I see her pulling behind me, starting to pull into the left lane, like just because I'm fat and she's thin she can't stand it that I passed her, and she's going to pass me now—"

Joel felt his own chair swaying as on a bumpless highway, saw the road that curved into darkness, and the glare of the headlights as they moved out of Andrea's rearview mirror.

"And then she was alongside me—I was already going pretty fast, I mean I just don't see why it wasn't fast enough for her—when she was alongside me, I . . . I . . ." Andrea's voice was suddenly very soft. "I speeded up." She was silent a moment. "And she speeded up, too, and so did I, and we were going about neck-and-neck, her in the left lane and me in the right, and that road is so curvy and narrow I knew it was dangerous, but then," Andrea squeaked, "it was like those times when I just sort of lose control, like the time I broke all those dishes of my mother's and pretended it was an accident. . . ."

Joel became aware of a clammy film that had formed between his hand and his motionless cheek.

"Then all of a sudden, there was another car coming the other way. I remember, I saw the headlights way up ahead and then they disappeared around a curve, and then they appeared again. So I knew it was coming, but still, it happened so fast. We were still together, me and the Jaguar. The other car honked and kept honking all in one stream, and I braked and went off the shoulder. If there hadn't been a little shoulder there I wouldn't be here now. The MAR GO car—she went off the cliff."

Joel listened for a moment to the loud, grinding ticks of the clock. Then he asked, "What did you do then?"

"I pulled off the shoulder and just started going again," Andrea said. "I just kept driving. I mean, it was like I blocked it out." She entreated, "I mean, haven't you ever hit a parked car when no one was around, and then you just drove off because you just couldn't deal with it? And you thought about it later, and you didn't think you could do something like that, but you knew you did? But then it's like you feel that if you just don't think about it, then it will go away?"

"Are you saying that's what you did?"

"I didn't think I could do something like this," Andrea whispered. "But if I tell what happened *now* then it's so much worse. Hit and run. Vehicle Code section 20001. It's a misdemeanor. I could go to jail for a year."

Joel closed his eyes. Maybe Andrea *had* imagined the entire episode. That was all he could hope.

"I got to Jennifer's house and somehow I just put it out of my mind." Andrea sounded calmer now. "I don't think I meant to get her. I thought there'd be an accident, but I thought it'd be me, and then you and my parents would come to the hospital. . . ."

"Was it—was it a steep cliff?" Joel asked.

"I don't know. It was too dark. None of the cliffs are that steep there, though—it's not like they go straight down to the ocean or anything. You could skid to a stop." Pause. "Maybe."

"Did you see what happened afterward at all? Did the other car stop?"

"The other car?" She seemed surprised by the question. "No. I

don't think so. But I guess he's at fault, too?" Pause. "Maybe not."
Pause. "Should I turn myself in?"

Joel took a Kleenex and used it to pat his forehead. "You want
me to tell you what to do," he observed. For once he was
tempted.

"Oh, God, I feel so guilty." Andrea spoke softly. "No. I don't
feel guilty. Well, I do, but mostly I'm just scared."

"Scared . . ."

"That you're going to call the police and tell them."

"You just asked me if you should tell them yourself."

"But I won't," Andrea said promptly. "I can't. My father would
cut me up and feed me to our neighbor's gross little terrier. And
you know, if I ever want to practice law, which I doubt, because
I'm sure they're going to kick me out now—but if I ever wanted
to, then I can't have a criminal record."

Suddenly Joel wanted to laugh. If what Andrea said were
true, then surely the Jaguar and Margot would have been
found by now. Even if Margot had been unconscious, she
would have been carrying her license, and the auto registration would be in the glove compartment. Ted would have been
notified. Joel remembered how once Andrea had given him a
detailed but completely invented account of sleeping with her
civil-procedure professor, though Joel had suspected that
fabrication immediately because of the physical difficulty of
certain positions she described.

"I was so jealous of her," Andrea was saying, "that Mar Go
lady. It's like there's another person inside me. A person who
knows when I'm weak and takes over. A person who hates me. I
know I just want to fuck things up. But knowing that doesn't
help! I love you, I mean not that way, but I really care
about you—I've never never felt about anyone the way I feel
about you. It's like you're God, but a boyfriend, too. When I hear
you talking behind me, I shiver all over. It's almost like—I hope
this won't gross you out—like coming. Or like dying, but in a good
way. But I know you're a real person and that this is another
patient of yours and it's my fault. If you love someone, you want
him to be happy, and look what I've done instead."

"Maybe you don't only love me," Joel said. "Maybe you have
other feelings, too." Negative transference.

"But I *do* love you! I just don't want to share you." She sounded confident now. "Maybe I don't need to feel guilty. It really was an accident. I didn't mean for anything to happen to her, I thought it would happen to *me*."

Joel rubbed his thumb against the stubble on his chin.

"And you'd all be at the hospital, standing around the bed—I'd have all these wires and tubes in me and they wouldn't think that I was going to live. And my father would be crying, and so would my mother, and our priest would be there. . . ."

"That's all you want to say about the accident."

She stiffened. "Well, no, I mean, I'm not sure. . . ." Then she added coyly, "Was there something in particular you wanted to know?"

"Did you come back the same way this morning? Did you see anything then?"

"I knew you were going to hate me."

"You think I hate you because I asked you a question." *And I sure would appreciate it if you'd answer me.*

"It sure *sounds* like it."

Joel rubbed his eyes under his glasses, damning himself. Was he going to throw away two years of work in one morning? *Go ahead, see if you can pry it out of her! See how far you get!*

"I *didn't* come back that way," she said petulantly. "Once you've had an accident somewhere, it's sort of scary to drive that way again, I mean, don't you think?"

Joel said nothing. *Don't panic. Do what you're supposed to do.* There was the rule, the basic rule, and it had been his creed and motto all these years: *The patient says whatever comes into his mind.* He'd always thought the rule was for *their* benefit, but maybe it was for his, too. Let her do it her way, slow as that way was, drive him crazy though it might. . . .

"I wish you'd say something," Andrea sighed.

"You want a response from me." There, that was by the book.

Now it was her turn to be silent, while Joel's mind clicked on. Her story must be a fantasy, or a lie—but even if it wasn't, could he make her go to the police? Here in this room, the border between fantasy and reality was so wavy—and as subject to change as Poland's. At this moment, he couldn't draw that border for himself, let alone for her.

Andrea finally began again, picking up the thread of her fantasy about her death in a hospital room. He tried to listen. He was aware of the paintings on his wall, hovering blurred in his peripheral vision.

And he realized, as she talked on, that he wouldn't make her go to the police. Not even if he could. Not even if her story were true. Here in this room, even killers had to be safe.

CHAPTER 4

SUSPICIOUS MINDS OR JUST BECAUSE YOU'RE PARANOID

But that didn't stop him from trying to check out her story.

After all, though there may in fact be no coincidences, the universe does allow for bad jokes. For example: Joel had freed up his afternoon so as to allow for the possibility of committing adultery with Margot, which was why he had time that afternoon to follow Andrea's alleged route of the night before, driving across the Golden Gate Bridge and down the long curvy stretch of Highway One that passed through Muir Woods and went on to Stinson Beach.

The sky was overcast, but the light was clear, so that he could see the cliffs for miles ahead, looking jagged and sinister; they made him think of one of Ibsen's fjords. The ocean was slate, with thin lines of stark white foam where the water met beach or rock. The foliage along the road was already turning summer brown.

During the first part of the drive, he scanned the cliffs, actually afraid that he was going to see the battered hulk of a white car. Of *course* the car would have been found by now: The road was regularly traveled. But this was the only way that Joel could eliminate the possibility that the Jaguar had slid down the cliff and remained undiscovered, or dismiss the picture of Margot, unconscious, sprawled across the bucket seats.

The curves went on and on, like a hypochrondriac describing his symptoms. Gassing, turning, braking, Joel reflected that this highway, especially at night, would be a natural migratory path for someone who wanted to act out an impulse, self-destructive or otherwise. No wonder Andrea found an excuse to drive here. If she didn't have a friend in Bolinas, she would have had to make one. Joel thought it plausible that she had forced *someone's* car off the road last night. If so, then her jealous and guilty mind could have afterward superimposed Margot's hated personalized plate on the one she had actually seen.

Either that, or she had invented the whole thing. But he didn't think so—at least not the *whole* thing. She wasn't delusional, and her lies were usually more transparent.

He stopped on a turnout about a mile before Stinson Beach and got out of the car. A chilly wind blew his tie over his shoulder. The ground sloped at about forty-five degrees down to the water; it was rocky and covered with shrubs. Even if a car rolled over, it looked as though it would stop before falling very far.

He kicked a small stone, then watched it skid through the metal barrier and disappear down the hill. Denise would be willing to believe that Andrea had simply ended up behind Margot's car. *Synchronicity*, she would call it. Things happen the way they're supposed to. But then, Denise also believed in God and that God might be female. Joel did not believe in God, though he would have liked to: a God who—as male, female, or burning bush—would make for a little justice in the world.

None of this solved the problem of Margot's whereabouts. Joel had checked with Ted before leaving the office: Ted still hadn't heard anything, although he said he was still phoning her friends. Even so, he hadn't wanted to notify the police until Joel had challenged him, *Does she do this often? Just go away and not tell you where she is?* No, Ted admitted, and finally agreed to call.

But now Joel began to wonder if Margot, feeling more conflicted about her situation, had decided to take off by herself to think things through. Joel would be hurt, even angry, because of the worry she had caused him, but he would try to understand. Even if it meant that she had changed her mind about their future affair. There was something about looking out over the Pacific Ocean, breathing in salty air, alone on a narrow road, that made you feel independent of the need for romantic love. Joel was himself exhausted after only two days of *considering* an affair, so he could empathize with how she might feel.

He decided to drive the rest of the way into Stinson before turning back for home. But he got back into his car feeling relieved, and even slightly ridiculous for having wasted a precious free afternoon.

"Here's to Margot." Ted raised his shot glass.

"To Margot." Joel grasped his orange juice, but did not lift it. The calm he had felt on the cliff above the ocean had lasted until he had driven back into the city and checked his mail, his answering machines, and the message board at the office. He realized then that he had been expecting Margot to contact him. She would whisper huskily that she had simply needed to get away from Ted. Perhaps she had gone to Carmel after all. "Why don't you join me here?" she would ask.

This time he would say yes.

"The first lady of my heart, the only woman in my life," Ted slurred, "Margot Iddele Harvey, the Princess of California Street." Ted downed the shot of tequila and refilled the glass. The bottle of Herradura was half empty. Or half full, Joel thought.

He and Ted sat on the floor, in the pit of the living room: The pit, two steps below the main floor, was bordered on three sides by the horseshoe-shaped couch, custom-made in Italy. Joel and Ted rested their backs against ottomans. The house was huge and empty around them, like the crumbling, dark castle of an extinguished noble family. Ted had lit a single candle in a silver candlestick, and the flame cast the wavy shadow of his head on the gaping space against the wall where the stereo cabinet had been. Joel remembered the tiers of chrome knobs and green-lighted gauges. The creaks and sighs of the house sounded like Margot's footsteps on the path, like her key in the door.

"I was never good enough to her. I never appreciated her." Ted rubbed his thumbs against the shot glass, then hiccuped. He covered his mouth with his hand.

"H'm," Joel said neutrally.

"She's okay, don't you think?" Ted asked. So far, he had drunk just enough to be talkative, almost cheerful.

"I hope so."

"No, really."

"What do you want me to say?" Joel's orange juice was sour; Merlin must have squeezed it a couple of days ago. "You should know better than I what's going on with her."

Ted raised his eyebrows and wrinkles appeared on his forehead: his new venetian-blind look. He'd had it about a year.

"I'm sure she's all right," Joel amended. "If not, we would have heard something by now." Wouldn't they?

Actually, except for the small matter of Margot's disappearance, this was like old times: hanging out in the triangular living room of their apartment in Westwood. How grown-up they felt, with underwear they didn't have to put away. If not for Margot, Joel would have stopped seeing Ted years ago. But as it was, he had jollied himself along, letting his mild contempt pass for friendship—friendship made more tolerable by Ted's private box at Candlestick Park and access to the pool at the Spartan Club.

"Remember the gorilla suit?" Joel asked suddenly. "I still can't believe you did that."

"Did what?"

"Wore it to that exam. It was Spanish, wasn't it?"

Ted gave a short, gurgly laugh. "I never did that."

"Yes, you did, you—"

"I know you're trying to make me feel better, Joey. Thanks."

"I *am* trying to make you feel better. But you did wear the gorilla suit."

Ted picked a shriveled lime wedge up from a plate on the carpet. Ted usually still went through the motions of mixing water into Scotch and putting onions into martinis. But Joel had recently noticed that he would also run to the kitchen to get more ice, or more glasses, or fresh crackers more often than was necessary, presumably so he could belt down a secret shot or two. "Margot cared about you a lot, you know."

Joel started. "Hey, none of this past tense stuff, okay?"

"I just want you to know, whatever happens, that I really appreciate all the support you've given her, with Playground and all." He reached out to squeeze Joel's arm; Joel recoiled inwardly. Ted was passing into Stage Two: sentimental.

"I mean," Ted went on, "I was busy with my business a lot of the time. . . ."

Playing office is more like it, Joel thought, but said nothing.

"Margot and I talked about you a lot. We wanted to see you get married. Marriage can be really special. I mean"—he poured another shot and held the bottle nearer to the candle, the better to see what remained—"I shouldn't try to analyze a shrink, but it seems that you've always gotten involved with very possessive women."

Joel was wishing he hadn't come here after all. He had thought he wanted to comfort Ted (and maybe he did, in part), but the real reason was that this was Margot Headquarters—the first stop for any official news. "I can't believe that no one's seen her," he grumbled. "Have you tried to find Rosa or Merlin? Did you call their families? Their friends?"

"Joey, I was on the phone all day," Ted whined, rubbing his ear. "I've got a cramp in the whole left side of my body. I tried everyone—I mean, Merlin's school and"—he whimpered—"don't you think I want to know where she is?"

"Yes," Joel said absently. He unknotted his tie. "Then there's the mess upstairs. . . ."

Ted dribbled another shot of tequila into his glass. "The police came to look around up there," he said, "and I noticed that Margot's ring was gone. It was the only good piece of jewelry she kept at home, but she never wore it, because—"

"I know," Joel interrupted. Margot didn't mind driving a Jaguar, and she owned a couple of fur coats. But the engagement ring was more ostentatious, and it advertised *family* wealth: Margot's maternal grandfather, the department-store tycoon, had given it to her grandmother. The ring, worth a small department store itself, had come down to Margot. It was God-knew-how-many karats, a marquis the size of a small candy easter egg; it flashed miniature rainbows like the spray of a waterfall. Margot and Ted joked that it was part of her dowry; Joel had derived unconscious satisfaction from Ted's metaphoric impotence in not giving Margot a new ring. "Did you tell the police that it was gone?"

Ted nodded. "I told them about the stereo, too, though I sorta thought I shun'ta." He stifled a belch.

"Why not?"

"'Cause I think Merlin took it. I wouldn't want to see him get into any trouble. He always liked that stereo. I remember—he was such a nice guy, really—he'd come up here late at night—"

Joel interrupted, "Do you think Merlin took Margot's ring, too?"

"Margot's ring?" Ted looked confused.

"You said her engagement ring was missing."

"That's right. I did. It is."

"Well?"

"*I* don't know." Ted eyed Joel's glass. "More o.j., José?"

"No."

"Hey, I don't mind. I'll go get it for you."

"No need . . . Rosa, then? No." He answered his own question. Rosa might be a pain in the butt, but she wasn't a thief, and she was devoted to Margot. "Margot must have taken it with her," he said. His back was hurting from leaning against the ottoman.

"Oh, God." Ted rubbed his eyes with the heels of his hands. "She musta gotten kidnapped." His eyelids looked swollen, and his face was pale in the candlelight. "It's the only thing that makes sense. They broke in here to rob us, and then she put up a fight, you know she would have put up a fight. . . ."

"Then how come we haven't gotten a ransom note?"

Ted fingered the front of his hair for a moment. "Maybe it's just too soon," he said.

"I don't think we have to worry yet," Joel said. His voice was reassuring, deep. Psychoanalytic. But he was starting to get almost panicky himself. What if Ted was right? A lot of it made sense. *Wait, wait.* It was magical thinking, really: his fear that his sexual impulses toward Margot had harmed her. *But what if Ted was right?*

Ted made a wet sound, half laughter and half tears. "It's all my fault. . . ."

Passive-aggressive trick #387: Take all the blame before anyone can blame you. Joel gave his tie one sharp tug, pulling it free through his collar. He rolled it around his hand and put it in his pocket. "I want that address book. I'm going to call those people myself."

Ted was slumping a little closer to the floor.

"Come on, up," Joel said, unbending his own legs. He couldn't sit here any longer, feeling his back twinge and watching Ted lose the battle against gravity.

"Oh, God, Joey, give me a minute." Ted's neck was flush with the ottoman, and he let his head roll backward onto it. The motion had its effect: He gagged.

Joel stood. "You can stay there if you want. Where's the book?"

"Everyone's already heard from me," Ted moaned. "Why would they tell you something they wouldn't tell her husband?"

Joel did not move. Then he heard the words come out of him. "Ted, you need help."

"That's right. Bring the crane around here, wouldja?"

"No. I mean, you drink too much." *You should wait until he's sober.* "You've got a serious problem. You're an alcoholic."

Ted gave a splattering laugh. "Oh, Joey, you're funny. Like I don't know. Like I care."

"Well, what are you going to do about it?"

"What do you want me to do about it? I'm under a lot of stress right now, wouldn't you say?"

"You've been an alcoholic since I've known you." He spat them out, these helpful words, "You just had it under control for a while." But now here he was, a thirty-three-year-old, losing his hair, rolling around on the floor like a teenager. *Our pasts lie in ambush for us.*

Ted laughed again. "Your timing sucks, you know that?"

Joel folded his arms across his chest. "Seems like a good time to me."

Ted started to sit up, but fell back against the ottoman again. "You don't know what it's like. Things are easy for you."

"Bullshit."

"You've got all the answers, don't you? Like you fart pink clouds." He raised his upper lip to sneer, "You had the hots for Margot, too."

Don't admit anything. He's fishing. "Forget it, then," Joel said. "Where's that address book?"

"Joey, don't be mad."

"I'm not," Joel lied.

"It's just I'm *so* worried about her—it's making me crazy."

Joel almost felt sorry for him then. "Then do it for Margot. Get help *now*." Did he really want Ted to recover? Maybe; then it would be a fair fight.

"You're right." Ted nodded very slightly. Ingratiatingly. "I'll stop. You'll help me, Joey, won't you?"

"Yes," Joel said. But he was feeling uneasy. It was something about Ted's sudden docility. As if Ted had something to hide. Or maybe he was just pissed off, that Ted had gotten him to make a promise he didn't want to keep.

. . .

The call came at ten that night. Ted had fallen asleep on the sofa, and was snoring adenoidally. Joel had finally gotten hold of the disputed address book and had made several calls, with no more luck than Ted had predicted he would have. Then he had picked up his messages: Andrea had called to say that she was having "flashbacks about that thing I told about," but specifically requested that he not return her call, since her parents were having company and she would be hiding out in her room. The head psychologist at the halfway house had called to ask if Joel could take on another new patient for them ("I'm afraid it will be a very low fee," she said). Alex Forans, self-appointed office manager, had called to say that they needed to have another meeting about the cost of supplies. Nothing from Betty. Nothing from Margot.

He had just finished returning the calls that needed to be returned when the cordless phone emitted its weasely little buzz. It was the San Francisco Police Department. Was Mr. Harvey there, please? *No, Mr. Harvey passed out after a bottle of high-grade tequila*, he wanted to say. *I'm Mr. Harvey's therapist. You can tell me everything.*

"Mr. Harvey's here, but he's indisposed. I'm a close friend, so if there's any information, I'd really appreciate it if you'd tell me." He heard Ted snort in his sleep, as if in response to his name.

No, they had to talk to Mr. Harvey directly, the Police Department said. This was Sergeant Someone speaking.

"Hold on," Joel said. He stepped down into the pit. The candle had burned down to a stub; wax had melted over the candlestick and dripped to the carpet; the flame cringed and swelled. Joel shook Ted. "Come on, dammit. Wake up."

"I've got to go now," Ted muttered in his sleep.

"*Wake up.*" Joel shook him harder. As Ted's eyes opened he immediately started to gag. "Oh no, you don't." Joel held the receiver of the cordless phone next to his head. "Speak," he hissed. "Say, this is Ted Harvey."

Ted obeyed.

Joel bent down, closer than he wanted to, smelling booze and unshowered armpits and an unchanged undershirt, near to the space that he created between Ted's ear and the phone.

Margot's car had been found on the cliffs near Stinson Beach. They guessed it had been there about twenty-four hours.

Joel took the phone away. "How can that be?" he demanded. "Why did you take so long to tell us?"

"The license plates had been detached," the sergeant explained. "The vehicle ID number had also been removed. We had to run several computer checks—"

Joel noticed that Ted was trying to right himself, his legs wriggling like a fly's, attempting to crawl out of something sticky.

"And where's Margot?"

"Let me speak to Mr. Harvey."

"Where's Margot?"

"We don't know that, sir."

"No body?"

"No body."

Joel sank down. Ted had given up the fight to stand, and was crawling toward the bathroom. His foot hit the candlestick; it toppled over; the candle went out. Joel heard him moan.

Joel lay on the sofa with the phone on his chest. They must have already towed the car by the time he drove out there. But the license plates had been removed. The room was dark, but there were track lights hanging from under the eaves of the house, so that through the French windows Joel could see the backyard where he and Ted and Margot had spent their last night together.

Joel and Ted were able to learn that the Jaguar was only slightly dented. The hubcaps and the tape deck had been removed, too, indicating that person or persons unknown might have vandalized the car after the accident. There was a small amount of blood on the driver's seat: Type O-positive, which was Margot's blood type, but also the blood type of another million or so residents of the nine-county greater Bay Area.

This promptly gave rise to Joel's new theory that the accident had caused Margot to have hysterical amnesia. Since there was no body, she must have walked away from the car. His theory would not only explain what had happened, but would mean that she wasn't purposely letting them worry. He pictured her at a woodcutter's cabin, somewhere in the John Muir Woods, drinking tea and eating whole-grain muffins. Or perhaps the modern equivalent of the woodcutter would be a gentle dope farmer, who along with his wife might even now be puzzling over Margot's driver's license, family snapshots, and stack of credit cards. More likely, though, Margot had lost her purse and, along with it, all forms of identification. The dope farmer, because of his need to hide his own illegal activities, would not want to take Margot back to town.

It was a pretty, if bizarre, story, and Joel clung to it.

Friday morning came. Waking up at home, Joel was amazed: The sky was light again, the weather report was on the radio, and the *Courier* had landed at his door with the usual dull thud.

Joel knew that there would be something about Margot's disappearance in the paper. That was Margot's own fault, in a sense: With her family background, she had an immediate entrée into the society column, and she had always taken advantage of that, while cultivating an acquaintance with as many "hard news" editors and TV people as possible, too. She needed, she said, to keep up a certain level of name recognition, for herself and Playground, in order to keep the donations rolling in; but even she admitted that she didn't mind the attention for its own sake. Recent mentions by Jody Daniels of a fashion-show–fund-raiser and the Harveys' last trip to Europe alone guaranteed that a journalist reading the police report would consider Margot's sudden absence noteworthy.

And so the morning paper ran a small page-three article about just that. The piece, though, somehow gave the reader the impression that she had gone on holiday and didn't want her whereabouts known for the sake of her privacy. Since Margot's cousin Frank was in charge of the newspaper, he and Ted had agreed that this was the best way to handle it. Ted explained to Joel that actually they probably *could* have kept it out of the *Courier* altogether, except that the rival afternoon paper, the more sensational *Deliverer*, would have their own people reading police reports.

Betty did not appear for her scheduled appointment that afternoon. Joel called her, but there was no answer; no machine, nothing. Was there some connection between her and Margot's disappearance? If so, it was only in his soon-to-be-demented head, where Margot's disappearance (and imminent return) might be linked with the number of steps that led to his building, with the rise and fall of the Dow Jones Industrial Average, with the sight of a woman with a ribbon in her hair.

In lucid moments, Joel knew that Betty had probably decided

he was more dangerous than whatever inner threat had originally prompted her to contact him. At least when he read the *Courier*, he had determined that no little boys had been abducted.

Between patients he went out to get the afternoon paper. Ted was right: The *Deliverer* carried the story, in an article that began at the bottom of the front page, and was continued on page eight, with a sidebar about Margot herself. The latter included two sentences about Playground and approximately six paragraphs on the more lurid scandals of the Iddele-Jordan family, including (but not limited to) Margot's father's second marriage, the rumors surrounding the divorce, long-disproved allegations of Mafia connections, the rumors surrounding the divorce from his third wife, and his death from cirrhosis (Margot had always said it was cancer of the liver). Somewhat less space was devoted to the celebrated feud that had caused Margot's maternal great-uncle to open Le Frère Jordan's, a women's clothing store which competed with her grandfather's.

Joel stood in front of the vending machine while he skimmed the articles. He also learned from them that Margot was two years older than she had said she was and that she had been engaged once before she married Ted, to a man with a noble title of dubious authenticity.

Only Margot's mother's suicide was not mentioned. Joel imagined that Margot's father had bargained with the devil to keep just one family secret an actual secret, and that this was the one he had chosen—for it was commonly believed that the first Mrs. Iddele had succumbed to a congenital heart condition. Margot had not even told Joel the truth; for his knowledge Joel was indebted to the three flasks of Chivas Regal that Ted had zipped into the pockets of the down jacket he wore to a Forty-Niner game.

The article concluded, "Francis Iddele's will stipulated that day-to-day management of the *Courier* pass to his nephew, Francis Iddele II."

"As if I wanted to run a newspaper!" Ted shouted that evening to Joel, crumpling the offending sheet into a ball and kicking it across the room. "Margot and I had more important things to do."

Joel had started to gather the scattered papers and to pick up the empty bottles, but he stopped now, and not only because he didn't want to play maid. He didn't care to know what Ted's definition of "more important things" was. Certainly Playground qualified, absolving Margot of the sin of self-indulgence in Joel's own critical mind. But he wondered at the value of all human pursuits in a world where a phone can ring and you can find out that someone you love is gone forever.

Joel often went to the office on Saturday morning to catch up on paperwork; the solitude forced him, eventually, to concentrate on forms and reports.

Bad move today. That same solitude quickly drove him out into the hallway, where he soon confirmed that he was the only one in the building. He paced the narrow passage. At that moment he would even have welcomed a lecture from his neighbor "Alex Forans, the toilet paper man" a.k.a. Mr. Obsessive, on the relative merits of various long-distance phone companies.

The uncertainty was the hardest part, because he didn't know whether to grieve or to be angry, and so had to do both together.

Someone rang the bell about eleven o'clock. Joel skidded down the stairs, squinting to see the form on the other side of the venetian blind that hung over the door. He would have been grateful to the Fuller Brush man for the company, but he was thinking—praying—that it might be *her*.

Betty stood on the porch, the collar of her blouse turned up, and her sleeves carefully rolled. Joel might have preferred Margot, but he was almost as glad to see Betty: She was safe, and somehow that, too, became a harbinger of Margot's return. "Hello," he greeted her. "Come in. We'll talk."

"I can only stay a sec," she said, as she swayed ahead of him into his office. She carried a beige leather tote bag that looked, from the way it dragged on her shoulder, as if it must weigh fifty pounds. "It's run-run, on the go, for me these days. I'm meeting with the CEO of Babes-In-Arms—you know the toy store? I'm going to redecorate their corporate headquarters."

"You're a decorator?" Joel motioned to the armchair, and Betty sat, squeezing the enormous tote bag next to her. There was a puffy sac under each of her eyes, like a smooth crescent pastry, but her hair was sprayed into neat sloping curves, with the ends tucked under. Joel found it comforting to think of her going to the beauty shop, having coffee handed to her, being thanked for a tip.

"My mother told me I should have something to fall back on. And boy, was she right. My ex-husband now, he's a gynecologist. Isn't that disgusting—a man who spends his whole day looking at women's private parts?"

"You called me the other night," Joel reminded her, settling into his own chair.

"Yes, I did."

"And we were going to meet here that evening."

"And I hope you know that I appreciate that, Dr. Abramowitz. You're one of the good ones. Now Al, my ex-husband—"

"Was there a reason you didn't come?"

"My next-door neighbor asked me to baby-sit her little boy."

Joel massaged the bridge of his nose, letting his glasses ride on top of his thumb and forefinger. He was tempted to ask, like a Jewish-mother-turned-psychologist, *So why didn't you call?*

"I'm very good with children, you know. That's why I went by the Playground Center last week, to volunteer my time, even though I'm very busy right now." Betty unzipped the tote bag and brought out a small stuffed giraffe. "See? I got this from the store, Babes-In-Arms, to give to my neighbor's little boy." She stroked the giraffe's neck.

"You like children." Joel again had the idea that Betty had lost a child. He wanted to suggest she try the couch, where the associations would come up faster, but he had to wait for the right moment.

"Then I wanted to see you the next night but I couldn't because my ex-husband is having me followed. He wants to reduce my alimony. If he knew I was coming here . . ."

"Yes?"

"Well, Dr. Abramowitz" —Betty grinned, wiggling her wide rear end deeper into the chair "you *are* a very attractive man."

Joel waited a moment before he spoke. "I wonder if it might be that when you have what you consider to be bad thoughts, that those are the times you think that other people are watching you. It's really the way you watch yourself, to make sure you don't have those thoughts. Bad thoughts you might have about me, for example."

"My ex-husband sent these men. They're detectives."

"Your ex-husband seems to represent the same process. It's as if he's one of those people who disapprove of everything you do—when maybe you're the one who really disapproves. And maybe of something in particular."

Betty tilted her head and looked at him evenly. Her eyes were hazel and sad. "You're right," she said. "The reason I didn't come that night was that I had done something terrible, and I couldn't face you. It's about Mrs. Harvey," she added, "that nice lady from the Playground Center. The paper said that you saw her last, but actually I was the one. In fact, you may not know this, but we're very good, close personal friends."

Joel wished again that Betty were on the couch, but this time for his own sake: so that he wouldn't have to worry about keeping his expression blank. "You knew her before—before last Tuesday?"

"Oh yes—didn't she tell you? The day that you and I met at the Playground Center, I had a meeting with Margot there. Of course we're on a first-name basis."

"Mrs. Klass, do you remember *how* you and I met?"

She looked at him, puzzled, for a moment. Then she clucked, shaking her head. "Don't you remember how you had to come up to the roof to fix that thing?"

"You were on the roof. You were very upset about—um, a little boy."

Betty carefully smoothed her skirt. "I think you have it a tiny bit wrong, Dr. Abramowitz. But that's all right. Let me tell you about me and Margot. We just hit it off right away. You know how it is sometimes, you're just like sisters." Betty held up crossed fingers.

"You say you were the one who saw her last."

"That's right. We had dinner Wednesday night at a *posh* little café on Nob Hill. It's so elite, most people don't even know about it. From the outside, it looks like a dry cleaner's. Well, Margot had the grilled shiitake mushrooms and crab cakes. I just had an endive salad, because I'm watching my figure." Betty frowned as she straightened one of the giraffe's ears, both of which appeared to have been crushed in her tote bag. "I told her my secret."

"Your secret."

"I was having an affair with her husband."

"Ah." *Sure, what the hell, why shouldn't you get in on this, too?* No, he thought, calm down—it wasn't surprising that Betty would fantasize something along these lines. Schizophrenics often believed they were involved with celebrities; this could be Betty's equivalent.

"He's charming. He holds a door for a lady. Not like my Al—*he* just walks on through, like an elephant."

Betty could have overheard Margot talking about Ted. "How did this—um, affair come about?" he asked.

"We met at a party. We were very, highly attracted to each other." Betty smiled, lowering her eyelids. "It was like electricity. He couldn't keep his hands off me, and I couldn't keep mine off him. We made love that night in the back of his car. He told me he was married, but that he was going to get a divorce. I believed him. I didn't know he was married to Margot. Imagine how I felt." She primly patted the bottom of her hairdo.

"He didn't—he didn't tell you his last name?"

"He pronounces it differently," she said haughtily. "Like the French—Ar*vay*."

Joel thought briefly of Melanie. He would have been reluctant to admit this to Denise, but it really did seem as though certain themes overlapped in his patients' stories sometimes. This was obviously Marital Infidelity Week.

"So you told Margot," Joel said, "that you were having an affair with her husband."

Betty turned the giraffe so that it was facing outward on her lap. "I told her I was pregnant," she said, "that Ted was the father, and that we had to do something about it."

Joel's thoughts danced around this last revelation, as if it were a fire he needed to put out. "Are you pregnant now?"

Betty looked confused. "I must be," she said.

"And you told her that."

"Yes." Betty nodded vigorously, and the giraffe's head bobbed up and down. "She was distraught. I tried to calm her. Finally she got up and ran out of the restaurant, weeping. That was the last time anyone saw her."

"How—if I may ask a personal question, Mrs. Klass, how old are you?"

She wagged her finger at him. "A lady never divulges her age."

"Do you—do you have other children?"

Her face darkened and she clutched the giraffe. "No," she snapped.

Joel nodded slowly, encouragingly.

"But what worries me, Doctor"—storm passed, Betty leaned forward, and the gold chain she wore around her neck touched the giraffe's head—"is that, you know, her mother committed suicide. That's what I'm afraid has happened to Margot."

Joel felt his ears grow warm, felt the warmth travel down his neck. "How did you know that?"

Betty smiled. "She told me." She held up her crossed fingers again. "Like I said. Sisters." Her smile disappeared quickly and she sighed. "I guess we have to get on with our lives, don't we, Dr. Abramowitz? I bet *you* don't have problems like this. You and your wife must be very happy together. But you really should wear your ring." She made a wide gesture with her arm and looked at her watch. "I really have to be going. This is such a hectic time of year."

Joel reached for his appointment book. "Perhaps we could set another time," he suggested. He knew he sounded too eager. His therapeutic composure—that detachment so necessary to helping someone—had shattered in pieces around him, like a broken clay mask.

"Let's see." Betty unzipped her tote bag. She pulled out, in succession, a canister of Mace, a toy fire truck, a tape recorder, a makeup bag, and a particularly unwieldy ring of fabric swatches. At the appearance of each item, she shook her head in an exaggerated gesture of dismay. "Oh my. Darn me anyway. I forgot to bring my 'Zip 'n' Go.' I can't remember anything I don't write down in it. Let me call you."

"Of course it's up to you." *Shut up, Joel.* There was urgency in his voice—even a trace of sarcasm. Unacceptable. He had already let Betty know that he wanted to see her. That was enough. And he could always call her later.

Okay, so Betty had displaced some of her transference to Joel onto Margot's husband. Big deal. Obviously she had met Margot only once, the same afternoon she had wandered into Playground. . . .

If only she hadn't known about Margot's mother. But there was some explanation for that. There had to be.

Betty stood. "You've helped me so much already," she said.

Joel wished he could agree. He stood as well.

She held the giraffe out in front of her. "Will you keep this little animal here for me? I'm afraid to keep him with me. I'm afraid something might happen to him."

"I'd like to talk about that," Joel said, almost involuntarily. "Your fear that something will happen to it—him."

Betty shook her head. There were tears in her eyes. "Take him," she begged.

She was continuing to act out. The analytic taboo. He should give her the opportunity to discuss it but refuse to take the giraffe. "All right," he said, taking the stuffed animal. "Where shall I put him?"

Betty stared at the bookcase for a moment, then lifted the blue cushion of the couch. Suddenly she pointed to the top right-hand drawer of the rolltop desk. "There," she said, her voice shaking. "No one can get him"—she broke off—"there. He'll be safe there."

As Joel interred the giraffe he thought that it was likely she would return for it, and he was glad.

Denise had offered to postpone their date. Joel did not want to be alone, and he certainly couldn't face another night of sodden self-pity at Ted's house. "No, I'd really like to see you."

"Then come to my house. I'll cook."

Denise was a vegetarian, too, but she insisted on currying tofu, making paste from black beans, and doing far too many devious things with miller's bran. "I want to take you out," he said. "Somewhere nice. You deserve it. Besides, that was our deal."

They went as planned to the Chinese restaurant Stix, which had just opened on Van Ness in a spot which had been host to three different, and now failed, restaurants in the last two years: Japanese, California cuisine, and then Cajun.

During dinner Denise asked him if there was any news about Margot. He said no, then changed the subject to Alex Forans' latest wholesale paper-towel supplier. He wanted to tell Denise about Andrea and Betty, and he could do so without breaking confidentiality—but although he had often consulted with her in the past, he had always maintained an I-can-handle-this-but-I'm-curious-what-you-think demeanor. This time, he was afraid that she would think that *he* was crazy. And indeed, in the neon glow of the pink-and-turquoise restaurant, Betty's True Confession story of her affair with Ted, and even Andrea's tale of an accident on a dark, curved road seemed products of his own latent psychosis—or a dream, the psychosis of the common man.

Afterward, Denise suggested that they go to the piano bar she had recently discovered. "It's a dive, but it's fun," she said. She had tried to take him there a couple of times before, and Joel had demurred, but tonight he didn't really care where they went, and he certainly didn't have any ideas of his own.

The Last Act was on Geary, across from the theaters. Joel and Denise sat at the bar on swivel-top stools, facing numerous small mirrors with the brand names and logos of beers printed on them.

The walls of the bar were almost completely covered with autographed black-and-white glossies of obscure movie stars. Joel recognized Jean Seberg and George Sanders, but most were unknown to him: With their pompadours and arched brows, they had the fungible appearance of portraits unearthed in one's mother's closet. Yet each one had probably shared Melanie's pulsating desire for fame. Melanie must have hundreds of photos of herself, tiny icons to her beauty; someday those photos would be equally anonymous. *You see,* he wanted to say to her, *it doesn't matter whether you're remembered by ten people, a hundred, or ten million.*

At the rear of the bar, a spotlight illuminated a young woman playing a piano; a half-dozen patrons sat at the semicircular bar surrounding it, singing along with her "You Are My Sunshine."

"I wish you'd talk about it," Denise said. She was stirring her piña colada with a straw.

"Talk about what?"

"I can tell something's bothering you. It must be Margot." She grimaced, just for a second, as if she had turned the wrong way and revived the pain of an old injury.

"I'm all right."

"There's no shame in expressing your feelings. A good friend of yours is unaccounted for. It's normal to have a response to that." She twirled the stem of her glass, jerkily. Her fingernails were short and unpolished. "I mean, what if you were your own client? Wouldn't you want you to open up?"

Joel was touched by this logic.

"You feel responsible, don't you?" she asked. She gazed at him intently.

"What *ever* gave you that idea?"

"You always feel responsible for everything. You think you can make everyone happy." She smiled timidly, churning the crushed ice with her straw. "It's very grandiose, you know."

Joel made a circle on the bar with his wet cocktail napkin. He was getting Denise's sympathy under false pretenses: She probably thought he was one heck of a sensitive guy to be so distressed about a friend's wife. Especially since that friend's wife, as the *Deliverer* implied, might have simply taken off on a pouting expedition after a fight with her husband.

"I mean, who knows what was really going on with her?" Denise removed the pineapple wedge from the edge of her glass and shook the moisture from it. "If you ask me, her husband was fooling around."

Joel laughed shortly.

"He came on to me once," Denise said, narrowing her eyes. "And don't laugh at *that*, or I'll never speak to you again."

"When did that happen?"

"At their house. One time when you took me over there for dinner. The time that Margot—" The grimace again. Joel remembered with a corresponding muscular twinge an evening when Margot had asked Denise if the cape she was wearing had been part of a Halloween costume. He had been wrong to assume that Denise was oblivious to those unkindnesses. "Whatever, I mean, it was around Easter. We were in the kitchen and he sort of grabbed me. Maybe I imagined it," she added, and bent over to suck hard on her piña colada. The final drops gurgled in her straw.

"Want another one?"

She nodded. He signaled the bartender, a young man with a Fu Manchu mustache and wearing a denim workshirt. "I don't think you *imagined* it," Joel said. "But he was probably drunk, right? Maybe he just made a grab for you to keep from falling."

"Yeah, you're right," Denise sighed.

Joel laughed again, looking at the little-girl despondency on her face. *Bless you, Denise, for being my friend tonight!* "Not that he shouldn't *want* to come on to you. You know I didn't mean that. It's just hard for me to see Ted getting excited these days about anything that was less than eighty proof."

Denise did not look any happier, and he thought he'd better change the subject before he got his foot the rest of the way down his esophagus. At the end of the bar, the group was singing "New York, New York." "He might like this place, though." He motioned with his head to the singers. "He likes to burst out into song when he's had a few."

Denise looked over her shoulder. "Oh. Heh-heh." She bent over the second piña colada.

Joel shoved his Calistoga out of the way and put one elbow on the bar. "Okay. There *is* something I want to talk to you about."

At last she looked pleased. And once he began the tales of Andrea and Betty (with identities appropriately masked), she listened with a puckered brow, black eyes on the jukebox, and her straw held lightly just above the ice.

He told her everything, except the part about Margot's mother. "*Jesus*," she said when he had finished.

Joel blinked. "I don't like the way you said that."

"No, I just mean that I'm amazed, that's all. They're such incredible stories."

"You don't think any of it's *true*, do you?"

"Well"—she shrugged—"you know about synchronicity."

"Y-yes."

"There's a Jungian analyst in New Mexico doing work on psychic phenomena. I'll give you an article about him. You see, what he's found out is that the people we get involved with are people that we've known in past lives but haven't resolved our conflicts with."

"I'm having enough trouble with conflicts in *this* life."

"I know, but don't you see how it isn't really a *coincidence*, it's more like—"

Joel tuned out briefly, experiencing the same mild irritation he felt when someone told him that the fish was divine and he should *really* have a bite.

"The point is," Denise was saying, "that *they* think what they're telling you about Margot is true. And even if they don't—*your* job is to find out what it means to *them*. You've got to give them that unconditional regard, accept what they tell you, for the time being. Let go of having to have the answer."

She was right about that. Joel actually felt relieved.

She touched his hand with her fingertips, then quickly drew them away, as if his skin were hot. "You'll find out what happened to her." Then she tittered, a little noise in her throat like a bird's wings against a cage. "Will you let me prescribe for you? I have a very exciting evening planned."

This last was said in an affectedly sultry voice. He started to smile. When Denise tried to be sexy it aroused him just because of how hard she was trying. He had assumed that they wouldn't sleep together that night; without exactly planning for it, he had thought he would tell her about Margot, or at least let her know that his situation had changed. But suddenly he wasn't sure how it *had* changed. Or maybe that was just the rationalization beginning, because he was having that response, deep in his groin, that did not seem entirely part of him, and yet was so much part of him that he could never escape it. Or want to.

Well, he had plenty of time to worry about that.

"Step one." Denise tapped the bar. "Have a drink."

He shook his head.

"*Please.* One of these." She licked the foamy end of her straw. "They're so weak—they taste just like pineapple juice." Leaning forward, she whispered, "I think they even water the wine."

"All right, then." He smiled, feeling like an indulgent parent. He would just take a few sips.

When it arrived, Joel sucked almost absently on his drink. *Yuck. They should give out insulin samples with these.* He was suddenly feeling sorry for himself, missing Margot, and remembering again how he had thought that tonight he would be telling Denise about his lunch with her. But now he couldn't, or didn't want to—now it seemed like so much gossip. He glanced at Denise, who was listening attentively to the singer, and was grateful again for her company. Then he noticed that the end of his straw had been so mashed by his teeth that he couldn't suck any liquid through it.

Denise's mattress and box spring were on the floor; the sheets were of a leopard-skin pattern, and the comforter an imitation fur that resembled seal. She had jazz on the stereo—Coltrane, she had said—it was dark, smoky music and he felt the percussion like fingertips running lightly along his spine.

"What do you think? Carl gave them to me." Two scraps of black leather material dangled from Denise's hands. Joel remembered that Carl was the psychiatrist whom she lived with in Berkeley, though she had mentioned him only a few times.

Joel had made himself at home on the fake seal bedspread; shoe- and tieless, but otherwise as overdressed as ever. After a second piña colada, fearful of diabetic coma, he had had a tonic water. With vodka in it. Joel hadn't had anything stronger than fruitcake made with rum in ten years, and now, besides being slightly under the influence, he felt as though he had violated a taboo as absolute as incest. As soon as he got entirely sober he was going to have to analyze this.

"Shall I try them on?" Denise asked hesitantly.

"Oh, I don't know. We don't *need* that." Once he saw Denise naked and plump, he was erect and eager and it was always good. Denise tended to moan and twist a lot; he liked that.

"No, we don't *need* it, it's just . . ."

"Well, go ahead, then."

She still hesitated, fingering the garments. Joel swung his legs off the bed, came over to her, kissed her forcefully, and placed his hands a little clumsily on her breasts. "Go on," he said. Kissing her made him hard.

When Denise went into the bathroom Joel remembered that he had what had seemed like a compelling reason for not sleeping with Denise, and that it had had to do with having exchanged murky vows with Margot. For a few moments he tried to rationalize what was happening: He needed the company, it would be awkward to explain now. The fact was, whether this was right or wrong, he was a bowling ball halfway down the alley. He started to undress.

Then Denise returned, wearing the black underwear. He had not expected it to be quite so—erotic. He felt like a twelve-year-old sneaking his first look at a girlie magazine. The black leather bra was too small, scooped out in front so that her nipples were squeezed forward. The garter belt was also too tight and a small roll of pink flesh swelled over the top. She wore black stockings and a pair of black high heels that he would never have imagined she possessed.

She strode over to the bed with a look of grim determination.

He was still wearing his jockey shorts and she pulled them down. His penis sprang up with an almost audible *boing*. She bent over it, enveloping it in her mouth, and he felt the tickling around the tip, the deep plunge, the softer, slipperier version of a cunt. He put her hand on her sleek hair.

He was getting too close. He tugged her away. "You like that, don't you?" she asked. His chest tightened. It was dark, he wasn't wearing his glasses, and this shadowy woman was too aggressive to be Denise. He pushed her—gently enough—down on her back. Outlined in black, she had a new body, was only a body, a woman. She raised her hands above her head, spread her legs. He touched her and found she was already dripping wet. He thrust his fingers deeply inside, felt her muscles contract around them. She started to moan. He took his hand out—he was going to make her wait.

He put his mouth on her breast, tasted perfume. His cock

ached, as if someone were pulling it away from his body. He held her wrists, and nudged her legs farther apart with his knees. Then he kissed her, his tongue licking hers. She felt so soft, all around her mouth, and the words he thought of then—that there was *no resistance*—made him grunt with wanting to possess her entirely, all to himself, his only, only.

She pulled her head away. "Now," she whispered.

"Wait," he whispered back.

"Please."

"No."

She tried to squirm away from him but he wouldn't let her go. He dimly realized that she wasn't trying very hard. He felt her legs thrashing and felt her nipples, pushed forward by the bra, rubbing against him. He could hardly stand to wait but he didn't want the waiting to end.

Finally he plunged into her. He let go of her arms and she gripped him, and *uhhed*, and they rocked for several minutes like a fast-swaying cradle, until everything spilled out of him in a whirlpool, and he was empty, limp, exhausted, and wanted nothing but to sleep.

But he stayed awake a while longer, his head on Denise's stomach. He smelled himself on her, listened to her raspy breathing, and felt her fingers entwined in his hair. *Thy belly is a mound of wheat, edged with lilies.* Denise murmured something about wanting to get out of these darn things, something about loving him, but her voice mingled with the flickering, indistinct images behind his eyes.

Then he was awakened by the sensation of falling. A myoclonic jerk. He lay motionless and afraid. He realized that he had forgotten about Margot, and he had the superstitious feeling that he should not let that happen again, as if, wherever she was, his thoughts were what kept her alive.

Denise stood barefoot on a chair, looking into her cupboard. "I've got hibiscus tea, chamomile tea, ginger tea, saffron, rose hips, lemon, apple, SleepyTime, cinnamon—"

"Nothing, thanks." It was the next morning and Joel was tightening the knot of his tie.

"If you'd leave a razor here, you could shave in the mornings."

"Oh, that's all right," he said, knowing that he didn't want to have a razor, a toothbrush, running shorts, or his favorite brand of mineral water *any*where except in his own apartment.

She stepped carefully down from the chair. Her toenails were polished, but the polish was chipped. "I try to have what you like, but every time you come over it's something different." She peered into the refrigerator. "I have orange juice, but it's from concentrate, gross. I have apple juice, though. Organic."

"Really, nothing. I have to go home and go out running." He also had a pronounced headache; if Ted's hangovers were much worse than this, then he had been adequately punished for any suffering he had ever caused.

Denise retied the belt of her old purple terry-cloth robe. "So soon?" she asked.

"Um . . . well, yes." He was politic enough not to mention that he wanted to check for news about Margot.

Denise closed the refrigerator and walked past him into the bedroom. He waited a moment, then followed.

"What's the matter?"

"Nothing."

"Obviously something's the matter." When she made no reply he said, "You always say that *I'm* uncommunicative."

"All right, I'll tell you what's the matter. It can't be like this anymore."

"What can't be like what anymore?"

"Like *this*. Us."

"Us?" Why did this feel like that moment when you see a car coming at you and don't know if you'll have time to get out of its way?

Denise sat on the edge of the bed, hands between her knees. "I'm sorry. I didn't want to say anything. But I'm always telling my clients that they have to be honest and say what they feel, and finally I realized that I was being a hypocrite if I didn't do the same with you."

"Well, say what's on your mind," he encouraged her, though he was wishing that he were somewhere safe, like Three Mile Island or the Mekong Delta.

"Well . . . we've been seeing each other for a year now, and I just wonder where we are."

"Russian Hill?"

"*That* is not funny."

He raised his hands as if it were a holdup. "Well, what do you

mean, where we are? We're just where we've always been—
having a good time."

"Is that all I am, a good time?"

"Isn't that a good thing to be?"

"Just like a psychoanalyst," she muttered. "To answer a
question with a question."

"Jesus." He sank down on one of her drop-bottomed chairs.
The woman clearly did not believe in comfortable places to sit.
Pound, pound, went his head. "How do *you* see our—um,
relationship?"

She rubbed the beauty mark on her cheek for what seemed like
a long time. "I want more," she said.

"Like . . . how much . . . more?"

She laughed, but her face wore the old grimace. "I've never
seen you look so scared," she said.

He shifted in the chair. "It's just that I don't see what's wrong
with things the way they are."

"Shit! We go out and we have a great time and then you don't
call me for a week—sometimes longer."

"But . . . you could call me," he said lamely.

"Well, I do sometimes. But you know you wouldn't like it if I
called you a lot. You'd suddenly get busy."

"So . . . you want to get together more often, is that it?" He
wanted to assess the situation and propose a quick solution. He
hated to see her so upset, and especially to think (or be made to
feel) that he was the cause of it. He *did* like things the way they
were, but he was willing to make some adjustments.

"No! I want you to *want* to get together more. Like to spend
the whole weekend together."

But I don't want to. "I don't know what to say." He should go
find some aspirin, or something a little stronger, like Demerol
maybe, and then they could continue this conversation.

She rubbed the nap of the bathrobe belt. "I feel so used," she
said finally. "I swore that I'd never get involved in another
self-destructive relationship like this."

Self-destructive? How dare she! How could she invalidate
everything they had done and been through together? Make him
feel like one of those grunting, insensitive pigs described by the
self-help books as hopelessly immature? The Peter Pans, the
Casanovas, the Men Who Think Their Pricks Are Gods . . .

"Denise." He went over to her, put his arms around her. He

rarely spoke her name aloud and she looked up as if startled by the sound of it. "I care about you a lot. *How* did I use you?"

"By asking me out all this time when you really didn't care about me."

"But I *do* care about you."

"But not that way."

"*What* way?" He was genuinely confused. "If we want to see each other is there something wrong with that? I never beat you over the head and dragged you out." He wondered if she would see the humor in it if he reminded her about the performance piece she had dragged *him* to, the one with the man on the unicycle for eighty minutes. Probably not.

"And then you asked me to take that class for you, and said you'd take me out to dinner."

"It's bad to take you out to dinner?"

"Well, do you think I keep track of those things? You have to keep the score *so* even. You're so afraid that I'll get something on you." She fixed her black eyes on him, Grand Inquisitor eyes. "And *then*—you just assume that I'm available on Friday and Saturday."

"If you're not free, just say so. I don't care."

Ooops.

"That's just it! You don't *care*, goddamn it! And besides, you know I'm always going to be free. Reliable old Denise!"

"I didn't mean I didn't care. I meant I didn't mind."

She dabbed at her eyes with the terry-cloth belt. "You would have just gone home last night after we ate if I hadn't begged you to come to the bar."

"No, I wouldn't have." Actually, he *might* have, but why was that wrong?

She shook herself free of his arm. "I think you need to go home so you can go out running."

He felt as though he were being sent to his room. "What does this mean, exactly?"

"I don't think we should see each other for a while," she said coolly. She stood and, with great dignity, drew the belt tighter.

"I'm sorry you feel that way." He was surprised at the depth of his sense of loss. And he was angry, too, because he felt that he needed her now more than ever. So maybe he *was* selfish, and *did* take her for granted. Like she said. "Very sorry." He debated kissing her good-bye, and decided that he'd better not. But he felt her black eyes, like spiders on his back, as he walked out her bedroom door.

CHAPTER 5

THE PAST CREEPS IN ON LITTLE CAT FEET

There were six narrow lanes on the Golden Gate Bridge. At quarter to three in the afternoon, on Monday, all six were in use, and traffic moving in two directions was separated only by tiny yellow markers, shaped like one-handled rolling pins, stuck at intervals into the roadway.

Sometime during the night, the body of a woman had been washed ashore on Stinson Beach, then discovered by a predawn jogger when he tripped over it in the darkness. Now Ted was going to see if the body was Margot's, and Joel had canceled the afternoon's appointments to accompany him.

Joel did not try to make conversation. They could do nothing to comfort each other until they knew, and the dead woman could be anyone. Except that they had said that it looked as though she had been dead for about three days. Ted did not speak either, though he cursed occasionally as his right tires strayed onto the raised bumps of the next lane. Joel was undistracted by this flirtation with death. Let the other drivers watch out for them. He was busy: He had to make himself ready. If Margot were dead he could still assemble an inner photo album that would preserve his best memories of her.

The album would start with her at Playground, with the children—those unguarded moments when she dropped to her knees to button a jacket or wipe jam from a face. Thank God, she had left Playground behind. And Joel would make sure that it flourished, would take over her job there if he had to. He tried to picture himself in Margot's office, saw Mrs. Tuttle bring him tea and those doughy cookies she made. . . .

Ted didn't even know the Playground Margot. He only thought of her as the woman who had given him a scholarship to the rest of his life: a BMW, a big house, his name on the door of an office where he could talk on the phone and take nips from a drawer. Not that Joel could have lived like that, on a woman's money. But if Ted knew Margot the way Joel did, then he would have taken better care of her and this never would have happened.

But this was bullshit. This had nothing to do with Margot, how she smelled, the way she laughed like a xylophone, and how she had fit into his embrace the one and only time he had really kissed her. If he knew for sure that was all over then he'd jump out of the car.

He looked up as the second red tower of the bridge passed over them. Was it the second tower already? "Damn!" Ted muttered, as the car ran over the bumps again.

Joel caught himself chewing on the joint of one finger. Ted, the old bastard—*he'd* get to mourn in public. Joel imagined Ted at the funeral, drunk—Margot's cousin would be there, and her friends, and for once they would understand how Ted was acting. *How can I think like this?* What did anything matter if Margot was dead? But it did matter. Back on Thursday night, even Friday night, he could still have told Ted about him and Margot, gotten a share of the grieving action. Now it was too late. He'd have to keep the secret of what had almost happened as closely as he would if a patient had told him. And there was simply no one else he could love, no one else who was like her, whom he would ever want to confide in. His loss was so personal and unique, so insurmountable, so unrivaled by anything that Ted could possibly feel . . .

You are being narcissistic.

And people do get over things like this. After a while, you get out of bed because bed is boring; you put on clothes because you're sick of your pajamas; you make appointments and remember to keep them. Suddenly you hear yourself laughing at a funny movie. It's just too exhausting to mourn forever. Only a few people have the stamina for it.

Ted put on the radio and pushed buttons. A psychologist was

talking about his weekend seminars on How to Create a Loving Divorce.

There were rainbows painted on the mouths of the twin Waldo Tunnels. The car plunged in, and for the few seconds that they were in the hollow tube, Joel felt a sort of elation, as if the worst thing possible were about to happen to him, and with that out of the way, nothing else would ever trouble him again.

Marin County was too small and inadequately violent to have its own morgue. Bodies that came under the jurisdiction of the coroner's office were taken to the nearest mortuary, in this case the Dove of Peace in Mill Valley.

The mortuary was a freestanding cottage, with ersatz stained-glass windows and a crewcut lawn, down the road from a 7–11 and a Shell station.

In the parking lot Joel and Ted met a detective from the Marin County Sheriff's office. "Lieutenant Emory Epcot," he introduced himself. "You're the doc, I bet. Call me Emory. I hate titles. So pompous, like somebody's better than someone else." He shifted his bomber jacket and Louis Vuitton pouch to his other arm and indicated his fuzzy sweater and pleated corduroy pants. "That's why I don't dress the part." Emory was pudgy, red-cheeked, and red-bearded; he wore a fedora with a yellow button pinned to the hatband, and a pinpoint diamond in his left earlobe. Joel did not like the way he was grinning, as if identifying bodies was the most fun thing he got to do all week.

"Listen, it's okay to be nervous." Emory put his hand on Ted's shoulder. "Everyone is, their first time. And remember, I'm here to help."

"It must have been an accident, though, don't you think?" Ted asked. He was bent slightly at the middle, hugging himself. He hadn't even had anything to drink today, at least not as far as Joel could tell.

"Not necessarily," Emory said. He winked at Joel. "Somebody offs somebody, throws them out to sea, sushi-to-go, right? Only problem is, bodies don't sink—they float. People don't realize that, they don't weigh them down. So we do know it's an amateur job."

Joel heard his own sharp intake of breath.

Emory glanced from Ted to Joel, and for a moment his eyes

were narrowed, calculating. Then he slapped his own face lightly. "Oh, Lord, what am I saying? I'm *so* sorry."

"Don't worry about it," Ted mumbled.

"How can I not worry about it?" Emory protested. "I feel horrible. I'm overworked, that's the problem. But don't worry, I *promise* we'll get to the bottom of this, *whatever* happened. I'll put *all* of my energies into it."

"Can we get this over with?" Joel asked. His heart was beating as if he'd run three miles uphill.

"Let's go," Emory said, setting his fedora at a more rakish angle. He rested his hand on Ted's back as they walked.

Inside, a woman in a dull peach sweater greeted them. "You must be Mr. Harvey," she whispered to Joel. "I'm Mrs. Guernsey. I'm so very sorry." Her voice was rattly, cheerful, even when soft; her lower teeth were crooked and tobacco-stained. Joel noticed the sheen of her dark fuchsia hair and then realized it was a wig: it sat like a bird's nest on top of her head.

"This is Mr. Harvey, here," he corrected her, storing away the tiny tribute of her mistake.

"Hey, Fran, how's it going." Emory slapped her on her frail shoulder.

Ted furtively grabbed Joel's wrist, squeezing it hard. But Joel would be damned if he would let him know it hurt.

"Just come this way," Mrs. Guernsey said.

The front room of the mortuary was done in brown and turquoise; there seemed to be too many sofas. Mrs. Guernsey took them through a side door to a short, white-painted hallway, all the brighter in contrast to the imitation wood paneling of the front room. At one end there was a screen door that led to the rear of the parking lot. Joel could hear a hum that sounded like a refrigerator. He knew that they were going to the room where they did the embalming and his stomach felt the way it had the last time he had eaten a hamburger. He did not like blood or dead animals or even graphic horror movies. It occurred to him that he might faint and he was momentarily afraid of the embarrassment that would cause him.

Through a white door. Inside, there was a single table, slightly tilted, with a sink at the bottom, and a hydraulic pedal for raising and lowering it. The table was covered with a sheet, the contours describing a human form. A rusty kettledrum light hung from the ceiling.

On the other side of the table a man in shirt-sleeves was taking notes on a spiral pad. He looked up as they entered. "Rich!" Emory greeted him. "*Que pasa*, buddy? This is the coroner's investigator, Rich Thackeray."

The coroner's investigator kept writing. "Ready for the ID?" he asked, without looking up.

"Yep. Wouldn't it be great if we could wrap this up right away?" Emory said.

Thackeray went to the head of the table and raised the sheet. Joel was distantly aware of Ted's fingers pressing into his wrist again, and a sound which might have been Ted's teeth chattering. Thackeray pulled the sheet down a little farther and Joel saw a purplish head with bulging eyes that looked like a giant fish's. The skin was macerated, wrinkled, and translucent; the features were swollen into tumorlike masses. Joel's tongue curled, but the spasm passed and then he saw and knew and cared only that it was not Margot. The face was unrecognizable, but the head and neck were too long to have been hers, the shoulders too wide; the few strands of hair remaining were blond.

"No!" he heard Ted wail. "No! No!"

"Ted." Joel stepped between Ted and the body. His own limbs were shaky, but regaining strength. "It's not her, it's okay now."

"Christ, he's so upset," Emory said. "Poor guy! Are you sure it isn't his wife?"

Thackeray still held the sheet aloft, uncertain whether Ted's reaction constituted a positive identification.

"It's not his wife," Joel snapped. "Can't you cover her up?"

The sheet fell.

Ted leaned to one side of Joel to stare at the body. He raised his arms as if to push Joel away, but when his eyes caught on Joel's he dropped his arms. "I'm not feeling well," he mumbled. "Maybe I'll step out for a second, okay?"

"The men's room is to the left," Mrs. Guernsey told him.

Joel started to follow Ted, but Emory touched his shoulder. "Can I talk to you for a sec, Doc? Alone?"

Joel hesitated. "Sure."

"You can use my office," Mrs. Guernsey said. Then she clucked, "We've still got to find a home for *this* one. It's a shame, isn't it? You can even tell she was pretty."

"Looks like something from *Alien* now," Thackeray said. "You know what causes the skin to do that? Gases form in the body. It's like the way wine ferments."

Joel hurried out, moving ahead of Emory.

Mrs. Guernsey's imitation-wood-paneled office had a vase full of silk flowers on the desk, next to a customer questionnaire. HOW DID WE SERVE YOU? it said across the top.

Emory closed the door. "What's the story with your friend, Doc? Is he out of it, or what?"

"I'd say he's had a bit of a shock." Joel leaned against the edge of the desk. There was perspiration on his neck and forehead; waves of euphoria alternated with faint nausea. But he was determined to act professional now, whatever that meant—it probably *didn't* mean loosening his tie and unbuttoning the top button of his shirt, but those were the breaks.

"Post-traumatic stress syndrome? Is that what you're saying?"

"Maybe."

"You're not covering for him, are you?"

"That woman isn't Margot Harvey, if that's what you're asking."

"Damn. I was hoping that we could solve this right away."

"I hope we aren't inconveniencing you too much."

"You're right, that was tactless. It's just they *really* have given me too many cases to work on. I'm a victim of the Peter Principle." Emory winked and twirled the pinpoint diamond in his ear.

Joel couldn't decide whether Emory was out of it himself, or whether he was putting on some sort of campy act to disarm him. An odd but possibly effective way of building trust.

"You thought that Ted might be hiding something?"

"Just a feeling. I rely on that a lot." Emory winked again.

The wink, and Emory's bristly grin, sent another wave of nausea washing over Joel. The image of the drowned woman's face rode on the crest of this one—the sunken nose, and the jawline. Now there was something disturbingly familiar about it. Joel felt his tongue spasm again, and he concentrated on the button on Emory's fedora. It read, BORN TO MAKE HEADLINES. "Let me ask you something. If no one ever claims that body, what happens to it?"

"First we'll take it to a hospital for an autopsy. After they determine the cause of death, if there's no further investigation, we send it to the mortuary college. Eventually they cremate it. They keep the ashes for a year."

"What do you think happened to her?"

"Well, she didn't go for a swim. When she washed up, she was still wearing the better part of a dress."

"And no one has reported her missing?"

"No. Tragic, isn't it? This is the part of my job that I hate."

His grin was broader, revealing pointed teeth; Joel thought of a vampire. Joel felt dizzy; the drowned woman floated up at him again. Why did she seem *so* familiar? It *wasn't* Margot—he was sure of that.

And then he understood. *Someone* was looking for this woman, and that someone wasn't going to be happy when he found her. Like the sole survivor of a plane crash, Joel felt guilty toward the unknown people who were not as fortunate as he.

Having accomplished that bit of work, Joel felt his nausea fade. "Tell me," he asked, "do you think there's any connection between Ted's wife and—this body?"

"Wish I could say. I've been doing this ten years now, and one thing I've learned about the job is that it never runs out of surprises. I'm working on a screenplay now about my experiences."

"Congratulations." Joel pushed himself away from the desk. "I should get Ted home now, I think." *And myself.*

"Be sure you drive carefully," Emory said, taking one of the silk flowers from the vase on Mrs. Guernsey's desk and sticking it in his buttonhole.

Ted was waiting for Joel in the foyer. His face was pale and his forehead damp. Next to him, Thackeray, the coroner's investigator, was biting furtively into a thick sandwich made with dark bread.

"Sorry I lost control there for a moment," Ted apologized to Emory. "I've been pretty stressed out. That poor woman."

"You go home and take care of yourself, Ted." Emory patted him on the back. "Get some rest. We'll be in touch if we need you."

As they walked across the parking lot, Joel held out his hand. "Give me the keys."

Driving back across the bridge, Joel kept wondering what it would be like to be making this same trip, looking at this same view, if the dead woman had been Margot—and he knew that even the whitewashed panorama of the city would be flat and ugly, like a prison he had to return to. Each time he thought of what could have been, he silently said, *Thank you, God*, feeling a little hypocritical, but so grateful that he had to thank someone. He even cherished a tiny hope (a hope he planned to take out and examine later) that, after all, wasn't it just *possible* there was a God who had answered his prayers and spared Margot? For all things seemed doable and forgivable and endurable, as long as she was alive.

So what was Ted's problem? His friend sat slumped and wordless in the passenger seat. True, they still didn't know about Margot, but Joel was riding the crest of a wave of euphoria and determined to enjoy it while it lasted. Margot was okay. He'd beaten the odds with this body; there weren't going to be any others washed ashore.

Unused to the BMW's more responsive brakes, Joel stopped too suddenly for the traffic backed up at the toll plaza. Ted jerked forward and Joel saw that he wasn't wearing his seat belt. He almost said something about it, but then he just let the BMW creep closer to the old Thunderbird in front of them and turned his attention inward. A week ago he had thought he was in love with Margot, but he had continued to wonder if he was just infatuated, or merely lusted for her. Since he'd thought he was obsessed with her then, he would have been scared if he could have seen himself now.

It almost seemed that that was why she had disappeared: to permanently eliminate all his doubts, to lodge herself in his consciousness at her most desirable. If that was her plan, it was working. The imperfections of the real Margot would always dim in the radiance of that idealized one, who grew brighter every hour.

Unlike the real woman whom he knew as Denise. He hoped that eventually they could be friends again. But in the meantime, she had made things easier by breaking up with him, eliminating the necessity of any dramatic confessions followed by Q-and-A. Now, perhaps once Margot returned, she and Joel could start up very quietly, and no one would get hurt.

No one would get hurt? What a nice idea. And what next, voices from Jupiter?

When Joel stopped in the driveway of the Harveys' house, Ted bounded out of the car before Joel could shut off the engine. Ted lumbered across the lawn to the porch, where he dug in his pockets for his keys; when he couldn't find them, he started pounding on the door.

Joel lifted the mailbox. He had always thought that the key taped there was a concession to the Harveys' unconscious guilt about their wealth, a purposeful hole punctured in the otherwise tight web of their burglar-alarm system. He had never said anything to Margot or Ted about it—perhaps because he found it an appealing puncture—but now he wished he had. He looked at the key and wondered if it was taped at exactly the same angle as before. The last wave of euphoria spread out, thinned, and receded, leaving him beached.

As soon as Joel unlocked the door, Ted bolted for the kitchen. He returned holding a bottle of Stolichnaya by the neck, and stumbled into the pit of the living room. "Well, that's it, Joey," he said. His mouth was fixed in a masklike smile. "She's gone. I'll never see her again." He unscrewed the cap and held the bottle near his thick lips. "Never is a long, long time and I'm going to have to get very, very drunk as fast as possible."

"I wish you wouldn't," Joel said. Now he was frightened by Ted's reaction to viewing the body. Post-traumatic stress syndrome? Ted gave new meaning to the term.

"I bet you doooo," Ted sang. He squeezed his eyes shut and tilted the Stolichnaya into his mouth. "Aaargh." Then he collapsed, facedown, on the sofa, his thumb stuck in the opening of the bottle to prevent spillage.

Joel sat behind Ted, in the bottom of the U of the sofa. He had gravitated unconsciously to the analytic configuration: Ted lying down, with Joel out of sight. "We don't know that Margot is gone," he said gently. He'd have to talk Ted down from this before he left.

Ted pressed his face into the crook of one arm. "Not Margot." His voice came up muffled from the cushions, followed by a low chuckle. "Melanie."

"Melanie?" Joel echoed. "Melanie?" He was puzzled, suspended like a clothesline between knowing and not wanting to know. There were so many Melanies in the world. Melanie Klein. Melanie Hamilton. Melanie Griffith.

"Melanie Hardwicke," Ted turned over on his back. He was

still chuckling. "That's who that lady was. Mel-an-ie Hardwicke. You didn't even recognize her."

Melanie Hardwicke. Melanie the model, who wanted to be famous. Melanie with the long legs and long hair. What was left looked like an unfinished mannequin. Joel recalled the slimy dull sheen of her skin, and almost gagged again. "How did *you* know her?"

"She was a friend of Margot's," was Ted's response, cryptic but sufficient.

Melanie who was involved with a married man.

"You sent her to see me, didn't you?" Joel asked. He remembered how evasive she had been about where she had gotten his name.

Ted rested the bottle upright on his shirt, keeping it steady with his fingers wrapped securely around its base. The Harvey Monument, Joel thought. Phallic, too. "I thought you could help her. She was all fucked up."

"*She* was all fucked up?" Joel felt his throat tighten. He was going to grab Ted and throw his sorry ass across the pit and smash him into the wall until he looked like a plate of spaghetti . . . but not yet. That wasn't a good way to get information. He could take a lesson from Emory, if being a shrink himself wasn't enough.

"You were having an affair with her, weren't you?" His voice was unnaturally low, but as neutral as a white dress shirt.

Ted flicked the ashes off an imaginary cigar. "That's the most ridiculous thing I ever hoid."

Joel said nothing.

"But maybe, just *maybe* . . . you're right. I was having an affair with her."

Spaghetti with meatballs. But Joel dug his fingers into the spongy cushions of the custom-made sofa. Ted *wanted* to tell him about it—Joel simply had to become that blank canvas, that empty mirror. "You say she was a friend of Margot's."

"That's right. They met at one of those women's networks where women go to talk about how men have screwed them over."

"H'm." Encouraging. Supportive. *I can't wait to kill him.*

"You know how Margot likes to help people. Me, too." On the defensive, Ted's voice was squeaky. "Melanie was new in town. She didn't have any friends. She was—shy. Yeah."

"Ummm h'm." Joel remembered how much he had relied on vaguely encouraging syllables in the beginning of his career, when he was wary of silence, and trying to sound like a psychoanalyst.

Ted pounded the bottle slowly against his thigh. "It's not my fault what happened, it's not my fault what happened, it's not my fault what happened," he singsonged. "You're gonna help me get over this, Joey, I know you are."

Joel felt something like the pressure of a dull needle against his scalp. "How *did* it happen?" A *murderer*—was that possible? Everyone was a murderer in his head, but a real one . . .   He couldn't believe it. Ted would look different, would have horns or a tail.

"I swear to God, Joey, I don't know. I hadn't seen her since Wednesday. And even then I was trying to break up with her."

Now Joel's stomach churned like the engine of a car that refuses to start. But Ted had the band out for a chorus of "It's Everyone's Problem but Mine," the tune that always topped his hit parade. "God, poor thing, she needed help. She depended on me. I sent her to you, 'cause I thought you could tell her how to get over it." Ted sighed, and Joel imagined strangling him, how his eyes would bulge out. "I guess you couldn't do anything for her, either. Well, I'm sure you did your best."

"Sounds like you did *your* best," Joel said, trying to keep the sarcasm from leaking through his clenched teeth.

"I felt so awful about cheating on Margot. That's why I've been drinking more."

"My heart's breaking."

"God, Joey, I didn't mean for it to happen. It was perfectly innocent."

That was it. "Innocent!" Joel exploded. "Jesus Christ!"

"No—it's true. Margot had Melanie over for dinner one night, to be nice, you know, and I took her home."

"So? So what is it, you can't control yourself for ten minutes? What are you, a walking dick?" Melanie had told him that she'd known her lover was married. Why hadn't he figured this out? How could he be so stupid?

Ted sat up.

"I just took her home, that was all. She wanted me to walk her to her door, just to be safe. I couldn't say no to that, could I?

Could I? Then, I don't know, she started to cry about something, her sister I think, and then I don't know. . . ."

"What do you mean, *you don't know?*" Joel was shouting now.

Ted didn't answer, because he had his tongue halfway down the neck of the Stolichnaya, slurping faster than Joel thought anyone could slurp vodka without puking. Joel was about to grab the bottle away from him—even started to reach for it—and then he remembered Saturday night with Denise, and stopped. *That was different*. Totally different. But he had to admit that he hadn't planned to sleep with Denise either, and once she'd gotten him to a certain point, trying not to sleep with her would have been like trying to climb back on top of the Empire State Building after you jumped off. "Besides, if it was so *unintentional*," he growled, "why did you keep seeing her?"

Ted moistened his lips. "There was something else, too."

Joel guessed in the moment that followed: a razor-thin silence sharp enough to cut an artery.

"She was—"

"—pregnant."

Ted hugged the bottle, keeping its head up. "There's something wrong with this vodka," he said. "I can't feel it at all."

And I don't want to feel anything. Somehow this was his fault. Why hadn't Melanie told him? If she'd told him just a little more, he would have figured it out, done something.

"It happened that first night," Ted explained.

"No drugstores open?"

"Joey, please, don't you think I'd change everything if I could?"

"I don't know, would you?" Now would be a good time for a confession. A little morality tale. By the way, Ted, I almost went to bed with your wife, but I didn't. *Almost* is a good four yards short of the goal line. But Ted would only turn it around and say, *You see! Hypocrite!*

"It wasn't like we were having an affair. We'd get together— but just to try to decide what to do. I mean, that's all I wanted. I guess"—*sigh*—"she thought she was in love with me. But I was hoping if she went to see you then you'd fix it for her."

"Do you have any idea how stupid that is? What do you think, I've got magic powder I sprinkle over people?" *Wait.* Melanie hadn't said anything about being pregnant. That didn't mean for sure that she wasn't—obviously she hadn't told him everything— but pregnancy would have interfered with her ambitions, unless she was planning to do a cover for *Modern Parent* magazine. "Did Melanie know that Margot was having problems getting pregnant?"

"I don't know, maybe . . . maybe even Margot told her. Why? What are you getting at?"

"Just curious. How pregnant was she?"

Ted blinked. "I'm not very good at dates," he said. "Does it matter?"

"Not anymore." But if Melanie hadn't been pregnant, she wouldn't have had very long before she either had to start producing visible evidence that she *was* pregnant or admit her deception. And if she were pregnant, she'd have a deadline for an abortion. Either way, she would have had to up the pressure on Ted, a man who clearly did not respond well to stress, as weeks went by.

"If it hadn't been for that, I swear I wouldn't have kept seeing her. But don't you see? If I'd broken up with her, she would have gone out and gotten rid of it. I couldn't stand that. I mean, that was my baby, goddamn it. Don't men have any rights?" The front of Ted's hair was sticking up; he tried to flatten it with a shaking hand. Then he stared at the bottle furiously. "When is this shit going to kick in?" He turned the stare at Joel. "You don't know what it's like. *You* don't care about having kids. That would cramp your style. But it's like—you look around and you wonder how all those people clogging up the freeways ever got born, when it's so fucking hard to get your wife knocked up. You feel like a eunuch."

"It didn't sound like you were trying very hard."

"Did Margot tell you that?" His eyes narrowed. "Maybe she just wanted to make you think that it was all out-of-it Ted's doing, that it had nothing to do with *her*."

"Anyway, I didn't know you were so desperate for a child."

Ted smiled sadly. "I wasn't. Not like she was. But for her sake, for Margot, I wanted us to have one." He went on, almost tearfully, "I wanted to repay her, you know, for all the beautiful things she'd given me."

I may throw up. "So you had a baby with Melanie. To repay Margot."

"It just worked out that way!"

Joel grimaced. "I don't think so. I think you wanted to *prove* it wasn't your fault. As in 'big man with high sperm count'?"

Ted waved this off. But he looked pleased.

"I take it Margot didn't know about any of this?"

Ted held the bottle between his legs, rubbing it. "No. I kept trying to work up the nerve to tell her, but, oh, God, she would have lost it."

"That's putting it mildly," Joel said. But he felt relieved. Because if Margot had known about Melanie, that might have been the reason she told Joel that she was in love with *him*.

"Joey . . ." Ted started to peel the revenue stamp off the neck of the bottle. "Do you think—do you think Melanie killed herself over me?"

"Don't flatter yourself," Joel said. "In my professional opinion, which you sought out in such a forthright manner, she was not suicidal." *Oh, God, listen to me! My professional opinion isn't worth jack shit, if I could be so wrong about this. . . .*

"If I can't get drunk, I'll have to kill *my*self," Ted whispered. "You don't know what it's been like."

"Tell me, then," Joel said. "Tell me about the last time you saw Melanie."

Ted thought a moment. "I was at her apartment late Wednesday afternoon," he said finally. His head listed to the side, felled by the effort of remembering specific events and linking them to the days of the week. "We were having—a discussion, about what to do."

Wednesday afternoon . . . that was right after Joel had last seen Margot tucking her blue dress into her Jaguar. "So?"

"So . . ." Ted's fingers played the bottle like a saxophone. "So . . ."

"You don't remember, do you?"

Ted looked down.

"Oh, Christ."

"She wanted me to leave Margot, I know that. I kept trying to explain why I couldn't. I *love* Margot. But Melanie said that if I didn't leave her she was going to get rid of the baby. I told you, I couldn't stand that. It made me crazy."

"What did you expect her to do, then?"

"I don't know. Have it."

Joel almost laughed. "Then what? You and Margot would adopt it?"

"But Margot *wanted* a baby," Ted pleaded. "I don't think she could have one."

"Do you really think Margot would have gone along with you having a baby with someone else? And be grateful to you, for God's sake?" This time he did laugh, vibrations that hurt his chest. "How could you be married to her for so long and think that?"

Ted gave an exaggerated shrug, like a little boy who can't explain why his homework is late.

"All right, forget that," Joel said. "Is there anything else you *do* remember from Wednesday?"

Ted spoke slowly. "Sometimes I'd fall asleep at Melanie's place. But I never stayed over very late. Anyway, I got home somehow, at some point, and I must have passed out on the sofa here, 'cause that's where I was when I woke up. I could just tell something was wrong. I could tell that there was nobody in the house. It was Twilight Zone city." He grinned conspiratorily. Joel and Ted had often watched reruns of "The Twilight Zone" together, back in Westwood. "I went upstairs to find Margot, and when I saw the mess in the bedroom, I called you."

"Well," Joel sighed, "you can feel better about one thing. I don't think Melanie was pregnant. I think she just told you that to force you to make some decision."

Ted's grin vanished. "Fuck you."

"I meant . . ." He had thought that he meant to mitigate the loss of Melanie's death, but looking at Ted's face, Joel realized that he had his own motivational U-boats, swimming around unseen.

"Anyway, you're wrong. She was." Ted took a swig. "I'm scared, Joey. I'm so scared that I'll never be able to get drunk again."

"You will if you try hard enough," Joel said, and stood up. "Listen, it's been real, but I've had a long day. We might as well call the coroner and get it over with."

"What are you talking about?"

"You have to identify Melanie."

"No way, I don't."

"Ted. Be serious. The very least you can do is let her family know what happened to her. You owe her that."

Ted blew air into the top of the bottle and was rewarded with a low, tooting sound. "Joey," he wheedled, "don't you think it's better this way? There're bound to be questions, the autopsy. . . . I'm sure one of Melanie's friends will report it eventually—"

"You said she didn't have any friends."

"Well, not very many."

"Come on." Joel moved toward the phone. "You want me to dial for you?"

"Joey," Ted tried again, "think how Margot would feel."

"You should have thought of that before."

"No, I mean, the publicity." He tilted his head. "All the stuff in the paper about me and Melanie? It will kill her. She'll be brokenhearted."

Joel looked down at Ted. He was human garbage, certainly, but in this case he was right. People who had envied Margot would appropriate this scandal as their private revenge. And when it came right down to it, how could he call the police and turn in a friend? Okay, not a *real* friend, but someone he'd known a long, long time, someone he'd stayed up late with, been drunk with, talked about women with. And *maybe* Ted had killed Melanie or arranged to have her killed, but he swore he hadn't, and Joel had no proof that he had. It was hard to believe that a man with his shirttails hanging out and clutching a bottle of Stolichnaya was any threat to anyone.

Maybe they could hold off, at least for a day. Maybe by tomorrow Margot would be back, and he could break the news about Melanie himself, let her get used to the idea. She could go away on a real vacation after that, if she wanted to avoid the media coverage. He might even go with her. Meanwhile, Ted wasn't a psychopath who was going to go on a rampage with a machete in Union Square.

"I'll call Emory and tell him she was a patient of mine. I'll tell him that she looked familiar and I didn't figure it out till we got home. Okay?"

"That's a good idea, Joey." Ted nodded. "That works out perfectly for everyone."

On his way out, Joel remembered a conversation/argument he had once had with Denise about the process of helping other people. Denise said that you had to *want* to help. That desire must be as pure and unselfish as possible. Call it love, *agape*, friendship; it was the power that healed. Joel took issue—you didn't even have to like someone to help him, if you had the right technique. A surgeon could be vain, greedy, and selfish, and still save lives. To which Denise had countered: What about those *male* doctors who do all those hysterectomies that don't need to be done, but they do them because they want to finance their vacation homes? Joel knew from experience that as soon as feminism was an issue, he'd better change the subject.

But he thought of the conversation now, because here he was, going through the hedge to California Street, and wondering how to help Ted! Wondering exactly when and how he could make the intervention that would make Ted get some treatment of some kind . . . preferably a frontal lobotomy. *What do I care about Ted anyway? I want someone to help ME, to love ME.* But maybe it was just a reflex, after all these years, to think in terms of a treatment plan.

Joel stopped for an afternoon paper on the way home. Margot's story had been moved to page two: SOCIALITE STILL MISSING. Damn them, Joel thought. Margot had worked very hard so that she wouldn't be called a socialite. Other rich women traveled to Cannes, collected art; Margot let babies dribble on her blouse. In a town with a decent newspaper, there wouldn't have been an article at all.

Ted was right; Margot would be furious about this. So why didn't she come back and put a stop to it?

Well, he had to call Emory. But first things first. He needed a good, long, hard run. He needed to run until his leg muscles turned to lime Jell-O.

"So you say that this woman was a *patient* of yours. Is that why *Harvey* started screaming?"

Emory Epcot had pranced into his office at 7:30 A.M. Arms akimbo, he had glared at the couch as if it were a suspect in a particularly grisly murder. "Do people really *lie* on that thing?"

"Like you said," Joel replied, "your job never runs out of surprises."

"Hey, it's quaint, you know, kitsch. Ever see that DePalma film with the shrink who turns out to be the killer?"

"Missed that one." Joel smiled. "Sounds like you like movies."

"You got that right." Emory even looked like a film director, with his mirrored sunglasses, long wool scarf, and beret. Only the handgun in his shoulder holster spoiled the effect. He had first revealed this last when he tossed his brown suede jacket on the couch—too casually, with the follow-through of a good tennis serve.

Now he dug the toe of his cowboy boot into the carpet. "What *exactly* do you expect me to believe, Doc?"

Joel twirled a pencil between his fingers. "She *was* a patient of mine. I only saw her once, so I didn't recognize her at first yesterday. Apparently, though"—he hesitated, feeling like a snitch and a tattletale—"she and Ted Harvey were involved."

"I love it," Emory said, and Joel wasn't sure whether he was being sarcastic. "Tell me more." He sat in the armchair, and laced his fingers over his knee.

"I'm not sure there's more to tell." He felt relieved. He hadn't wanted the burden of Ted's secret. How many times, in college, had he lied to Ted's parents, pretending that Ted was out (when in) or sick (when hung over)? How co-dependent he had been! Enough was enough.

"Listen, Doc, do the words 'accessory after the fact' mean anything to you? You're a nice guy. Don't make me get mean." Emory took off his sunglasses for the apparent purpose of raising one eyebrow.

Joel discarded the pencil. "Why don't you just talk to Ted?"

"What a *good* idea!" Emory slapped his own face. "Why didn't I think of that? He'll just tell me the whole story. Like how he strangled this woman."

"She was strangled, then?" Joel asked quickly.

"Results of the autopsy. I suspected as much from the bruise marks—turns out there was also a broken hyoid bone."

Joel assumed that was a bone in the throat. He didn't want to ask.

"So why don't you just tell me what *you* know about this lady, for starters?" Emory got out a small black notebook. "We'll just keep it real friendly."

Joel obliged with what little he did know. Her address and phone number. She hadn't even told him what modeling agency she'd been with. But he did tell Emory, "She might have been pregnant. Did that show up on the autopsy?"

"Hey, who's the detective here?" Emory massaged his temples. "Lord, I am getting me one of my headaches."

"I have some Tylenol." Joel indicated one of his desk drawers.

"Kid stuff." Emory produced a prescription bottle of pills and popped two in his mouth at the same time. "I've been around

the block a few too many times for that." He *mmm'phhd* through
the pills, before swallowing them without benefit of liquid. "So
she was knocked up. Did she tell you that?"

"No." Joel hesitated. It wasn't easy to talk to "the authorities"
about Ted, no matter how clearly right was on his side. "Ted
seemed to think so."

"And here I was looking for a motive." Emory *tsked*. "The
things I waste time on! Tell me, Doc, you weren't screwing her,
too, were you?"

"No," Joel said coolly. "I told you, she was my patient."

"*And* she was screwing your friend." Emory chuckled. "How
do I know the three of you didn't get it on together? Believe me,
Doc, I've seen weirder things. Bet you have, too."

"That's true enough." *My father raped me. My mother made
me eat from a dog dish.* "Nevertheless."

"See, that's what pisses me off." Emory bent over to flick a
piece of lint off the toe of his cowboy boot. "There's so much
prejudice against gays—I swing that way myself—but the breed-
ers are much worse."

"On the subject of breeding, then, can't you tell if she was
pregnant?"

"Sure, and I suppose you want to start reading my mail, too."

"You can see why it's important," Joel pressed.

"Which is why it's none of your beeswax at the moment. I
mean, it could up the charges to *two* counts of murder." Emory
winked. "That has been known to make the difference in whether
or not someone does the old bail skip."

"H'm." Joel's vision went slightly fuzzy for a second as he made
one of those dreamy, intuitive leaps: He had a feeling that Emory
simply didn't know himself whether Melanie was pregnant.
Maybe he hadn't gotten that far in reading the autopsy report
last night.

"So what about Margot?"

Emory rose, stretched languorously, then placed his hands on
the small of his back and gazed at the couch. Then he slid across
the room and flopped down sideways on it. "No," he said, after a
moment, shaking his head, "I just don't see it."

"Margot," Joel repeated tightly and not very analytically.

Emory swung his legs back over the couch. "We'll want her for
questioning, of course. If you hear from her, let us know right
away."

Big help you are! Joel thought. "What about the car? No clues from that?"

"The Jag? Looks like it just drove off the road." Emory added, with one eyebrow raised, "Whoever was at the wheel coulda been drunk."

"You mean, maybe Margot wasn't driving it."

Emory tapped a forefinger against his temple. "Smart."

Maybe Ted and Melanie had been trysting somewhere near Stinson Beach. Maybe Margot had found out they would be there and was rushing to catch them when she had her run-in with Andrea.

Or maybe Ted was driving the car, as Emory implied, on his way to meet Melanie. Joel almost wished he could tell Emory about Andrea; perhaps Andrea had information that Emory could piece together with something he wasn't telling Joel. Maybe the Jaguar was swerving. Maybe it had gone off the road on its own. Maybe she could remember whether she saw more than one person in the car. But his promise of confidentiality to Andrea came first. He wouldn't tell Emory about her even if he knew she'd strangled Melanie herself. He did think that Andrea would eventually go to the police on her own; the criminal justice system, the social embodiment of the superego, existed for those whose own superegos didn't function properly. Andrea's worked overtime.

Emory grinned. "I'll tell you the inside dope, Doc, 'cause I like you."

Joel was wary of people who told him that they liked him, just as he was of salesmen who said "I'll be perfectly honest with you," friends who assured him that his secrets would be safe, and women who swore that they weren't fertile that week.

"The boys in S.F. got Merlin Davis, just last night. Seems they found him living in a minivan on Ellis Street, high as a kite. That minivan had a *really* nice stereo in the back. Remember the stereo?"

Joel remembered.

"The Harveys tried to help him out, didn't they? Bleeding hearts. I was in three foster homes, after my parents gave up on me and threw me to the streets. This kid was just hustling them, which is okay, if they're stupid enough to be hustled, but he's stupid, too. The last thing he should have taken was the stereo."

Who cares about a stereo! Margot had told him once that

Merlin wanted to open his own restaurant. But pulling on Merlin was an undertow of history that extended much further back than his birth, and that—if you had to get into the area of blame—would involve you in psychology, sociology, and economics, and still leave you with no one. Against these currents, Joel didn't consider Merlin to be either stupid or a hustler. He was, so far, simply not a strong enough swimmer.

"He's in juvy now. He'll probably do some time. But that pretty much eliminates him as a suspect. So that's one down."

"What did he say about the night Margot disappeared?"

"He was tired of the straight life, no pun intended. So when he came home that night and there was no one there"—Emory snapped his finger—"he saw his opportunity."

"What about Rosa Avera? I wouldn't think she'd be so hard to find."

Emory was stroking the cushions. "Think again, Doc. She's got no family left in the States except a brother." He twirled a finger around his ear. "Ricky Retardo."

Joel clenched his teeth. "I beg your pardon?"

"You know, not a full deck, two quarts low. A snooze alarm that doesn't ring. His name's Danny, he works at a garage on Leavenworth."

Joel glanced at the tree outside his window. "How can I say this diplomatically? Only a real asshole would talk like that."

Emory's eyes widened. "Hey, Doc, don't go into a tailspin. Try to see it from my point of view. Here's my best lead so far, and I can't get a thing out of him."

"Um . . . you went down there to talk to him?"

"Yeah, that's right."

"Which garage on Leavenworth?"

"What's it to you?"

"My car needs a tune-up." Joel added piously, "Given my profession, you know, I like to patronize businesses that hire the mentally handicapped."

"Bleeding heart," Emory snorted. "But I won't stop you from doing a good deed. It's the Crown Garage."

"Thanks."

"Well"—Emory slapped his hands down on the cushions, then looked dissatisfied by the lack of noise he had made—"I'm history." He fixed Joel with his penetrating stare again. "But we'll talk again soon, eh, Doc? Don't get any ideas about vacations in Rio."

"The last time I took a vacation," Joel replied, "was to attend a conference on 'Ego Psychology and the Disturbed Adolescent.' I had a stunningly functional room, overlooking the parking lot of the Santa Rosa TraveLodge."

Emory surprised Joel by laughing. "I'll see you around, then. And don't worry, I'm not going to grab your buns, even though they are awfully cute."

"I'm flattered," Joel said.

"You should be." Emory winked and was gone.

Joel remained at his desk. He took off his glasses, as he sometimes did when he wanted to think. He wanted very much to talk to Denise, and she was only two doors away. But obviously she'd misinterpreted his interest in her from the beginning; he'd feel like an even bigger jerk if he unloaded all this on her now. On the other hand, if she were just a tiny bit more reasonable . . . Why was it that women couldn't separate sex from romantic love? There were plenty of theories about that, but none of them made him miss her less for the way she listened sympathetically to anything he wanted to tell her. (Granted, her proffered solution to his problem might be to cast the *I Ching*.) The only other person he could really talk to was Margot.

For the first time in years he wished he could talk to Dr. Schneider, his old analyst. If only the lousy bastard hadn't died. He'd finished his work but left it vulnerable, and now Joel felt like a regular Venus de Milo. The severed arms must represent castration anxiety.

But after analysis you should be able to carry on your own internal work. And Joel was beginning to see what his mistake had been: He had abdicated responsibility, waiting for the Teds to confess, the Emorys to locate, and the Margots to reappear.

He cleaned his glasses on his handkerchief, and put them back on. At lunchtime he was going to have someone take a look at his car.

CHAPTER 6

REPAIR WORK

The Crown Garage was squeezed between a laundromat (apparently out of business, since its windows were covered with Chinese newspapers) and a tenement, where several Vietnamese children played on the porch.

Joel's Dodge Colt could penetrate no deeper than the driveway of the garage; the rest was packed with dusty autos, most with panels and hoods removed, exposing cables and batteries. He thought of an overcrowded ward in a county hospital. "My car needs servicing." He addressed the blue-coveralled rear end of a man whose face was bent low into the dusty eviscera of an Escort. In fact, Joel couldn't remember when he had last had a tune-up, and sometimes he noticed the disturbing odor of burnt oil after he turned off the engine.

"You'll have to leave it overnight," the mechanic said. "Let's take a look." Opening the hood of Joel's car, he shook his head the way Joel's mother once had over the state of his sock and underwear drawers. "Did you know your radiator's leaking?"

"Is it?"

"Yeah, and the fuel pump is about to go, too."

"How much is this going to cost?"

"Three, four hundred dollars. Plus labor." The mechanic twisted something under the hood. Joel read his oval name patch: R.B. "When was the last time you had your brakes checked?"

Joel was scanning the darker reaches of the garage, where he distinguished a young man in the corner leaning over a car. "Can you write me an estimate?"

"It's gonna be a little while. Customer's coming to pick up this Escort in a few minutes. I've got a guy out to get some parts. As soon as he gets back he can do it."

"What about him?" Joel pointed to the young man in the back.

"Him? You don't want *him* to do it."

"I'll wait, then." Joel took a few steps deeper into the garage; at the same time, the young man in the corner stepped aside and Joel saw a brightly restored, cherry-red-and-white car. "That car over there . . ."

"That's mine," R.B. said, slamming the hood of Joel's Colt. "A fifty-seven Buick Super. Belonged to my father. He passed away about five years ago, and I put a whole new engine in myself." He held out his blackened hands.

"It's beautiful. Mind if I take a look at it?"

"I can't have you back there."

Joel had already noticed the sign: OUR INSURANCE DOESN'T COVER CUSTOMERS IN THE WORKPLACE. "I really admire old cars that have been kept up."

"Wellll . . . okay, go ahead. Don't be long. As soon as my guy gets back with the parts—"

"Write me an estimate for the dent, too."

"Which one?"

"All of them." That, Joel reasoned, should give him plenty of time on his own.

Joel picked his way through the cables on the floor, feeling his shoes stick to the oil and sawdust, turning sideways to squeeze between the dusty fenders of cars.

The Buick Super was the only automobile surrounded by some clear space. The car had thick white sidewall tires and a row of little portholes on its swelling fender. The grill was huge, with two conical shapes protruding like dinosaur's teeth. But it was the rectangular breeze windows that brought Joel's childhood back to him like a faint odor on the wind. He could remember riding in such a car, how modern it seemed, a vision of the future.

The young man polishing the hood looked about seventeen. The smooth, dark planes of his face, the flat tip of his small nose, his Clark Gable mustache, and his slanted eyes gave him the appearance of a lithe cat. He, too, wore an oval namepatch on his green workshirt. Danny.

Joel lightly caressed the hood. Danny held up the hand with the cloth in it. "Please."

"I'm sorry. It's a beautiful car. You take good care of it."

"Thank you." His accent was soft, lilting.

Joel took off his glasses and wiped them with his handkerchief. "My name is Joel. Joel Abramowitz. I need your help."

Danny smiled, showing small and very white teeth. His expression was both pleased and fearful.

"I'm looking for a friend of mine."

Danny ducked his head. The dim fluorescent lights made his curls glisten.

"She's a friend of your sister's, too. Rosa. Do you know where Rosa is?"

Danny shook his head vehemently.

"My friend is Margot Harvey."

"Mrs. Margot," Danny echoed. He rubbed the hood more ferociously. "Spots," he said. "Spots won't come out." He gently pushed his fingernail against the edge of a mark that only he could see. "Mrs. Margot has a big, pretty house."

"Yes."

"I go there a lot. But Rosa says I'm not supposed to touch anything or she will get me sent away."

"Can I help you?" Joel asked.

"Help?"

"The car."

Danny wrinkled his nose. "You make streaks."

"No, I won't. I promise."

Danny shrugged again. This time Joel isolated three distinct stages: Danny would shrug deeply, bringing his shoulders as close to his ears as they would go; then he would tilt his head to his right and smile diffidently; then he would flinch: blinking and jerking his head slightly.

"Show me how," Joel said.

Danny removed the extra cloth that was tucked into his belt and gave it to Joel. "Like this," Danny explained, moving his own cloth in gentle circles.

"Like this?" Joel imitated Danny's movement.

"Yes. Good."

"Tell me about going to Margot's house."

"I do lots of good stuff for her," Danny said proudly. "I wash the car. Mrs. Margot say I do the best job on the car."

"What else do you do there?"

"I fix the hoses. I am good in the garage. They have me there lots. Once they had a party, and I comed to help." Danny shook his head. "It was not a fun party, though."

"Why not?"

"Everyone was unhappy, because they had to eat snails." Danny stuck out his tongue. "Then Mr. Ted started acting silly. He was pretending to be a dog." Danny chuckled. "I thought it was funny and the other people liked it, too, but Mrs. Margot was very unhappy. That's when she sent me down to the basement, to watch TV with the black man." He whispered, "Rosa hates Mr. Ted. She says he . . ." Danny paused and thought a minute. "He thinks like a fish."

"So Rosa was there that night?"

"Oh yes. She's *always* there."

"Tell me about Rosa."

"She likes Margot." He paused and repeated, as if by rote, "She says Margot is her mentor and her roles model."

"Did you ever live with Rosa?"

Danny's smile disappeared. "Yes."

"What was that like?"

Danny shook his head.

"Can you tell me more about that party, then? The one that wasn't fun?"

"The TV in the basement is very big, like the movies. Do you like the movies?"

"Yes, I do."

"I've been to the movies lots."

"What happened in the basement?"

"The black man wanted to watch 'Twilight Zone' show, and I am scared of that one. Then he wanted me to smoke marijuana with him, but Rosa says if I ever smoke marijuana she will get me sent away, so I didn't."

"Sent away where?"

"Not supposed to tell," Danny mumbled.

"What happened then?"

Danny looked down.

"I won't tell anyone."

"I was hungry," Danny said softly. "I still wanted more ice

cream, and Mrs. Margot said I could have it whenever I want."
He looked up. He was a few inches shorter than Joel.

"And you saw something."

"Mrs. Margot was very, very mad. She was yelling, like Rosa
yells at me. I was standing behind the door, but she didn't see
me."

"Whom was she mad at?"

"Mr. Ted." Danny squatted down to wipe one of the big
headlights, then looked up knowingly at Joel. "She said he was
going to regret it."

"Regret what?"

"The day he was born."

Joel wondered if this could have been the same dinner party
that Ted had described, the night he had first met Melanie. Then
he wondered why they hadn't invited *him*.

Danny was rubbing harder. Joel hoped that the guy who had
gone to pick up parts had stopped for coffee. Maybe doughnuts,
too. "Mr. Ted yelled, too," Danny said finally. "He said very bad
words. If I say them, I am curtains with Rosa."

"Ted was angry, too, then."

"Yes." Danny whispered, "He called her a *bitch*. And he said
the other one, the *really* bad one, too. Do you know what that is?
He said—f-f-*fuck*." Danny flinched. Joel wanted to pat his
shoulder, but feared it would be a mistake. Danny wasn't
retarded, as Emory Epcot had so endearingly suggested, but he
was developmentally arrested, and might misinterpret a touch.

"Then Mrs. Margot put a pot on his head." Danny grinned
suddenly, staring into the giant headlight as if it were a crystal
ball. "I saw from the door. They didn't see me."

Joel squatted down next to Danny, balancing himself against
the Buick's grill. "Don't worry. I won't tell anyone what you saw."
Danny's eyelids drooped. "Danny, do you know where Rosa is?
Or how I can try to find her?"

Danny flinched. Then he shook his head.

"It's very important. You see, she might know where Margot
is, and I want to find her very much."

"Has she done something bad?"

"No, she hasn't—she's just missing."

"Do you like Mrs. Margot—like girlfriend?"

Joel had to smile. Danny had intuited how Joel felt about

Margot in about four years' less time than it had taken Joel himself. "Can you keep a secret?"

"I keeped many secrets," Danny said grimly.

"I do like her."

"Mrs. Margot is very nice," Danny said. He reverently wiped the grill of the Buick. "She said I could have all the ice cream I wanted." Danny rolled his eyes. "There is not that much ice cream in the world, especially the marble fudge."

"That *is* nice of her."

"And she tells Rosa not to yell at me. Rosa never yells at me when Mrs. Margot is there."

"Rosa shouldn't yell at you at all."

"Rosa doesn't like me because I'm stupid," Danny explained. "She says she has big plans. She says it's my fault that she can't do her plans."

"What plans?"

"To be rich. Like Mrs. Margot." Danny held his hands far apart. "She want to have a big store and sell clothes. She went to a big school, but I'm too stupid to go."

"I guess Rosa likes Margot a lot, too," Joel said. But he didn't mean it—at least not entirely. Rosa's devotion to Margot appeared as smooth and flawless as ice on top of a lake; but as ice melts with a slight change in temperature, so could Rosa's absolute loyalty crack.

Perhaps Danny sensed this as well. He shrugged.

"Does Rosa have any friends that you know about?"

"Oh yes. Chuck. They go dancing. Do you like to dance?"

"I'm not very good at it . . . but yes, sometimes."

"We have dances where I live. It's fun." Danny's head swayed in rhythm to some remembered music.

"Where do you live, Danny?"

"At a house, with other people. I can go there by myself. I take the bus with the big three."

"Do you like it there?" Joel hoped his anger didn't show. Danny could have been living at home if he'd had a loving family. *And if I had wheels I could be a bus.*

Again Danny went through the ritual shrug, smile, and flinch. "I like the dances. There's a girl I like to dance with the most," Danny whispered. "But she makes me feel funny. Rosa says it's bad."

"Rosa's wrong. It's okay when you feel like that."

"Rosa makes me do bad things. But she says it's okay when she says so."

"What bad things?"

"I can't never tell."

Joel wondered how to probe this. *Bad things.* "She told you not to tell."

Danny nodded.

"Did she say why?"

Danny flinched twice. "Never tell."

All right. "Do you know where Chuck lives?"

"Yes, on a big street. I've been there. I don't like it. The toilet is always fulled up with smelly things."

"Do you know his last name?"

"Only Chuck." Danny grinned. "He says, call me Chuck Only, and it's supposed to be a very big joke. Everyone pretends to laugh, like this." Danny ho-ho'd, like Santa Claus.

"Hey!" The mechanic shouted. Joel looked up to see him coming toward them, squeezing his bulk between the cars. "I've got that estimate for you. You gotta move your car, it's blocking the drive."

Joel rose stiffly. His knee—the old running injury—twinged.

The mechanic handed him a slip of yellow paper. "I can do it all for fourteen hundred." He pointed down the list of repairs with a grimy ballpoint. "I'm giving you a deal. We checked your brakes, they're almost gone."

"Jesus," Joel mumbled. "This is everything but the transmission."

"Want me to check the transmission?"

"No, thanks. Can I leave it now?"

R.B. clipped his pen back in his pocket. "Sure. I can have it back for you in ten days. Call first."

Joel studied the estimate, reflecting that, whether by luck or design, he was continuing a long pattern of not being able to save any money. He shouldn't take so many low-fee referrals.

"Aren't you finished with that yet?" R.B. shouted at Danny. "Move your butt, I want you to hose down the drive."

"I was talking to him," Joel said. "It's my fault."

"He's got work to do." Louder: "And this time you're not going home till you finish." He turned to Joel. "Some jerk comes around from the city with a little fairy briefcase, says I can hire this guy and be a hero. Biggest mistake of my life. He's in trouble already.

Yesterday there were a couple of cops in here, spent an hour with him, screwed me up for the whole day." Loud again: "If you've been stealing, you're out on your butt."

"Can I talk to you?" Joel motioned R.B. aside. "You get subsidized for employing Danny, don't you?"

"Yeah, so what?"

Joel stepped back a few feet, indicating that R.B. should follow. "I shouldn't be telling you this, but I'm a psychologist." He cleared his throat. "I have colleagues who work for the city, who started this program. They're doing spot checks. They want to make sure that the conditions are good for the employees."

"What kind of crap is that?"

"It's this new administration. The bleeding hearts have control."

"That's a fucking fact." R.B. squinted at him. "You're not one a them spot checkers, are you? If you are, you can—"

"Oh no, not me," Joel assured him. Then he whispered, "They also want to find the best employer, to give him a special award. In cash."

"I'm real nice to Danny," R.B. grumbled. "I let him keep all kinds of his crap here. He's got a whole box of garbage in my office."

"I'll certainly give you *my* recommendation, if I get a chance."

R.B. stuck his thumb in the direction of a gutted automobile. "I'm just trying to make a living. We specialize in American cars. Who drives an American car? I've got to compete with those Japanese mechanics, they work for slave wages, live eight to a room. And you seen this neighborhood? It looks like Cambodia out there now, with all those refugees. Give me a wino any day, he's too drunk to steal your customers from you. Listen," he broke off, "you want me to work on your car or not?"

Joel crammed the yellow sheet into the inside pocket of his jacket. "Sure, sure. I need it today, is the problem." He looked over at Danny, who was crouched behind the Buick. "But I'll be back very soon," he promised.

As he came up the stairs, he recognized Denise's black tights through the bars of the balustrade. She was standing outside her office, and for a moment his fight-or-flight instinct was weighted toward the latter. He'd wanted to talk to her, but even before he climbed high enough to see her face (his eyes meanwhile traveling up to her knees, then to the black skirt and black leather belt), he knew that her mouth and brows would be set in a distinctly confrontative expression, and they were.

"Hi," he said. Not his most brilliant opening, but unobjectionable enough.

"Had lunch?" she asked. Joel hoped this wasn't female code for *I want your balls, mister.*

"No. I thought I'd skip it."

"Anorexia?"

"Mild."

"I brought some soybean burgers I was experimenting with at home. You could tell me what you think."

"Sure," he agreed, then glanced at her open door with dread. He was suddenly afraid that she only wanted to lure him into that small enclosure whence he might never escape. Behind her, he saw the sinister eyes of a thousand small creatures, real and fantastic, on her crowded shelves.

But he entered and heard the door click shut behind him. And then the words he expected all along, spoken in a lower, more serious tone than before: "I really wanted to *talk* to you." He knew what that meant: A lecture on Relationship Failure. He could hear the theme from "Dragnet."

All right, he thought grimly. I deserve it, I guess, so let's get it over with. There was a student coming to confer with him at one. She would have to let him out for that.

"First I'm going to feed you." Denise removed oily wax paper from two soybean patties on paper plates. Some red juice had soaked through the whole-grain bread.

Joel lowered himself into one of the beanbags, though he always felt silly, scrunched up down there. He cautiously sniffed at the soybean burger; it smelled like the Crown Garage. "What did you want to talk about?"

"I—I . . . This is hard for me." Denise, who looked equally silly scrunched across from him, was folding the wax paper into smaller and smaller squares, creasing each fold, and drawing her fingers slowly along the edge until it was scalpel-sharp. He noticed with relief that she hadn't started to eat. "I realized I was way out of line on Sunday. I'm sorry."

Joel exhaled fully for the first time since entering her office. "Don't worry about it," he said magnanimously. "I mean, I don't think you were."

"You weren't leading me on. I was just projecting." Denise

traced the outline of the beauty mark on her cheek. "But I thought, because you always wanted to pay for everything—"

"I didn't want you to know how poor I was." Joel suspected that by keeping his financial independence marginal he was trying to protect his so-called emotional independence, just as his living in a studio apartment prevented anyone from offering to move in with him. "Also, I admit it, I'm old-fashioned about that."

"And you always spent the night. . . ."

"I thought you wanted me to."

"I did." Her eyes widened. "You didn't do it just because I thought I wanted you to, did you?"

"No, of course not." If only the rules were published somewhere, so he could go look them up.

"Well." Denise picked at the crust of her bread. "I want to go back to the way things were."

"Are you sure?" he asked. He was suddenly, unforgivably reluctant to show any concern in the matter. Unforgivable, when he had so misjudged her. She had once said that he wanted to see everyone happy; *that* was the projection, for it was she who was one of those people who make the planet bearable: people who actually think of others first.

Denise nodded.

"I'd like that," he admitted. "I'd like that very much. I've—I've missed you. But maybe we should be clearer this time . . . about . . . I mean, it sounds like you didn't *like* the way things were before."

"I liked the way *you* thought things were, I just thought they were different than that."

"So we'll go back to the way—why don't we start from the beginning?" *Come one, come all, see two shrinks negotiate a relationship!*

"Okay." Denise folded her hands neatly on her lap. "We're friends. Sort of a garbage-can term for men and women who fraternize without plans to wed."

And who sleep together? Joel knew that he couldn't do that anymore. There was no *technical* reason for him to be faithful to Margot, but he was too wrapped up in her for sex with Denise to be anything but mechanical—exploitive—now.

"But"—Denise still had the resigned expression of someone about to go in for a root canal—"I don't think we should sleep together anymore, if you don't mind."

"I understand," Joel said quickly. He was glad that they wanted (or didn't want) the same thing, even if for different reasons; he was also dimly aware of his narcissistically wounded male ego.

Denise sighed, pulled off a corner of the bread, and put it on her tongue like a pill.

"What's the matter?" Joel asked. "This can't be about me."

"It's not," she said. "I'm taking it out on you, that's all. I don't want to lose having you in my life. I'm just upset that I haven't gotten over this . . . pattern."

"What pattern is that?" Joel was feeling much more relaxed, almost brave enough to try the soybean burger.

"I've always been attracted to men who aren't available. You know that. But my radar is so good that I'm attracted to men who aren't *emotionally* available, too."

She had, in fact, told him that about the high school history teacher to whom she lost her virginity, and her long-standing crush on her sister's husband. She had only hinted, though, at some of the cruelties of Carl, the psychiatrist. "That's why I fell in love with you. You really didn't know, did you?"

"No," he said, maybe a little too forcefully. He hadn't—but when he had reviewed the past year, he realized that there had been many signs he had chosen to ignore: If he called after a week or more of not talking to her, she would be in a mysteriously sullen mood, which he could, however, dispel with a few compliments. Then, too, she kept mementos from their dates: cocktail napkins, theater programs, ticket stubs, and the little slips of paper from fortune cookies, a veritable drawerful of which he had stumbled onto by accident when she had asked him to get Scotch tape from the kitchen.

But he felt embarrassed by her declaration. "You aren't missing out on anything, you know—I'm poor, I can't fix a toaster, and I always forget to put the mayonnaise back in the refrigerator." Sonja had often complained about the last.

"It's not that. If you really were available, I mean, wanted to get involved, I wouldn't be interested in you at all."

Joel nodded. So much for thinking too highly of himself.

Denise covered the beauty mark with her palm. "I think I finally had my breakthrough insight about this. You see, I figured out about you and Margot."

"Margot?" Joel echoed, ingenuously. She hadn't figured it out, *too*, had she? He felt as exposed as he had the first time he had lain on Dr. Schneider's couch. He couldn't let her know! He'd simply deny it.

"It's so obvious now. When I think of seeing the two of you together. The way she was always finding an excuse to get you into the other room to tell you *secrets*. And she hated me. She was always talking to you about people I didn't know."

"That must have seemed rude, but I don't think she meant to exclude you." Joel told himself he still wanted Denise and Margot to be friends one day.

"Hah!" Indignation burned—rather attractively—in her eyes. "You don't know her as well as you *think* you do, Joel Robert Abramowitz." She took her first and very large bite of the soybean burger. "I have to tell you honestly," she resumed as soon as she could swallow, "because I'm really trying to be honest, even though it's hard, I don't think it was fair of you to sleep with me without telling me you had other sexual partners. I—I have *feelings* about that. These *are* the nineties, after all."

"I've never slept with Margot."

"Oh." She hastily wiped her mouth with her napkin. "Well, okay, then." She hesitated. "I wasn't trying to be nosy. But I respect you more now. I don't think adultery is a very individuated thing."

"Neither do I." Joel smiled. "So Oedipal." He glanced up and noticed the elf whose head Denise had been repairing when he had come into her office last week. Before he knew that Margot was gone. The elf was an evil-looking creature, with tiny, sharp teeth, and Joel imagined it giggling.

Denise was clutching the moist bread tightly. "But you do love her, don't you?"

"I . . ." Once again, he wanted to break camp and head for higher ground. But he owed her the truth. "Yes, I do."

And once he said it, he felt something else—such relief. How sweet to turn a secret over to another's care. How erotic to confess. To be known. It made him shiver, like a cat having its belly stroked. "Very much," he added. "But it was really just in the last few weeks that I realized it."

Denise rolled her eyes. Her hands opened, and the sandwich dropped onto the plate.

"Are you all right?" For a moment he was afraid she was choking.

"Fine, fine." She grimaced. "I'm just sorry I asked, that's all."

"Ah." There was a short pause. He did not want to tell Denise that from the beginning she had been too eager to please, too . . . available. He wanted to feel that he was pursuing a woman, while dimly sensing that she was causing him to pursue her. Then one of those it-seemed-like-a-good-idea-at-the-time ideas came to fill the vacuum. "Let's go out this weekend."

She stroked her cheek, eyes narrowing.

"I'm not assuming you're free, and I'm not trying to keep the score even. We're friends, right? So I'm just suggesting to you that we go out and have dinner, but feel free to say no." He grinned. "I'll be crushed, but I'll survive."

"We have to split the check."

"Why?"

"Friends split checks, unless one of them is an insecure male trying to prove something. Besides, you just told me how poor you are."

"All right." For the first time Joel noticed the sand tray behind her, only half shoved out of sight. The figure of a bride and groom stood in the center, surrounded by prehistoric monsters. "And . . . we'll be honest from now on. No more mixed signals."

"Right." Denise nodded, compressing her lips, a return of the abscessed tooth.

Joel lifted the top slice of bread from his soybean burger. Cold to begin with, it now not only smelled like the Crown Garage, but resembled a used-engine part as well. "And in the name of honesty, I am going to tell you that—I'm not very hungry."

Denise began to dig herself out of the beanbag. "Thank you for sharing that," she said.

"I don't mind that you canceled our session yesterday," Andrea said, as soon as she flopped on the couch, "but it was at the last minute, practically. I was like really upset."

Joel rested his chin on his hand and detected the odor of soybeans. Andrea might be pleased if she knew how much he had been anticipating this session: He hadn't seen her since she had first told him about her "accident" near Stinson Beach. "You mean, if I'd given you more notice, you wouldn't have been upset?" He was almost tempted to remind her how she had cried when he told her about his plans to take Memorial Day off, although he had let her know a full month in advance.

She giggled. "Well, okay, maybe I would have been. I just wish I knew *why* you canceled. And it does make a difference, that it was at the last minute. . . ."

"And what are your thoughts about that? About why I canceled at the last minute?"

"It was just something more important than me that came along."

"Like?"

"Jesus. Maybe you had to get your teeth cleaned."

"Do you really think I would cancel our session at the last minute for that?" *Wait.* Andrea *did* believe that she could be that easily dismissed. She didn't know that he had gone to Mill Valley to identify what turned out to be the body of a former patient. He remembered the psychoanalyst's prayer: *Let me respect the autonomy of others.*

"Okay." Andrea caterpillared down the couch a few inches. "So I guess it was an emergency."

"An emergency."

"I was thinking. . . ." One by one, Andrea pulled on her fingers, yanking off invisible rings. "Maybe you went to see that MAR GO woman in the hospital. Maybe you told her that I'm the one who did it to her."

Joel looked out at the tree, marveling at how a living thing could remain so still.

"It's been bugging me so much the past few days. What I can't stand is not knowing. It's driving me crazy."

"Not knowing . . ." Joel prompted.

"Not knowing what happened. Whether MAR GO is all right. I thought of calling the hospitals, but I knew they wouldn't tell me anything."

"Have you read the paper?" This morning's *Courier* had demoted the story to the society column. Jody Daniels implied that Margot had slipped away to a fashionable retreat to recover either from plastic surgery or a dependence on prescription drugs. Joel guessed that the *Deliverer* was good for at least one more day of unearthing scandals about Margot's family, and he hoped that their dedicated journalists wouldn't make the connection between Ted and Melanie.

"Oh no. I don't have time."

"Watch the news?" The body on Stinson Beach had been television-worthy for the first day at least, before being crammed

out by the usual run of stories on drug busts in Oakland, cor-
ruption in Sacramento, and debate about whether to build a new
downtown stadium. Melanie's name had not been released pend-
ing notification of her family.

"I don't see how you can ask that," Andrea replied irritably.
"You know I'm studying for exams. Don't you even care about
that?"

Joel did not reply.

"Was she . . . Margot I mean . . . was she your patient?"

"Would you want me to tell you if she was?"

"No," Andrea said finally. "I wouldn't want you to tell other
people about me, either."

"I think you ask for other reasons. If you really wanted to
know, you could find out in other ways—maybe even by reading
the paper."

"I don't get you sometimes. I already explained why I
can't . . . anyway, I'm going to tell you whether you care or
not—I've got an appointment with the dean this Thursday, to
talk about whether I can take my antitrust exam over." Andrea
clapped her running shoes together. Joel noticed that the laces of
the right one were untied. "Don't you care a *little*? If I can't take
the exam over, I'll flunk out."

He did care, but his telling her wouldn't make her believe it.
Meanwhile, he would have to struggle to be patient. He was
pretty sure that she had more to tell him about Margot, but she
would also know damn well what a fishhook that was in him, and
she would give that fishhook a few tugs before dispensing her
information. Masochists make the best sadists: They know what
hurts.

"I had another big blowout with my father last night," Andrea
said. "He's handling that case, the one where the private airplane
crashed into the Jack in the Box last year? He was bragging
about it, about how he was going to get zillions of dollars from the
'deep pockets,' for the plaintiffs. What got me was that he was
acting like that was a *public service*. And I said, What, are we
going to have signs in every fucking Jack in the Box from now on
that say, warning, this fast-food restaurant may double as a
runway? And if he *really* wanted to perform a public service, I
said, why didn't he take the case for free? So he said—" Andrea
did a deep-voiced and (Joel guessed) accurate impression of her
father—"'Young lady, whose house are you living in? Who puts

that food you're eating on the table?' I guess he was telling me I'm fat, but he should talk, the old porko. Besides, every time he talks to me, it's like I'm the jury and he's doing closing arguments." Andrea cackled. "So I just left the table right then. I think it was important that I stood up for myself. I didn't even finish dinner, if you can believe that. Although I had a couple bags of Potato Skins in my room. They're not as fattening as regular chips, though, 'cause they're natural.

"And I ended up eating them all because I was feeling so guilty. Not because I finally stood up to him, but for all the money I spent of his for cocaine when I was into that. And not because it was his money, either—but because of how he made it. I mean, he made it off of people losing their arms and legs, right?

"I told you he wants me to work for him. But I'd just be a slave. He fires about seventy-five people a week. I don't want to be a lawyer at all. I guess that's why I want to flunk out, because it's easier to do it that way than to just tell him how I feel. I can just see myself stuck there, working on all the car accidents that are too bloody for anyone else."

Long pause, stretching into silence. This silence was like a drop of water, clear to the human eye, which when viewed through a microscope would reveal itself full of squiggly creatures. Joel breathed through his nose, waiting.

Andrea sighed, and folded her hands across her chest, like a body arranged in a coffin to look peaceful. Somehow he could tell her eyes were closed. "I really don't want to talk about the accident. I can't deal with it. I keep hoping it will just go away, you know, but I have nightmares every night. I keep seeing myself on the road and then I'm going off the cliff, but it's like I'm flying. Then my father's there, but he looks like this picture I saw once of St. Joseph.

"I'm afraid to drive anymore. I keep thinking people are going to throw themselves in front of my car. I walked here today. I've been taking the bus to school. I even let this pukey guy who likes me from school give me a ride home yesterday, even though he has zits covering his entire body." She suddenly stuck one finger into her mouth, and he could see that she was chewing on it furiously. "I thought maybe I should go to the police."

"Why haven't you?" Joel asked, though he thought he knew the answer.

Andrea stiffened. "I was waiting for you to tell me to go," she said. "Because I thought maybe you *wouldn't* want me to go, too—like it would be our little secret."

Joel almost sighed now. "Tell me again what happened that night."

"Well, I was driving up the coast highway about midnight, and I was following this car and I honked twice and passed her and she tried to pass me back and I speeded up, and when another car came the other way she went off the road."

More silence; this one, too, filled with wiggling bacteria. It was not impossible that she had just happened to find herself behind Margot's car, but Joel still believed that it was no coincidence. He slid a little lower in his chair. Funny, though, how at times like these he *could* be almost as still as that tree.

Finally Andrea said, "Believe it or not, that wasn't the really terrible part."

"What was, then?"

Andrea's elbows twitched. "I guess I'd better tell you the whole thing from the beginning."

I certainly wish you would.

"When I left here Wednesday, I told you I had a feeling about that woman in the blue dress who came to see you. And then I went outside, and down to the corner, and that was when I saw the Jaguar, and I just had a feeling it was hers. It was so *pretentious.* I was going to leave then, you know, the exam was at two, but I couldn't stand it, I just had to wait to see what was going to happen, like how soon she was going to come back to her car. I figured she was your next patient, but I was afraid maybe you gave her more time than you give me. So I thought I'd sit in my car and wait and see how long it was till she came out. That would still give me time to get to the exam.

"So I sat in my car. I was parked just a couple of cars ahead of her. Then . . . then I saw you guys coming back together. That was like so unfair I couldn't stand it. She's your patient, but you walk her to her car! How come you won't walk me to my car? I mean, would you walk me to my car if I was thinner? I know you wouldn't, because she's probably smarter than I am, and funnier, that's why you like her.

"I watched you guys in my rearview mirror. I slouched down so you wouldn't see me, but you didn't even look my way. I saw you stop at her car, and talk, then she got in and drove off. You were still standing there, watching her. I just wanted to kill you, or kill myself, or someone. And I knew you'd be going back to the office, so . . . I just decided to follow *her*. I didn't even think about the exam then.

"It's funny," Andrea went on after a pause. "I keep dreaming about accidents and all, but it hasn't really sunk in that I might have killed someone. I think I can stand it, though, because I didn't do it directly. People kill people every day. Like all those guys who went to Vietnam? Maybe they didn't want to, but they did. It was kill or be killed." Her voice was thick with melodrama. "And all those big companies that pollute the environment, they're killing people, too, when those people get cancer. And then there's abortions—if I ever got pregnant, which I won't, 'cause no guy likes me enough for that, but then I'd have an abortion and not feel guilty about it. A bunch of my friends have had three abortions apiece. And what about the doctors who do the abortions, or who fuck up and their patients die when they're in surgery—"

"That still begs the question of your responsibility."

Pause. "I hate you when you say stuff like that. You're supposed to make me feel better."

"So you followed her."

"Well . . . I followed her home, like I said. I guess you know where *that* is," she added. "I mean, I bet you've been there, haven't you? There's a big, high hedge so you can hardly see the house. But there's a gate in the hedge and it opened up automatically for her car. The driveway curves, so I couldn't quite see where the garage was, but anyway, the car drove in there. I swear, that was the *whitest* white car I'd ever seen. I mean, what does she do, get it repainted every week? Except there *was* some bird shit on top, I saw her try to wipe it off when you were standing with her.

"Then I just waited for a while. I remembered the exam then, but I thought, since I'm flunking out anyway, it doesn't matter. I had this whole scheme in my head. I was going to go up to the front door of Margot's house and pretend that I was selling magazine subscriptions to work my way through law school. I knew I looked kind of sloppy, but it fit in with the Hastings sweatshirt I was wearing. I was just getting up my nerve to do it when the car drove out again."

He could picture the hood of Andrea's sweatshirt bouncing up the Harveys' walk, and he smiled. "What were you going to do after you convinced Margot that you were selling magazine subscriptions?"

"I'm not sure. I just wanted to meet her. I don't know why you ask me these stupid questions. Maybe I was going to tell her that I was in love with you and she should keep her grubby hands off. And I guess I wanted her to know how pathetic I am and to feel sorry for me. I wanted to debase myself as much as possible. It was like I had sunk lower than an ant's rear, and everyone knew what a twerp I was, and now I was going to see if I could sink even lower than that. I felt like I'd enjoy all my suffering more if someone knew about it."

"Someone does."

Silence again. "Don't say that," she said finally, and her voice was thick. "I want you to feel sorry for me, but not that much. Anyway, I didn't get to meet her, because, like I said, the Jaguar drove out. By then it really was too late to go to the exam, so I started following her again.

"She just went straight down California Street. I almost lost her about halfway, when I missed the light at Arguello, but she got stuck at a light a few blocks down. She drove all the way from Seacliff to Nob Hill. There's a big highrise there, across from Grace Cathedral. You know the one I'm talking about? It sort of looks like a hotel, and there's a restaurant on the ground floor, Nipper's or Puker's or something. There's a garage for the building off Jones Street, that really steep hill. She turned the corner on Jones, and when *I* turned the corner the car was gone again, so I figured she must have gone in the garage there. I drove in, and the Jaguar was there, and there was an attendant getting into it to park it, but MAR GO was already gone. I got paranoid that maybe she knew I was following her and went to call you. But I thought, well, if she went to call you then you'd have to come to get me, and that would be sort of fun, almost."

Joel thought he knew the highrise she was talking about, and he thought it was where Melanie lived. Had lived. He suddenly remembered that tomorrow would have been his second appointment with her, and his arms tingled.

"The parking lot is for people who live in the building and for people who come to the restaurant. Oh, God, I bet you've been there with MAR GO and it drives me crazy. Why can't some guy like *me* the way you like her? There's that guy at school, but he's pukey. Whenever I look at him I want to cry, 'cause if I don't like him I'll never have a boyfriend, but I can't like him—"

"You were in a parking lot," he reminded her.

"All right, all right. *Jeez*. There were two attendants there, they park your car for you. I had rolled down my window and one of them was coming over to my car, and the other one called out to him, 'She said she'd be back in an hour.' I figured he meant MAR GO, so I thought, what the fuck, I'll just stay and wait for her.

"So I told the attendant that I wanted to park there and sit in the car for a while. He must have thought I was banana-brains. I told him that I had an exam to study for and that there was too much noise at my house. He said that it got pretty noisy in the parking lot, 'cause there were so many people coming and going, and I asked him, 'Look, is there a law against me sitting here? I'll give you a big tip,' and that shut him up. They let me park the car near the guardpost, so I knew I could make a quick getaway if I had to, and follow her when she came out.

"Well, you aren't going to believe this, but she did not come out for *eight fucking hours.*"

Eight fucking hours. Or eight hours fucking. Because Ted and Melanie must have been together in Melanie's apartment that afternoon.

"See, I'd thought she'd gone to the restaurant in the building, but nobody can spend eight hours in a restaurant, I mean," Andrea reasoned, "not if they're thin. So that was when I figured out that maybe you guys had rented an apartment there so you could get down. Maybe after she left you took your own car and met her there.

"Well, after a couple of hours I had to go to the bathroom so bad, my eyeballs were turning yellow. Finally I got out and went to the restaurant upstairs to use their john. I was sure MAR GO was going to get away from me then, but the Jaguar was still there when I came back. A couple of times the attendant asked me what I was studying for—I think he was trying to pick up on me, but I just scratched my armpit while he was talking to me, to sort of put him off. Sometimes when a guy is trying to pick up on me I do something gross like that, like try to make myself fart. If they think you're crazy, they leave you alone. I should try that with the pukey guy at school I was telling you about, if you remember.

"The garage attendants go home at ten, because that's when the restaurant closes. At ten, I asked the attendants if I could stay. I said I'd pay them in advance for a whole night. The one guy said that wasn't allowed. But the other guy . . . 'Member I said one of them had been trying to pick me up? You're probably thinking he had rotten taste, but I have a theory, that some guys have a thing for fat redheads. It's a sickness. Or maybe he was just nearsighted. Anyway, this guy said, 'All right, honey, just don't tell anyone, okay?' He winked at me and he said, 'I bet you're meeting someone down here, that's okay, too, he's a lucky guy.' I wanted to cry then, 'cause no guy ever wants me, except the pukey ones, like the guy at school, or this one, he had a really big nose and dandruff.

"Okay, so the garage attendants left. It was real creepy down there, I was afraid there might be cockroaches, or you know, maybe one of the building security guards would come down, and no one could hear me scream if one of them did. . . .

"For a while I listened to Bruce Springsteen. I just go nuts over him, I listen to this one album all the time. It's one of the early ones, those are the ones I like the best. Do you know that song where he sings 'I came for you'? I like to listen to that in the dark. It always makes me think about dying, and how you would sort of . . . of *come* for me.

"Then I started going over the rules for tracing community property, because I still have my C.P. exam coming up. I should have known better, because that really *did* put me to sleep.

"I was dreaming about an engine revving up. And then I realized it wasn't a dream, and I woke up. Right ahead of me the Jaguar was starting. She'd come down and gotten in while I was asleep. I waited till the garage gate opened and she was driving out before I started my own engine. It's a one-way street, so I knew she had to turn left out of the garage, and the next street down, Pine Street, is a one-way street, too, so I knew that when I got out of the garage, if I couldn't see her, she would have turned right on Pine Street, and unless she really peeled out I could probably catch up with her." Andrea cackled. "You know, I bet when she got that hotshot MAR GO license plate, she didn't know it would get her into so much trouble. It's a reflective plate, too, so those things together made her easy to follow the whole way."

Joel leaned forward and the leather of his chair squeaked.

Andrea, asleep, had not seen the woman who got into the Jaguar in the garage—and that that woman wasn't the same petite, dark-haired, blue-dressed one with whom she had seen Joel after lunch. Ted must have driven Margot's Jaguar over to Melanie's. Maybe Ted and Melanie had had a fight, then, and Melanie had taken the keys from Ted and the Jaguar from the garage, driving off to a friend's house to sulk, or to give Ted a scare. Instead, she had ended up on the beach.

"We drove out Van Ness," Andrea was saying now, "and then down Lombard, and out to the bridge. That's when I really got scared. I don't like to drive the bridge at night, at least not the Golden Gate Bridge. The lanes are so narrow and there's that oncoming traffic so close. There wasn't very much traffic that late, but it was even spookier that way. You can't tell the water from the sky—it's all black. Now that they light up the towers they look even creepier, like something that's landed from outer space in one of those fifties horror films. When I was little and my parents took me across the bridge I always cried, especially at night.

"But we got to the other side, and I followed her through the tunnel, and then she turned off on Highway One. By that time it was like I was hypnotized. I was afraid I'd fall asleep again, so I had the Bruce Springsteen on. His voice on that dark road, it was . . . it was the only thing I could hear, and it was sort of religious. Like listening to God. His voice sounds just like yours. I imagined then, Bruce Springsteen was like a priest or a saint, and you were God. When I see you here, you're like Jesus—like God in a body, right? That song I was singing, I think it's about a suicide attempt, 'cause there's this stuff about an ambulance and oxygen masks.

"By the time we were getting close to Stinson Beach, it was after midnight. I was thinking about all the weird cults that hang out there, all the bodies they say they've buried up in the hills. I hadn't seen a car in like ten miles. I started thinking, what if I had a flat tire, maybe one of those goony cult people would find me first and use me for a ritual sacrifice."

Andrea didn't say anything for several moments. Joel finally observed, "You say you were following her."

"I *admitted* that. Don't try to make me feel worse."

"If you were following her, then you wanted to see where she was going."

"All *right*. I said I'd turn myself in, if you tell me to. What more do you want?"

"I was just wondering. If you wanted to see where she was going, why did you pass her car?"

"Because . . . I thought . . ." Andrea was silent a moment, then she giggled nervously. "Did I say that I passed her?"

"You were quite definite about it. You passed her, and it was when she tried to pass you in return that you speeded up so that she ran into another car."

"I don't remember that now." Andrea rubbed her head against the antimacassar. "It's all kind of fuzzy in my mind. Maybe I thought I passed her, but I didn't really. Is that possible?"

"You tell me."

"But you're the one who said . . . I mean, it's true, why would I pass her car?" Pause. "I really don't think that I did. I *know* I didn't. How can I make you believe me?"

Joel waited, seeing again the dark road, feeling almost as if he were a passenger in the car—and wishing he could read minds the way his patients so often imagined he could.

"What I remember is that it was real spooky. And then . . . I was scared because suddenly there was this car behind me. Yeah. I don't know where it came from. I thought he had his brights on, he was like blinding me in the rearview mirror. He honked to pass me, but I speeded up, 'cause I didn't want to lose the Jag. I was driving faster and the Jag was driving faster, and the car behind me was driving faster, but none of us was going more than about forty. That's 'cause that road is so curvy that even driving that slow you keep swinging over into the left lane."

After another pause, she laughed shortly. "Maybe I'm not so self-destructive after all. 'Cause now I remember that there was this big curve and I slid over in the left lane so far that I really freaked out, so then I slowed down after that. Then—then"—she chewed a finger—"the car behind me was still like honking and flashing its brights, so I finally pulled over on the shoulder, when I saw a place to stop. And that car passed *me* then."

She examined the callus on her thumb for a moment. "I understand why I forgot that part. Because I felt totally humiliated, like I failed at everything, like I couldn't even *follow* someone, even when I missed an exam to do it."

"And what happened then?" Joel asked. The room around him

had dimmed; as though she had hypnotized him and he was remembering what had happened along with her.

"Well, then I thought, if that other car is in such a hurry he'll probably pass MAR GO, too, and then I can still follow *her*. So I started after her again. I lost both the cars around a curve, but then the cliff sort of hooked around, and there were the two cars real clear up ahead, and I saw the second car, the one that passed me, was bumping up against the back of the Jaguar. Then they disappeared again, and I speeded up a little more. I took the next turn and I saw them again—just when the Jaguar skidded off the cliff. I think the other car pulled over then."

Andrea slowly let out a breath that she seemed to have been holding for a long time. "It's funny, because it's like I can see it two ways now, like two different movies in my head—the way it happened and the way I thought it happened. The second way is starting to lose something now. It's starting to seem more like something I made up." Pause. "I think you believe me. I hope you do. I don't blame you, though, if you don't." She crooked her thumb and started on fresh calluses. Her entire body was stiff, down to the running shoes crossed at the ankles.

"It was a powerful experience," Joel said. "It would have affected you in many ways." He should know. He'd been affected himself—he hadn't realized how much until now—now that *his* muscles suddenly felt as if he'd been lifting weights for twelve hours.

"I was so freaked out, I drove on past the accident without looking at anything, at either of the cars. It was like my eyes were frozen on the little bit of road right in front of my car. I drove ahead until I could cut over to 101, and I came back that way. You probably already figured this out, but I didn't go to Jennifer's." Andrea relaxed slightly. "What I don't understand is why I thought I passed her in the first place."

"Perhaps it was something you wished you *had* done."

"To kill somebody?" Andrea giggled. "How could I wish that?"

"She was your rival, after all."

"But to *kill* her . . ." Andrea laughed. "Come on."

"But you *didn't* kill her," Joel said. "What bothered you, I think, was that you wanted to. That made you feel guilty enough, perhaps, to feel as though you had. To want to punish yourself for it."

"It's true," Andrea said. "I didn't kill her. I *didn't*."

She hadn't. Joel was relieved that she wasn't directly involved. But someone was. Ted was in that other car, bumping up against the Jaguar.

"God." Andrea's back arched off the couch. "I feel so *high*. Wow. Maybe they'll let me take that exam over, and I'll really ace it."

"The other car," Joel said, "the one that passed you. Can you remember what it looked like?"

"It was so dark."

"I know. . . ." What was the point? Ted drove a BMW, which in outline looked like a dozen other makes of cars. And how reliable was Andrea's memory? She would try to figure out what he wanted to hear, and tell him that, or the opposite, depending on her mood. It wasn't fair that he should have felt so relieved and then have to start worrying again right away. Still, there was Andrea, and Andrea's whole existence separate from this private drama. *She* had accomplished something today, and he was going to hold on to that for a moment, like a gift he had to return, before he went back to his own problems.

He glanced at the clock next to the tissues. They had exceeded the end of the hour by a couple of minutes, but Joel let another moment pass before he said, "We're out of time today, Miss Griswald."

CHAPTER 7

HAIR OF THE DOG

They booked Ted at the Hall of Justice on suspicion of murder. The damning evidence was a torn piece of Ted's driver's license, and his Carte Blanche, buried deep in the sand on Stinson Beach, near where Melanie's body had been found two days before.

Ted's lawyer had confidently informed Joel that statutory bail would be set, and Ted released, by the end of the day. In the meantime, Joel was in a lime-green anteroom, waiting next to a door with a wire mesh window. Joel was the only adult male and the only Caucasian in this line. The eight women who waited ranged from svelte, with thick makeup and hair in corn rows, to potbellied, in housedresses and spongy pink rollers. About half had babies; some had more than one child. Mostly they were silent, though two women at the head of the line were discussing a new nightclub.

Joel had been here for half an hour. Goddamn Ted anyway.

Joel had had plenty of time to create a fragmented scenario, that played in his head like previews for a black-and-white foreign film: Ted and Melanie together in her apartment, last Wednesday afternoon; she leaves him, driving Margot's car; Ted pursues her. After forcing the Jaguar off the road, Ted helps her out; she's cut her forehead, bled on the upholstery—Ted sobs, begs forgiveness—and on they go in Ted's car, hands on each other's thighs. Ted is drunk. Maybe Melanie is, too. They talk about Nevada.

Here the film skips. Another fight. Ted stops the car, Melanie jumps out; she runs toward the beach. Ted follows. Slow motion.

Final scene: Ted and Melanie on the dark, cold beach. The film is grainy, and then it runs out.

Maybe the strangling was an accident, at least as much of an accident as the unconscious allows. But a driver's license and a credit card get left, like a patient leaving his coat in the waiting room, like Betty insisting that Joel take the giraffe.

Andrea's testimony wouldn't be needed now; Ted had incriminated himself.

Faster than a computer check; more judgmental than a mother-in-law; able to leave clues and forget about them the next day! Look—in the back of your mind! It's a childhood trauma! It's a recurring nightmare! No—it's Superego!

One of the babies in the line whimpered, and the mother cooed to it. Joel looked over to see the mother's onion-shaped behind swaying in snug jeans.

Joel tried to stretch unobtrusively, pulling his elbows toward each other, behind his back. He got restless just waiting for a teller at the bank. . . . He had to stop running the Ted-Melanie *film noir* through his mind before he started imagining it in French with subtitles. He already had a name for the movie: *Ted et Melanie sur la plage.*

He sometimes distracted himself by envisioning various forms of an afterlife he firmly did not believe in. (Anyone who read the shortest essay by Freud or had spent more than a few weeks horizontal in therapy knew that belief in an afterlife was simply wish-fulfilling and death-denying.) So it was a harmless fantasy to imagine that this was a line to Hell, and he'd been sent here for not calling his parents often enough or in the proper spirit, not writing to his sister. Then there was flushing the toilet too often and taking baths instead of showers during the summer months. Don't forget littering, and taking parking places someone else had seen first . . .

. . . And not leaving New York right away after his grand-mother had her second stroke, so that he didn't see her before she died; spoiling his mother's Thanksgiving when he announced that he had become a vegetarian after the turkey was served; walking out on Sonja when she was crying after they had had a fight . . .

. . . Failures of love and charity, lapses of attention, the patient he referred out because he was too busy; countertransference, sexual aggression, repressed wishes, sibling rivalry . . .

Guilt. The thinking man's addiction.

He was roused by the sound of someone crying. Without turning around, he realized that it was the woman behind him. He stepped aside. "Here," he said softly, "why don't you go ahead of me."

The woman took two steps forward without looking up. She had a tiny ruby pierced into her nose.

"Is there anything I can do?" Joel asked.

Her eyes were dry now. "Not unless you is Jesus," she said.

Ted and Joel were separated by a pane of thick, dirty glass, and Ted spoke to Joel over a phone receiver that made his voice foggy.

"Don't ask me if I did it," he said. "I know you think I did. I can see it in your face."

"I won't lie," Joel said. "But that's why they don't put your friends on a jury." On the stool next to Joel, a young mother held her baby up. The man tapped the glass to get the baby's attention. Ted glanced at the father, and envy flickered through his eyes.

"How are you doing?" Joel asked. Ted was pale, and his light stubble made him look more haggard. His eyes were swollen and red-veined; Joel noticed the capillaries were starting to become visible on his nose.

"Well, I haven't made this many new friends since Camp Beaverbrook," Ted replied a little shakily. "But I'm going to kill my travel agent. The service is lousy, I'm afraid to drink the water, and the group activities are just *too* supervised."

"Not your usual vacation spot," Joel observed.

"Didn't you always say *you* wanted to be a travel agent?"

Joel had kidded about that a couple of times. "Travel Agent to the Damned, that's me."

"It was nice of you to visit. But you got me here, you know."

"Come again?"

"You told Emory about me and Melanie."

"Ted, I couldn't lie about that."

"I forgive you. I know I deserve it." Ted pulled on his receding thatch of hair. "We had a special party last night. There was a guy in the psych cell who decided to kill himself by eating his jeans. Now, you would think if you were going to eat your jeans that you'd start with one of the legs, but this guy started with the waist."

"Maybe he was very hungry," Joel suggested.

"We told him it wasn't fair unless he brought enough for the whole class." Ted's eyes were blank now. "Joey . . ." He put his hand up on the glass.

"What?"

"I'm sort of scared."

Joel winced: at his own satisfaction, at seeing Ted stripped of his Seacliff castle, the titles of his wife, and the royal booze. At knowing that even Ted's miraculous luck didn't last forever. But Joel at his most vindictive was still a therapist. Ted would be vulnerable now, so this was Joel's chance to save his soul from repression and win it for sublimation.

"Joey, do you know what happened to that old bathrobe I used to have?"

"The gray satin one, with the red T?" Joel made a cross over his lapel. Ted had found it at a secondhand store, and was thrilled with the coincidence of the monogram. He used to call the T his scarlet letter.

"I wouldn't have thrown it away. I just can't remember what happened to it. You—you didn't take it, did you? You liked it."

"But my name doesn't begin with a T. I'd look sort of strange." Joel admitted to himself that he *had* once coveted the bathrobe. "Your lawyer told me he'd get you out later today."

"Up till now, my lawyer specialized in acquiring net-operating-loss companies for tax purposes. What's so funny?"

"Nothing." Nothing should be funny at a time like this—but the talk of lawyers had made Joel think of Andrea's father. Anyone with a six-figure bank account could hire Grisly Griswald, Andrea had said.

"Joey," Ted moistened his lips, "come pick me up when I get out, will ya?"

"Sure," Joel said. "Sure, I'll come pick you up."

The silence that followed was more awkward than any Joel had had to sit through with a patient for the last several weeks. He finally tapped the phone receiver. "I'd better get back now," he said. "Besides, I bet someone wants to make a call."

. . .

Joel hurried so as to get back before his appointment with
Betty Klass, but when he returned, there was a message from
her on his machine: "Dr. Abramowitz, I do hope this isn't going to
inconvenience you, but I can't make it today. I just had to go back
over to Playground and volunteer my services again, for you-
know-who's sake."

Jesus.

Joel went through a very stale yellow light driving across
California Street.

The Playground house looked quiet. He parked in the driveway.

Once on the porch, he could hear the sounds of fussing children
inside; the front door was unlocked, which it shouldn't have been,
and he entered.

Mrs. Tuttle sat cross-legged on the floor of the parlor. "Can't
you all play together nicely?" she was pleading to the dozen
children who waddled around her.

"Is Mrs. Klass here?" Joel asked quickly.

"Children, children, *please.*" Mrs. Tuttle covered her ears with
her hands. The children, however, did not respond to this appeal
to adult sensibilities. Instead, pants and diapers drooping, they
rummaged for toys, and hit each other for no apparent reason
other than fulfilling the demands of the separation-individuation
stage. "Lord help me, I'm getting a migraine."

"Is Mrs. Klass here?" Joel repeated.

"Who?"

"*Mrs. Klass.* The lady who broke in last week."

"No, Dr. Abramowitz, but I wish she was. I wish *some*one
was. . . ."

Joel dashed to the kitchen, poked his head into the hall closet.
Empty. That woman . . .

"I'm going upstairs to check," he called to Mrs. Tuttle as he ran
past again.

"Jasmine!" he heard her shout. "You come down from there!"

Joel took the steps two at a time until he burst out onto the
roof. Again the expanse of tar and gravel glittered, waiting for
him, but this time he was alone. He sighed, waited a moment to
catch his breath, listening to the cars and gazing at the phone
wires. Then he started back down, much more slowly.

When he reached the second floor, he noticed that the door to

Margot's office was open. That gave him an idea: Here, after all, was a place where Margot might have left footprints, unconscious messages—the way Ted had left his driver's license in the sand.

The office was cluttered; he and Margot shared a tendency to accumulate small objects. "I can't throw it out," Margot would say. "It has *sentimental* value." He, on the other hand, only saved items that had potentially practical use.

Margot had arranged a dozen snapshots in front of the eclectic books on the shelves. Photos of her and Ted: at the beach, sightseeing in Wales. There were some of Joel with Margot, some of the three of them. Joel counted quickly: He appeared in five of the twelve, while Ted was in seven. There was a picture of her father, looking very much like a newspaper editor with his graying hair and wire-rim glasses; as usual, no pictures of her mother.

The room still contained Margot's lingering scent, the faintly musky and yet childlike odor.

He sat at her desk and started going through her drawers, moving quickly, not wanting Mrs. Tuttle to catch him. The drawers were neat on top, but once he peeled off the uppermost layer of reports he found loose paper clips, receipts crumpled into wads, and half-eaten memo pads with Margot's familiar circular doodles. It was only then that his scruples returned, as he thought what an invasion this was, thought of peeling off layers of Margot's clothes.

But he kept on, smoothing out the receipts as he gathered them—American Express, Visa, MasterCard—they were for office supplies, restaurants, tune-ups for the Jaguar. One was for a hundred and eight dollars, from the Chocolate Dippery, and he remembered with an ache that she had loved chocolate-dipped fruit. *Had* loved? *Stop that, Joel!*

Then there was a receipt for thirteen hundred seventy-three dollars and blurry cents, from the Aurora Place Inn. He slowed down when he read that name, feeling it like a slightly dull razor blade against his cheek. Aurora Place. The address was on Pine, but the credit-card imprint was too smudged for him to read the street number.

He found a phone book and looked up the address: the eight hundred block of Pine Street. And then he remembered something that Margot had said, the last time he had seen her: *Whenever Ted and I have had enough of it all, we go to this little*

*bed-and-breakfast on Nob Hill, the quaintest thing you've ever
seen. A special suite with a grandfather clock.*

A real estate agent would call Pine Street Nob Hill, but a
native like Margot wouldn't. Still, maybe she was being charitable. And what could it hurt to go there and look around?

He put the receipt in his pocket and went back downstairs,
arriving just in time to help Mrs. Tuttle pry a puzzle piece out of
a child's mouth.

"These things are dangerous to have around, Mrs. Tuttle," Joel
said, holding up the soggy bit of cardboard.

"I can't do it all by myself!" Mrs. Tuttle whimpered. "I was
supposed to have an assistant come in and help me, but now that
Margot's gone . . ."

An assistant. "Mrs. Tuttle, Mrs. Klass told me that she was
going to do volunteer work here at Playground."

"Why, I do recall something like that. She was a nice lady,
Betty Klass. Just a little high-strung."

"Is that why she came here that day?"

Mrs. Tuttle was crawling after another child who was toddling
toward the stairs, but she moved somewhat ineffectively as her
knees rubbed against her long skirt. "Which day?"

"The day she almost jumped off the roof with Horatio," Joel
said impatiently. "I can't imagine that would be easy to forget."

Mrs. Tuttle rolled back on her heels. "Please don't you start
yelling at me, too. I thought you were my friend."

"I am, Mrs. Tuttle. I'm sorry." Joel guided the toddler back
into the parlor. "What I'm trying to find out is, did Mrs. Klass
know Margot before that day?"

Mrs. Tuttle wrinkled her nose as a child tottered past. "I think
Capricia Louise made a potty."

"Did she?"

"Let's see." Mrs. Tuttle picked a few crayons up from the floor.
"Yes, I do believe she and Margot had some sort of meeting that
afternoon. That's right, Margot was going to start training
volunteers, and I think that's why Betty dropped over. Then
Margot must have been late, or Betty was early, because Betty
was here and she offered to help me redecorate my kitchen. Did
you know that Betty was a friend of Elizabeth Taylor?"

"Wantit, wantit."

A little boy was reaching for a shelf of stuffed animals and Joel handed him a teddy bear. "How did Betty get hold of Horatio, then?"

"Well, she *said* he was her son. A lot of the black children have white mothers. Is that a crime? You're not prejudiced, are you?"

"Listen, Mrs. Tuttle, this is very important. If you hear from Mrs. Klass, you have to let me know immediately. And don't let her take any of the kids anywhere, all right?" Maybe the Betty scare was over. But Joel was almost as disturbed by what he was seeing here in the parlor at Playground. He had assumed that Margot had left enough gas in the tank, as it were, to keep the place running without her for a while. And maybe she thought she had. Because she might hide from him or Ted, but she wouldn't let Playground suffer.

"You were such a good friend to Margot," Mrs. Tuttle said wistfully. "She always spoke so highly of you. I know she'd be happy that you came by today."

"She's not dead, Mrs. Tuttle," Joel snapped. He'd always known he was a little superstitious—he'd just never known quite how much. "Don't talk about her like that. She's only *missing.* You won't forget what I said about Mrs. Klass."

Mrs. Tuttle started rebuckling one of her gladiator sandals. "Well, if you say so, but there's something you could do for *me.*"

"Sure." Joel was keeping an eye on a little girl with a Pebbles Flintstone barrette pulling on the drape cord. It looked long enough for her to get into some sort of imaginative trouble.

"There's a young upstart on the board who's trying to get me fired. Says I'm incompetent! Can you imagine!"

"Which—um, board member is that?"

"Jean Stone. She's acting president, now that Margot's—not here. And she certainly thinks she's something special!"

"I'll talk to her." Joel disengaged the cord from the little girl's hands and she wailed. *And I thought my job was hard.* "Maybe the board can send someone else out to help you." He swung the cord out of reach and glanced around for something safe to give her, settling on a plastic ball too large for her mouth, which she immediately threw toward the middle of the room.

"I would appreciate it. It wouldn't be easy for me to get another job, and my husband's retired, and he's starting to get a little confused, you know; he's always late to pick me up because he gets lost driving around the city."

"Well, I'm sure they can work something out." Mrs. Tuttle

couldn't be left in charge like this, but ideally the board could keep her on, as *de facto* assistant to someone else. "In the meantime, you have to watch them more carefully. I know it's hard."

Mrs. Tuttle rolled her eyes. "You have no idea." After a few false starts, she scrambled awkwardly to her feet. "Milk and cookies time, children! Would you like some milk and cookies, Dr. Abramowitz? I made them myself."

"No, thanks. I'm trying to cut down."

"I hope you don't skip lunch. It's the second most important meal of the day."

"I've got to get back," Joel said. He was going to be late for his next appointment. "Remember, if you hear from Mrs. Klass, call me immediately." He started to hand her a card with his number, but both her hands were gripping smaller hands, so he left it on the mantelpiece.

He stood on the porch for a moment, reluctant to leave. Only God and Betty herself knew why Betty had left him that message. Maybe she had sensed another episode coming on and then been able to fend it off herself; maybe she had started for Playground and gotten distracted.

But he had thought that somewhere in Betty's elaborately woven tapestry of fantasy there might be a loose thread of truth. And here it was: Granted that Mrs. Tuttle was not the world's most reliable witness, it did appear that Betty had known Margot from some time before that first day. The extent of that relationship—that they were "like sisters"—Betty had clearly exaggerated.

Joel could understand why Margot wouldn't have wanted him to know that she had asked Betty to Playground, since Margot had obviously mistaken her for a lovable eccentric with volunteer time on her hands. Still, he wished she had told him. And he wondered why she would have told Betty about her mother's suicide, something she seemed almost completely to have repressed.

For now, he couldn't stand guard at Playground. He had to move on.

Ted made the front page of the afternoon newspaper. Since it relied more on newsstand than subscription sales, and therefore suggestive headlines, the *Deliverer* might even have made Ted

the lead story, if there hadn't been an earthquake in South
America that morning.

Besides reporting Ted's arrest and drawing the inevitable
conclusions (*"We saw quite a bit of Mr. Harvey around here,"* one
*of the maintenance crew of Ms. Hardwicke's apartment building,
who asked not to be identified, told the* Deliverer), the article
added a new twist: *Friends say that Ted Harvey's wife, socialite
Margot Harvey, is vacationing in the Caribbean at an undis-
closed location.*

Joel threw the paper away.

Ted was released that evening. Joel waited while Ted's valu-
ables were returned: a watch, a hip flask, a handful of coins,
Certs, his belt, and business cards with the glittering embossed
logo of his PR firm. *Harvey & Fairfax.*

They left the Hall of Justice and drove up Sixth Street, Ted's
nose elevated as if offended by the smell of a musty Dodge Colt.
"Stop somewhere, will you?"

Joel had never really noticed how many stores sold liquor, how
many billboards promoted various brands. In just the two blocks
next to the Hall of Justice there must have been half a dozen
bars, most with a tie-in name: The Jury Room. The Bench. And
of course: The Bar. As they drove farther, the names became
more generic: The Hub. The Corner. The Lounge. The Pit Stop.

"Forget it," Joel said. "This conveyance carries no alcoholic
beverages."

"Fucking shit," Ted muttered. Then: "I didn't do it, okay?
Margot must have taken my wallet. Then after they found
Melanie there, Margot tore up the license and put it on the beach,
so that it would *look* like I killed her."

"But why would Margot have taken your wallet?"

"*I* don't know."

"Then stop blaming her."

Long pause, while Ted's anger filled the car like steam. Joel
ended the silence. "Ted, Margot knew about you and Melanie,
didn't she?"

"Yeah."

"So you lied to me before."

Ted slumped lower in the seat. "I didn't mean to lie to you,
Joey. I really wasn't sure. Those whole couple of days—I could
have spent them on Mars. That night you were over for the

barbecue? Maybe you didn't notice, but I got pretty drunk that night. Well, that was the start of a *real* binge. Now I sort of remember that Margot and I had a fight about Melanie after that . . . but I don't know how she found out. I didn't tell her. I don't think. Hey, I'm not *that* suicidal."

They were stopped at a light. Ted put his hand on Joel's sleeve. "I *wish* I could remember. I really do."

Repelled by his touch, Joel gripped the steering wheel more tightly.

Ted sighed. He looked out the window and pointed to a group of ragged-looking men loitering in front of a graffiti-splattered wall. FUCK LIFE was sprayed in dripping red letters. A man stood under this banner, wearing a blanket over his shoulders. "Look at those poor bastards," Ted mused. "It's a tough world out there. Now I know how people like that feel."

The birth of sensitivity. Joel turned onto Market.

"You know," Ted went on, "when they first brought me to the . . . cell, there was another guy there, and he was reaching for a cigarette that the guard was holding, or maybe he was a trusty, but he was holding it just out of this guy's reach. I thought . . . I thought that wasn't very nice, was it?"

Suddenly Joel felt Ted's fear turning over in his own stomach. When he was away from Ted, his Old Testament God wanted Ted's balls. But prison . . . green cotton trousers, warm tuna, the creaking of other men's beds all night long—Ted would never survive. His personality would break into the ten thousand tiny, irregular pieces of a jigsaw puzzle.

"Jesus, you could have brought me something to drink. I can't wait to get home. My lawyer says we should hire this guy from Boston. I don't know. I don't *remember* anything that happened, doesn't that count for something?"

"You said you didn't do it."

"I didn't! At least, I don't think I did." Ted sighed again. "My lawyer doesn't believe me, either. He's talking about diminished capacity as a defense." Ted rubbed his finger under his nose. "But that would still be manslaughter. I could still go to jail for that."

"I guess you could," Joel said. He remembered the lime-green anteroom, the line of poor women, and Ted's eyes behind the thick glass. There were "nice" prisons, of course, minimum-security facilities where they let inside traders play tennis. But it wasn't physical hardship that would destroy Ted, it was the anonymity. Joel was just beginning to realize how much Ted needed a gray satin bathrobe, embossed business cards, a phone in his car. This was the man he'd been competing with? He relaxed his grip on the steering wheel.

"How could Margot leave me now," Ted asked softly, "when I really need her?"

"*If* she left you," Joel reminded him. "*If* she's all right."

"I miss her."

"So do I." That seemed a good prelude to a confession—or a boast: *I loved her. She loved me.* But Joel went no further. It would be cruel to dump that on Ted now. Or was he afraid that Ted wouldn't believe that Margot loved him—afraid that Ted would be right?

Ted was leaning up against the window, as if wishing to reach out and pluck the nearest bottle from the nearest shelf. "If Margot was okay, she'd come back to help me out."

"Maybe not." Joel edged into traffic to get around a bus. The sun was in his eyes; he lowered the visor and a pencil fell into his lap. "Maybe not after you got another woman pregnant."

"But I didn't mean for it to happen. . . ."

"No, of course not," Joel said. "Melanie practically raped you, the way I understand it." The black-and-white previews were starting again. Highway One at midnight. NOW SHOWING AT A THEATER NEAR YOU. "Ted, do you carry an emergency road kit in your car?"

"Yeah." Pause. "Why?"

"So you could have stopped on the way back and taken the license plates off the Jaguar."

"I didn't!"

"But you don't remember."

"I'd remember *that*." Ted smoothed down the front of his hair. "Whose side are you on? This is a tough time for me. I need your help."

"When did you notice your wallet was missing?"

"God—I don't know—no, wait, I do remember—it was when I went to buy—something at the store Thursday morning."

"And you weren't worried about that?"

Ted laughed. "Joey, do you have any idea how many times I've lost my wallet this *year*?"

Joel stopped for a skateboarding teenager. It was still hard for him to think of Ted, the Westwood Terror, as a killer. But things got away from people sometimes. He remembered something Andrea had said—what was it? About women having abortions and men shooting each other in the jungle. Doing what you thought you had to do.

Joel drove on into the sun. Was he trying to excuse Ted? Well, maybe he had his own reasons for wanting Ted to stay free: He needed Ted to make himself feel secretly superior. Needed him to steal Margot from

"Why are we stopping here?" Ted asked.

They were in front of a Methodist church.

"There's an AA meeting downstairs tonight. A newcomers' meeting."

"I'm not going." Ted clung to his shoulder harness. "No way."

Joel put his hand on the tab of the seat belt. "Give me about seventy good reasons."

"It's supposed to be Alcoholics *Anony*mous. But everyone's going to know who I am."

"I beg your pardon?"

"Joey, after those articles in the paper today? *Front page* of the *Deliv*? I'm practically infamous." *Infamous stud*, his little grin seemed to say.

"Should have thought of that before."

"I'll go, but not tonight."

"If not now, when?"

"Tomorrow. Any time. Just not tonight. After what I've been through—"

"No good reasons so far. Only seventy to go."

"Joey," Ted whimpered, "I need a drink."

"No, you don't." Joel pushed the tab that released the seat belt. "You need help, is what you need." He had not forgotten Ted's haggard, frightened look, behind the thick glass, or even his nascent sympathy for the men on Sixth Street. This was Joel's opening. *Quick! Before his defenses all go up again.*

Ted pressed himself firmly against the door of the Colt, squinting at Joel.

"I'll carry you if I have to," Joel said, and Ted apparently believed him because, albeit with a withering look, he opened the door himself and got out of the car.

Joel sat on a folding chair next to Ted for the duration of the ninety-minute meeting, from the reading of the twelve steps to the recitation of the Lord's Prayer.

If Joel had had to write a paper on it, he would have described the meeting as attended by people from diverse socioeconomic backgrounds who had all recently suffered losses that were perceived as threats to self-esteem. "These losses," he would have written, "have proved the motivating factors in seeking counseling." A woman was fired three times in six months; a man depleted his savings; another man's girlfriend died while he was driving drunk.

And now they wanted to *change*.

The drive-model pitted one unconscious force against another to see what behavior would win out. Like a cockfight. You could be rather clinical about it then, and figure that some people would make it and others wouldn't. In this very smoky basement room, it was harder to think about drives; it was seductive, even for a reluctant atheist like Joel, to believe in that Higher Power which dispensed change as a gift, like grace.

It was a little after sunset when they headed back to Seacliff. Another fogless evening, slipping into blue.

"I'm not like those people," Ted insisted. "You know that."

"That's right." *The rich are different from you and me.* "You have more money."

"Did you see how they smoked? Did you see how they were dressed?"

Joel silently looked at Ted's rumpled white jeans, his soiled Lacoste shirt.

"All right, all right." Ted's hands were clenching and unclenching. "I know I drink too much. But I don't have to quit completely. I have more self-control than that. I could just cut down."

"You *know* that won't work, Ted."

"Yes, I know. I know all of that." Ted's voice rattled. "And I'm going to tell you something else, too. Right now every single fucking cell in my body is screaming to have a drink, I mean it's like the Watts riots in here, and if Margot were in the backseat holding a gun to her head and saying that she would pull the trigger unless I promised never to take another drink—"

"Okay, Teddy, relax." Now it seemed to Joel that he had actually expected this when he dragged Ted to the AA meeting.

Maybe he'd been hoping for magic. Or maybe he just wanted to feel that he had done everything he could.

There were lights on in the Seacliff house when Joel and Ted drove through the gate in the hedge. *Burglars* flitted through Joel's mind. "You don't have houseguests, do you?" he asked, before he thought of just who it really could be. So he didn't wait for an answer from Ted, but bounded out of the car, thinking, *It has to be her.* Or Rosa at the very least, come back to get something. He ran across the lawn, just missing a sprinkler nozzle; saw someone through the window but couldn't make out who it was. It did occur to him that there might be half a dozen hunting rifles trained on the door, but he couldn't wait—he was only afraid that she would slip away again before he got there.

The door was slightly ajar and he pushed it open, and found Emory Epcot, standing in the pit of the living room. "*Bonsoir, mon ami,*" Emory greeted him, with a swashbuckler's bow. "I hope you don't mind us making ourselves at home. Just got the warrant signed, you know."

Emory's *chapeau* of the evening was a top hat, and Fred Astaire's cane was tucked under one arm. Several uniformed men roamed around the borders of Joel's peripheral vision. Joel's heart rate was returning to normal, while his disappointment, and his anger at himself for hoping, rose in inverse proportion.

"Another bottle, sir." One deputy held up a fifth of Chivas Regal, with about an inch of liquid swirling at the bottom. "This was behind the cabinet."

"Nothing but the best," Ted muttered. He had come up behind Joel in the doorway.

Emory unscrewed the cap, sniffed, then drank. "Just want to make sure it hasn't gone bad," he said, then dangled the bottle at the end of his arm.

Ted reached out. He started to push past Joel; Joel caught him. "No. Don't. It's day one. Come on."

Ted stared at him as if he had been deprived of the power of human language. He grunted. He even looked like a pig, with puffy, inexpressive features. Joel tightened his grip; but he felt Ted's muscles stiffen, and he knew that the only way he could stop Ted from taking that drink was to beat him unconscious.

Joel let go, and Ted stumbled down the steps to the pit. Emory swung the bottle in front of him, until Ted's fingers touched it, and then Emory released it, and Ted held it like a baby holding its first bottle of milk. Then he raised it up, offering it as a sacrifice, and there was exactly one half of a second when Joel was uncertain, when he hoped Ted might throw the bottle down again, but instead he tipped the Scotch into his mouth.

Teddy, Teddy.

Another pair of deputies, these two in street clothes, came down the stairs. They carried several plastic bags containing tiny vials of clear liquid, collections of what looked like dust or powder, and—Joel squinted—hairs and bits of fabric. "We're all finished up here, Lieutenant."

"Good," Emory said. He wiped his forehead, and Joel saw that he was bald—at least as far back as he tipped the rim of his hat before he appeared to catch himself and push it forward again. "It's just amazing what you can learn from a person's bathroom," Emory continued. "That medicine cabinet! I've busted dealers who were holding less. But what I really liked was the Scotch in the aftershave bottle. It's wonderfully tacky. Do you really drink when you're on the can?"

"Only when my head isn't in it," Ted replied, blowing air into the now empty bottle. "I bet you didn't find *half* the stuff."

Emory laughed. "Maybe not."

"You haven't found Margot yet, either," Joel said, descending the steps.

"Hey, take it easy, Doc." Emory gave him one of his bristly grins.

Joel wondered if he could get away with strangling Emory Epcot. Andrea had it down, all right; at that moment, he felt that he could guiltlessly live with the crime. Too bad there were so many witnesses standing around.

Ted was groping under the sofa. "You moved all the little ones I had down here," he complained.

"Look, I don't believe there isn't something you can do. What about checking other cities, other police stations, something like that?"

"We *want* her for questioning. She shows her face around here and she's subpoena-meat. But isn't she in the Caribbean? If I had the manpower, excuse me, I mean person-power . . ."

"This is just incompetence," Joel said.

Emory started, then directed the one-eyed-raised-brow stare at him. "Doc, you seem awfully upset. I don't suppose you and Mrs. Harvey were more than just friends, were you?"

Ted righted himself quickly. He looked at Joel with semi-comprehension.

"Oh, for God's sake," Joel said, exasperated, "what makes you think *that*?" He never knew he was such an actor. But a few years behind the couch were as good as a stint at Juilliard.

"I don't know. I told you I go by instinct. Now here you are with your buddy, and you look like friends, but you seem more concerned with his wife than he does."

"I'm concerned," Ted protested. Groping under the cushion at the far end of the sofa, he produced an airline-sized bottle of Johnnie Walker Black, which he downed in one swig. "I'm innocent. She could help me."

"And you don't believe this story about the Caribbean, do you?" Joel demanded. "That's just a rumor the *Deliverer* started. Why would Margot go there and not tell anyone?"

Ted wiped his mouth with the back of his hand. "She *could* have gone there, Joey. She'd been talking about needing a vacation like that."

"She had *not*," Joel insisted automatically, but then he looked down at Ted, who was intent upon cracking open a tiny bottle of Cutty Sark, and he knew that he could not go on without telling everything—which he certainly wasn't going to do in front of Emory Epcot and his assistants.

"Sometimes she would just take off," Ted sighed, pausing between swallows. "Her and Rosa."

"He's the hubby," Emory snickered, scratching his beard. "He should know."

Joel took a deep breath. Emory clearly did suspect something about him and Margot, and was baiting him now. "It looks like I'll have to find her myself." *I have the receipt from that Aurora hotel*, he remembered. And he had an idea.

"That's a nice offer, Doc," Emory said. "But I'd rather you stayed local for a while."

Did Emory really think Margot had left the country? Joel looked again at Ted, who was crawling toward the center of the horseshoe sofa, holding the neck of the miniature Cutty Sark between his teeth. He lifted another cushion and uncovered several more tiny bottles. "God, *what* a relief," he mumbled. "What a relief, Joey, what a relief. . . ."

"I'm not going anywhere," Joel said, folding his arms across his chest. *But I'll find her anyway. And once I find her maybe the two of us can leave together.* He watched Emory polish the tip of his cane with his thumb, and thought of Danny at the Crown Garage, polishing the old-fashioned cherry-red-and-white car. People told Joel more secrets than he could ever want to know: the gritty, petty, fetid thoughts that polite people don't acknowledge but that collect in the crevices of one's mind. And from his couch he heard the wail of secrets that had gestated long past term, and were finally delivered, bloodied and defective. Joel took these orphaned secrets home with him, carried them around like the man on Sixth Street carried his bedding on his shoulders. Someone would tell him where Margot was.

Ted was arranging a group of empty bottles in a circle. "I'm feeling so much better," he said. "So much more relaxed."

"We finished the kitchen, sir." Two more deputies, wearing surgical gloves and carrying plastic bags, lined up behind Ted on the sofa.

"You can take the stuff out to the car." Emory pointed with his cane. "Listen, Doc, since you're here, I've been wanting to have another little chat with you."

"I certainly wouldn't want to pass up that opportunity." Joel wondered why Ted hadn't mentioned before that Margot had been talking about taking a vacation. Then again, Ted's memory was about as reliable as a politician's promises. "But it'll have to be another time. I've got a class now."

"So what's the big deal?"

"I'm superstitious," Joel said. He put his hand in his pocket and felt for the hotel receipt. Still there. The grimy feel of the carbon copy reassured him. He probably should give it to Emory, but that was the last thing he was going to do; it had become a very precious slip of paper, a connection to *her*. "See, I missed this same class last Wednesday, and that was the night a lot of trouble started for a lot of people."

CHAPTER 8

HEARTBREAK HOTEL

Early the next morning Joel called Jean Stone, now acting president of the Playground board of directors, at Easily Replaced, the temporary-help service she owned.

"How *lovely* to hear from you!" she almost shrieked. "You don't remember me, but we met at the May Day Gala last year. A shame what happened, isn't it?"

Joel was guarded. "What exactly do you mean?"

"I mean, the Harveys splitting up like this. Of course, I saw it coming."

"You haven't heard anything from Margot, have you?"

Jean Stone did not answer immediately. "If I did, I'd have a few things to tell her."

"For example?" Joel noticed her abrupt change of tone.

"Well, I probably shouldn't say anything, but since I took over I've made some *shocking* discoveries. Playground's finances are a complete and utter disaster!" Jean Stone lowered her voice to an excited whisper. "There may even have been some misconduct."

Joel had to laugh. "Not from Margot."

"Perhaps you'd like to see the books."

Joel felt lucky when he got correct change at the grocery store. "My main concern right now is the kids."

"And mine!" Jean Stone insisted. "I hope this won't upset you, but I think that Margot may have been a little lax in some of her policies. She hired Mrs. Tuttle purely out of friendship, and the woman is less than qualified."

"I agree. She needs help and I was thinking—"

"I appreciate your input," Jean Stone interrupted. "Why don't you come to our next board meeting? Maybe we can hire you as a consultant."

Joel had sat on the board of the halfway house for a year, before walking out of a two-hour meeting over whether a certain member could use the title "vice president of development" or had to settle for "chairperson of the development committee."

"I'm not interested in that," he said, "and this can't wait for another board meeting. Someone should get down there now."

Once again Jean Stone did not speak for a long moment. "I know you were a friend of Margot's," she said finally, her voice having made the impressive plunge from tropical latitudes to the Arctic Zone, "but she *left* the place, without a word to anyone, and *I'm* running things now. If you aren't happy, you can"—she cleared her throat—"file a complaint."

"Margot ran things, too, and she was down there every goddamn day, not giving orders over the phone. I suggest you do the same, unless you're looking for serious trouble."

"And you—can mind your own business!" Jean Stone sputtered at him, and then hung up.

Well, it was his own fault, wasn't it? He beat out an uneven rhythm with his knuckles against his desk, knowing that he'd lost his temper at Jean Stone because she'd usurped Margot's position. She'd probably always wanted it, for the glamour of parties and press releases—she obviously didn't want to do the real work. *Consultant, my ass.*

But Margot did leave without a word . . . Then again, she might have had a very, very good reason.

During Joel's morning session with Andrea, she told him that she had arranged with the Hastings administration to retake the antitrust exam she had missed. She had gone to the student nurse to explain, in confidence, that she was under stress because she had just discovered that her father was molesting her younger sister. Joel hardly needed to point out that Andrea didn't have a younger sister.

Andrea was pleased with herself. Joel privately wished that she would move away from home.

. . .

Joel had dinner with Denise the following night, Friday. They went to Beans, a vegetarian restaurant run by a group of Buddhist monks.

Joel liked to eat simple, recognizable food: cheese sandwiches, Campbell's tomato soup, chocolate milk, Cheerios, and occasionally, bagels and cream cheese, strudel, dill pickles. That is, after rebelling against his mother's Donna-Reed-meets-Mogen-David cooking, he had ended up eating pretty much what she had always served, minus only the pastrami, lox, and Hamburger Helper. Besides, these were things he need never depend on anyone else to prepare. Sonja, as a graduate student, was too busy to cook, but since then he had feigned enthusiasm over a lot of soufflés that were pretty much wasted on him.

The waiters at Beans had shaved heads and wore white robes. They also smiled as if they had just emerged from three rounds of electroshock. "We're lucky we got a table tonight," Joel observed. "I hear you have to book ahead for your next incarnation."

Denise frowned. "Don't you like it here? I thought you did, or I wouldn't have suggested it." She had abandoned her usual leotard and Native American jewelry for a tight-fitting skirt and silk blouse. He could tell that she was wearing a bra, but it was a loose one of flexible material, and the top three buttons of the blouse were undone. Thin bands of eyeliner made her eyes appear tilted, feline.

"It's fine. What a lovely blouse. What is it, peach?"

"You *really* like it? It's new."

"Lovely."

She fingered the brooch which was pinned over the fourth button, at the base of her cleavage. "What's the matter?" he asked.

"You're being charming. I don't trust you when you're charming."

"How shall I be, then? Rude? Vulgar?"

"You *want* something."

Right into the end zone. He had been working up to it slowly, but not slowly enough. "You could do me a favor. As a friend," he added. "I'm checking into this hotel tonight, and I was wondering if you'd go with me."

Her lips parted.

"I mean, this is a place Margot used to stay."

Now she pressed her lips together tightly.

"I mean—" Damn! Now what? He could explain that he wanted her to go with him for company, not sex—but he didn't think that would save him.

"You look like a man who knows he's in trouble." Denise grinned suddenly. "I'll give you a chance to start over."

Relieved, he told her about the receipt in Margot's desk. "I want to go check out the place. Get the feel of it. Maybe there's some way I can even get into the suite where she used to stay."

"I heard that she had gone to the Caribbean." Denise shrugged. "To get away from it all."

"That's how rumors start."

"I don't know." Denise used the tines of her fork to pull a row of tofu and vegetables off a shish kebab skewer. "It makes sense to me. She knew that Ted was having an affair, right?"

"I guess so." There wasn't any *guess* about it. Of course Margot had known. But he hated the fact of it, because it meant that Margot had asked him to go to Carmel knowing that her husband was being unfaithful, and that changed a lot.

"So"—Denise stabbed a cherry tomato, spurting red juice on her plate—"why wouldn't she want to take off?"

Especially, Joel thought, *if she had reason to believe that Ted killed Melanie.* And maybe Ted didn't do it in a drunken frenzy; maybe he had even planned to have her killed, hired someone to do it. Maybe Margot knew that, too, and was afraid for her own life. Maybe her invitation to Carmel was part of a more elaborate escape plan. Maybe she was afraid to get in touch with him now because she thought that he was being watched, or that she might endanger him.

Denise cut into a chunk of grilled tofu. The glistening beige flesh made Joel feel just the slightest bit queasy. He pushed his own salad plate forward. "Okay. There's another reason why I don't think that Margot has left town." He explained, a little vaguely, how Betty knew more about Margot than she should. At some point, he realized, he had made his own leap into faith or madness: He thought that Margot might be in touch with Betty, who, ironically, could probably be trusted with the secret of her whereabouts.

"You think she's in touch with your *patient?*"

"You're expressing a lot of skepticism for a woman who believes in astral projection."

"I didn't say I believed in it, I said it was *possible. Jesus*," she muttered softly. "What does Ted think?"

"He did say that she might have gone away," Joel admitted, resenting Denise's implication, *Ted should know.*

But Ted was wrong, that was all. Ted had been wrong about a lot of things, and pretty soon everyone would know that.

"It's just . . ." Denise was smearing a thick layer of butter on a whole-grain roll. "It's just that I hate to see you obsessed about this."

"I'm not obsessed," Joel said. *Just because I know that it's been nine days and six and a half hours since I saw Margot drive off.*

"Then why aren't you eating?" She looked at him with a deep frown between her eyes, the way his mother did when he had the flu.

"Anorexia, remember? The disease of the week." He felt vulnerable enough with Denise, without admitting to nausea.

"I'm worried about you."

"No need."

"Well, Caribbean or not, I'm sure she's all right. And intuition is my dominant function." Denise bit into her roll, then started on another shish kebab. "And when you do see her again, what then?"

"I don't know," Joel said uneasily. "I won't know until I find her." The oddest part was how, after only nine days (well, almost nine and a half), his former relationship with Margot seemed so distant. They used to talk on the phone so often—sometimes just long enough to run their fingers over the texture of each other's lives. He thought of how Margot always wanted to hear about his sex life in general, and recently, about Denise in particular, though she usually expressed her curiosity indirectly. "Anyway, that's where you come in . . . if you want."

"Look, I wouldn't mind a free night in a fancy hotel. But don't you think it'll be a little awkward?" She sliced another hunk of tofu. *Gurgle*, went Joel's stomach. "We used to be lovers, you know. You can't have forgotten that *yet*."

"I promise I won't try to take advantage of you." He was encouraged by her slightly mocking tone; she seemed to have forgiven him his former callousness. He felt no desire for her, in spite of the loose bra. "Seriously, I could go myself but I think I'd stand out less if I was with someone. At least, I'll feel much more comfortable. I know it's a lot to ask."

"Just don't get any ideas," she warned, pointing the fork at him.

They went from the restaurant to Denise's apartment on Russian Hill and he waited while she packed an overnight bag. Joel could travel with a shaving kit in a briefcase, although he'd brought an overnight bag for appearance's sake; Denise, however, seemed determined to pack the entire contents of her medicine cabinet. Joel thought that if he wandered outside it might subtly encourage her to hurry. He left her choosing among jars of herbal cold cream as if the bathroom were the *Titanic* and her plastic-lined makeup bag the only lifeboat.

Denise's apartment opened onto a scaffoldlike wooden porch; in two directions Joel could see streets swooping down and then up again, like giant roller-coaster tracks. And now a Technicolor sunset was spread against a 70mm sky, unblemished as a movie screen: On the western horizon, a band of pink deepened into mauve and then pale blue. To his left the waters of the Bay glowed turquoise. The beauty of it made him long to believe in a transcendent purpose that he was fulfilling—Travel Agent to the Damned, as he'd described himself to Ted. Booking flights out of Hell. But if Hell was so bad, how come the people there were so reluctant to leave?

It was called the repetition compulsion: the apparent need to re-create and relive painful situations. Joel always thought of one particular "Twilight Zone" episode he had watched, years ago, with Ted: Nehemiah Persoff played a German U-Boat captain who sinks a passenger ship. Later his own ship sinks, and the drowned captain wakes up on the deck of the passenger ship he destroyed. He knows what's going to happen, but he can't stop it; he drowns again with the passenger ship, only to reawaken on the deck of the same passenger ship. And the viewer knows he's going to spend eternity going down with it again and again.

Beneath the vast smooth dome of the sky there were the rows of houses, and the moving red and white dots that were the head- and taillights of cars. Margot was somewhere out there, only one tiny piece in this jigsaw puzzle, as was he, but she was the piece that would fit precisely next to him.

Someone tapped him on the shoulder and he jumped. "Ready?" Denise asked.

The Aurora Place Inn was just below the Mark Hopkins Hotel. What Margot had called "the quaintest thing you've ever seen" was more like a giant jewel box, or a miniature palace. The base of the building was an old Victorian which had been meticulously restored, painted a rich forest green, and trimmed in white. The original facade, with its elaborate cornices and friezes, had been preserved; the porch was framed by pillars, and there were stained-glass windows in the front entrance. Inside, the obvious intention had been to re-create an elegant, turn-of-the-century hotel. The carpeting and wallpaper were conch-shell pink; the furniture was in the style of eighteenth-century French drawing rooms (curved and decadent, making Joel think of wealthy ladies taking lovers in the afternoon), and a three-tiered chandelier hung from the ceiling.

There were cocktails being served in the lobby. The waitresses wore long black skirts with the hint of a bustle, expansive white lace aprons, and ruffled caps: modest outfits except for their plunging necklines. The guests wore evening clothes and seemed to have the long legs required for true languor. One woman even had a cigarette holder.

The gentleman behind the registration desk—a high, marble-topped counter—was thin, graceful, with a perfectly groomed mustache.

"You go ahead," Denise whispered. She moved toward a Louis XIV rest bed that could have been an analyst's couch, but then hung back.

Joel asked for the suite with the grandfather clock. The desk clerk frowned as if Joel had asked him to compute the distance between Coit Tower and the Andromeda galaxy. "I am so sorry, *monsieur*. That suite is occupied."

"How unfortunate. Then let us have the nicest room you have available."

"Very good, *monsieur*." The desk clerk made a couple of birdlike pecks at a computer keyboard. "You are lucky. I have one room left." He took Joel's only and seldom used credit card, and rang the bell. "Armando! Front, please!"

The bellman took their bags. The elevator had an old-fashioned accordion gate, but the metal-paneled interior was equipped with

TV camera and recessed lighting. There was another guest riding up with them, his face hidden by a *Wall Street Journal*; he was attended by his own bellman, who was dressed, as was Armando, as if about to negotiate peace with the Prussians. This second bellman asked Armando, "Do five for me, will you?" and Armando used a tiny key which hung from a chain on his wrist to turn a lock on the panel. Then he illuminated the five button. Five was the highest floor.

Joel's and Denise's room was on three. And a lovely room it was, if a bit too froufrou for Joel's taste, with the pink bedspread and lace curtains. French windows opened onto a balcony overlooking an enclosed courtyard with a small fountain.

As soon as Joel had tipped Armando, Denise flung herself across the high four-poster bed. Her ankles waved in the air. "Isn't this amazing? It must cost a fortune."

Joel was looking inside the armoire. One side was closet space, big enough to stand in; the other contained a fully stocked bar and a television, complete with remote, VCR, and several unmarked videotapes. "It's not bad."

"You have to let me pay for part of it."

"No, thanks. I asked *you*, remember?"

"That's nice, but . . . we discussed this, I thought, and—"

He closed the armoire. "You're doing *me* a favor."

Denise was looking at the ceiling. "It's important to me to feel like I'm participating, that I'm not dependent."

Joel shrugged. "All right. Hey, you can buy me a new car, if that will make you feel more independent."

"Well, don't get snippy."

"I'm sorry. We'll split it. How's that?" He *was* being defensive, and then he realized why: The subject reminded him of Margot's wealth. He'd never take money from *her*, and on what he earned . . . Maybe he would have to give up some of his low-income patients in favor of a more upscale clientele.

Denise's attention was caught by something else. "Wow." She scrambled off the bed. "Look at this!"

On the writing desk there was a leather blotter, an inkwell, and vellum paper. The paper bore the Aurora Place logo: a tiara crowning two cursive letters, an A and P, whose curlicues embraced each other.

"I feel as though I should write love letters to the count," Denise cooed. "Oh, and look at *this*. The *room*-service menu.

Room service is my very favorite thing in the universe. It really represents the good breast for me."

"Right. Eighteen dollars for toast with the crusts shaved off."

"Don't be grumpy. You could learn to like it."

"We just had dinner."

"We didn't have dessert. You rushed me."

Joel paced behind her. "It's all so *wasteful*. Look at this." He gestured toward the ceiling. "We don't need all this space. What about all those people living in cardboard boxes at United Nations Plaza?"

"Well, then"—Denise turned her black eyes on him—"why don't you invite them over?"

Joel stopped. Margot used to call what he was doing Automatic Lecture. "Do you want to order room service?"

She relented. "Maybe later. I'll unpack first."

"Did you like the desk clerk's accent? I bet he spends hours with a tape recorder, getting it just right." Joel was also imagining how Margot would have imitated him.

"Grump," Denise laughed. "You know what you are? You're the kind of man who actually *wants* a tie for his birthday."

"What's wrong with a tie?" Joel asked, touching his fingers to the end of the striped one he was wearing. "Listen." He started pacing again. "I thought that I would find out which suite Margot used to stay in and then maybe just hang out when the maid was in the room. But did you notice how the bellman used a special key for the fifth floor? That must be where the suites are, and obviously there's limited access."

Denise was unzipping her suitcase. "It's too late to look around. It's bedtime. Tomorrow you can do whatever you want."

"H'm. I just wonder how I'll get up there." Joel sat on the bed. The top floor must be reserved for guests who paid for the privilege of extra privacy. The forbidden room compelled him, like the secret cave he dreamed of as a child, and tried for years to find in Griffith Park. *You felt excluded from your parents' bedroom*, Dr. Schneider might have said. Maybe that was why he was so convinced now that the suite held a clue.

"I'm not tired at all," he said. "Maybe I'll go for a walk."

Denise looked at him with sharp disapproval. He wondered what he could possibly have done wrong this time. She was putting her things away, and it seemed to him that she was walking strangely—sort of backing up with garments in her hands behind her. He saw something black go into a drawer: a garter belt. He felt a stab of heat in his groin. So much for being just friends! Well, he wasn't a goat. He wasn't Ted. This wasn't anything he couldn't handle.

"Well," Denise sighed, holding up a nightgown, "I have to admit this is pretty awkward. Should I go in the bathroom to change?"

"It doesn't feel like a pajama party, does it? Whatever you're comfortable with." He, too, felt suddenly modest; if she went into the bathroom he might try to change quickly himself. Of course, once she went into the bathroom he would probably have a whole hour alone.

"Oh my God, look at this! Joel! Come see the bathroom!"

The tub was a sunken gray marble square. The floor and ceiling were black marble. Two of the walls were mirrored, so that he stepped into a gallery of Joels and Denises, reflecting charcoal suits, peach blouses, and black hair into infinity. The light came from frosted pink sconces in the shape of fleur-de-lis.

"Joel," she squealed, "isn't this *fun*." She hugged him, and he thought that what was fun was to see her so excited: like watching something being born.

Then he felt Denise's lips against his ear. The heat returned immediately to his groin. *We weren't—I wasn't—* But when she tilted back her head and parted her lips, he didn't think anymore, he just put his tongue in her mouth. They kissed a long time, and then he rested his forehead on her shoulder.

He felt her stroking his hair. He was already hard. In the mirror he could see the back of her head, and the back of his head, and both of their faces, all at the same time; in her dressier-than-usual clothes, he noticed curves of her body that he hadn't been aware of before: the rounded muscle at the top of her calves, the slope of her hips. But the fullness of her breasts—he put his hand there now—*that* he had always appreciated.

"We weren't going to do this," he reminded her, although he was quickly arriving at the point of no return, or at least the Point from Which You Have to Be Dragged Back Screaming.

"It was your idea to come here," she said.

"True." Pulsing throb below; cautionary whine above. He wasn't going to make promises he couldn't keep.

"And I said yes," she sighed. "Wouldn't it be nice if we could just stay here forever? Right in this room?"

"Mmmm." If she didn't want him to sleep with her, she was doing all the wrong things, like curling her fingers around his hair and pressing her chest against his. His penis felt like an animal trying desperately to burrow out of a too-small cage. "We won't be here forever. But I'd like to make love to you now."

She answered by touching the tip of her tongue against the very edge of his lips. No more thoughts. He wouldn't let her object or bargain, past this point. He was just going to have her.

He grasped her around the waist, began pulling her back into the bedroom. "Just what the doctor ordered," Denise giggled, as they scuttled crablike toward the bed. "A good object to incorporate."

Usually they made love only once, sometimes twice. Tonight their first time, on the bed, only made Joel feel more aroused. There were candlesticks on the mantelpiece and Denise had found candles in the nightstand drawer (no Bible here); she slipped only a little awkwardly into the underwear she had worn for him before. She must have packed it when he was on the porch.

The second time they ended up on the floor. The carpet pile was quite thick, almost as if it were intended for this use. Joel was worried about staining it—but Denise, apparently with the same concern, suggested a towel.

"We should do it on the balcony," Denise said, after the second time.

"That would be a boost to our careers. Can you see the headlines? Besides, it's freezing out there."

"Admit that you like the idea."

He did like the idea. He was surprised and a little frightened by all the ideas of his own he had. Joel's id had knocked his superego out for the evening and only once in a while did the superego regain enough consciousness to protest before the Id Kid kayoed him again. And then there would be long times, unmeasured by minutes, when he was the star of his own pornographic movie, and there was only him and her, their breathing and grunts and gasps, soft and wet.

Denise wanted to strip for him and he let her. They were both embarrassed and kept laughing, and he didn't notice when the laughter stopped.

Yes, there was something about the Aurora Place Inn. No wonder Margot liked it here.

He didn't even know what time it was when they huddled naked under the covers. (Denise's undergarments had long since vanished—somewhere.) The bed was high and the mattress a little too soft. Denise fell asleep right away, with her arm across his chest. He waited a few minutes before he gently dislodged it, so that he could turn over comfortably. Sonja had told him (quoting *the* definitive study done at Harvard or Yale or maybe it was just Definitive Study U) that most men fell asleep more quickly than most women. He wished it were true in his case. He wanted a sandwich—peanut butter on whole wheat—but he doubted that was on the room-service menu, unless they had something called *pâté à noix*, or Puree of Country Nuts.

God, he was exhausted. Too exhausted to sleep. It was almost too quiet here. He longed to hear a siren going by.

Wasn't that a little intense, for sex between friends? How could he explain that? Was it his desire to have one last uncommitted sexual experience before settling down—with another woman whose whereabouts were unknown? Had it simply been a way of releasing the tension that had built up in him over the past week?

He couldn't explain it, that was all.

The self-conscious moments, and the jokes they made to cover them, had been the touches that turned the porno movie into art. The only part he hadn't loved had been when Denise had to go inject more spermicide into her diaphragm. He even hated that word, *spermicide*. It made him think of swarms of those little wiggly things gasping and choking and then shriveling up, like electronic enemy creatures massacred in a video game.

Not that he wanted Denise to get pregnant. He still regretted Sonja's abortion. The baby would be . . . *don't think about that.* The baby wouldn't be a baby anymore, he—she—it would be . . . Sonja had wanted an abortion; that had been his excuse. But he hadn't tried to talk her out of it, hadn't wanted to; and that remained his burden. I was twenty-three! he protested, turning over. Too young, in school . . . He hadn't known yet where he wanted to live, whether he wanted to stay with Sonja. He had been afraid of not being able to travel, of having to earn enough money for three.

And didn't he know what inadequate parents could do to a child? Betty Klass and Andrea Griswald had started out as infants: mounds of wet clay, pummeled by incompetent hands.

But Joel had been waiting all these years for the baby-for-the-baby punishment. Perhaps it had come at last. Because maybe Margot couldn't have children.

I always said that I didn't want kids. Being a father was obviously a tough job, from the reports of his patients. *But what I meant was that I didn't want kids YET.* He suddenly realized that he had been carrying around an image of a little girl who for some reason looked like Sonja, and a little boy who wanted to learn to play football.

So? No self-pity. His patients would have to be his foster children. He sometimes thought of them that way already, especially the low-fee ones, to whom therapy would have been less accessible. But it wasn't the same.

He felt a tickle, and wondered if it was a breeze from the partially open window, or if it was Denise, edging closer and breathing on his neck. He lay still, pretending to sleep.

He awoke early. Denise was lying with her mouth open, her hands curled in front of her face, and her body skewed across the bed. He'd felt her feet against his legs a few times during the night. How tame and undemanding a sleeping woman is. He kissed her forehead. *"Mmmm,"* she murmured. He had awakened with an erection but he was eager to get moving now.

He showered and dressed as quietly as he could, and put on his burgundy V-neck sweater. The one Margot liked.

The previous evening he had noticed the assistant manager's office in a hallway right off the lobby. The office—visible through glass doors—had been empty then, but Joel had decided that he would talk to whomever might be there now.

It was just after eight, and the lobby was almost deserted; he had noticed that checkout time wasn't until 2:00 P.M. For a moment, Joel thought that the same desk clerk was on duty, then realized that he was simply another ectomorph; he even had a similar mustache. He posed with the grace of a ballet dancer, pecking at his slim computer keyboard like an anorectic chicken.

The assistant manager was already in. Joel saw her through the glass doors: She was a woman in her mid-twenties, wearing a gray uniform that was a skirted partner to the bellmen's, minus the gold braid and epaulettes. She bent over a table with thin, curved legs; behind her there hung an award from an association of hoteliers, gleaming with stars.

She stood when Joel entered: She was tall and leggy, with long, tawny hair that flipped up at the ends. Her name tag said Tami. "May I help you, sir?"

"I hope so." Joel wondered if he could offer her a bribe—but what? How about a hundred hours of free psychotherapy? Now, that would make a good gift, especially for the holidays. "You see—um, I'm a reporter for *Here* magazine and I'm doing a story about, uh, small luxury hotels in the city."

"Really?" She had creamy skin, and a doll's tiny features.

"Yes, and—uh, what I need to do is follow someone around, maybe one of the maids, while she's cleaning up, you know, to do a full report on what it's like to work here."

"That's an interesting idea, Mr.—"

"Doctor," he said, without thinking. *Damn!* "I mean, Mr. Abramowitz. I have a doctorate in journalism, forgive me for being so pretentious."

"Ah."

"It would be good publicity for the hotel."

Tami sat again. "Actually, our hotel doesn't really *want* any extra publicity. In fact, we keep a low profile on purpose. Our guests prefer it that way."

"They do? You mean you have celebrity guests?"

"Some," Tami admitted modestly. "But now don't ask me who, because the whole point is to keep them anonymous."

"Well, this isn't an exposé," Joel tried. "This is going to be more a day-in-the-life kind of thing. I wouldn't even have to mention the name of the hotel, if you prefer."

Tami lifted a stack of papers, evening the edges with long fingers that reminded him of Margot's. "No photos?"

"No—I take a harder news approach than that."

"Well, I'd have to clear it with the manager, and he's out this morning. Maybe you could check back with me tomorrow."

"It can't wait," Joel insisted. "My deadline is this afternoon." He smiled. "It's terrible—I'm such a procrastinator."

"Let's see, then—I'd like to help you. Maybe you could try the Swantree, down on Sutter Street."

"Aurora Place came so highly recommended."

"Mr.—I'm sorry, I don't remember your name."

"Abramowitz."

"Mr. Abramowitz, you don't happen to have press credentials, do you?"

"Well, no, you see, I free-lance."

Tami rested her chin in one hand. "You know this story is starting to sound a little flaky, don't you?"

"I suppose," Joel sighed. "Okay, then, the truth." He was better at the truth; he'd trained for it. "The wife of a friend of mine disappeared a week and a half ago and I'm—I'm writing a story about that." *The truth can only get you so far, after all.* "Nothing trashy—it's a *zeitgeist* type piece about the evolution of class structure in post-Watergate America. By the way, my friend's wife is Margot Harvey."

Tami raised her eyebrows.

"Perhaps you read about her?" The newspaper coverage mostly focused on Ted's case now, but the *Courier* gossip columnist had yesterday reported that an unimpeachable source had seen Margot at the Curaçao Hilton.

"Mrs. Harvey told me," Joel went on, "that she used to stay in one of the suites. That it had a grandfather clock. Perhaps at least you could tell me—*is* there such a suite here?"

One corner of her mouth turned up. "Well . . . yes. But it's leased full time by a corporation." She evened the papers again. Her eyes were golden brown, the color of her hair: They reminded him of a very crisp autumn leaf, trembling on the sidewalk, waiting for a foot to crush it. He looked at her hands again: no wedding ring, but a large cubic zirconium stone on her right hand.

"I honestly don't know if Margot Harvey uses it," Tami went on. "I've heard her name, but I don't know what she looks like. Sorry I can't help you."

"You could, though. You could let me take a look at that suite."

She laughed. "Mr. Whatever Your Name Is, you look like a nice man, but why would I want to do that?"

"Because you look like a nice lady. And because if you do let me take a look, then I *will* leave the name of the hotel out of it, I promise. Otherwise—there are all sorts of rumors I could give credence to."

"Blackmail doesn't sound like something a nice man would do."

"Don't think of it as blackmail. Think of it as incentive." But her words stung. "Let me put it another way. Have you ever wanted one thing, one thing more than anything else, and you'd do anything to get it?"

"Maybe." With her thumb, she turned the stone of her ring toward her palm.

"You might say that's the way I feel about writing this article. The suite is part of the whole background. I just need to take a quick look."

Tami rose and removed a file from the top drawer of a carved rosewood chest that served as a file cabinet. "You realize I could lose my job over something like that?"

"You said your boss was out this morning," he reminded her.

Now it was her turn to sigh. "You know, I was thinking of quitting anyway. Going back to school. I have a B.A. in art history from Stanford."

"Graduate school." He nodded. "What a good idea."

"It's just possible that I need to check that suite out. It's just possible that I could take someone with me, if he could be very quick." She shut the drawer. "But if anyone found out—"

"They won't," he said. "They won't, and thank you."

Tami had a tiny key like the bellman's, which she wore on a chain around her wrist like a charm bracelet. She dismissed the elevator operator and used the key to take them to the fifth floor.

When they emerged from the elevator, Tami took him straight down the hall, decorated with green-striped wallpaper and green velvet parson's benches. They didn't pass any doors, and Joel guessed that there might be as few as two suites on this floor.

At the end of what seemed like a long walk there was a solitary carved wooden door—501. "Wait," Tami said, with her key in the lock and her hand on the knob, "isn't Margot Harvey the one who went to the Caribbean island after her husband got arrested?"

Joel nodded. "That's the one."

The suite was decorated similarly to the room he was sharing with Denise, but there was a sitting room (with a fireplace), as well as the bedroom; also a second, smaller bath. The ceilings were higher, and there was a skylight in the bathroom. There was indeed a grandfather clock. Seeing that, Joel wanted to throw up his arms and shout, *Margot was here*. If the suite was leased by a corporation, then that corporation must be Margot— she must be the only one who ever used it.

In the bedroom there was an iron spiral staircase, like the stairway that leads to the upper deck of a 747. Joel caressed the cold metal of the banister.

"Where does this go?"

"There's a roof garden," Tami said, "though I don't know what the point is, it's always so windy up there." She bounced on the edge of the bed. "Listen, I wouldn't mind if you blew this place open in your article, if you really could keep my name out of it. You know why we don't advertise?"

"Why?" Joel looked in the nightstand drawer. There were only the same candles as in his and Denise's nightstand, except that these were half used up. He squatted down to check beneath the bed ruffle. Nothing under the bed.

"They don't want tourists here. It's all for *liaisons*. *Les rendezvous*. Translate that into *le F-word*. The first staff meeting I went to here, they told us that the whole purpose of this place was for the 'A list' to have their affairs in peace. There's got to be someplace for the rich and beautiful to boff their brains out and have the maids bring them champagne and not have anyone gossip about them."

Joel opened the armoire. Several padded hangers swung from the bar: all empty. If Margot had been here recently, she had left no sign of it. He felt a ball descending from his throat down to his stomach.

"At the meeting, the manager said, 'The Fairmont has the entertainment, the Mark Hopkins has the view, but we have the *ambience*.' The maid's uniforms are supposed to subliminally remind you of *The Story of O*. Then they have four-posters so you can have bondage if you want."

"Do you remember when someone stayed here last?" Joel asked.

Tami raised her ankle and looked down at her long slim foot in its sensible and drab navy pump and heavy nylons. "I wouldn't even know when she used it last—there's another entrance for the suites, if people want to use it. Our clientele's privacy is paramount."

It was the privacy that would attract Margot. Wasn't that what she had said to him over lunch? That she and Ted had wanted "to get away from it all"? That didn't mean she had ever . . . Funny, he was so used to the idea of her making love with Ted that he could pretend that she didn't, but with someone else . . .

It was an unacceptable idea, so his only option was to forget it. He started on the drawers, moving quickly. And in the bottom one, staring back at him, was a small red leather purse with diamond stitching and a gold shoulder strap. He resisted the urge to grab it immediately, instead looking up suddenly. "I think I heard something. Out in the hall."

Tami jumped off the bed. "Oh, great. I knew this was a bad idea."

The moment she was gone he opened the purse, just to glance at the contents. A few tubes of makeup, a package of Ex-Lax, a tampon, a $20-off coupon at a boutique on Union Street. And something very bright at the bottom, shooting off little rainbow flashes . . . a diamond . . . an enormous marquis diamond ring. Margot's engagement ring. The one that Ted had reported missing.

Was this Margot's purse? He tried to remember seeing her with it, but couldn't.

No time; Tami would be back. He pulled his sweater over his head, and wrapped the purse in it, remembering how he and Sonja used to sneak bottles of soda into the movies that way. He could always mention to Tami that it was very warm in the suite.

"No one there," he heard Tami say from the next room. "But come on, let's get out of here. I don't hate my job that much."

Joel was beginning to hate his. He held the sweater tightly to his side.

Denise was still in bed. Joel came in bearing the *Courier* and the single bloodred rose that had been delivered to their door. At first he could see only her hair, like a black cat napping on the pillow. Then she rolled over and smiled. "Good morning," she said. "Isn't this the most fun you've had since the NCAA playoffs?" She sat up; her large breasts bobbed over the satin bedspread. "I had a great dream. I can't wait to analyze it. You and I were on a plane going to Seville, and I had a white dress on. But the plane was like a big tube, and the way it was going to take off was by going round in a spiral really fast, then springing into the air, so I was afraid of suffocating or falling out." She shuddered theatrically. "What did you dream?"

"I don't remember." He really didn't, and he wasn't sorry— because he'd been plagued for several nights with dreams of Melanie's drowned body.

"Oh well, enough shop talk, h'm? Will you hand me the room-service menu? We got so *distracted* last night. I thought bran muffins and coffee and I bet they have fresh orange juice—"

"I need to get going," he said. He was stuffing the sweater, pregnant with the red purse, into his overnight bag. He glanced over his shoulder at Denise, and the moment he saw her face he knew he had made a significant error in judgment.

"Oh, *well*." She threw back the blanket. "Excuse *me*."

"I'm sorry," he apologized. "I really am." He had been so eager to be by himself, to examine the purse more closely, figure out what to do next. "We'll order room service first. Bran muffins and—"

"No fucking way," Denise said. "I wouldn't stay here another second."

CHAPTER 9

THE LOWENBRAU DIET

Denise did not speak to him as they drove toward her apartment on Russian Hill. All right, he had been thoughtless to announce their departure so abruptly, but couldn't he apologize and be done with it? Men just weren't as sensitive as women, he decided. If you did something a man didn't like, he either told you or he forgot about it. He wouldn't *punish* you like this.

As the wheels of Joel's car wavered on and off the cable-car tracks on Hyde Street, he thought of how he had announced his decision to become a vegetarian in front of eleven assembled Thanksgiving relatives and how, later, he found his mother crying in the kitchen over the Jell-O mold.

"You know," he said finally, "sometimes with you I feel as though we're shooting a movie, only I don't have the script. Care to Xerox me a copy?"

She turned and glared at him. *Oh shit.* That would teach him to try to open the lines of communication when he was still feeling ambivalent. Funny how his anger could leak through the smallest holes in his words.

He did not trust himself to speak again until he pulled up in Denise's driveway. "Four out of five doctors," he began, "would say I was a real jerk."

"I'd be one of the four." Denise looked out the window but made no move to get out of the car.

He spoke to the back of her head. "I like you a lot. You know I do. But I said from the beginning that I just wanted to be friends—I said that maybe ten *months* ago." Hadn't he said that on their second or third date? He was sure now that he had. "And you act as though I've been lying to you."

"I didn't propose marriage. I just wanted to stay to have breakfast."

"And I said we could stay."

"But you didn't *want* to."

"On second thought, I don't think a copy of the script will be enough. I need the Monarch notes, too."

"It's hard for me to be just friends." She turned to look at him, and the blackness of her eyes made them seem more accusing. "I don't understand how *you* can, when we have such great sex."

"Well, yes, we do have great sex, and I enjoy it very much." And he shouldn't be enjoying it, shouldn't even be *doing* it, if he was so in love with Margot. . . . "Maybe there's something wrong with me."

"Huh. Probably."

Joel gazed at the splintery redwood of Denise's garage door. Part of mature adulthood was committing to one person, but *couldn't he have just a little more time?* "Great sex is a wonderful thing," he began ponderously.

"But 'what's sex got to do with love?'"

"I didn't say that, I just meant—"

"Yes?"

"Um . . ."

"'Great sex is a wonderful thing,'" Denise repeated. "But what?"

"But that doesn't solve our other problems."

"Like Margot."

"Well, like Margot." He looked all over the car, then finally looked at her. "But that's not all. Listen, I don't know what I want. I'm confused. If you think we shouldn't see each other, I'll respect that." He raised his right hand. "I won't even nod at you at the office. I swear."

She put her finger on her beauty mark, then drew a circle around its edge. "You know," she said after a moment, "while we were driving home just now, I was analyzing that dream I told you. I've been analyzing my dreams a lot lately—I keep a journal of them."

"Isn't that sort of a busman's holiday?"

"Do you want to hear about it or not?"

"Sure." Guilt. His non-Jewish friends claimed to suffer from it, but he couldn't help believe that there was a special strain, unchronicled in the textbooks, a virus that was carried, like the Tay-Sachs gene, only by people of his religion.

"The woman in the white dress isn't me at all. She's *you*. Or she's Margot, but Margot is you."

"Try me again."

"Margot is your *anima*, and you're having the archetypal experience of the *quest*. That why you and she are flying to Europe. When you find her, you'll be able to integrate her and then have a relationship with a *real* woman, in this case me."

"Do you want me to be honest? That is the most ridiculous thing I ever heard."

"Well, then, let's just say it's *Oedipal*. Would you like that better?"

"Jesus." He hated to argue about this. Surely no one person—Freud, Fairbairn, or Murray Schwartz—had been given The Answer like the tablets on Mount Sinai. But if you didn't have theory, you only had mysticism, pure faith, and he was hardly comfortable with that, either. He managed a smile. "See, the problem is that you're so experiential."

"No, Doctor. The problem is that you're a *putz*." She smiled, too, but he couldn't tell if she was masking fury or beginning to be amused. He wanted to tell her then that he was grateful she put up with him, grateful for her humor, her companionship, her patience; he wanted to tell her that he knew he had used her and the fact that he hadn't planned to was no excuse; but she was already out of the car, her overnight bag bumping against the banister of her crooked wooden steps.

Still, he was relieved to be alone, so he could get home quickly and examine his catch: the small red purse, which serenaded him from his own overnight bag in the trunk.

From the street, his building looked dreary, and he wondered if his pride in shabbiness was failing him. Perhaps he'd been corrupted by his night at Aurora Place.

Once inside his apartment, he undid the clasp of the handbag and emptied the contents on the floor. All the way home, he had been worried that he had imagined the ring earlier—Aurora

Place, he decided, could play tricks on a person. But it was still there; shining like something alien and magical. Joel sorted through the other items—the tubes of makeup, the Ex-Lax (it was a large package, and half used), the tampon, the discount coupon, a small calorie-counting book he hadn't noticed before, a few tissues.

He knew these things didn't belong to Margot, as surely as he knew that the ring did. Joel held it up to the light. So many surfaces. He thought of Danny polishing the great insect-eye headlight of the Buick Super. Jordan's money: Racks of women's clothing had been transformed into this hard object. Pretty, yes, but what purpose did it serve? Women with big diamonds always made him think of therapists on the consciousness circuit, comparing the depth and convolution of their insights: *I'm more aware than you are, and my penis is bigger, too.* He was glad that Margot didn't wear it often.

Had she simply left it there the last time she was at the hotel? It was hard to imagine that even Margot would forget a ring this size; not because of its worth, but because he knew she never threw out so much as a hair ribbon. If she invested even those with "sentimental value," how about a ring that had been in her family for three generations?

Still, dancers forget steps, bankers forget money, and lovers forget to kiss—all with the right unconscious motives. This could be the symbolic rejection of her marriage, or the wish to expel her internalized image of her mother. . . .

Enough. He bent back over the pile. A bit of foundation had dribbled over the side of one tube, drying to a flesh-colored streak. He flicked the tube with his finger and watched it roll across the floor, bump up against the side of the bookcase, and roll back a couple of inches. Makeup. Model. Melanie.

Of course it was Melanie's purse. He grabbed it and turned it upside down again and shook it, though he knew that it was already empty. He could not remember whether she had carried it on the day that he had seen her; still, it looked like her: slim, stylish. There was no identification, but still he knew.

Suddenly it seemed to Joel that Ted had noticed Margot's ring was missing pretty early . . . especially considering how befuddled he was on every other point. Joel thought of him sitting in the rocking chair, whining, *I don't remember.* What crap! Well, Ted was calculating but stupid. Or not so much stupid as self-destructive. You didn't need a Ph.D. to figure that out about a man who consumed his own weight in ethyl alcohol every six hours.

Ted might very well have given Melanie the ring—a grandiose, self-centered, and therefore quintessentially Ted-like gesture—to prove that he was serious about her, and stall her threatened abortion. Then he was smart enough (if you could use that word at all with regard to him), after he strangled her—God! that sonofabitch!—to remove the ring and to take her purse.

And he brought them back to hide them at Aurora Place. That would have been easy enough even for Ted. He would have his own key to the suite—Margot had said they stayed there together. He could have used the private entrance—and even if he didn't, at Aurora Place, nocturnal comings and goings were supposed to be ignored.

It was obvious that Margot hadn't been there for a while, and hadn't been planning to go back. If she leased the suite full time she would keep some things there, and he hadn't seen as much as a lipstick.

Joel rapped another makeup tube against the floor to the rhythm of *Ted et Melanie sur la plage.*

The sonofabitch. He had suspected Ted until now, but this was too damning. No more Mr. Nice Guy. Joel rewrapped the purse in a different sweater and hid it in his closet. He could take this evidence directly to the police, but he wouldn't have the pleasure of confronting Ted and finally making him confess. Ted wanted to, anyway, since he'd obviously left the purse there on purpose so that he could be caught. Of course, since he'd done that unconsciously, he didn't *know* he wanted to be caught. Joel would explain it to him if he felt like it.

Then Ted could turn the evidence in himself, which would look better. And if he wouldn't, Joel would cram the purse down his throat.

He was out of there, and sailing down California Street by the time he could catch a fully deep breath.

He pounded once on the door of the Seacliff house, but didn't wait before he tried the knob. It was unlocked.

Ted was in his bathrobe, with his bare feet on the glass coffee table. He had a bottle of Lowenbrau in one hand and a remote-control panel in the other. Joel paused just long enough to take in the champagne bucket behind Ted, and the blanket crumpled in the base of the U of the sofa.

"Joey! I was hoping it was Pizza Prince." Ted tooted into the top of the bottle. "Have a beer. To what do I owe the honor, Big Man on Campus?"

Joel leapt into the pit. "You *asshole*," he said.

Ted opened his mouth and belched.

Joel felt his hands clenching around the lapels of Ted's bathrobe. Ted rose lightly, almost effortlessly, under his grip. He heard Ted yelp, felt his hands flailing at him. Joel swung him around once, heard the crack of something against the coffee table.

Ted groaned.

Joel shook him. "I could kill you," he announced. "I wish I could get away with it."

Ted sank to the coffee table and massaged his calf. Joel stood over him, with arms folded across his chest. So he was unprepared when Ted sprang up like a jack-in-the-box, and aimed a fist that almost hit him on the nose but only struck the side of his face because he ducked in time. He saw Ted's fist drawing back again, and he dived forward and tackled him. Joel felt the floor rise up to meet them, and the two of them rolled over and over, locked together—Joel felt the carpet on his back, Ted's breath near his ear, then the dizzying sensation of rolling over once again. Suddenly he was able to stop it. He pinned Ted's arms near the shoulder. Ted tried to raise himself, but couldn't. "You killed her, didn't you?" Joel panted. There was blood under Ted's nose and the sight of it fed his fury. He vaguely remembered hitting him there and he wanted to do it again, with Ted under him, unable to get away.

"*Uh.*" Ted made a final effort to get Joel off him, and failed.

"I found Margot's ring," Joel said.

"Where?"

"At Aurora Place." Joel tightened his grip on Ted, although Ted was offering no resistance.

"Joey . . . do you mind? I'm losing the feeling in my hands."

Joel waited another moment before he slid off. Ted sat up, smoothing down his hair. "Feel *better*, BMOC?"

"Much, as a matter of fact." But his heart was still pumping his fury straight to his brain. "I'd feel even better if I bashed your head in."

Ted moved a few inches away.

Joel laughed. "I won't, though. At least I don't think I will." He got out his handkerchief and wiped the smear of blood from his knuckles before he gave the handkerchief to Ted.

Ted rubbed under his nose. But there wasn't as much blood as there had seemed at first. Joel was disappointed. For the first time in twenty years, he'd been in a fight. He suspected it would be another twenty before the next. And it had felt good! He laughed again—suddenly, inappropriately. "I hate you for doing what you did. I don't even *want* to understand it."

"But what did I *do*?" Ted wheedled, folding the handkerchief. "At least tell me that."

"I told you, I found Margot's ring at Aurora Place. You must have left it there."

"Why would I leave it there? It was Margot's ring. Whoever stole it left it there."

"Margot told me that the two of you used to stay there."

"She did?" Ted elevated himself to the sofa in stages, grasping hold of the coffee table and then the cushions. He knelt on the sofa cushions to reach behind and above it, and into the metal champagne bucket, whence he pulled out another beer. *Beer all of a sudden.* Ted was really going back to his roots. "When did she tell you that?"

"Uh . . . right before she disappeared."

"Maybe she lied."

Asshole, Joel thought. "Why should she lie? You're the one who's been shoveling it from the start. You killed Melanie, and now you're whining that you can't remember and it's not your fault." Joel's throat constricted. "I have the evidence and I'm giving you a chance to turn it in yourself."

"What evidence? Margot's ring?"

"I found Melanie's purse there, too."

"You didn't say anything about Melanie's purse."

"I'm saying it now."

"Melanie's purse . . ." Ted looked sad. Then his drooping eyelids rose a little. "Maybe we should get rid of it," he suggested. "Don't you think? It's only going to hurt a lot of people."

Joel laughed at this, too. "Nice try, Teddy." *I should hit Ted more often. Could do wonders for my cholesterol count.* "That you did it is bad enough—if you'd just be *sorry*."

"But I didn't do it. I've never been to Aurora Place. I don't know how Margot's ring got there. *Or* Melanie's purse." He squinted at the Lowenbrau. "Maybe I'm a drunk. Maybe I'm an adulterer." His eyes were misty, the lids at half-mast again. "Okay. But I didn't kill anybody." He leaned forward, brandishing the bottle. "Do you really think I could, even if I wanted to? Do you think I'm strong enough for that?"

Joel leaned against the nearest ottoman. He was coming down from his battle high. "No, you're not."

"Well, then." Ted toasted Joel and drank.

"But maybe you're weak enough." Although the blood-thumping anger had passed, its waves had washed Joel onto a new shore, where thoughts that he had once censored now became words.

Ted blinked. "I'm not even that. If you say Margot was there, she was there without me. Maybe she went there with someone else. Maybe with *you*?"

"No," Joel said automatically. He saw the remote-control panel lying on the floor near him and only then became aware of the sounds of a baseball game on the TV behind him. He clicked it off. But the new silence seemed to demand the truth. If truth it was. "But she almost did."

Ted's eyes narrowed. He took a quick gulp of beer. "What do you mean?"

"Last Wednesday she asked me to go to Carmel with her. And not for the golf tournament, my friend." Joel looked into the empty TV screen, at his distorted reflection. They'd talk about it now. Good.

Ted fingered the front of his hair. "I don't believe you," he said finally.

"Believe it." *And maybe then I will, too.*

"You were in love with her, weren't you?" Ted asked wistfully, and Joel almost felt sorry, but not quite, because he had made it to the Island of Spilled Beans, like a man who has just escaped drowning. And perhaps Ted sensed that self-pity would get him nowhere, because now he spat, "I always knew you were! What a joke. You always wanted her. You always wanted everything I had."

"Bullshit," Joel retorted, already allowing, as he had to, for its possible truth. And then a runaway thought, like a child darting into the street, right in front of his car . . . *Wanted what I had.* "That's why you sent Melanie to see me, isn't it?"

"What are you talking about?" Ted hugged the bottle close. "I was *hoping* you could help her."

"You wanted to make sure I wouldn't go after her!" Because Ted knew that Joel might not have been as loyal to *him* as he should be, but he also knew that Joel could never pursue a woman once she had been his patient.

"That's crazy. I wish you *had* taken her off my hands! I didn't want a divorce. Margot and I would have worked things out just fine if you'd stayed out of it." He stretched out his legs. "You must have got it wrong. *You* must have asked Margot to go to Carmel. Otherwise you'd be in Carmel!"

"I wanted to wait until she talked to you," Joel snorted. "Can you believe it? Did you think I was that stupid?"

"I see." Ted made a foppish gesture with pinky extended. "You wanted it *civilized*. So then no one could find fault with the great Dr. Abramowitz."

"Civilization." Joel laughed shortly. "Highly overrated. It has built-in discontents."

"Well, you're pretty damn civilized, all right." Ted scratched the dried blood under his nose. "Shall I turn the other nostril?"

Joel bounced his fist against his knee. "No regrets, Teddy." It was what Ted used to say when he woke up with a Salsa and Extra Onions hangover.

With a grunt, Ted raised himself up again, and stuck his hand into the champagne bucket. Joel heard the remaining fragments of ice swishing in the water, as Ted plucked out another beer. "You are something else," Ted carped. "You were really thinking of fucking my wife, weren't you? We have you to our house, we treat you like a friend—"

"You never treated anyone like a friend. You wouldn't know how. You're a taker, Ted. You only want Margot to come back now so that she can take care of you. Well, she's outgrown charity cases."

"And you think she wanted to take you on next?" Ted bared his teeth in an ugly sneer.

"She was about to leave you anyway."

"That's crap. If Margot came on to you—and I say *if*—it was only because of Melanie."

Fight or flight. "You know goddam well that she and I would have gotten together years ago—but *you* had us feeling so guilty we couldn't move. And let me tell you something else"— Joel made a fist—"she was too smart and beautiful to be married to a passive-aggressive drunk, and if you think she was going to wait around much longer for you to get it together, you're a sorrier case than I thought!"

Ted raised his nearly empty beer bottle, and Joel tensed, thinking that Ted was going to throw it at him. But then, just as suddenly, Ted sagged, his shoulders and chest shrinking within his bathrobe. "You're right, Joey. *Mea maxima culpa.* Everything is my fault."

I wished he'd thrown the bottle. "Yes, it *is*." Joel's voice was loud. "Don't start that 'how can you hate me when I already hate myself' routine. Don't even *think* about it. It ain't gonna work."

"Well," Ted sighed, "it was actually *your* fault that Margot found out about Melanie." He treated himself to a victory swallow of beer, finishing the bottle.

"God." Joel took off his glasses and rubbed his eyes. "I can't wait to see how I get blamed for this."

"Remember that day that there was that woman on the Playground roof?"

"No, I'd completely forgotten." There was a sour taste in Joel's mouth. "Since that kind of thing happens to me so often."

Ted looked quizzical for a moment before he went on. "I called her a looney. I said, you have to take Looney Tunes on as a patient. You probably don't remember."

"I do, though."

"Margot was mad at me, because I used that word. Maybe it wasn't a technical term, but you can't say it wasn't true. Margot said"—Ted mimicked her in falsetto—"'Joel wouldn't have said that. If I were married to Joel' . . ."

"She said that?" *If I were married to Joel* . . . He inhaled slowly, playing it again in his head, trying to simulate the exact timbre of Margot's voice. So she *did* care about him. How could he have ever doubted it? He felt her presence now, as surely as if she were in the next room; he could almost smell her; any moment she would walk in. "And *you* say she didn't want me."

"She didn't. She just said that to make me crazy."

"And what happened after that? And tell me the truth this time, just for a change of pace."

"I've always told you the truth. Okay, I've had to cover some things up. But don't you see, I had to?"

"Just go on." Joel folded his hands between his knees. He

thought of Margot's hands, trembling like hummingbirds in the air—how she caught them together when she was upset, as if to keep them from flying away.

"Okay. I barbecued that night. Steaks. But of course Merlin had to make *you* special fettucine. Then it got late, and for some reason you were still here, but I went to sleep. The next thing I knew Margot was waking me up so she could scream at me."

"H'm," Joel said, more skeptical than analytic.

"That's right. She did that sometimes, like if I hadn't put the toilet seat down, or if I didn't straighten the towels right. You never saw her when she got like that, but it would take me all night to calm her down." Ted rolled his empty bottle under the sofa. "That's when she started on me about calling that woman Looney Tunes. I just couldn't take it anymore. I mean, I already had things on my mind." He paused. "So I finally told her about Melanie."

"Good," Joel nodded. "Your wife's upset, so you tell her that you're having an affair. You really are suited for public relations."

Ted reached for a third beer. "See? I'm cutting down. Nothing but beer before one P.M. And *you* thought I couldn't do it."

Joel didn't say anything for a moment. *Oh, God, he's serious. He really thinks this is an achievement.*

But Ted seemed to interpret Joel's silence as approval. He thoughtfully held the bottle to his cheek. "I don't hold any grudges against Margot. That was just the way she was. But it was pretty hard to live with. She had these screaming-meemie fits. I never knew when one was going to start. The littlest thing could set her off. Once a button popped off her dress, and she went crazy. Totally crazy. She screamed and screamed and I couldn't get her to stop. We were on our way out to a party and we couldn't go. And wait till you hear this—sometimes I'd pull the drapes shut with my hand. You know, I wouldn't use the cord?" Ted chuckled in a kind of amazement. "She'd *lose* it."

Joel sank back against the ottoman. If there were any missed parties, it was more likely due to Ted's drunkenness. But he wasn't going to argue—he was curious to hear what Ted had to say. It might be good for another laugh.

"You know what I think?" Ted peeled some of the foil from the neck of the bottle. "I think she inherited whatever her mother had. I think it's just in the genes. That's why I don't believe in therapy. No offense, Joey. I just don't think there's jack shit you

can do about stuff like that, because God knows I tried everything. Margot could have inherited the crazies from either of her
folks. Her father was the lush to end all lushes.

"So that night she lost it *entirely*. I mean, after I told her about
Melanie. Hey, I wanted to *share* the problem with her. What did
she want me to do, keep it secret forever?

"Margot kept screaming until Rosa came upstairs. I thought
maybe Rosa would calm her down, but she said to Margot that I
was a shithead and they should just leave! Can you believe that?
Rosa always hated me. I think she was a dike, but if she was, that
was the least of her problems. Even *Margot* knew that Rosa was
a sicko. She told me once that Rosa had raised a couple of her
brothers and that she used to beat them up." Ted stared into the
small opening of the Lowenbrau bottle for a moment. "Okay.
Confession time. Margot was the one who wrecked the bedroom.
That was when she was having her fit. She was throwing things
at me and then she just started emptying drawers and pulling
stuff out of the closet. I left it like that so it would look like we
were robbed. I shouldn't have, but I was scared."

Ted paused, then nodded, as if Joel's continued silence was all
the forgiveness he needed. "You know what else? *Rosa* started
hitting me. I think Margot finally pulled her off. Isn't that funny?
I wasn't even defending myself. I couldn't hit a woman. Besides,
I guess I felt I deserved it. That's why I don't need a shrink. I
already understand everything about myself—but understanding
doesn't change jack shit, Joey."

It changes everything, Joel started to say, but decided to let
Ted go on.

"Like I said, it was Rosa who made Margot leave me. She said,
'You have no self-respect at all if you stay with this big shithead.'
They left that night. They just drove off. I must've gone back to
sleep finally, in the yellow room, and when I woke up I felt like
someone was doing brain surgery on me. I mean, I've had
hangovers. 'Member how we used to rate them?" He smiled
faintly. "You were more fun when you used to drink. Anyway,
this was one of those hangovers where you can feel the little
ropes of the shag carpet when you walk.

"I had a couple of shots just so I could function, and I dragged
myself over to see Melanie. She lived in that highrise on Nob Hill,
across from the cathedral. It was one of those two-level condos.
I was helping her out with the rent, because she couldn't work as

much after she got pregnant. She said she had morning sickness real bad. I figured okay, Margot knows, what's done is done, Melanie and I will go off somewhere for a few days. Margot will miss me then. Maybe she'll, you know, get this in perspective.

"When I told Melanie what had happened, *she* started screaming at me, too. Saying things like why couldn't I handle my own wife. Joey, you're a shrink, why are beautiful women always so crazy? Here she'd been trying to get me to tell Margot about us all along, and when I do, she yells at me that I'm stupid! Does that make sense? On the other hand," Ted grunted, "I have to admit that in my condition she could have been whispering and it would have sounded like a primal scream.

"Then we figured out that we would go up to the Sonoma Mission Inn that night. I wanted to take off right away. I'll tell you the truth, I was sort of scared. If Margot's father was still alive, I would have been even *more* scared, but I was still feeling paranoid, like Margot was going to get Cousin Frank to come after me and take my balls off. And Rosa—I seriously think she had connections to the Filipino Mafia.

"Then Melanie got a phone call, and she said she had some stuff to do first. What, I said, do you have to go *shopping* again? You know, maybe there was one color bathing suit she didn't have and we couldn't go to the SMI until she got it. But she said she had a doctor's appointment, that it was very important for the baby." Ted winced. Joel thought that he must suspect by now that there was no baby, but he wasn't going to push it.

"I'd made us a pitcher of piñas, you know, Melanie liked them, but after she went out I decided to hit the Chivas. She was gone a long time. I got a little suspicious then, I guess. I knew she'd seen you that morning and I just had this crazy thought. And she wouldn't really tell me anything you'd said, though she knew that you and I were friends.

"But then she came back and she was pretty upset. I asked her how was the doctor and she said what doctor, so I caught her at *that* lie. You know, whenever she didn't want me to know where she was going, she said it had something to do with the baby. But she still wouldn't tell me where she'd been.

"We kept trying to pack and get out of there, but then we started fighting again. She was crying. She said she wanted to break up with me but I really owed her. I almost called you then.

I wanted her to talk to you, I thought you could help me, I mean, help *her*."

Poor Melanie, Joel thought. She was like a real estate investor who ends up with forty acres of swampland, but who would prefer to spend a few million more to build a luxury hotel and watch it sink, rather than admit that the original investment was wasted. She had probably come very close to breaking it off with Ted that afternoon, and if Joel had had just a little more time with her, or maybe if Ted *had* called him . . .

"It seemed like we packed all afternoon, but somehow we never got ready. She'd called for reservations, and put them on my credit card. I didn't mind—but I got mad at her for doing that anyway. It was all so weird, that whole day. It was really hot in her apartment. Then it was like . . ." Ted frowned, deepening the venetian-blind wrinkles on his high forehead. "There's still a lot I don't remember, but it was like, all of a sudden we were in the bedroom and she was standing there with her clothes off and she wanted to make love. I couldn't figure out how we'd gotten there. I was dressed. And she was standing there, and her hair was wet—I guess she'd just gotten out of the shower. That was was when she looked her absolute best, with no makeup on or anything. But then she said she wanted to make love, *right then*, or it was all over. Does that make any sense to you? I didn't feel like it right then. I was worried about Margot. Can she blame me for being worried about my *wife*? Melanie knew I was married from the first night! Jesus!" Ted pounded the bottom of the empty bottle against the back of the couch. "She was always trying to get me to prove I loved her and not Margot. She wanted me to let her call me at home. She would have these screaming-meemie fits.

"Joey, you saw her. She was gorgeous—like Rapunzel, with all that hair. She always had this damp look, like she'd just woken up. And her shoulders—she had the most beautiful shoulders in the world. I wanted to make love to her. I just couldn't."

"How long had it been?" Joel asked. Joel and Ted had once spoken very graphically to each other about sex, naming body parts in the vernacular, and asking how-many-times and did-she. That continued even after college, on those very rare occasions when they spoke on the phone—until Joel met Sonja and found that he had a new loyalty which transcended the old.

"It'd been a while," Ted admitted. His thumb squeaked against the neck of the bottle. "I admit it, I hated her then."

Silence. Ted's bathrobe had fallen open and Joel could count the folds of his stomach. Ted was taller than Joel, but Joel knew that Ted had always envied him his deeper and hairier chest. And while Ted's hairline was receding, Joel's remained unchanged.

"The next thing I remember is that I was back at the house, in the bedroom. It was like someone dropped me there without a parachute. That's when I called you."

Good old Joey comes running. "Maybe Melanie got tired of waiting for you to get ready to leave, and she left to go to the Inn by herself. Maybe you followed her in your own car."

Ted seemed genuinely curious. "Why wouldn't I just go with her in *her* car?"

Joel was thinking of Andrea's story of seeing the two distant cars on the road to Stinson Beach. "What if she left without you and you went after her?"

Ted's eyes were watery, not with tears, but with his chronic liquid befuddlement. "I suppose I could have."

"You followed her across the bridge, into Marin. You followed her toward Stinson Beach. And you followed so close behind her that finally she skidded off the road. You were scared. You got her out of the car. You were so glad to see she was okay that you promised to marry her. So the two of you started driving down the hill together, then you started fighting again."

Ted's eyes had widened—empty and colorless, like a paint-by-numbers canvas that Joel could fill in.

"She jumped out of the car, and you went after her. You were trying to get her to come back with you, that's all. But she wouldn't, and then she started shouting. Maybe you put your hand over her mouth to stop her. Maybe you liked the way it felt. Maybe you put her hands around her throat. Maybe you kept them there a little too long."

Now Ted's eyes were full of the mottled knowledge Joel had put there. "Maybe."

"Maybe?"

Ted groped for another bottle.

"Well," Joel said, "it's not first-degree murder, at least."

"That's easy for you to say. I *spent* a night in jail. I'd shoot myself before I'd go back." Ted moistened his lips. "I know what else could have happened. When Melanie left me, she went to

Aurora Place. She left her purse there." He looked up plaintively. "Don't you think? Don't you think that's what we should tell Lieutenant Epcot? If you'd agree, it would make my side of the story look that much more convincing." He added, with pitiable confidence, "We really don't know where Melanie was that afternoon, I mean, when she went out and I was in her apartment. Maybe she was even with Margot."

"And Margot's ring? How did it get in Melanie's purse?"

"Uh . . ." Ted shrugged, then looked up at Joel with a hopeful smile. "Margot gave it to her?"

Joel sighed. He didn't know how conscious or intentional Ted's lies had been or continued to be. In a way it didn't matter. Lies were lies. It was hard to draw the line of responsibility between levels of consciousness, especially with the constant border disputes going on in there. "What have you told the police about that day?"

"Not much. It's been coming back to me slowly. My new lawyer—the one from Boston—says my only hope is to keep claiming that I don't remember anything." Ted looked down heavily at his current bottle. "What time is it? Is it after one yet?"

"Ted, you've *got* to stop. Think what a good impression that would make. 'Your honor, this tragedy has caused Ted Harvey to reform.'"

"You dragged me to that stupid meeting. Well, it didn't work."

"Because last week you didn't *want* to stop. That's the miracle of human beings. They can always change their minds." Joel wasn't optimistic about the effect this Automatic Lecture would have—but wasn't he obliged to try? His missionary fervor had burned away even his rage.

Ted leaned forward, showing his teeth again. "Everyone I meet is in therapy. Lots of men, even. If therapy is so great, and everyone's doing it, then how come the world isn't full of wonderful, with-it people?"

"It doesn't work that way," Joel said. *It works for the privileged few. It works like the grace of God.* "The world has never been full of wonderful, with-it people, and it never *will* be, people being who and what they are. And then people think they can go in for a personality change like their souls were flat tires—"

"Now tell me that the tire has to want to change."

"Well, it does, as a matter of fact. That tire has to pop its own lugnuts and pump its own jack. At least you can still do it, if you want. At least *you're* alive. You're still young, and I wouldn't say healthy, but you're alive. And you'll probably never win the Nobel Prize for anything, but maybe you can be the kind of person who gets dressed occasionally."

"So what do you care if I end up getting butt-fucked at San Quentin?"

"Oh, God, Ted, I might even like that a lot. I think I'd *like* to see you drink yourself to death. I *know* I would like to see Margot divorce you. I care very much about seeing you punished for what you've done. I can't stand to think you'll get away with it. But maybe you shouldn't go by what I want."

Ted stared across the pit of the living room. His eyes looked even more bloodshot than usual. "Does it ever end? Do things ever get easier?"

Sometimes, Joel thought, but he said, "Yes, I promise they will, but you've got to try. Pop those lugnuts. Besides, Teddy, whether you killed Melanie or not"—*and I think you did*—"look at the mess you've gotten yourself into. Wouldn't you say it's now or never?"

"I don't know." Ted shrugged.

Joel tapped a knuckle against his own teeth. He didn't love Ted—didn't even *like* him—but does a travel agent have to like his clients in order to book them on a Mediterranean cruise? "All right, then, are you going to the police or am I?"

Ted hesitated. "Joey, do you really think that's such a good idea? I mean, how am I going to explain it? I don't know how it got there—isn't it just going to confuse things?"

"If you're so sure you're innocent, what are you worried about?"

"Because if *you're* so angry at me," Ted explained, humbly, "imagine how all those people who don't even know me are going to feel."

"Sorry, Teddy-O." Joel got up. His knee twinged. "I'm not going to cover for you anymore."

On his way back to his car, Joel noticed a van parked outside. The words PIZZA PRINCE were printed on the side, in ornate red letters.

By the time Joel got home, his muscles were crying for a good, hard run. He put in a call to Emory Epcot, and hit the sidewalk, taking his Lake Street route, a route heavily associated with

Margot, which led him back in the direction from where he had just come.

Joel had an elaborate and frighteningly obsessive system of running routes, in which he always took one of four paths and always turned around at one of several predesignated points. With all extensions added, this particular route ended at the Palace of Fine Arts.

He started, not knowing how far he would go.

Soon he had what he wanted—the rhythm of his arms, the shudder of pavement through his legs, the exhilarating rush of air in his lungs. The scenery passed with the skipping tread of a home movie.

But then he had to run even faster, so that he wouldn't think about Margot. His knee throbbed, but he ran through it. *Masochism.* Sadism, masochism, the oral stage, the anal stage, the genital stage, latency. The pain receded, and he was only his head, a passenger on top of his body.

At his Seventeenth Avenue turnaround (a point he had "arbitrarily" predesignated because a woman he had once dated lived on the corner there), he couldn't quite face going home, so he added another mile, and went out to the Palace, passing very near Ted's house again. Thus he fell into the runner's trap. By the time he got back to Arguello Boulevard, he couldn't run anymore, and so he had to walk the last mile to his apartment. Then he couldn't stop his thoughts about Margot, Ted, and Melanie.

While Joel was having lunch with Margot on *that* Wednesday, Ted was with Melanie. And Margot already knew about Melanie then. Margot knew, and didn't tell him. Well, she was hurt. Still . . .

Ted was with Melanie, but Melanie had had to go out. She had probably gone to Margot's. Margot had probably arranged the meeting. She would have wanted to confront Melanie herself. Melanie would have wanted that, too, might have wanted it from the beginning. After all, the real bond was not between Melanie and Ted, but between Melanie and Margot—Melanie wanted to become Margot, to have what she had.

There was a bond between them, all right—but slack, like a ligament sprained too often, healed only with scar tissue; easily twisted, not so easily torn.

Two strong women, one weak man. Even so, Joel felt some residual jealousy of Ted. *Two* women. Was it his looks? It *couldn't* be his lovemaking. Maybe it was his manipulativeness, or his immaturity or his puerile sense of humor. Joel had had plenty of patients, men and women, who were "in love" with people whom they also detested. Sometimes hearing their stories was like watching the same "I Love Lucy" episode for the fourteenth time. It was dated slapstick in low-contrast black and white; boring, unfunny, but comforting, because you know exactly what's going to happen next. Stories of masochistic love. But it wasn't love at all—it was just transference.

After Joel had walked Margot back to her car, Andrea had followed Margot home to Seacliff. Where Melanie was waiting. The two women would have confronted each other and, somehow, Melanie had gotten Margot's car keys away from her. Melanie must have driven the Jaguar off like a stolen trophy, proof that she could take Margot's place. She'd driven the Jaguar back to her two-level highrise apartment, and to Ted . . .

. . . With Andrea right behind her.

At some point—later—Melanie's purse had gotten left at Aurora Place. By Ted. Joel thought of it now, hidden in his closet, a prize he dared not show.

Margot might have gone into hiding at first to spite both Ted and Joel himself, for not going to Carmel with her when she asked. But once she realized what had happened to Melanie (and who had done it), she would have become too frightened to return.

Joel was just a couple of blocks from his apartment; the rest of the way was uphill. He imagined the first spray of a cold shower on his face and chest, and the hill seemed to steepen and retreat. His run-out leg muscles wobbled beneath him. He hated walking uphill. But something else was bothering him, too, some minor irritant he couldn't identify. He stopped and shook out his leg. The sweat on his face was warm. What was it? Margot? Well, yes, that was *always* bothering him, but it wasn't that right now . . . it was a feeling . . . that he was being followed. He turned around, his breaths still shallow: There was no one behind him, except half a block away, where two black women wearing identical cellophane rain hats and bulky, mustard-yellow coats, were slowly climbing the hill. One of them returned his stare.

Paranoia. His unconscious was reminding him of Betty, lest he forget that *she* was still out there, too—possibly the keeper of some information.

But when he reached the corner he was struck by the feeling again. He clenched his jaw and did not turn around. Instead he pressed on to do the final uphill block.

Emory Epcot, wearing a Stetson, and suspenders with his pleated corduroy pants, was waiting for him by the mailboxes. "I could have busted down the door." He winked. "But I was sure you'd be back soon."

Joel took him upstairs. He felt oddly naked in his running shorts, with the hair on his legs still lying flat with perspiration. And the faint odor of sweat, inoffensive enough to himself, didn't heighten his feeling of social grace.

"Rather *monkish*, isn't it?" Emory asked, when they entered his apartment.

"Poverty, chastity, and obedience," Joel said. "I thought I could handle one of the three." He brought the sweater from his closet, and Emory unwrapped it.

"The ring's inside the purse," Joel said. He wondered if Melanie had taken that from Margot, too, or if Ted had given it to her. Either way, Ted had thought to stash it there, so it wouldn't be found on Melanie's hand.

Using the sleeve of Joel's sweater, Emory lifted the stitched red flap of the purse. "Did you put everything else back?"

Joel nodded.

"This is tampering with evidence, you know."

"But how could I know it was evidence," Joel asked innocently, "until I tampered with it?"

"Well, we'll see. We might have to search your"—Emory touched his tongue to his upper lip—"little cell here."

"Fine with me." Joel shrugged, though it wasn't fine at all. He went to the refrigerator, where he found three yogurts, two of them well past their sale dates, and a few bottles of lemonade Calistoga. One had been opened and he knew it would be flat, but he drank that one anyway, in deference to his mother's admonitions against waste.

"I'm taking this down to the station." Emory was carefully wrapping the purse up again.

"I'd like to keep my sweater."

"Sure, Doc." Emory tossed it on a chair. He tucked the purse under his arm and posed. "Like it?"

"It's you."

"We'll let you know if you're in any trouble."

"I beg your pardon?" Joel chucked the empty Calistoga in the trash, which needed taking out.

"Doc, give me a break. What made you decide to go to Aurora Place all of a sudden? No offense, but it doesn't sound like your scene. And how can I be sure that you found this there?"

"Maybe you'll just have to trust me."

"Now why would I do that?"

"Trust is the basis of *all* relationships." Joel smiled, reaching for one of the unopened Calistogas. "Like some?"

"No, thanks." Emory laughed. "You can never tell where it's been." He walked to the bookcase, and ran his finger lightly over the spines of the books, his lips moving as he read their titles. "Yes," he observed almost absently, "it's pretty funny, that you found this before we did."

"I think it's funny, too. But you haven't been looking for *Margot*, and I have. That's why you didn't find it first."

"H'm." Emory pulled down a book on countertransference. "Property of Columbia University Library," he read from the flyleaf. "Nice of them to give you this." He replaced the book. "I know Aurora Place. When I was working S.F., I cornered a big securities-fraud man there." He rolled his eyes. "You wouldn't believe what goings-on *he* was up to."

"Shock me," Joel encouraged him, between gulps.

"He had a harem. We came in on them crawling around naked on all fours." Emory tucked his thumbs into his suspenders. "It made me *real* happy to be gay, let me tell you. I was off my Shredded Wheat for a month."

Joel recapped the Calistoga. There was a feeling in his stomach which he suddenly identified as hunger. He realized that he hadn't eaten that day.

"I think I could recover from the trauma if I solved the murder of Melanie Hardwicke, and it became a movie-of-the-week, and I got real famous."

Joel winced at the word *famous*. "Any current theories about that?" he asked.

Emory shoved aside several file folders so that he could sit. "Doc, I've always got a theory. I think Ted Harvey had this little red purse stashed somewhere, and he gave it to you to turn in before *we* found it. So you come up with some cock-and-bull story about finding it at Aurora Place." He paused to raise an eyebrow.

"You remember what I said about being an accessory after the fact."

Joel almost regretted that he had persuaded Tami to let him see the suite. He turned to the cabinets, to rummage for something to eat. "I hope that won't stop you from searching Aurora Place."

"No. But it won't stop me from dragging your name into this, either, if necessary."

"Oh, come on." Joel slammed a cabinet shut. He had found nothing but stale crackers, instant coffee, and a jar of peanuts that were about ready for a Carbon-14 test. "You have no evidence against me."

Emory leaned back on his elbows. "But maybe we'll turn some up."

Joel returned to his search. In the next cabinet, there was only the fruitcake that Denise had given him last Christmas. He was not afraid of being implicated in something he hadn't done, but if his name was in the papers . . . He was obsessive about his privacy, had chosen psychoanalysis in part because it allowed him a degree of anonymity. And how would his patients react to this? Would his referrals dry up? "Listen," he said, noticing that Emory was looking awfully comfortable, reclining on his sofa, "don't think I'm rude—"

Emory sat up. His Stetson started to fall off but he quickly righted it. "You're not kicking me out, are you, Doc?"

Joel raked his hand through his sweat-sticky hair. "I'm tired, hungry, and I could use a shower. Or let me put it another way." He opened the front door. "I'm kicking you out."

CHAPTER 10

FORGOTTEN TOYS

If a workaholic dreads the weekend, then at least Joel had a job
to do.

Later on Saturday, he made phone calls to everyone he knew
who knew Margot—mostly people with whom he was acquainted
from her parties. "Oh yes, the *psychoanalyst*," they murmured
when they recognized his name. Had they heard anything? No,
nothing. If they did they would tell him, really. In the meantime
they had to . . . Joel was still amazed how people who identified
him by profession only could sometimes be struck catatonic by
the sound of his voice, as if he were plotting to include them in a
research paper on sexual dysfunction.

On Sunday he went to the office, made more calls, left a lot of
messages, read the final papers from his class (Wednesday night
had been the last meeting of the term), even paid bills. His only
interruption came when Alex Forans slunk by, hinting that Joel
had taken more than his share of teabags from the coffee room. "I
don't even like tea," Joel said, but he promised to keep watch for
the thief.

At home that night, Joel was able to reach a couple of people
who had been away for the weekend. "Why, she's in Curaçao,"
one woman purred. "I had a postcard from her." But when Joel
asked—insisted—that the woman read the card to him over the
phone, she couldn't find it: The postcard had slipped through the
crack between memory and junk mail.

Sunday night. Bachelor Night. Joel usually spent it with Ted and Margot. It happened that last Sunday there had been a family potluck at the halfway house: Joel (who brought potato salad from the deli) had comforted an obese girl who wept in the corner, convinced a budding schizophrenic that no one had stolen his nonexistent Fender amps, and mediated an argument over whose turn it was to lick the frosting off the Saran Wrap.

But the Sunday before he had played Scrabble with Margot while Ted conducted an invisible orchestra and sang along to a tape of *Oklahoma!* Later, a few others dropped by to pay homage: a gallery owner looking for a partner, a county supervisor looking for a reelection committee, and an architect who wanted to build an indoor fountain in the front hall. By that time, Ted had wandered off to another room to finish the Chivas Regal in private.

Tonight, Joel would have liked to go out running—but he wanted to be home in case he heard back from someone he had tried to reach earlier. He kept thinking—hoping, actually—that Denise would call, too; then he had to remind himself how they had parted. Still, she might call him. He couldn't call *her* because that would be "sending mixed signals." *You'll be okay*, he told himself. *It's just Sunday night.*

It was probably better if he and Denise didn't talk. So why was he thinking about her so much? He didn't love Denise, and he didn't want to marry her. But he would have liked to see her, make love to her again. He would have preferred to sleep in her bed that night instead of his own, just to see her smooth black hair on the pillow.

What if none of this had ever happened? If Margot had never said she loved him, never disappeared, what would he be doing tonight—would he be back from going to another street fair with Denise, looking forward to another evening of double entendres over Scrabble? (And by the way, had Margot been *letting* him win?) When he thought of it that way, he was surprised at how dull and static his old life seemed. Almost as if he was *glad* this had happened. That didn't make sense, because he still felt very bad about Melanie and anxious about Margot. But he would find her, and when he did, whatever happened, there would be no more nights of vague longings.

He ended up calling his parents, who wanted to hear about Denise. (He'd mentioned her to them just so they'd take a short break from worrying whether or not he was gay.) "Denise is fine," he said cryptically. *Just fine without me.*

His mother went on to ask him if he'd gotten a wedding invitation from Doug Greenfield. Joel had never heard of Doug Greenfield, but his mother insisted he'd gone to Hebrew school with him, and now Doug was marrying a lovely young woman who had gone to Columbia, the law school, actually three years after Joel was there, but maybe Joel knew her?

Sorry, Mom.

Then his father wondered—for the eleventh time—why a nice girl like Denise would move to a city where there were so many homosexual men. Joel was about to explain—for the eleventh time—that she had grown up there, but opted instead for pretending to hear someone at the door, a noise he simulated by kicking the wall.

Then he settled down to spend the rest of the evening watching TV, with a peanut butter sandwich and the last of the lemonade Calistogas. When he saw that there was a "Twilight Zone" rerun on, he turned to that channel; either out of nostalgia or masochism, because his youthful fascination for the show had long passed.

Rod Serling was smoking a cigarette.

It was the episode in which a band of neighbors blame a power failure on the strange family that just moved to the block. Joel admired the camera angles, the sharp black and white, and the long shadows, all of which seemed the visual counterparts of paranoia.

By the time the commercial for easy-credit diamond rings came on, Joel was thinking of Betty Klass again.

Oh, why not?

He called her, but got her machine. He'd expected that, but he cursed technology as he hung up, and was then afraid that one of his ill-chosen words had found its way onto her tape. She'd love that.

If he kept calling, he was sure that he'd keep getting her machine. But he knew where she lived.

He went the next day. The ethics of this were marginal, but his entire relationship with Betty had strained conventional boundaries, and he felt he had nothing to lose.

Betty's house, a narrow Tudor that needed paint, was not far from his office, on Jackson: a leafy street with a slight incline. Pacific Heights. But then, she'd been married to a doctor.

What makes me so sure she's home? he wondered as he stood on the sidewalk. But there wasn't any real doubt in his mind. Somehow he knew not only that she was home, but that she'd been home for days, wearing a bathrobe, eating from cans, watching Oprah.

He knocked and waited. Then he heard something to his right. He willed himself not to turn to look. It could have been curtains being pushed aside, a window pushed up. Betty checking him out. He composed his features and stared straight ahead.

He knocked again, and after a minute the peephole opened and He thought he recognized a murky hazel eye. Then he heard a long series of clicks. Betty opened the door but left the chain on, so that she revealed only a three-inch column of herself down the middle. Her face, stripped of makeup, looked a decade older and a century more sad. She was wearing a navy-blue housedress of a spongy-looking material, with a red stripe in front.

"I knew this would happen," she said glumly, but she unhooked the chain.

Ah yes, she might have known all right, might have been silent because she knew he'd come around. But he didn't care. He knew it was an emotional risk for her to let him in, and he was grateful.

The house was surprisingly dark; every curtain was drawn, every chink that might emit light was blocked off. The living room looked as though nothing had been moved, or cleaned, for years. A thick gray-brown layer of dust preserved a shelf of leather-bound "Great Books" and a painting in the style of Rembrandt.

"Can I offer you something." Betty spoke without inflection as she sat in a chair next to an ashy fireplace. The chair was dusty blue, with a pleated skirt around the bottom. "A Dubonnet."

"No, thank you." Joel wrestled with an urge to open some drape, any drape. "Mrs. Klass, I remember that you said you've known Margot Harvey for some time. You—you haven't heard from her, have you?"

Betty nodded. "It's such a coincidence that you should ask, Dr. Abramowitz. I got a call from her last night, about two A.M. She was crying."

Joel tapped his knuckles against his teeth. Ask a straight

question, get a straight answer—don't expect to know whether the answer is true or not. Don't get greedy.

Betty folded her hands in her lap and crossed her legs. She was wearing old beige leather slippers. "I tried to calm her, but then she hung up. I have to admit, I was partly just relieved that it wasn't Al. He used to call me in the middle of the night and breathe heavily."

Joel shifted, wondering if he'd made a mistake in coming here. Then his gaze drifted to the couch to his left.

"Dr. Abramowitz," Betty hesitated, "do you still have my little giraffe?"

"Yes, I do. He's perfectly safe. You can come get him whenever you want."

"Ah." She sat back, and a few lines vanished from her face. Still, she was so pale that she looked like an unfinished sketch of herself. "I'm going to have to return him to the store eventually. They say I didn't pay for it, and there's been some unpleasantness—a letter. But it was a gift to me, from the CEO."

So what could he say, *Mrs. Klass, would you like to lie down and talk to me?* Then he noticed the box of Kleenex on the end table next to her chair. That gave him courage. "Mrs. Klass, you know I have a couch in my office."

"Oh yes," she said absently, patting her disheveled hair as if smoothing a perfect coiffure.

"Lying down—it helps some people to talk." He was remembering suddenly, vividly, his own first day on Dr. Schneider's couch—how he had sunk down, not knowing what would happen, terrified of the water that would cover his head, drown him—but *wanting* to drown, wanting his lungs to explode, so as never to end the moment. When he heard Dr. Schneider's voice behind him, it felt like the hand of God squeezing his intestines.

"It does?" she murmured. "It's hard to see why."

Actually, it is. "I wonder if you'd like to try it."

Later his resistance could go twelve rounds with Dr. Schneider, dodging every cross and hook. Later still, he had less resistance. But during those first few minutes on the couch, he might have jumped out the window had Dr. Schneider told him to—and it was during these minutes, during this once-a-millennium alignment of conscious and unconscious, before the two systems resumed their separate orbits, that he hoped he could get Betty to tell him what she knew.

"Here? Now?" She raised thin, almost-invisible eyebrows.

He smiled and shrugged. "Why not?"

She looked at the couch. "I don't see what good it would do. It seems like a waste of time."

"I think . . . it might be scary to think about what *would* happen."

Betty stood up shakily. "And I think maybe you'd better leave." She folded trembling arms under large, shapeless breasts.

No, no. "I'm not promising anything," he said. "But would it hurt to try?"

Her arms dropped. A deep line appeared between her eyes as she stared at her own blue couch with the pleated-skirt upholstery. Then with a sigh and the air of a parent indulging a pesty child, she lay down.

Without rising fully, Joel reached across the room to grab the box of Kleenex, which he then slipped on the floor near her head. Once it was there, he was at home: He had the essentials. It didn't matter that this was an unfamiliar room, a lumpy chair. The semidarkness would help his concentration.

Betty grunted, and tugged at her housedress. And yet, gazing at the top of her wispy blond hair, he could imagine her a young girl. The ethics were less than marginal now, but once the rollercoaster pulls away from the station you're on it for the ride.

Betty had not spoken. He waited a few more moments before observing, "You've been quiet for a while."

Silence.

"What is it?" he asked.

"I don't like this."

"What don't you like about it?"

"I feel funny." Now she sounded younger, too; he detected a slight lisp. "Like I want to cry for absolutely no reason." She *tskked.* "Isn't that silly? You really want me just to lie here without looking at you?"

"Tell me what you're thinking right now. Whatever it is."

"Why, nothing. My mind's a total blank."

"Right now."

She giggled. "My sisters. Did I tell you about my sisters?"

"Tell me about them."

"I have three sisters. Doris, Rosalie, and Arlene. I was the third of four girls," she said, with obscure pride. "They're all successful, professional women in the top of their fields."

"What do they do?" He noticed a clock on the mantelpiece. In the gloom he could just make out that it was stopped at 10:17. Betty started a complex litany of her sisters' accomplishments; he had trouble following them, since they were vague and not quite credible. "You're impressed with their achievements," he fed back, and almost continued, *perhaps you don't feel you can measure up.* Was that the connection with Margot—a successful woman?

"Oh yes. Doris—she'll be mayor of Indianapolis soon. That's where she lives."

"Are you close to your sisters?" The third of four girls . . . Betty might have had trouble standing out. Going crazy was always a good way to stand out, though there were alternatives, like discovering radium, or becoming an astronaut. . . .

"Well . . . sort of. I mean, yes. I would say definitely yes."

"And Margot—"

Betty made a choking sound.

"What is it?" he asked quickly.

"This is stupid," she said.

"You thought of something upsetting." It suddenly occurred to him that it could have been Margot herself who had driven Betty to the roof that day, by inadvertently being harsh with her. Was that what Betty had recalled now? Betty had come to talk to Margot about doing volunteer work. Suppose that Margot, once she spent some time with Betty, realized her mistake and turned her down—triggering Betty's episode. Margot would feel responsible for the Horatio incident, then, and be afraid to have Joel know what had really happened.

"My sisters all have children," Betty whispered. "They all have children but me!"

"That upsets you."

"Why shouldn't it upset me?" she demanded. "My sisters call each other every day and say vicious, nasty things about me. They talk about how it was my fault."

"What was your fault?"

"I just left him for a minute!" she whimpered. "I just left him for a minute!"

"Left who?"

"I went to get the giraffe. Once he started having a tantrum, I couldn't stop him unless I did what he wanted."

"What who wanted?"

"Robbie. I told you about Robbie, I know I did."

Joel thought of Betty holding Horatio's hand. She had called him Robbie then. "Who was he?"

"My son."

"What happened to him?"

"I don't know. But something must have happened, don't you think? I mean, he must be somewhere I can see him someday, otherwise it just wouldn't make sense. Why would God go to all the trouble to make a baby and then just take him away and put him nowhere?"

Joel thought he saw the tip of a small shoe poking out from beneath the skirt of the chair that Betty had first sat in. But a moment later, it seemed to merge with other shadows. "You miss him," Joel said.

"All the time. There are so many things I think of to tell him. I tried to talk to him when he was little, but he couldn't understand then. I—I write him letters. I put them in the mailbox sometimes. They came back until I stopped putting the return address on. So maybe he's getting them. He was too young to read, but maybe they have schools in heaven. Or maybe when you die you just automatically know everything. If he were alive he'd be in high school now."

"Can you tell me how he died?"

"I took him outside to play," she began, after a moment. "I forgot one of his toys. It was his favorite. A stuffed giraffe. He started to have a tantrum. He would call me 'bad mommy.' I couldn't stand it when he did that. I came back into the house—just for a second! He wandered out into the street. I don't know why. I always try to figure out why."

Joel waited.

When she spoke again, her voice was much lower. "A car hit him. I can't stand to tell you the rest. It *was* my fault, wasn't it?"

Joel saw Betty standing on the sidewalk. Her scream was not audible but he could feel the pain of it against his eardrum, and he knew how it hurt Betty even to feel the warmth of the sun on her skin ever since that day: the day she came back into the house—this dust-choked house—just for a second. "It doesn't help to blame yourself," he said.

She covered her eyes with her hand, and her shoulders twitched.

"There's Kleenex beside you," he said.

She reached down, groping for a tissue. "I put a towel on him, waiting for the ambulance. Then, at the hospital, they gave me the towel back. It was all—bloody. I don't understand, why did they give it back to me? I wish they hadn't. I still have it. I can't throw it away. I should, but I can't." She blew her nose. "Al said it was my fault. He called me a bubbleheaded dodo-brain. He looked so ugly when he cried at the funeral. I didn't cry. He yelled at me because I didn't cry." She placed the wadded tissue on her chest and sniffed. Then her head rolled to one side.

Joel waited. There seemed to be more shadows now, moving to an invisible breeze—stretching and then shrinking around the heavy drapes and the old, heavy furniture.

After a while Betty spoke flatly. "I wish you could let me live that day over. Just that one day."

"You feel as though you failed," Joel said. "As though it was your fault. Maybe you imagine other people know about what happened—and blame you, too, so that you think they're angry at you, want to punish you. Maybe that's why you sometimes think that your ex-husband is having you followed—or that Margot Harvey calls you on the phone and cries."

And why, perhaps, Betty had sought out Margot, the childless caretaker of children; Betty, the mother whose care had not been sufficient.

Betty let out a long sigh. "I didn't forget what happened," she said finally. "I've never forgotten it. I just stopped thinking about it. You—you won't tell anyone, will you?"

"No, I won't tell anyone."

Shorter silence. Then Betty talked on quietly: about how Robbie slept so little and fussed so much when he was a baby, how he had thrown food at her when he was older and she tried to feed him; about her sister Doris's theory that Betty's inability to breast-feed had caused all of Robbie's difficulties. Then she talked about Al's second marriage.

Joel listened, absorbing it all. He gazed at the unmoving clock, occasionally believing for a moment that it would tell him when their time was up.

But after about forty-five minutes, Betty seemed to reach her own stopping point. She sat up in a single fluid motion, primly dabbing tissue on the pouches under her eyes. "I'm so embarrassed," she murmured.

"Perhaps you'd like to come talk to me again at my office," Joel said.

She sniffed, then nodded.

And Joel felt the old excitement, absent from his work since Margot had been absent from his life, that here was someone ready to work and ready to be helped. "Wednesday at ten-fifty?" He knew that it was his only opening that week, but if she couldn't make it, he'd try to rearrange some other things.

She looked directly at him. She seemed so calm, so lucid; all her delusions had fallen away. He knew it wouldn't last. It wouldn't be that easy. *Get ready to sift through ten thousand jagged pieces, all of them sky.*

"All right," she said.

You won't forget? he almost asked, but didn't. If she came, she might tell him more about Margot—if he hadn't found Margot himself by then. But for now, he wasn't going to push anymore. Maybe he'd be sorry later. But he wasn't going to disturb what fragile trust Betty had in him.

She smoothed the back of her hair, suddenly looking doubtful. "I *was* going to go to the beauty shop that day," she muttered. Then she added, with equally sudden cheerfulness: "I'll make it, though. Felice can take me a little later, I'm sure."

"Good." Joel rose to leave; Betty smiled, but did not get up to see him out, and he almost stumbled against the furniture a couple of times as he groped for the door.

Back at the office, Joel checked his machine and found three messages. Andrea had called to cancel her session, explaining that she had to take her mother's parakeet to the vet to be put to sleep. Damn, Joel thought. Andrea generally pulled this trick when something big was about to come up in the analysis: first she would cancel several sessions at the last minute, with just this type of excuse (last time she had said that she had symptoms of Epstein Barr-syndrome). When she returned they had to spend some time working through her resentment toward him for charging her for the missed sessions (Joel had his own issues about that but remained firm). When Andrea was done fretting that he only saw her because of the money she paid him, the repressed material emerged.

Joel wondered what it was this time. Well, there would be psychic aftershocks from the car accident she had witnessed for a while yet. That was good; it would stir things up. It was like a mild earthquake, knocking dusty old knickknacks off from shelves that had been too high to reach.

The second message was from Ted: "Help, Joey, the Cleveland Gestapo has arrived."

The Cleveland Gestapo? But then Joel remembered that Melanie was from a suburb of Cleveland. So it had something to do with her. Maybe her parents, come out to see how the investigation was going?

Lieutenant Epcot had also called. "Doc, give me a buzz, will you?"

Joel made a less-than-necessary trip to the bathroom, fully aware that he was hoping to run into Denise on the way. But her door was closed, the slim, blue IN SESSION—DO NOT DISTURB sign facing out. He felt as though the sign was personally directed at him. Damn, she was unreasonable! No, she wasn't. This was the way he had wanted it, right? But they were still going to share office space, so they should at least be on good terms. They could at least be *adult* about it.

He had hoped to talk to her for a few minutes before he returned Emory's call. He was feeling some trepidation in that department, remembering how he and Emory had parted. But then his desire for news made him put that aside.

"Hey, Doc, it's been two whole days. Have you missed me?"

"Dreadfully. Did you search Aurora Place?"

"*Fait accompli.* But listen, I didn't call to tell you about my childhood. I want to talk to you down here at the Hall of Justice."

Now Joel was standing in a pool of guilt, the level rising steadily around him. "Why?"

Emory laughed. "I want you to answer a little question for me. What kind of car did what's her name—that Rosa lady—drive?"

"A Ford Mustang." Rosa had been very proud of her blue Mustang with the V-8 engine.

"Would you recognize it?"

"I think so."

"I just want you come on down and take a look, then."

It was indeed Rosa's car. It was parked in a gated section of the underground garage of the Hall of Justice, along with the battered and rusty carcasses of ancient abandoned autos, and some newer cars, which had been impounded after they were used to commit crimes against man and the state.

"Where did you find it?" Joel was circling the Mustang, reassuring himself that his first impression was correct. Margot could have been in this very car, just a few days before. He stuck his head through the open window and detected an odor reminiscent of her—she *had* been in it! But then, Rosa favored the same floral perfumes. There was a faint dent in the passenger door. He could hear Rosa swear.

"In the Mission. Dude swears up and down that he bought it from a friend who just *happened* to have lost the pink slip. We've got him upstairs now—he's waiting for his buddies to sell enough dope to bail him out."

"Why didn't you ask Ted to identify the car?"

Emory twisted the pinpoint diamond in his left earlobe. "He's been charged in the Melanie Hardwicke case. Doesn't make him *real* reliable. Now you, Doc, I don't know—you might be a bit off-the-wall, but I know you want to find this little Margot lady." Emory narrowed his eyes. "Seems like you want to find her real bad."

"What about Aurora Place?" Joel wanted to know.

Emory shrugged. "*Nada.* There's a suite there that Mrs. Harvey rented, but she didn't leave anything behind."

Joel was relieved that Emory didn't repeat his threat to search his own apartment. He knew just how thorough Emory would be, combing through every notepad for love notes and examining his underwear for stains. But what about Margot? Were there other suites she had rented in other hotels? Why not? She was proud of her philanthropism, and her poor, artistic friends; she was more secretive about her self-indulgent side: the money she could spend on building an indoor fountain, or perhaps on an entire network of hotel suites around the city.

"They switched the license plates," Emory was saying. He tapped the bumper of the car with the toe of his cowboy boot.

"Of course," Joel murmured, remembering that Rosa, too, had had personalized plates: RO ZA. "But it *is* her car." He was sure of it now. An automobile somehow assumes the character of its owner: Even the grill of the Mustang had the disapproving shape of Rosa's brow. "The guy you picked up, who was driving the car—do you know who he got it from?"

Emory snorted. "*I* think Rosa Avera just junked the car in the Mission. She knew it'd get stolen. She probably thought that would throw us off the track." He put his finger to his temple. "You can't think like a shrink, Doc. You gotta think like a cop."

"Uh huh." Joel nodded slowly. He remembered that Danny, at the Crown Garage, had told him Rosa had a boyfriend, Chuck. He smiled at Emory. Emory was an authority figure, so crossing him inevitably involved a little Oedipal guilt. But Joel had been analyzed enough to handle *that*.

It was nearly closing time at the Crown Garage and a gaggle of tired, dressed-for-success young professionals stood at the cashier's window, waiting to pick up their tuned cars. Joel was able to slip in without attracting any attention.

He found Danny in the back, his head stuck deep in the bowels of the Buick Super, vacuuming the inside with a long yellow tube.

Joel touched him on the shoulder and Danny jumped, with a yelp that he quickly swallowed.

"I'm sorry, I didn't mean to scare you," Joel said. "It's only me. Remember? Joel."

Danny held the vacuum up; the nozzle sucked in air like someone being strangled. Danny stared at Joel for a moment, frozen, then quickly doubled himself back into the Buick.

Joel went around to the other side. The door was unlocked and he leaned into the car so that he was eye-level with Danny over the backseat. "I just want to talk to you," he said.

Danny backed out of the car. He shut off the vacuum cleaner and disappeared through a small door.

Joel followed him, ignoring the hand-lettered EMPLOYEES ONLY sign. There were in a storeroom, lined with shelves: Tires were propped along the upper tiers; battered cardboard boxes predominated on the middle shelves. Greasy Michelin reference manuals were stacked on a metal desk. On the wall above the desk there was a calendar with a picture of a naked Japanese woman and next to that a poster of a large sparkplug with the banner USED PLUGS TELL A STORY.

Danny had retreated to the corner, next to a stained Mr. Coffee pot which held half an inch of murky liquid. He turned and performed the three-stage tic that Joel remembered from their first meeting: tilt head, shrug, and flinch.

"I need your help," Joel said. "I need to ask you about Rosa."

Danny shook his head. He bent down behind the stand that held the Mr. Coffee and took out an old shoebox from behind it. He slowly removed the top, which was torn at the seams. Joel looked inside. The bottom of the box was covered with buttons, of various sizes and colors, some with a fragment of thread still attached.

"I collect these," Danny said. "I hide them here. At the place where I live, someone would steal them."

"They're very pretty," Joel said. He wanted to take an interest but he was distracted by his own heartbeat, elevated to running speed.

"I'll show them to you."

"Danny—"

But Danny sat at the metal desk, hugging the box close to him; then he shook it like an old prospector panning for gold. The buttons whooshed back and forth. "I have so many now," he said, looking at Joel.

And Joel sucked in a breath, lowering his pulse. "Yes, show them to me," he said, trying to sound calm. He sat across from Danny on a wooden crate, and rested his chin in his hands. "Show them all to me." *Play therapy.* The *whooshing* of the buttons lulled him, calling up that slower, meditative state he needed to listen. To hear.

"You can't touch them."

"I won't," Joel promised. He was fascinated by all the things that people hoarded: matchbooks, snapshots, personal slights. What did buttons mean to Danny? Clothing, manual dexterity, money? Had someone once told him to button his lip?

The collection was as sparkling and multicolored as a pirate's treasure chest. Danny picked out a big pink one. "This belonged to Rosa. I stoled it from her, but she never knowed. If she did, she would hit me."

"How could she hit you, where you live? Aren't there people around to take care of you?"

"Sometimes Rosa comes to take me out." Danny wrinkled his nose and stuck out his tongue. Then he squinted into the box and carefully selected several small navy-blue buttons. "From a boy in my house. He let me take them from his shirt, when he didn't want it anymore." He rubbed the buttons, smiling with eyes half closed, and Joel thought of the curator of a museum, holding a relic from a pharaoh's tomb.

"How does she hit you?"

Danny demonstrated with two more of the buttons from the box, clapping them together. "With her hands, on the side of my head. Or sometimes with a towel. *Snnnaaap.*"

"Tell me more about her." *The bitch.*

"My mama left, then there was just Rosa and our father." Danny examined a gold button, then placed it next to the pink one. "Our father was not very nice, but Rosa, she tooked care of me."

"Did she hit you then?"

"Only when I was bad."

"What did you do that was bad?"

"Things she didn't like."

"Just because Rosa doesn't like something doesn't mean it's bad."

"Rosa worked very hard." Danny frowned. He didn't speak for a few moments, as he leaned over the desk; his hair had been cut since Joel's first visit, into the severe flattop style that was currently popular. Joel watched as he arranged his buttons in rows according to some inner scheme. "She was very tired and she said it was my fault, that she couldn't do nothing she wanted to do."

"It must have been hard for Rosa," Joel said, not very convincingly. "She was angry about what had happened with your mother. You know when you get angry you want to blame someone, and if the person you're really mad at isn't there, you might blame someone who is, especially someone who's younger or littler than you are."

Danny nodded. "Our father hit Rosa and Rosa hit me." He sighed and shrugged as if to say, *Such is the lot of all mankind.* Then he made a scoop of both hands and deposited most of the rest of the collection on the desk—careful, though, that none spilled over the side. He stared at them, awed by his own riches.

"Make me a picture," Joel encouraged him. "With the buttons."

Danny shoved all the buttons into a pile, then began to draw them out, one at a time, arranging them in new lines and curves. He hummed faintly as he worked. *Patience,* Joel reminded himself.

"Rosa says I have to do what she wants," Danny went on after a few moments. "She says if not, she can put me in one of those places where they have those electric chairs." Danny vibrated his head, apparently imitating a man receiving shock treatments.

"She can't do that. I'll make sure she doesn't."

Danny smiled, amused at Joel's naïveté. "No, Rosa can do whatever she wants."

"No, she can't," Joel insisted. "And Rosa doesn't know. *You* know what's good and bad for you, only you know that."

Danny glanced up and there it was—the tiny, tiny dot of light in his eyes—the look that Joel longed for and hoped to see every day, every hour. The look of someone about to see the world in a different way. Then the light snuffed out, and he went back to his buttons.

"Rosa's just your sister," Joel went on. "You can do what you want—what you know is right," he amended.

Danny blinked.

"I think you know where Rosa is now," Joel pressed. "I think she told you not to tell anyone."

"I see her. She told me where to go to see her. But I don't remember where it is."

Forgetting has as many uses as a Swiss army knife. For Danny now, it was an act of self-preservation. Even the design he was creating with the buttons was abstract, meaningless. *Damn.*

"How did you get there, to see Rosa?"

"I drived. I am a very good driver."

"I'm sure you are."

"I drive everywhere. I know my way around." Danny looked up from his work, raised his chin.

"Do you have a car of your own?"

"No. Rosa won't let me drive her car." He selected a final button from the box and studied his design for a moment before he placed it at the end of a row. "And her car is the most easy to drive! I drive the pickup truck, the motorcycle, the van. Everything."

"M'mm," Joel acknowledged, gazing at the pattern of buttons again. Danny was apparently finished; he was evening out two rows. *Wait* . . . the figures on the right-hand side could be numbers. Upside down, they looked like 1011. And next to them . . .

Joel got up quickly and stood over Danny's shoulder. Danny didn't like that; he huddled over the desk, started to squirm away. But Joel had a chance to see what he had written, in wobbly button shapes: 1101 GERRO.

"Guerrero Street," Joel whispered, stepping back. *It must be.* Guerrero was in the Mission. "Is that where you saw Rosa?"

Danny's head swayed. Then he held the box at the side of the table and swooped his arm across the desk, blotting out the design. "Brown house," he whispered.

"Is that where Chuck lives?"

Danny stuck out his lower lip. Then he nodded.

"Thank you." Joel played for a moment with the leather button of his sport coat, then he grasped it firmly and yanked it off. "For your collection," he said. Danny's fingers closed over it.

CHAPTER II

PRISONERS

He left the Crown Garage with the intention of going straight to the Mission to find Chuck. But then he had an idea. It was one of those stupid ideas that, once had, cannot be easily gotten rid of, because they gain strength from their very stupidity.

He wanted Denise to come with him. That was a big favor to ask, and he didn't deserve to have her say yes. But he realized now that he needed her there, someone he could trust, to balance his newfound impulsiveness. Maybe, he thought, he was beginning to believe in her as a good-luck charm.

Or maybe he was looking for an excuse to see her again.

But that was all right. Obviously, there was something unfinished between them, or she wouldn't have been so much on his mind since Sunday. She might welcome the opportunity to discuss their feelings; to get closure, so they could get on with their lives.

Rationalizations.

He didn't want to discuss feelings, and he already knew exactly where they stood. He just wanted to see her.

Well, what was the big deal about that? Maybe he would just drop by and act very casual, as if there had never been anything wrong. *Hello, how are you, I was just buying more peanut butter at the grocery store, and I thought you might like to take a drive to the Mission with me to look for my friend's wife's assistant and a possible car thief.*

Wait—he'd bring her a gift. What, though? Women never wanted candy, or anything to eat; the thinnest of them were always on diets. Clothes? He didn't know the sizes. Besides, she might think that he didn't like the way she dressed. Something for the house? No, that was too—*domestic.*

Flowers.

At the flower stand off Union Square he debated among the tiny nubs of color—baby roses, sweet William—and the longer-stemmed, more dramatic flowers. Now he understood why men liked to give women flowers: not because they symbolized virginity or because they were the genitals of plants, but because they died so soon, conveniently disposing of the evidence. That would also explain why women pressed them between the pages of books.

Finally he chose a half dozen each of the blue irises and the white gladioli. They'd stand out in that brown-toned apartment of hers, a little life among all those bowls of shriveled-up leaves she called potpourri.

When he drove past her building, there was a strange car parked in her driveway—a neighbor's, he wondered?—which postponed his arrival while he hunted for a space of his own. It was still light, but the fog had rolled in during the last hour; the view was so completely obscured that he might have been on a hill in Tibet.

He climbed her stairs and knocked, then held the flowers in front of his face, like a child holding his hand over his eyes and peeking through his fingers. He saw her open the door through the stalks. "Oh!" She stood blocking the tiny opening she had made.

"I was passing a flower stand," he said, lowering the bouquet. "And these were crying out, 'Buy me, buy me.'"

She rubbed the big silver heart that hung from her neck. "Well, that's very nice. I'll put them in water." She held out her hand.

"Aren't you going to ask me in?"

"Uh . . . I can't."

Joel felt the faintest thud in his groin, the echo of an invisible kick. "Why not?"

"I . . . do you really think that's any of your business?"

"No." The wind was blowing hard against him. "But tell me why anyway."

"There's somebody *here,*" she hissed.

"No problem. I'll leave." But he didn't move. "Who is it?" He thought of the other two male therapists from the office. He thought of the men she might know from the psychology school in Berkeley—there were a few older graduate students in his own class, the class she'd taught for him . . . and what *other* men did she know? She'd been to bed with *him* three nights ago. Didn't she have any sense of—of—loyalty? "I'm coming in," he announced.

"No, you're not." She started to close the door.

"Yes, I am." He had to see, he had to know, he was going to drag the bastard off her fake fur bedspread—

"Joel!" She held up her hand. "It's a *client*."

He paused, with one foot in the doorway, wondering if he could believe her. "What are you doing, seeing a patient at home?"

"He's in crisis."

"Huh," Joel grunted. He looked down at the flowers. "Do you do that often?"

She drew up a few inches. "Sometimes," she said icily.

"Huh." He pulled a leaf off one of the gladioli.

"Aren't those for me?" Denise asked.

"Yes."

"Then don't ruin them." She grasped the damp violet paper that was wrapped around the flowers. "Yecch, they're wet." She shook out her hand. "Why don't you come back in twenty minutes?"

She had put the flowers in a chipped vase on a chest of drawers. Joel, sitting in one of her drop-bottomed chairs, glumly loosened his tie, then took off his glasses to clean them, dipping into the underwater world of his myopia: The flowers were an impressionist painting, the blossoms were smudges of blue and white. He stopped rubbing his glasses for a moment, wondering, had he chosen blue irises and white gladioli because blue and white were Margot's colors?

"I'm too nice to you, you know." Denise came in with a tray, which bore a teapot and cups, all with the same picture of a tiger in a meadow, chasing a butterfly. She sat down on one of the big square cushions. "I mean, you don't call first, you just come over—" She frowned. "What happened to your button?"

He pulled on the black thread dangling from his sportcoat. "I lost it."

"God, you need looking after." Her tone was exasperated, but she was smiling. "It's a dirty job, but somebody has to do it."

"Was it really a patient?" Joel asked.

Denise unfolded a cocktail napkin and spread it on his lap. "Yes. I love to see you jealous. It's very tempting to take it as proof of love."

"I'm unreasonable and boorish."

"Yes, you are. Two of your more *appealing* qualities." She held the lid of the teapot while she poured. The liquid was almost blood-red. "That's why I'm trying really, really hard to stay mad at you, but it's not working."

"I'm glad."

"Honey?"

"I beg your pardon?"

"Honey in your tea? I don't have any cookies. Sorry."

"I don't want any tea, thanks."

"It's hibiscus. It stimulates your liver and reduces stress." She extended the cup.

"I don't know that my liver needs stimulating, but all right, thanks." He sipped. The steam fogged up his glasses. He held the cup lower, and the lenses cleared to the sight of Denise pouring her own tea. A woman pouring tea—what could be less erotic than that? But maybe hibiscus acted as an aphrodisiac, too, because he was starting to feel aroused; a strange, feverish sort of arousal. Denise's head was level with his thigh, and he had the urge to stroke her hair, but if he touched her like that he wouldn't be able to stand it. And she might be angry, as if that was all he had come for. His desire was completely illogical, when he was hotter on Margot's trail than ever, but it was invading him as ferociously and inconveniently as a virus. He had to talk about something neutral, just to distract himself. "Do you think it's wise to see patients at home?" he asked.

She dribbled honey into her cup, then licked the spoon. "He called me here a little while ago. I don't think it's a big deal."

"I don't know. It's—there's the therapeutic frame, and you need to keep it secure. I mean, *one* needs to keep it secure, not you in particular."

She clinked the spoon against the rim of the cup. "I think that's one of those outmoded analytic ideas. What difference does it make where we are, as long as he knows I care?"

"Sometimes the people who care the most about each other do the most damage."

"That is *so* cynical."

"No, it's not. It's like being a surgeon. If you *care*, you'll sterilize your instruments." He heard his gears grinding into Automatic Lecture, but he forged ahead. "You've got to be consistent. Patients want love, but they need limits, too. You need to isolate the transference, you know, separate his needs from yours—"

"And I think," Denise interrupted, plunging her spoon into the honey jar again, "that you should stop trying to enlighten me on your preferred method of therapy."

He sank back. "You're right." *I'm lecturing myself.* After all, what had he just done with Betty? Hypocrite! But that was exceptional. He wouldn't do it again. Look what it had led him to, though! Maybe Denise was influencing him more than he realized. Maybe that was even good . . . ?

Denise put the second spoonful of honey straight into her mouth. "Why don't we change the subject?" she offered. "I can tell you're depressed. Tell Dr. Walters all about it."

He smiled. "Do you want to get the sandbox out?"

"Sand *tray*. I'm not charging you for this, but you have to be a good boy." She helped herself to another spoonful of honey. "I'm not sure it wouldn't do you some good. The thing about the sand tray is that it isn't so left brain. It taps more into your spiritual side." She squinted at him. "I know what you're thinking. But Jung started out as a Freudian."

"That's right." Joel reached for his tea. "And Jesus started out as a Jew."

"You're going to have to loosen up a bit," she warned. "At some point your unconscious is going to need to compensate for all this thinking. You've got to acknowledge your Shadow, not keep running from it."

"Are you trying to enlighten me on *your* preferred method of therapy?" Even with Betty, he'd stayed with the couch.

"All right, all right." She let her spoon clatter to the tray. "Why did I eat all that honey?" she asked.

He couldn't resist the urge any longer: He leaned over and stroked her hair, which felt as sleek as her furry bedspread. "Truce?" He felt her nod. "What's amazing to me is how otherwise very decent persons can instantly change into raging assholes as soon as they get sexually involved with someone."

"Speak for yourself."

"I was."

She was silent a moment. He kept stroking her hair. "No, I do, too," she sighed. "I get so possessive—"

"Haven't you heard? It's a proposed category for the DSM-IV. Sex-o-assholia. The diagnostic criteria include increased levels of paranoia and sleep disturbance."

She hugged his leg and laughed softly. He liked her so much, he really did. Unfortunately, the way she was hugging his leg, he couldn't reach her breasts without appearing like a sexist pig with the usual thing on his mind. You had to make it appear natural.

"It's good with us," she was saying wistfully. "We balance each other. I know you like me, because you keep coming back."

"Of course I like you." Did they have to go over this again? He wouldn't have asked her out if he hadn't liked her. (Or had she asked him, the first time? Well, he wouldn't have said *yes* if he hadn't liked her.) He'd always found her attractive, too—dark and soft and voluptuous—but as soon as he had sensed her making more permanent plans for them, he had begun finding fault. He didn't like the way she almost always wore black. He wished she would pluck her eyebrows. He thought her hairstyle was too old-fashioned.

Uncharitable, petty criticisms. As long as they were just friends, she didn't have to be perfect.

Margot wasn't perfect, either. He knew that—but he knew it the way he knew that the earth was hurtling through space around the sun. In the meantime he thought of her with the longing a Southern Californian can feel for that same sun during a summer in San Francisco. That warm, dry heat you can count on.

He sighed.

"I heard that." Denise let go of his leg. "I know what you're thinking about. *Whom* you're thinking about."

"No," he lied, "I was thinking of Ted, actually." And the image of Ted came to him: cringing on the sofa in his bathrobe. Joel realized guiltily that he had "forgotten" to return Ted's distress call about the Cleveland Gestapo. No accident, that.

"How's he holding up?"

"Not well." Joel tried to look stoic. Martyred, maybe.

"Any news—on *her*?"

"Well, *since* you asked . . ." He told her about Rosa's Mustang being found in the Mission; about his visit to Danny and the lead to Rosa's friend Chuck.

"That sounds like our next stop then."

"'Our' next stop?" Joel asked innocently.

"You don't mind if I come with you, do you?" Kneeling, Denise was gathering the cups onto the tray. "I'm curious about all this myself."

Number 1101 Guerrero was one unit of a triplex, a few doors from a Kentucky Fried Chicken stand. The odors of grease, salt, and something that might have been chicken wafted over to where Joel and Denise stood on the porch.

Joel rang the bell. No one came, but he could see a distant light shining through the dirty lace curtain that covered the beveled glass in the center of the door. He rang again. The curtain moved slightly, and after another moment the door was opened by a bare-chested man in jeans. He had a broad, high forehead and a pointy yellow beard; he wore a small gold cross around his neck, and held a trumpet in one hand.

"Sorry to keep you waiting, pal. I didn't hear the bell." The man held up the trumpet. "I was practicing."

Joel introduced himself and Denise, explained that he was a friend of Rosa Avera's, and that they were looking for someone named Chuck.

The man scratched his hairless chest. "I'm Chuck," he said. "But I don't know no one named Rosa. You mean Rosie, maybe? There's a Rosie lives down the street, next to the Buddhist temple." He started to shut the door.

"Wait," Denise said. "Can we talk to you just for a moment?"

"Ma'am, you're not selling magazines, are you? We already get *Time*, *Newsweek*, *TV Guide*, *Ebony*, *La Raza*, and the *New Republic*. My old lady tells me if I get any more she's going to beat the shit out of me. But they sell 'em to raise money for Big Brothers, and I'm a pushover. I'm also a large contributor to United Way." He pointed with the mouthpiece of his trumpet to a sticker on the door which confirmed this.

"What about Margot Harvey?" Joel asked. "Do you know her?"

Chuck shook his head. "I sure wish there was something I could do for you nice people."

"We don't have anything to sell," Denise pleaded.

"Maybe something you want to buy?" Chuck held the trumpet near his lips and played a silent flourish on the valve keys.

"That depends," Joel said. "You may not know, there's a large reward offered for information leading to the discovery of Mrs. Harvey, or to the arrest of person or persons responsible for her disappearance."

Chuck stroked his neatly trimmed beard.

"So if you happen to hear anything about Margot Harvey, or Rosa Avera . . . or maybe you know something about Ms. Avera's car, a blue Mustang? The police found it. They don't know who fenced it, though . . . yet." He added, "I got your name from a mutual acquaintance."

Chuck smiled. "Oh, you mean Rosa *Avera*. Shit, why didn't you say so, pal? I must have had her mixed up with someone else. I used to know a lady named Rosa Avera. Hey, come in." He opened the door wider. "My old lady loves to have company, she's a regular hostess, she'll fry us up some food stamps."

They entered a long, dark, high-ceilinged hall with all the rooms off to one side: a railroad flat. Battered Halloween decorations—cardboard ghosts, witches, and pumpkins—were taped to the walls. The only light came from the kitchen at the very end.

"I hope you didn't think I was unfriendly or nothing," Chuck told them over his shoulder. "You can't be too careful in this city. You never know when people are going to turn out to be ax murderers. Or IRS auditors. Prissy!" he shouted. Then, over his shoulder again, "You'll like my old lady. She's what keeps me going when times get rough."

They entered the kitchen. A long-limbed, emaciated woman stood at the sink with her back to them. Her spine, visible under a skimpy tank top, was curved and knobby.

A little girl—Joel guessed she was about three—squatted under the table, rattling one of the legs and making a growling noise that sounded remarkably like a dog's. The black T-shirt she wore, with the picture of a heavy metal rock band, came down to her knees. There were magenta half-moons under her eyes and a red stain around her mouth.

The sight of her made Joel's arms tingle. He knew right away that there was something wrong with her, something more serious and specific than living with two adults who were no more qualified to care for her than Joel was to make a night landing on an aircraft carrier.

"This is Basha," Chuck said. "Prissy here is her mom—her father got killed, so now it's like she's my own daughter." He called out again, "*Priss!*"

The woman turned around slowly. Her mouth, like Basha's, was stained with red, and Joel saw that she was eating a pomegranate. She had very pale red hair, light blue eyes, and skin so white that it was tinged with blue: as though she had been washed too many times. Her arms were marked with short ridges, which might have been from a needle.

Joel glanced from Prissy to Chuck. He didn't like the smell of things here, not one bit, and he wasn't just thinking of Basha's obviously unchanged diaper. But it was an ancillary benefit of practicing psychotherapy that you could maintain a neutral expression under most circumstances.

Chuck smacked his lips against the side of Prissy's head, which had the hint of an hourglass shape. "These are some nice folks from the DEA." He winked at Joel and Denise. "Just a little joke. We're always putting each other on. Come on, honey, wake up. 'Nightline' is on pretty soon, you don't want to miss that." He gave the woman a gentle shake. She bit into the pomegranate, squirting juice on her tank top.

From beneath the table, Basha hissed, catlike, and swiped at the air with her hand. Her head, too, was slightly indented at the temples, as if she had been delivered by forceps and it had never quite regained its natural shape. Joel wondered if she could talk. She might be autistic. He bent down to her. "Hi, Basha."

"When was Rosa here?" Denise asked. "Was it in the past couple of days? Was Margot with her?"

Chuck laughed. "Did I say that Rosa was here?"

Joel straightened. "Did you meet Rosa, Prissy?" he asked.

Prissy turned slowly, like an old horse who recognizes the sound of the stableboy. "Yes," she said finally. Her voice was low and lugubrious, a monotone.

"You're too smart for me, pal," Chuck laughed again. "I was just having some fun with you. But you knew that. You're smart folks. I bet you have letters after your name that I wouldn't even be able to pronounce."

Basha was imitating a siren now, first the warble, then the Klaxon. Denise started toward her. "She just does that," Prissy explained, "It don't mean nothing."

"*Was* Margot with Rosa?" Joel suddenly grasped at the frantic hope that Rosa was still here—out on an errand, or even in another room—and that Margot was with her.

"This place is like the Motel Six, you know?" Chuck interjected. "But cheaper. I don't charge. I like to help out my friends. So, Rosa's a friend of mine. I let her stay here for a while. She said she was in trouble."

"What kind of trouble?" Denise asked. She had knelt down beside Basha, who had lain on the floor and wrapped her tiny thighs around the table leg.

"I don't ask my friends what kind of trouble they're in," Chuck said indignantly. "I'm not like one of those Pacific Heights shrinks. I mind my own business."

Joel stiffened for a moment. *Chuck knew who he was.* Rosa had told Chuck—or even Margot had told him!—enough about Joel that Chuck recognized him. That was good, somehow, he was sure. He was flattered.

"Now, now," he said placatingly, "a good friend wants to know what his friends are up to. So he can help out. Like maybe if she had a car they had to get rid of. Or maybe if she needed some cash. You look like a generous man."

"Nah—I just try to help out, that's all." Chuck had lit a cigarette and he modestly waved smoke away from his face.

"I think Basha needs changing," Denise muttered. "Do you have any more diapers, Prissy?" She addressed this to Joel.

Prissy tossed what remained of the pomegranate into the sink, as if she hadn't heard.

Joel nodded at Denise. "Why don't you help Prissy change Basha, and then I can talk to Chuck."

"*Eeeeeh, eeeeh.*" Basha scuttled deeper under the table, away from Denise's arms. But Denise crawled after her and gripped her around the waist, and Prissy, with a small shove from Chuck, followed them out of the kitchen.

Chuck opened the refrigerator, humming. "What can I get you, pal? You look like a Scotch-and-soda man. Too bad I polished off the Cutty last night."

"How about a beer?"

Chuck popped open a can of Coors, took an overflowing

ashtray down from the top of the refrigerator, and gestured toward the Formica table. He pushed the ashtray toward Joel. Among the snowy-gray cigarette ashes was the finer ash of marijuana and the tiny tips of several roaches. "Look, I got some real good weed here," Chuck said. "Grown on a farm in Mendocino. It's my cousin's place and he just grows enough for himself and his old lady, and a couple of friends. That's why he ain't never been busted. He gives me maybe two ounces from the harvest, because I saved his life in 'Nam. Best stuff you ever had. He fertilizes it with his *own* B.M., that's how dedicated he is. I bet you want to turn your girlfriend on, am I right? Uptown, where you live, they don't have weed like this."

"No, thank you," Joel said. He was perspiring and he hoped it didn't look as obvious as it felt. "Just tell me about Rosa."

"Rosa and me were friends, you know? We used to go dancing at Guadalupe's. Last week she called me up, said she needed a place to crash for a couple of days. No sweat, I tell her. When my friends are in trouble, I go out of my way. It's not a sex thing, either. We weren't like that, you know?"

"And was Margot with her?"

"Margot? Margot?" Chuck stroked his beard. "Is this the Margot you say whose husband is looking for her? Are you sure you don't mean Margie, the lady that makes the bootleg lottery tickets?"

Joel squeezed the can, and beer spurted up. Chuck laughed. *Maybe*, Joel thought, *if I throw this beer can in his face he'll know I'm serious*. But patience was Chuck's greatest advantage at the moment. Joel dredged up his most banal smile, the smile of a shrink making rounds at a locked-bed facility. "Margot Harvey has been missing for almost two weeks. I'm a friend of the family. Her husband was devoted to her, and now he's severely depressed. The police are looking, but I decided to scout around a little myself, just for Ted's—her husband's—sake." He made circles with his beer can; he didn't want to drink any more. "Any information you have would be very valuable to him." Let Chuck fill in his own zeros. "We could both benefit—if the information were true."

"What are you saying, that I wouldn't tell you the truth?" Chuck looked up at the ceiling. "That hurts me." He dropped his cigarette butt into the overflowing ashtray.

"Just tell me if Margot was with Rosa."

Chuck gazed at the ceiling where at least one spider was constructing some low-income housing of its own. "Say, pal, I guess it's true what they say about smoking too much pot. I can't remember what you said about a reward."

"That there was one."

"Yeah, sure, but how do I know I'm gonna get it? I mean, where does an alien go to register, you know what I'm saying?"

Joel produced a checkbook from his back pocket. "A guarantee," he said, signing the top check, "until you can collect." He thought he had something like a hundred and thirty dollars in his account—he never balanced his statement—but this information would be a bargain at the price. "I'll leave the numbers blank. What's your last name?"

Chuck guffawed once. "I'll take care of that part." He rubbed the corner of the check. "This your current address?"

Joel nodded.

"It's a pleasure doing business with you, pal." Chuck put the check on top of the refrigerator. "Now, I can tell you're a busy man, so I'm not gonna waste any more of your time. They were here together, all right, and let me tell you, you can have that rich do-gooder friend of yours. I'm a hospitable guy, I try to make this place nice for my guests, and what does she do? Nothing but complaints, complaints, complaints. I think she wanted me to get down on my knees and give her a fucking pedicure."

Joel could picture that, and for a dreadful second he sympathized with Chuck. Then everything was burned away by the heat of this news. "When did she leave? Did she say where she was going?"

"She split a couple of days ago. Dunno where she was headin'"—Chuck grinned suddenly—"she said something about the open road beckoning."

Joel doubted that, and was about to say so, when he heard Basha scream.

He was up immediately, following the sound into the next room. But in the hallway he collided with Denise, who held the squirming child in her arms. "It's okay now," Denise said.

Behind him, Chuck laughed again. "Basha don't like to be hemmed in with diapers. I think when she grows up she's going to be an urban guerrilla. C'mon, Bash."

Denise let Basha go; the girl dropped to her knees and sprang, froglike, down the hall. "Don't you get into my CD player!" Chuck went after her.

"How's Prissy?" Joel asked softly.

"I gave her the standard lecture about toxic relationships, and I left her the number of the women's shelter."

"Good." But what he meant was, *It's better than nothing.* He was remembering that Freud had once written something about how simply telling people what their problems were was like passing out menus to victims of a famine. "I guess we're finished here."

CHAPTER 12

TICKET TO MARS

Joel lay next to Denise in her dark bedroom. A few minutes before, his whole body had been taut as a violin string, all his energy funneling down toward that funnel which funneled into her. Even his mind had narrowed to a phallic corridor, too cramped for anything but fragmented images of naked females and their indistinct faces in the contortions of prolonged orgasms.

He was tired now, and satisfied; but still semi-erect, still a conductor of postcoital electricity. He'd come a long way in the few hours since leaving Chuck.

"Pretty romantic dates you take me on." Denise had laughed softly, as they pulled up to her house. The fog had thinned and the night was misty blue and still.

"Are you inviting me in?" Joel didn't want to go home. There was something so addictive about a woman's bed, the sleep-perfumed smell of it, as subtly, invidiously addictive as coffee—the tenacity of the addiction not apparent because the substance was readily available.

So he put his hands around her waist—her hips were curved at exactly the right angle—then leaned down to kiss her. *Love the one you're with.* He could think of at least two songs which offered that advice.

But tonight's lovemaking had been nothing like it had been at Aurora Place. Well, he had always been a traditional guy, really, with a fondness for the missionary position. Maybe it had been their way of reassuring themselves that they could still sing the standards together. Kind of like going to your high school reunion and having the band play "Bridge over Troubled Water." Predictable, but somehow still with a sense of discovery: kissing, fondling above the waist, fondling below, penetration. He made sure that she had an orgasm before he got too excited; she lubricated, and came easily (twice, he was pretty sure). He was lulled into feeling safe inside her, contained; where it was soft and snug, but not too.

He stayed there for a little while afterward, keeping his weight off her by supporting himself on knees and elbows. Then, as he slipped out and rolled off, he made a long series of guttural vowel sounds, which he hoped she would interpret as "thank you very much I enjoyed that if it's okay I'm just going to think my own thoughts for a few minutes now."

By the mooney light of the shadeless window, those thoughts were still sexual. Fleeting memories of adolescent fantasies. *Hump-hump-hump.* The perfect breasts of his first high school girlfriend. And Ted razzing him for going to Sherie Myer's parents' house one Sunday. *Watch out you don't get pussy-whipped, Joey.* The plaintive sound of Joel's mother saying, *Someday you'll get married and settle down.* The unconscious decision to prove her wrong.

Later, on Dr. Schneider's couch, trying to decide what to do about Sonja . . . *Are human beings meant to be monogamous? Didn't Freud suggest that sexual repression had been too easily accepted as the price of civilization?* And on and on, until he heard Dr. Schneider bark, *You're intellectualizing.*

Denise was breathing more loudly and regularly; he hoped she had dozed off.

Someday you'll get married and settle down.

At the Greek restaurant—almost two weeks ago now! —Margot had blinded him: the sun backlighting her hair, the shine of the gloss on her lips. . . . He'd wanted her so much then, he would have been happy to give up all other women forever. *I can't have wanted her that much or I would have gone with her that afternoon.* But how was he to know that she was giving him a once-in-a-lifetime, limited offer?

Still, you sorta have to wonder, Joey old boy, what you're doing in bed with Denise right now. Okay—what if a patient described this to me? Let's see—in bed with one woman while the one I "really" want is Somewhere Out There? He would say, *You want to preserve the fantasy image of the perfect woman in your mind.*

The thought froze the scene around him in all its blurry dimness. The pool of light from the window, the silhouette of a floor lamp against it—without his glasses, he could hardly tell that it was a lamp; its neck curved like an old woman's. He gripped the fake sealskin bedspread.

I'll prove that I don't think Margot's perfect. I'll think of something I don't like about her. Like that Jaguar she drives . . . drove . . . There's nothing wrong with a Jaguar, I guess, but it was like a piece of Kleenex to her—she could just throw it away and pull another one from the box. And the furs. I don't approve of wearing furs, the way they kill those animals. . . .

Perhaps it serves another purpose for you to long for something—or someone—you can't have.

No!

Maybe I did idealize her a bit. But everyone does that when they first fall in love. Pay now, get disillusioned later. My problem is that I haven't seen her since I fell in love with her, so I haven't been able to lose the fantasies gradually.

But why exactly—enough rationalizations already—why hasn't she gotten in touch with me in all this time? Even if she knows that Ted killed Melanie and thinks he might kill her, by now she could have thought of some way to let me know that she's safe.

Unless she was hiding from him so that he could prove the depth of his love by finding her. He could understand how Margot might want that. He hadn't gone to Carmel with her; *ergo*, she felt rejected. According to the mathematics of need, the original rejection was only the cube root of the act required in compensation. So she had set this task for him, something wild and romantic. QED. But what kind of woman would put other people—him—through this much uncertainty?

Margot?

Then there was the worst thought of all. That Margot had only said she loved him because she had found out about Ted and Melanie. That would explain why she had been in such a hurry that day to consummate not love but revenge.

But he couldn't face losing her—or even the fantasy of her—yet. He turned over on his side, toward the window. And he was close to finding her—he knew it, he knew it! He felt his heart speed up and put his hand superstitiously on his chest, as if pledging allegiance to this wish. This was that same slightly racy feeling that he sometimes had when a patient offhandedly delivered a key piece of repressed information. He had to keep loving Margot, because if he didn't, then maybe he *just wasn't capable of loving anyone.*

All right—he knew where she had been until just a couple of days ago, when Chuck had said that Margot had left. Though it was always possible that Margot had gone from Chuck's to the airport to get on a plane to Curaçao, Joel still didn't believe that she would remove herself from the action that way. There's not much point in punishing people for hurting you unless you stay to see them punished; and you can't get rescued unless you stay within reach of potential rescuers.

He was startled by Denise's hand on his arm. "How about some tea?" she offered. He was between her and the window; her face reflected the ghostly light.

"No, thanks."

"Calistoga? Cranberry juice? If I *knew* when you were coming, see, I'd have more in stock."

He turned over in her direction. "I'll just hold you." It felt good to squeeze her plump breasts against his pectoral muscles. He pushed the black hair off her face, then kissed the beauty mark on her cheek.

She turned her head away. "Don't."

"I like it. It's sexy."

"Joel, I want to ask you something."

Uh-oh. He loosened his hold on her.

She wriggled free, and propped up on one elbow. "If you couldn't be a therapist, what would you do?"

He chuckled, relieved. "That's easy. A travel agent. Your clients come to see you when they're happy. They tell you where they want to go and you send them there. When you tell them where Paris is, and what time the plane arrives, they believe you. You have brochures and itineraries. You can hold things like that in your hand, you know exactly what they mean. No one ever calls you in the middle of the night in crisis over whether to go to the Grand Cayman Islands. And no one ever looks at a ticket and says, 'You don't understand—it says Chicago but I'm really going to Mars.'"

"It's a metaphor, isn't it? We're all travel agents, really. Our patients want to journey into themselves."

He rolled on his back. "I guess you could say that."

"I know, I know. When I say it like that, it sounds so *California*."

"Well, you're right, too." And when he didn't hate his work, he loved it. Or was addicted to it, which wasn't quite the same thing. Either way, he added those hard-won letters after his name with a slight flourish. He sometimes wondered what he would do if there was a Communist takeover and psychoanalysis was banned as counterrevolutionary. Maybe he should have more self-esteem separate from his work, but still, he felt he *was* his work. He liked, too, that it didn't matter how old he got or what he looked like or, to a great extent, where he lived. If he were blind or in a wheelchair—even deaf—he could still practice. Have couch and Kleenex box; will travel.

Denise was curling some of his chest hair around her finger. "Okay, now we've got your work life settled. So where do you think Margot went?"

"I think they've gone on to another friend of Rosa's."

"Why not one of *Margot's* friends?"

In the darkness, without his glasses, it was hard for Joel to see Denise's expression; still, he thought he detected a smirk.

"Maybe she's afraid she can't trust them." He *scooched* backward. Denise's bed had no headboard, and he pulled the pillow up to support his shoulders. Then he groped around the top of the nightstand until he felt his glasses; it was time to put the world back into focus. "I'll go back and talk to Danny again," he said, though he suspected that Danny had told him everything he could.

He rested his hand on the back of Denise's neck. "Listen, I want to tell you something."

He heard her draw in a breath.

"It might even make you more understanding about why I didn't want to stay to have breakfast at Aurora Place."

"Oh." She bent a little closer to him, and the ends of her hair grazed his chest. They tickled. "I doubt that, but tell me anyway."

Joel described how he had found Melanie's purse in the suite, and Margot's ring inside the purse. "Ted's the only one who could have put them there. I gave it all to the police, but they haven't found anything else. Still, I just don't see it any other way."

"Why didn't you tell me about that before?" A reproach.

He pushed her hair back behind her ear. "You didn't give me a chance. Besides, I didn't know what I had until I could really look at it. But you see, I think Margot knows that Ted killed Melanie, so she's hiding out. She'd want to stay with Rosa, so that Rosa could spy for her, keep tabs on what's going on. Maybe she's even in touch with that other patient of mine that I told you about." He meant Betty. "I know you think that's crazy."

"Don't go by me."

"I hate to think about what might have happened. I feel guilty."

"Why do *you* feel guilty?"

"Well, for one thing, I'm Jewish. I feel guilty when I wear the red tie instead of the blue one."

"Oh—heh-heh—I know that joke." Pause. "You're not so religious, though, are you? You don't go to synagogue."

"No." He had actually joined a temple—there was one on California Street, just a couple of blocks from his apartment—but had never attended a single service. It was the kind of thing he thought he might do when—if—he had a family.

"I'm sort of interested in Buddhism," Denise said.

"H'm." *What a surprise.* He sighed. "I keep thinking I might have been able to stop this whole thing. I should have guessed when I saw Melanie that day."

"It's wasn't your responsibility."

"I never lost a patient before." It occurred to him suddenly.

"But you didn't really lose her."

"I wouldn't say that she was misplaced."

"I mean, she didn't kill herself."

"A lot of murders are really suicides."

"What are you saying, that there are no accidents?"

"What are you saying, that there are?"

Denise lay back and put her hands behind her head.

Joel stared into the mottled gray cloud of darkness above him. "It's a loss," he said finally. "She was really beautiful"—he thought he saw Denise wince—"and then I saw her after she'd been in the water, and it was pretty horrible." He tried to make it a joke: "I mean, I won't even go to mad-slasher films."

Not funny. But he was embarrassed to tell her about the nightmares that he'd had for several days afterward. They'd only stopped when he'd slept with Denise at Aurora Place. "Maybe if I'd never seen her like that, it'd be easier for me to deny what happened. And even if it was only once, she was still my patient."

"That's the trouble with all this Freudian stuff, you see. It just adds to guilt. Freud is like this harsh father-god. He believed so much in that because of his hang-ups about his own father."

"Let's please not start that again." He loved the way Denise had of reducing the complexity and brilliance of psychoanalysis to a few dismissively glib phrases.

Denise was silent. A loud, hostile silence.

Joel raised himself up on one elbow. "Maybe you can help me."

"I'm available for consultation at reasonable rates." Rising from the shadowy pool of her face below him, her voice had taken on an unexpected anger.

He decided to ignore it. "I think both of those patients of mine know something more than what they're telling me."

"I guess you'll just have to use your *fine* analytic skills," she snapped at him.

Joel sank down, so that now both of them lay on their backs, in the confessional position of the couch. *Okay*, he thought, *have it your way*. Applying the emotional mathematics, he was going to have to come up with a big apology for what he'd said a minute ago—and he wasn't even sure what it was that he had said. Jesus, *she* was the one who questioned, over and over again, his entire *weltanschauung*.

After a moment she nuzzled against him. "I'm sorry. I get nasty when I feel insecure. Maybe if you and I—"

"That's okay," he interrupted. "My fault." It wasn't—but that was all right, if it put an end to it.

"So tell me," she went on, still in the conciliatory mode, "how did Margot's ring get to Aurora Place?"

"Ted must have brought it back there. My theory is that he gave the ring to Melanie, and then after he—he got rid of her, he reported it missing. He thought that the hotel was the best place to hide it, because Margot had been there and it might look like *she* left it behind."

"But what about Melanie's purse?"

"A purse is a purse. There was no ID in it. At first, I thought it might be Margot's, too."

"H'm." Denise tapped her fingers on his chest. "Didn't you say that Ted never went to Aurora Place?"

"That's what *he* said," Joel pointed out, a little irritably. "Why, do you think he'd admit it?"

"No, but . . ." Denise shrugged. "I just don't see it. He just doesn't seem like the type to kill someone, even if he was drunk."

Joel looked at her, uncomfortably suspicious that she was making excuses for Ted. Surely *she* wasn't fooled by him, too? "Do you have any *other* explanations?"

"No."

She wasn't suggesting Margot had anything to do with it? That wasn't possible, because—no. He wouldn't even try. Joel was an accomplished architect of those elaborate, gravity-defying edifices of rationalization that are just as fragile as they look. One topple and you fall to your death. For once he was going to rely on instinct, and his instinct told him . . .

Denise had started rubbing his stomach. His *lower* stomach. And speaking of death, a certain friend of his was making a surprise return from the grave. One more for the road? Making love with Denise might be immature and irresponsible, but like a compulsive eater who'd eaten forty-one Oreos, he saw little point in leaving the last one in the package. Tomorrow he might find Margot; everything might change.

But Denise had her hand around the base of his now-erect companion. "You're not thinking of going home, are you?" She was smiling.

He reached down to squeeze her soft, plump behind. "I was thinking of a lot of things," he said, "but not of that."

At the office, early, he listened to his messages. There were already three from Ted. Joel wouldn't have even expected him to be awake for a few hours. "Joey, aren't you *ever* at home anymore?" the last one began. "Wouldja *please* give me a call?" Then, in a whisper, "They won't leave me *alone*."

Joel felt a shiver down in his intestines. Ted spoke in the quavering tones of a very guilty man. And who was it who wouldn't leave him alone? Maybe Ted was starting to hallucinate: Melanie's ghost come to stand naked before him and taunt him into permanent impotence.

Then Joel remembered "the Cleveland Gestapo," and his guess that that referred to Melanie's parents. Joel grinned. Parents—

the two-headed revenge! This would be worse than any ghost.
Ted could hardly talk to his own parents. If he hadn't felt much
sorrier for the Hardwickes, Joel might even have felt sorry for
Ted. No wonder he was screaming for help. Well, that was too
damn bad.

The fourth message was from Emory Epcot: "Not sleepin' at
home these days, eh, Doc? Give me a buzz when you get in. I'm
lonely without you." This was followed by a loud *smaacck*.

And finally, another message from Andrea: "Oh, hi—was that
the beep? Dr. Abramowitz, this is Andrea Griswald, and I can't
come in today because, because—I'm not feeling well, and my
mother wants me to help her clean out the garage."

Terrific. Maybe her next excuse would be, "A UFO just
dropped on our lawn and my mom wants me to stay here until the
FBI can come." The smell of resistance was enough to make you
gag. He rewound the tape. Why was he so tempted to call her, to
insist that she come in? He knew he had that kind of power over
her, and that power was a sacred trust, one that he must refrain
from abusing. Always, always . . .

He dialed Emory.

"I need you," Lieutenant Epcot told him. "Tomorrow."

"I'm flattered. Did you have anything in particular in mind?"
Classic defense: humor against anxiety. Joel ran his hand over his
cheek, grateful for the electric razor he had stashed in his bottom
desk drawer.

"*Very* particular. It seems the higher-ups, in their infinite
wisdom, are thinking of dropping the charges against your
buddy, Commander Tequila-Head."

"What?" *Can't you people do anything right?* "What's the
problem?"

"The evidence is too circumstantial. None of Ted Harvey's
prints are on the ring or the purse. *Yours* are, I might add, but
that's another story. The driver's license on the beach, that was
enough for an investigation, but not for an indictment."

"What do you mean, not enough?" Joel demanded. "How did
the purse get in the hotel room if Ted didn't put it there?"

"Ho-ho! Don't we sound a little defensive!" Emory affected an
elevated tone. "How did the Jaguar get on the cliff? How did the
body get in the water? Hey, Doc—how did the moon get in the
sky? I ain't God, you know. I ain't got all the answers."

"All right. What can I do?"

"Come to the preliminary hearing tomorrow. I didn't think we'd need you, but we do. You can testify to all your little suspicions."

Emory made him sound like a busybody neighbor with a pair of opera glasses. "What time?"

"One. Come to the Marin County Civic Center Hall of Justice. Room 195A. They'll tell you which courtroom."

"I'll be there."

"Good. Now do me a favor. Between now and then, think as hard as you can about how weird Mr. Harvey was acting about all this and little things he might have said about Miss Hardwicke that make him sound good and guilty." After a pause that Joel was sure was meant to be ominous, Emory added, "I need a suspect. I don't really care who." Sniggering: "I want to do a screenplay of this, and I can't figure out how it ends."

"Just make it happy," Joel sighed.

"Oooh, den we can awl cry." Emory blew him a final kiss.

Joel sank down in his chair. He was ambivalent about Ted going free. Convinced as he was of his guilt, part of him wanted to drag Ted by the collar, out of his Seacliff house and down California Street, to the nonexistent town square where he could stand him on a scaffold and cry, *J'accuse*.

But if there wasn't enough evidence for the state of California, why was there enough for Joel Abramowitz, Ph.D.? *Because I've known him for fifteen years*, Joel thought. *The state of California hasn't*.

Suddenly Joel thought of Andrea. A one o'clock hearing meant that he'd have to cancel his Wednesday appointment with her. He couldn't change it, because the rest of the day was already booked up—in fact, he'd have to cancel a couple of other people, too . . . so he had to call her.

He reached for the phone again, but didn't pick up the receiver. Instead he tapped his knuckles against his teeth.

Analyze the impulse. Don't act it out. At least don't act it out with a patient.

But this meant he wouldn't see her until Thursday . . . and what if she could tell him something else about the accident she had witnessed that would settle—if only for Joel himself—the issue of Ted's guilt?

The buttons of her phone number played the first seven notes of *My Country 'Tis of Thee*.

Mrs. Griswald answered. "Who is this?" she demanded when he asked to speak to Andrea. "Do I know you?"

"This is Dr. Abramowitz," he said, wishing that he didn't have to identify himself.

"Oh, is that so?" Mrs. Griswald hissed. "What has she told you about me?"

"Mrs. Griswald, if I could speak to Miss—"

"It's fate that you called. *I have to know.*"

"I'm sure you understand, I can't discuss your daughter with you."

"Just about this one thing, you have to tell me, please please please."

"Mother!" It was Andrea, on the extension. "If you don't hang up, I'm going to scream."

"If you told him what I did to the video recorder, I swear I'll—"

"Mrs. Griswald," Joel said firmly, "I'd like to speak to your daughter privately."

Andrea's mother began to cry, and hung up.

"Miss Griswald?"

"Y-y-yes?"

"I just wanted to let you know that I won't be in the office tomorrow." He flipped the pages of his appointment book. "So, let's see, since you can't come in today, that means our next meeting will be . . . "

"What's the matter?" she demanded. "Aren't you feeling well?"

"I've been better," he said, which was certainly true.

"You're not going to get sick on me, are you?"

"I hope not."

"You don't sound very sure."

"You mentioned on your message that *you* weren't feeling well."

"Uh, yeah."

"Could you tell me more about that?"

"I have a stomachache and a headache. Oh, and I feel kind of nauseous, too."

"I wonder if these feelings are caused by something you don't want to discuss."

"How can we discuss it if you're not coming in tomorrow?"

"I guess we can't."

Pause.

"Well, all ri-i-i-ight," Andrea said, her voice more nasal than usual. "I'll come in today. But I want you to know I'm feeling sicker already. I just hope I don't die in your office. When is our appointment? I swear to God I can't remember."

"Two-ten." He wasn't taking any chances.

"Two-ten, two-ten. I hope I can remember that."

"I'm sure you can, Miss Griswald."

He hung up, thinking, *Dr. Schneider never would have done that.* But Dr. Schneider probably never had a Margot to find, or a so-called friend who'd murdered his mistress. Besides, whatever you might say about autonomy, and professional ethics, and unconscious dynamics, the first thing you have to do is get the patient to come in.

Andrea flopped down on the couch; one pair of untied shoelaces flicked up in the air. "Wow, you really let me have it," she said. "I think you came down pretty hard on me."

"What specifically are you referring to?"

"This morning, on the phone."

"I came down on you?"

"Well, really on my mother." Andrea giggled. "God, is it any wonder I'm fucked up?"

"But you said I came down on you."

"Well . . . yeah. Not on the phone, though."

"When, then?"

"Well . . . you know." She balanced the heel of one shoe on the toe of the other. "Don't make me say it."

He waited.

"All right. There was a reason that I wasn't going to come in today. I was scared, because you acted so pissed at me last time I was here."

"When?"

"Oh, come on, you know."

He didn't. "Why don't you tell me anyway."

"Well . . . you know. This is hard. Okay. The last time— when I told you about—about—about how I made up that—told that story to the nurse at Student Health, about my father and my younger sister, and you said that I had made up a lie."

Joel had no idea what she was referring to. "I said you had made up a lie."

"Yes—don't you remember? I went to the nurse at Student

Health so I could get a medical excuse, so they'd let me take the exam I missed over again."

The antitrust exam.

Andrea snickered. "And the way I talked her into it was that I told her I'd just found out my father was molesting my younger sister, and you said, you don't *have* a younger sister." Andrea's voice rose defensively. "Well, that's not *my* fault, is it?"

Joel massaged his eyes under his glasses.

"You see, I could tell just how angry you were at me and that you wished I was dead." Andrea said this last very quickly. "So—there was a reason that I didn't come in for a few times there."

Joel wondered if he should just ask, *By the way, Miss Griswald, do you remember anything else about that night? I really need to know now.*

"But now I've had time to work it out."

"You've had time to defend against the feelings."

Andrea ignored this. "There was another reason I didn't come in, too. I—I have a confession to make. This is really awful." She twitched; a whole-body spasm that included jerks of her knees, elbow, and chin. "I—I—I—I followed you the other day."

"When?" he asked, more sharply than he intended.

"When you went running on Saturday." She cringed, her body sinking as deeply into the couch as the unforgiving cushions would allow.

Joel recalled how he had walked the last mile back along his route.

"I've done it . . . a lot," Andrea said. "You get this really intense look on your face when you run, like—like—I can't say it."

Joel wasn't surprised. And he knew that Andrea had her reasons. Unconscious ones—her need to keep him in view, to protect him from harm, to make sure he hadn't replaced her yet. But he felt invaded. Wasn't he entitled to have a life away from this? Before he could stop himself, he sighed.

"Oh, God," Andrea said. "I heard that. This is it. You're never going to want to see me again."

"How do you do it?" he asked. "Do you run, too? Or follow me in a car?"

"Oh no." She relaxed a little. "I can't run. I'm too fat, and I have weak ankles besides. You see"—and now she spoke with unmistakable pride—"you always follow the same paths. I can just lag behind and I know you'll always come back the way you went by. Sometimes I just hang out at that synagogue on Arguello, because I know you'll run past."

Joel rubbed his eyes.

Andrea resumed twitching, though the spasms were fainter now. She seemed to sense, at least unconsciously, that even this latest transgression was not the fatal one. God only knew what she'd come up with next! "You see, I realize now that I wanted to spy on you sometimes because it was like watching my parents make love."

"That may possibly have something to do with it." Even now, when his main concern was Margot, the story of someone's life was the one thing that could draw him out of himself. *This is the drug YOU need, Joel. Someone else's life.*

"So now that I've realized that—"

"But I don't think that's all of it."

Andrea hugged herself tightly.

"I think you want to make me angry at you."

"You *are* angry."

"You got your wish."

"Why . . . why would I wish that?"

"Maybe to keep me—us—from learning too much about you."

Andrea clicked her tongue a few times. Then she demanded suddenly, "When I didn't come in, why didn't you call to see if I was all right?"

"You mean when the parakeet had to go to the vet?"

"Yes."

"Did you think I was going to believe that story?"

"No . . . but you should have realized that it meant something more serious was going on."

"So it was a test."

"No! It was proof that you didn't care. I said to God, if Dr. Abramowitz calls to find out what's wrong, it will be a sign that he does care what happens to me. I mean, if I don't pass the exam this time, I could flunk out."

Joel tried to imagine God as a venerable but overworked CEO, taking Andrea's request from the IN pile. "Do *you* care?"

She stiffened. "What do you mean?"

"Do you care about whether you graduate from law school?"

"I'm just going because my father wants me to." Pause. "I

mean, I do care, sort of, but I identify law school with my father."

"So—"

"So you see, I also identify with my mother, and I can't reconcile the two, so I rebel by screwing up in school."

"And what if you just went to school for yourself, because you wanted to?"

"I don't know what you're talking about."

"I'm talking about what you want to do with your life for yourself. Not for me, not for your father."

Giggle. "If I knew that, I wouldn't be here."

"That's true, to some extent. But I think you know more than you want to admit."

Silence—a sullen one, sagging in the middle, like a hammock. Joel sank into it with her for a moment—and then what he had just said echoed in his mind, and he realized that it could apply to more than just Andrea's choice of career. He looked down at his hands, spread out on his thighs, and imagined silvery threads shooting out from his fingers, like a spider ejecting the raw material of its web. *Just ask her.* "I wonder if there's anything else on your mind about the day you followed Margot's car."

"I've figured that out, too," Andrea announced. "That afternoon—that night—that I followed Margot, or I guess it was really what's-her-name, but anyway, the Jaguar—it was like I was trying to recapture my past. I never told you, but my mother had a white car when I was growing up. So it has significance for me. I think I was thinking that Margot was like my mother, and I wanted to connect with her. It's Oedipal, because you're like my father and she's your girlfriend, so that's like her being my mother. Oh, and the other thing about the car being white is that it's like for a wedding dress."

"Sounds like you've got it all covered."

"Yes, I really think so." Pause. "Do you mean it?"

"Do you?"

"You could answer that one thing." Andrea sulked. "It wouldn't kill you."

He smiled, looking out his window at the old tree. How private it seemed in this room! You'd never think that there were seven hundred thousand people out there . . . most of them looking for parking spaces. "You like to hear the answer from me, even when you already know it."

Andrea exhaled air in a series of short puffs, a breathy Morse code. "I remember something else. I guess I hadn't really forgotten it, but—well, anyway. The car—the car that was following the Jaguar, the one that pushed it off the road, it was a big, funny car. One of those old two-toned monsters from the fifties. My grandparents used to have one, it was green and white. I think this one was just like it, but it was too dark to see the color."

At first Joel thought he hadn't heard correctly. "Red and white?" he asked after a minute. He was seeing Danny polishing the Buick, and remembered his modest claim, *I'm a good driver.*

"Could have been." Andrea hesitated.

"Are you sure? I mean, about its being that kind of car?" *God, it's hot in here all of a sudden.*

"I got a pretty good look when it pulled up alongside me." She paused. "Why don't you believe me? Why would I make that up?"

"I do believe you," Joel said. *I just don't want to.* He looked down at his hands again. They were gripping the arms of his chair, as if the world had turned upside down and he was trying not to fall off.

Andrea rubbed her shoulders against the cushions. "Well, I'm glad to hear *that*." She tilted her head back slightly. "You like it when I remember things, don't you?"

Sometimes. Oh sometimes. That is what I said, isn't it, that I wanted you to remember. If only I could forget it now.

Margot killed Melanie.

Fragments of Andrea's continuing monologue still reached his brain. "Remember when I remembered" . . . "my father said" . . . "I never did, but he's a sleaze. . . ."

Margot had killed Melanie.

Margot had killed her—but in the sanitized, all-loose-ends-handled way she might have purchased a furnished house or have paid for a tour guide to meet her in Europe.

No. There must be more to it than that. Margot couldn't do that. She might be spoiled, even selfish, and she must have hated Melanie, but she wouldn't kill her. . . . Except that she didn't—she had Danny do it. And the way Joel knew, the thought that was making his stomach roil, was this: Margot *just loved* to help clean up after a party, and she would hold a drooling baby against a new dress, and coo, *awrn't you a pwecious widdle young person?*—but if anything really unpleasant came along, there was Merlin or Rosa or Mrs. Tuttle, or even Joel himself, to take over.

So if she wanted to get rid of Melanie, she'd pay someone to do it, and she wouldn't have to see it done, any more than she would concern herself with what happened to her dirty clothes after they went into the hamper. This was death the way it happens in a child's mind: A person goes away and never comes back.

"Should I do it?" he heard Andrea demand.

"I'm sorry. What did you say?"

"You mean you weren't listening? Oh, God, am I that *boring?*"

"I was distracted," Joel admitted. Once again he looked down; his hands had become fists. Now they uncurled, the palms like the bottoms of little bowls, to hold the truth.

"Well, that's pretty fucked," Andrea said. "But at least—it was nice of you to admit that you made a mistake for once."

The urge to laugh descended on him quickly, and he succumbed. Not that there was anything funny. It was just tension, bubbling out of him in a stream.

Andrea giggled nervously in response. "Should I do the research for my father's new case, is what I asked you. I get so grossed out every time I read about the way this guy's arm got cut off at the elbow when the plane crashed. And my dad's not even going to *pay* me."

Someone else's life. They had twenty minutes left.

At the end of the session he started to say, "I'll see you tomorrow," when he remembered the hearing. "I'll see you Thursday," he amended.

Andrea sat up, but stayed on the couch. "You're not coming in tomorrow?" She looked at him directly, which she seldom did, narrowing her small green eyes.

"No."

"You don't seem sick."

"Let's hope not."

She bent over to tie one of her shoelaces. She was far too old to be his daughter, and much younger than his sister. There were calluses around her cuticles; her nail-biting had not been alleviated by two years of therapy, and he felt sad about that—because when he said he would see her Thursday he felt that he couldn't be sure that was true. He couldn't see that far ahead. Andrea's information had turned his map of the world upside down and he was still too dizzy to choose another road. Maybe some sadistic travel agent would come along and pull the map from his hands entirely and say, You're on the wrong planet, stupid. . . .

Andrea pulled the ends of the shoelaces tight. Still she did not leave. "You look sort of worried," she said. "I'm scared you *are* getting sick."

Joel didn't know what to say. Under no circumstances could he have promised to see Andrea forever; he was just as vulnerable to disease and muggers as anyone. But now he couldn't predict at all where he would be in a few days. Because Margot needed him more than he had realized, even when he had been his most worried about her.

If he didn't see Andrea again, what would she think of him? Would she be on someone else's couch in a few months, telling the story of her abandonment, rightfully furious at him, regressed to her pretherapy stage? He even felt a moment of jealousy— another analyst would hear all those secrets, secrets more naked than flesh, confessions more lasting than love.

He leaned forward, businesslike, elbows on the arms of his chair. "If something happened," he said, "something external, which made me unable to see you, then you would think that you caused it."

"You mean—like if you were sick."

"Yes. For example." By now she was probably convinced that he had pancreatic cancer at the very least. "Something that I didn't cause or you didn't cause—something that might have nothing to do with you, or even with me." "Huh." It was almost a laugh. "I guess I would."

Andrea shrugged. Then she smiled. "I guess I'm pretty egocentric, aren't I, Dr. A? I always think everything has to do with me. Well"—she got up, tugging on her heavy white sweatshirt—"see you Thursday."

He followed her to the door, as always. He noticed that her other shoelace was coming untied. She looked over her shoulder—this, too, was customary—to glance a silent, timid good-bye at him. He nodded. Then she was gone, and he closed both doors behind her.

Now what? Joel turned back into his office, stood in the middle of the room; sat down, jumped up again, opened the window, paced. He had all of about four minutes until he had to be able to focus his attention on his next patient.

Danny polishing the Buick Super. Danny would have known how to get hold of the car, or help Rosa get hold of it. And one of them, or both of them, or all three of them had followed Melanie down Highway One.

Joel stared at his bookshelf. *Non-cognitive Approaches to Moral Development. Object Relations in Psychoanalytic Theory.* The letters on the binding of the books seemed to grow very large.

Rosa had made Danny do it. Rosa had that kind of power over Danny, the threat of the "place where they give you the shocks"—and the years and years of bullying. So she'd figured out a way to get the Buick out of the Crown Garage. That would have been the car least easily traceable to Margot that was available right away. So it was really *Rosa's* fault. Rosa wouldn't have done it for revenge, but so that Margot would be bound to her, the same way Danny was. That was it! Now Rosa, who had always skulked after Margot, resenting Margot's power, would be the one in control.

And finally Joel had his explanation, why Margot hadn't gotten in touch with him. She was ashamed to ask for his help, afraid she couldn't make him understand. Maybe even afraid that Joel would turn her in, because she would hold herself accountable, even if Rosa hadn't been pummeling her with guilt, convincing her that she *was* responsible. Delicate, sheltered—what did Margot know about crime? She'd be disoriented, paralyzed, and as time passed, she would become less and less able to act.

Joel imagined Margot sitting in one of the torn chairs in Chuck's flat—her arms limp, her hands quiet. Her pupils reduced to pinpoints, the irises awash in blue. And Rosa bent over her, caressing those downy arms, those small hands. Rosa's waist-length hair covering her like a black sheet. Rosa's braces glittering.

Rosa had probably not even told Margot about the "accident," until it was *fait accompli. Don't worry. I took care of it for you. We'll go away, you and me.*

But we were only going to hide out for a little while, Margot would have protested. *To give everyone a scare. We weren't going to do anything like this.* Her heart-shaped mouth would barely move as she spoke.

I only did what I knew you wanted me to do. Rosa would have serenaded her, stroking her hair. *You couldn't let him get away with it and still respect yourself.*

That was what Rosa had said to Margot to persuade her to

leave Ted. According to Ted. But Joel could believe it—and believe that Margot would let Rosa take her further than that. Women always blamed themselves when they first learned that their husbands were having affairs. They came to Joel then, convinced that they were the ones who needed help. They were stunned. They put lettuce in the dishwasher; they wandered into traffic. Fix me, they begged, so he'll come back. Margot would have been in this weakened state. Usually strong-willed, she could have been tossed about as easily as a beach ball. And though that would have lasted only briefly, by the time she linked up with gravity again, it would have been too late.

By now she might even believe what Rosa told her, that she had *wanted* Danny to strangle Melanie, that *she* had arranged the whole thing. Rosa could even point out the intelligence of the scheme: that Danny couldn't be held fully responsible for his acts.

So that was why Margot had gone to Chuck's with Rosa— out of fear. Poor Margot, completely surrounded by ene- mies . . . by Rosa, whose devotion would have rolled over to play dead by now, rolled over to show the repressed belly that lies under all obsessions . . . Rosa who would torture her and blame her and hate her.

But Joel would rescue her. Find her, take her away, hide her. They could assume new identities. If there had been inequities between him and her—her money, for example—this would even things out. She had something to hide, and more to lose. God—he was no better than Rosa, then, exploiting Margot's guilt! No— this was different. Wasn't it love which healed? Denise thought so. *Don't think of Denise.* How could he explain this to her? *Denise always suspected Margot.*

Margot didn't do anything wrong. Not really. It's not possible.

You don't want to think it's possible, he heard the voice of the analyst inside his head say.

Shut your goddamn mouth, he replied to the analyst inside his head.

Even if there was some hope she was innocent, he had to find her before he could know for certain. Besides, even if she was involved, did that mean she was entirely at fault? Everyone was capable of murder—didn't he know that? Rosa had taken advan- tage of Margot at the moment she was capable.

He sat once again. It was time for his next appointment, but he needed just another minute to himself. *Ladies and gentlemen of the jury, everyone is capable of murder.* Joel was a middle-class white male, raised to believe the policeman was his friend, and he was living in one of the most liberal cities on earth. But he also had a lot of Jewish memories tacked to the walls of his DNA, little warning signs that said THE COSSACKS ARE COMING.

He and Margot could leave the country. Curaçao—wasn't that where she was supposed to be? Maybe in ten years he could learn enough of the Spanish Creole dialect to practice there. But how could he leave *them*? How could he leave the only thing he ever wanted to do?

He tapped his knuckles against his teeth, then looked at his watch. Maybe the very worst of it was knowing that he had been unfair to Ted: He'd squeezed the evidence into the crime he wanted Ted to have committed; to get him out of the way— guilt-free. Although there were still unanswered questions about that—the driver's license. *But Melanie might have taken Ted's wallet when she left him that night. She'd have wanted money to spend.*

Enough now. Joel gazed at the tree, emptying his mind into it, then got up. Someone was waiting for him.

Apparently the gardener had still not been back to Ted's house. The ivy hung more densely over the walls and the lawn was ragged. Joel imagined the neglected foliage growing thicker and higher until he had to hack his way through with a machete.

"Joey!" Ted embraced him. Joel, startled, was aware that something was different a moment before he realized what it was: Ted was actually dressed, and his hair was combed. But he could tell, from the slurring of Ted's words and the strength of his embrace, that Ted was already pretty swacked.

"Thank God you're here," Ted murmured, still holding on to him. He whispered in Joel's ear. "You'll get them off my back. They're like the Furies. Oh, Christ."

Even if Ted *were* innocent, Joel didn't care for having his nose pressed against the stale cotton knit of Ted's polo shirt. Besides which, Ted was sweating vodka—and whoever started the rumor that vodka was odorless never tried to pickle his internal organs in it. Joel disengaged himself and went ahead into the living room.

There, in the pit, was a middle-aged couple: Melanie's parents. Mrs. Hardwicke was surprisingly petite, tanned as Melanie had been, with honey-blond hair worn down over her shoulders and a skimpy white dress, reminiscent of a tennis outfit, that exposed the brown-patched skin of a sunken chest, draped with half a dozen gold ropes. He could see the outline of her skull emerging under her cheeks and forehead. She sat with her hands tight around her kneecaps.

"Are you this shrink I keep hearing about?" Melanie's father was long-legged, like Melanie; an athletic man, in a light-blue suit with white stitching on the lapels. He strode across the pit toward Joel.

"Mr. Hardwicke?" Joel held out his hand. "I'm Joel Abramowitz. I'm very sorry about your daughter."

"Sorry, my ass. You pimp! Why didn't you do anything to help her?"

Joel froze, hearing the accusation he'd heard so often from himself. "I wanted to," he said.

"Crap!" Mr. Hardwicke's features—hawk nose, thin lips— would have been dignified in repose, but now they worked violently, the lines darting in and out around his tanned skin. "You're a pimp!"

"Try to stay calm," Joel said softly, also thinking, *I'd better let him stay mad.*

"It wasn't really Joey's f-fault," Ted slurred. He had staggered after Joel and now he leaned against him, gripping his arm as if to give him moral support, but clearly needing him as a lamp post.

"Somebody's going to pay," Mr. Hardwicke boomed, like William Jennings Bryan defending the Bible. "I'm an important lawyer in Cleveland, and I'm going to make this sonofabitch pay for this."

"Mr. Hardwicke," Joel began, "you're very angry—"

"Talk to Dr. Abramowiss," Ted suggested, "and you'll feel mush better." Ted had never once before referred to Joel as "doctor." In the part of Ted's brain that still resided here in Seacliff, he probably had some idea that Joel could have them beat the sofa cushions in order to get-in-touch-with-their-feelings.

"What have the police told you?" Joel started to ask. But suddenly he became aware of Mrs. Hardwicke's contained, wheezy breaths. The sound reached him like a siren from many blocks away—and he went over to crouch beside her. "I am so sorry, Mrs. Hardwicke," he said.

Mrs. Hardwicke raised her upper lip a little. She seemed to be testing to see whether, if she spoke, her mouth and nose and other body parts would simply fall off. "She was the best at everything. She was a winner. A star," she said finally, without looking at Joel. He noticed that she had same faint underbite that Melanie had had. "I—I just can't believe it. When am I going to start believing it? That's what I'm scared of."

"Don't think ahead." Joel took her hand. "Just think about this minute, this second." He squeezed the hand—it felt bony, old. "Just think about right now."

Melanie's father clutched the material of Ted's Lacoste shirt; Ted wobbled in his grip. "I came here to bury my daughter," Mr. Hardwicke said. "Do you know what that means? Do you have any *idea* what that means?" He gave Ted a shake with each word. Joel even heard Ted's molars clicking together. "I'm going to make you know, you sonofabitch. I swear to God I'm going to make you know."

"Joey!" Ted called.

Some worn-out reflex almost got Joel to rise. But not quite.

"We *didn't* bury her." Mrs. Hardwicke lowered her head. She had pinned a large white bow at the back of her hair. "We had her cremated." She began to cry softly. She pulled her hand away from Joel's to cover her eyes. "Lawrence wouldn't let me see her first. I let him talk me into not seeing her. Now it's too late."

"Do you have many friends, back at home?" Joel asked.

"Thass right. Dey should go back home."

Mr. Hardwicke gave Ted another shake. "Maybe you California weirdos think that it's okay to screw each other in hot tubs, but I'm an important lawyer in Cleveland and we don't put up with this kind of bullshit crap. I'm gonna see you hang by your balls."

Take a photo for me, Joel thought. While Melanie's father was raging at Ted, his own grief would be postponed. *And better he thinks Ted than Margot.*

Ted made one concentrated effort and was able to loosen himself from Mr. Hardwicke's grip. He staggered back to the bar where he hastily gulped from a glass of watery-looking orange juice. "Dere gonna drop the charges tomorrow," he said, wiping his mouth with the back of his hand. He sloshed more orange juice from a carton into the glass, spilling much of it. "Vitamin C. *Verrry* importan'." He slumped against the counter.

Mr. Hardwicke didn't move. After a moment he said, "If they drop the charges, then I'm going to kill you myself. I wouldn't mind getting hold of your wife, either. The smartest thing she ever did was take a powder on you."

Joel studied the white pleat of the skirt of Mrs. Hardwicke's dress, feeling like something more than a minor shit for not telling them everything, rationalizing that if Ted hadn't slept with Melanie in the first place . . .

"The policeman told us that they were having an affair," Mrs. Hardwicke confided to Joel in a hoarse whisper, "and he strangled her."

"I *dint*. Joey, tell 'em I dint." Ted had his back to them, and he leaned forward over the bar—probably both to keep upright and to find the vodka. *As if we don't know what he's doing!*

"She wanted a horse when she was thirteen," Mrs. Hardwicke went on, "but we didn't get her one."

"It's okay," Joel murmured. "It's okay."

"See? I tol' you iss okay." Ted took a few cautious steps back toward them. "*I'm* feeling mush better." Then he tripped, landing facedown on the sofa that bordered the pit of the living room.

Mr. Hardwicke bent over him. "Get up, damn it!" He pulled on the back of Ted's shirt. Ted rolled off the sofa, onto the floor. His heels, elbows, and butt made a series of little thuds as he landed.

This finally got Joel to rise. He leaned over Ted. "That's it for him. He's out for a while." *Get him upstairs to bed. Make sure he doesn't choke on his own vomit. Call the paramedics.* Joel's hands, prodded by impulses that had worn grooves in his brain, even reached out to take Ted by the shoulders, to start to lift him up. But once he touched the cotton of the shirt, he stopped.

No. No more.

"Listen to me, Doctor-Feel-Good," Mr. Hardwicke boomed. His finger machine-gunned the air, peppering Joel with invisible shots. "I'm going to sue you for malpractice, I'm going to sue—"

Joel ignored him. He was hypnotized by the sight of the unconscious Ted. He wondered if he would see Ted in a mortuary the way they had seen Melanie; he wondered if Ted would die the way Margot's father had. But he wondered about it in the way he might have if Ted had been a case history that a student was presenting.

Then he heard Mr. Hardwicke turning on his wife. "You encouraged her! You told her to go to New York! *That's* when the trouble started!"

"I did not!" Mrs. Hardwicke raised her own voice for the first time. "You drove her away! She hated you!"

"You turned her into a tramp. This never would have happened if you—"

"You didn't let me see her! Why didn't you let me see her?"

Joel took one last glance at the comatose Ted, then looked away.

"Don't do this," he said to the Hardwickes, just loud enough to interrupt them. "Don't do this to each other. It's a terrible, terrible thing, and it isn't either of your faults."

"She—"

"He—"

"Can't you be good to each other?" Joel asked. "Can't you at least *try* to comfort each other?"

Silence—for half a second. Then Mr. Hardwicke seemed to compress, like a spring, and then just as suddenly uncoil. "It's her *own* fault! *I* told her not to go to New York! This wouldn't have happened if she'd listened to me!"

Mrs. Hardwicke had hunched over and was sobbing again.

"I'm so, so sorry," Joel said. This was what things always came down to. Pain without recourse or explanation. *And Margot did this to them.*

"I told her to come back from New York! I told her not to go out to Frisco. It's fairyland out here. Even that policeman was queer as a three-dollar bill."

They deserve to know what happened. Tell them.

No, no, that won't do any good. And I don't know for sure.

But if Margot did do this to them—how could anyone forgive that?

Mrs. Hardwicke rubbed under her eye with the heel of her hand. "We've been going through her things." Her eyes were light brown, shallow-set. Joel tried to remember what color Melanie's eyes had been, and couldn't. "She had lovely things, and all of them were clean. But then we found a"—her mouth moved silently for a moment—"a vibrator." She held out her hands. "A *huge* vibrator."

"And we read her diaries. *Pornography.* That man corrupted her."

Joel was silent. He sat down, halfway between Melanie's mother and the heavily breathing Ted.

Mr. Hardwicke kept pacing. "We were good parents," he mumbled. "We didn't let her date until she was seventeen. It's television. She wanted to be like those jiggle girls on TV."

Joel nodded. Silence was what an analyst did best, but it was more than just keeping quiet. You harnessed and tamed silence; and if you did it right, you could bring down the walls.

For another fifteen minutes Mr. Hardwicke ranted and Mrs. Hardwicke wept. When they started to blame each other again, Joel reminded them that they shared this loss equally. Too early to tell whether their relationship would survive. If he'd known Melanie longer, he would know more about her parents, too.

And he thought about Margot. He had carefully constructed that image of Margot and Rosa together, and it returned now: Rosa stroking Margot's paralyzed arms. Margot couldn't have known. She couldn't have done this on purpose. He would never believe that, never, never, or his head would explode. Or he would be on Mars himself, no bearings, no direction, no hope of getting back to the places he knew.

Finally, he said, "I'm sorry to have to leave, but there's someone I need to see." He carried a few professional cards in his wallet, and a pen in the inside pocket of his jacket. "Here's someone to call, if you want, while you're in town." On the back of his card he wrote the name of a colleague.

Mr. Hardwicke *harumphed*. "It's all bullshit. Crap."

"Please." Joel held out the card. When Mr. Hardwicke stopped blaming everyone else, he was probably going to start blaming himself, and then his nightmare would truly begin. "Now would be a good time. Just to talk a little."

"No, thank you," Mrs. Hardwicke squeaked.

But Mr. Hardwicke took the card.

Joel looked at Mrs. Hardwicke, at her soft blond hair and perky outfit. He suddenly remembered that Melanie had told him her mother's name was Shirley. "I am so sorry," he said once more, and tried to put into those four words everything he knew about how badly this was going to hurt. "Where are you staying?"

Mrs. Hardwicke murmured, "At her apartment."

"Get out of there," Joel said firmly. "Check into a hotel. God knows we've got enough of them." Levity? "Really. Please. Go do it now."

"What about him?" Melanie's mother asked, raising her eyebrows at Ted.

"He can rot in hell, for all I care," Mr. Hardwicke said.

Joel looked down at Ted. "I'll call his lawyer," he offered. "He can take over. Meantime, let's just leave him there." Ted was probably dreaming of a successful PR firm, of Melanie's long blond hair, of his own mighty manhood, and of a world in which the tenth whiskey sour has the bite of the first. "He must be comfortable on the floor, because he sleeps there a lot."

CHAPTER 13

OPERATORS ARE STANDING BY

That night, unable to sleep, Joel fretted about what to do next. Andrea had given him all the information she had. There was still Danny to try, but maybe the clue had to come from Margot herself.

What, what, what? Once again, he sifted through his history with Margot—but he'd sifted through it so many times, he was sick of his own memories. The baseball games. The cocktail parties. The plays she took him to, giving him Ted's half of their season tickets, always with the explanation that Ted had to work late—an explanation he pretended to believe, rather than hurt her feelings or risk unbalancing the triangle. Seven years of agonizing flirtation. Now he was embarrassed, looking back on that stint as Good Friend of the Harveys. Was it as obvious to everyone else as it was to him, now? He never should have left New York and Dr. Schneider. But there was Sonja to get away from then. . . .

It suddenly occurred to him that he should have called Denise. He wasn't even sure why, since he had nothing in particular to report. Anyway, it was too late to call her now.

At 2:00 A.M., he got up to go running. He quickly decided on Route One, the shortest of them, without extensions: to Alta Plaza and back.

Shorts, sweatshirt, shoes, street. *Thud, thud, wheeze*. The rhythm was always comforting. It was still a little foggy, and predictably cold.

Halfway to the park he had an idea.

Carmel.

Didn't it make sense? She wanted him to go with her, he wouldn't—so she went there herself, to *make* him come after her. But that was the unconscious part. Consciously, she was trapped with Rosa and scared to come home.

That had to be it—he was sure of it now! He ran faster, raising his arms as if about to break through the ribbon at the finish line. And the finish line was Carmel. But where would she be staying there? There must be hundreds of those OceanVu bed-and-breakfasts with paintings of orange sunsets in the foyer. *Thud, thud, wheeze.* The dark, grassy slopes of the plaza loomed in front of him, but his brain was just reaching that level of oxygen saturation which caused it to ignore the impact of concrete on his spinal column. *Keep going.* One more extension. Maybe two. He ran past the deserted park higher up into Pacific Heights. It was one of his tougher routes, but he didn't notice the hills or even the darkness.

Danny might know where they'd gone. Danny! He'd hardly thought about what Danny must be going through.

Joel was at the Crown Garage when they opened at 7:00 A.M.

"Bring that car back?" R.B., the mechanic, did not look at Joel, but eyed the Dodge Colt like a man at a singles bar who still hasn't scored at last call.

"I've got to talk to Danny."

"He don't work here anymore." R.B. stuck his head back under the hood of a car.

"Did you fire him?"

"Nah. Some lady came and got him, day before yesterday."

"Rosa Avera?"

"Those Japanese all look alike to me. I fought 'em in the war. Now they're driving me out of business. If you ask me, Harry Truman should've nuked the whole country back in forty-five. Then we wouldn't have these little tuna cans puttering all over town." He snorted, "Maybe I should say *sushi* cans."

"Danny is Filipino," Joel corrected him, though why he was bothering, he wasn't sure. "They didn't say where they were going by any chance, did they?"

From under the hood, Joel heard a few squeaks and then a clang. "Are you kidding? I don't want to know. That boy's been nothing but trouble."

In the murky corner of the garage, Joel saw the red-and-white Buick sitting still and quiet, like a sleeping cat.

Some lady came and got him, the day before yesterday. Joel tried to console himself with the fact that by the time Andrea had told him about the Buick, Danny was already gone. So it wouldn't have mattered if he had come straight to the garage then, as he should have. Still, it made him almost nauseous to think of Danny with Rosa. If Rosa could frighten him enough so he would kill for her . . .

Joel had new black-and-white footage in his head, grainy scenes of Margot cowering in a cheap hotel somewhere, while Rosa rode along the dark road, shouting to Danny to pass Andrea's Toyota. How could a fifty-seven Buick catch a Jaguar?

I put a new engine in myself, R.B. had said.

And the scuffle on the beach . . . Danny would only know that he had to do what Rosa said. Joel thought of Danny polishing the car, his gentle and rhythmic movements. He was bigger and stronger than his sister. All that power he didn't know he had—he could have turned it against Rosa instead, but he didn't, because Rosa was his goddess, tormentor, and only savior. What a little transference can do.

Joel left the Crown Garage and headed to Playground. He had found the charge receipt from Aurora Place in Margot's desk, so there might very well be one from her favorite place in Carmel, too. And here he'd thought that he'd been so much a part of her life that he would know these things about her. Talk about *el jerko* . . .

The building was unlocked. Joel entered and found that the parlor, usually full of children, was empty. The room looked smaller without them: A few toys lay scattered about, mostly damaged—a dirty beach ball, pages torn from coloring books, a doll missing an arm. The carpet was covered with brown stains.

He climbed the stairs, disturbed by the silence, wondering if Mrs. Tuttle was in Margot's office.

When he turned the corner at the banister, he was startled to see a skinny woman in a dress with a sailor-suit top sitting behind Margot's desk. Her shoe-polish-black hair was pulled away from her face and topped with a sailor hat, while reading glasses, trimmed with mother-of-pearl, balanced on the end of a long nose, courtesy of a nylon cord around her neck. "Who are you?" he asked, too abruptly.

"Well, who are *you?*" the woman demanded in return, but accompanying this was a shrill peal of laughter. She was flipping through a Rolodex—*Margot's* Rolodex.

Joel introduced himself. "I'm looking for Mrs. Tuttle."

"Oh . . . Mrs. Tuttle is no longer with us," the woman said. She lowered her head to look at Joel over the top of the glasses. "Are you a relative?"

"No." Joel suddenly remembered who she was. "You must be Mrs. Stone." The board member who had been appointed interim president in Margot's absence. He had argued with her about Playground. "We spoke, remember?"

"Oh!" She clutched the pearls that hung from her neck and laughed again, shrilly and at some length.

"Where are the kids?" Joel finally interrupted.

"Oh, the *kids,*" Mrs. Stone gasped. "Well, you know, the board has decided to temporarily suspend the child-care division in favor of more community outreach."

"More community outreach?" Joel glanced around the office. There were things missing, but he couldn't say what. "What does that mean? Going over to their houses to tell them to keep their bikes off the lawn?"

"Dr. Abramowitz, if you knew how hard I've tried to save this place, you wouldn't be so critical!"

"Then tell me what's been going on."

Mrs. Stone gave the Rolodex a few nervous flips. Now Joel realized that all of Margot's snapshots had been taken down. How dare she!

"Well, for starters, I had to let Mrs. Tuttle go. If Margot wants to go to the Caribbean for a vacation, that's perfectly understandable, especially in light of certain events, but . . ." Mrs. Stone bent deeply over the desk; her pearls made a loose figure eight against it. "Well, I shouldn't say any more," she whispered, "but I've been auditing the books, and I'm shocked, completely and utterly shocked. Those fund-raisers and—and *galas* Mrs. Harvey was always putting on—they were just an excuse for her to get her picture in the paper, if you want my opinion. The events lost money and she secretly made up the difference herself."

Joel realized now that Margot's old file cabinet had been replaced with a new one of solid oak. He thought the drapes were new, as well. He hoped some charitable interior decorator had contributed them. "If she made up the difference, so what? The important thing is that she helped a lot of kids."

"She *used* them. *And* she used Playground funds to cover her own trips and expenses!" Mrs. Stone pulled open the top drawer of Margot's desk. "I just finished cleaning out a rat's nest of charge receipts—"

Now Joel bent over the desk. "You did? Where are they?"

"I got them ready to mail." She leaned back away from him, indignation coiling into suspicion. "My accountant will want to see them."

"Are they here?" Joel quickly began to shuffle through a stack of manila envelopes and loose papers on one corner of the desk.

Mrs. Stone batted at his hand. "Leave that alone! I took them out to the mailbox already." She added snippishly, "We should have secretarial help to do that kind of thing, but we can't afford it."

Joel looked at the envelope in his hand; it was addressed to the San Francisco Education Fund. He was not so far gone as to think that Mrs. Stone had purposely mailed off the receipts to keep him from Margot. That must be the act of an even more devious force. Lucky he didn't believe in God.

"Sorry." He tossed the envelope on top of the pile. Then he gazed at the shelves, at the places where the pictures of Margot had been, and the picture of her father—and the pictures of her with Ted.

It was time to leave.

But he stopped in the doorway. "I wish you luck here," he said. "I hope you can do some good things."

"Oh, I have nothing but confidence!" Mrs. Stone called after him cheerfully. "Feel free to stop by anytime!"

Joel left Mrs. Stone in Margot's office, and left Playground, suspecting that he would never go back.

He drove to the office, retracing the path he had followed just two weeks before, when Margot had called him. In the length of a block, the neighborhood changed back to BMWs and croissanteries—and when he crossed California Street, he again noticed the black woman in fuzzy yellow bedroom slippers, leaning against the window of the pizza parlor.

Joel now had further evidence of Margot's profound terror. Otherwise she never would have stayed away long enough to let Stoneheart take over. Mrs. Stone had probably wanted the job for years, and Margot was plenty competitive about things like that.

After all, Margot's motives didn't have to be completely pure. Whose were? What mattered was what you *did*. And if most of therapy is like being called to the scene of a five-alarm fire just as the last embers are dying, then with children, the blaze was just beginning to spread. You still had a chance.

Was he the only one who had ever seen to the core of her goodness? Granted, he had his own transference to her. Hadn't he acknowledged that at the very start? And the tricky thing about transference was that furry, repressed belly. So that best-friends-for-years might suddenly stop speaking to each other; so that, among the fans of rock stars, there sometimes lurks an assassin.

That was why, in the end, reality—with its dirty dishes and dusty corners—was always better than the fantasy: the *Architectural Digest* interiors, shot with wide-angle lenses, where no one could actually live.

Well, he was in for a dose of reality now, dirty dishes, dusty shelves, and leaky roof thrown in. In a few hours he'd be on his way to Carmel.

"I won't be there," Joel told Emory. "Something's come up." He scanned the office walls for the appearance of a compelling lie. "An emergency."

"What kind of emergency?" On the other end of the phone, Emory snickered. "Somebody break a nail?"

Joel's voice automatically downshifted to a bass. "You *know* I can't discuss that."

"Doc, Doc, you're breaking my heart." Joel heard him inhale on a cigarette. "Doncha want to see justice served? Can't you get some other shrink to cover for you?"

"If you don't have enough evidence without me, you don't have it with me." Joel wasn't worried about Ted. Ted would get out of it—as per usual. In the meantime, whatever Joel's unwillingness to blow the whistle on Rosa until he knew that Margot was safe, he wasn't going to help Ted get tried for something he didn't do.

And he knew that the hearing would provide him the cover he

needed. A head start. Time to get away. Once Margot knew that the charges against Ted were dropped, she might panic and run farther away—if she hadn't already. Hopefully Joel's neurasthenic Colt would make the two-hour drive south to the Pacific Coast resort town.

"Listen, Doc. Maybe you don't think this is serious. Maybe you think I don't care about solving this murder." Emory was using his raised-brow, single-eyed-stare voice.

"On the contrary," Joel said soothingly, "I think you care very much."

"Damn fucking right I do. I care enough to be very suspicious that you don't want to show up after all. I care enough to get a search warrant and ransack that little rabbit hutch of yours. I care enough to subpoena your patient files."

Joel gripped the receiver. To let Emory Epcot snigger over his careful process notes, discover his patients' secrets—*I'll flatten your face against a wall first. I'll burn them first!* "Just try it," Joel said before he hung up.

But Emory would try it, that was the problem. Should he attempt to stuff the God-knew-how-many files into his trunk before he left? No—they were all in file cabinets; there wasn't room, anyway. He'd have to take his chances. He couldn't prepare for everything—he didn't even know how the hell he was going to find Margot once he got there.

He sat down behind the couch, automatically reaching for his appointment book. He could go to the library and get the Monterey County phone directory, and just look up the names of hotels, motels, and bed-and-breakfasts. Maybe something would strike him. Otherwise, he'd just have to drive the streets of Carmel. Not an appealing image, cruising like a horny teenager . . . But still worth a try. Joel had been to Carmel only once (with Margot, Ted, and a former girlfriend), but the actual resort-touristy district, as he remembered it, was fairly compact. Then again, Margot might not confine herself to that part—she might have a secluded inland villa.

What else, what else? Ted might know where Margot liked to stay in Carmel, but Joel didn't want to alert him to where he was going. Would Denise have any ideas? Maybe, but he'd have to be a real shit to involve her at this point—not that he couldn't be a real shit.

He tapped his fingers against the appointment book. It felt so comfortable against his palm, almost an extension of his hand. It was just one of those black, faux-leather jobs, bought at an office supply store on Polk Street, but he examined it now as if it were the Dead Sea Scrolls. He thought of his process notes and the copies of insurance forms, already nostalgic for the texture of his daily life, the seldom-varied pattern of running, seeing patients, visits to the library, consultations with students; the classrooms where he taught, the chair he sat in to read. Once he left for Carmel, could he ever come back and pick up where he'd left off?

Anticipating the hearing, he had already canceled his afternoon patients—Andrea and a few others—but he still had people to see this morning. Well, who were those Last Patients going to be?

At nine: Arthur, three times divorced, twice bankrupt (bad real estate), the father of four; also a member of that rare species, a true bisexual. Arthur was unable to be faithful to wife number four, AIDS scare or no.

At nine fifty-five: Kathryn, receptionist at a law firm, young and beautiful and promiscuous, with the stomach cramps and migraines for which no medical doctor could find a cause, let alone a cure. And then there was her seven-year relationship with a man who would neither keep a job nor marry her, and who occasionally drove off, stranding her in bars or restaurants.

And sometimes people get better. Sometimes they get so much better that you want to cry.

And Betty Klass at ten-fifty.

Betty who said she got phone calls from Margot.

"A lummox, that's what Al was, a lummox."

Betty was lying on the couch. She seemed quite comfortable. Joel had been able, the first time, to take advantage of her initial vulnerability there, but today she had eased herself down like a swimmer equipped with an inner tube. Then she had sat up again, to pull her tote bag a little closer. As she dragged it along the floor by its strap, Joel heard metal objects clanging against each other inside.

"I don't mean he *was* a lummox. He still is."

"You haven't mentioned how long it's been since you and Al were divorced."

"Eight years. Or maybe it's a little longer than that." She sighed. "The time just slips away."

Especially when you can't let someone go. "Has he remarried?"

"She's a nothing. I mean, she's very pretty, but in that cute sort of way that no one likes. *You* might think she's pretty, I don't know."

"How long have they been married?" He wanted to orient Betty in the reality of her divorce—but he wouldn't go so far as to ask whether Al had had other children.

Betty stiffened. "Not that long. He doesn't really love her."

"You said that Al used to call you in the middle of the night."

"Yes."

"Have you had any other . . . phone calls lately?"

"Oh well, my phone rings a lot. Sometimes I'm too busy to answer—you know how people are, gab-gab." She tilted her head. "Why, do you think no one calls me?"

"I was just wondering . . ." He gazed over the top of Betty's wispy blond hair, which seemed to have a new strawberry tint. She was wearing patterned stockings and stiletto-heeled pumps. "Have you heard from Margot again?"

She stiffened. "No," she said sharply. "In fact, I've never heard from her. Did I say that I had?"

Joel felt his entire body go limp. Betty had lied, invented the whole thing, and he'd been so desperate that he'd believed her.

"I had a dream last night," Betty went on. "Do you want to hear it?"

"You can tell me whatever you want." His voice was hollow with disappointment. No, he told himself, it doesn't matter. I can still go to Carmel. I *might* find her there.

"I was trying to climb a wall. It was covered with vines, but I couldn't hang on to anything, so I don't know what was keeping me up. There was something on the other side I wanted. Then I heard a siren. So I had to hurry and get away. Then I was at the dentist's because I'd broken a tooth and needed a crown, but the dentist was you, but your name was Al." She tittered.

Dentist . . . Al . . . that old expression, *climbing the walls . . .*

Someone else's dream. Someone else's life.

Isn't it amazing? It's a vocation, a life's work, a passion that burns your fingers! NOW how much would you pay? But wait— before you answer—you also get a sense of accomplishment—

*AND this incredible vegetable steamer! Call now! Operators are
standing by to take your order!*

Could he hide with Margot, live in obscurity, someplace where
people wouldn't tell him their dreams? Or could he forge himself
a degree under a fake name?

"What does it mean?" Betty asked.

"Maybe we can find out together." Neutral. No promises.
Analytic.

"Oooh."

"What does the dream make you think of?"

"Why, nothing."

Joel himself was thinking of the toy that Betty had gone back
for; the siren she must have heard when the ambulance came.
Himself as dentist, fixing something that was broken. But he said
nothing. Figuring it out was the easy part—sort of, anyway.
Getting someone else to figure it out, to recognize it as his
own . . .

"My business is going very well, you know," Betty said
suddenly, her tone lighter and more confident. "I'm about to get
a big commission, the biggest job I've ever had."

"Can you say more about it?"

"No, actually I can't. The person said it was a secret. She wants
to surprise her husband. If I tell anyone I won't get it."

His nostrils flared. "It's a decorating assignment, though."

"Oh yes, a big, big house, a mansion. I guess it's okay to tell
you that, but please don't tell anyone. Heavens!" Betty's hand
fumbled at the cushions at her side. "You don't have a microphone
under the couch, do you?"

"No," Joel said, "I don't."

"I thought I heard a tape recorder clicking on."

"You're afraid of being overheard." Joel stared at the tree
outside his window. *Betty was talking about Margot.* She had to
be. No, he wasn't crazy, or maybe he was, but still—*Betty had
been in touch with Margot all along, from the very beginning!*
And now Margot had summoned Betty to her and promised her
a job in order to secure her silence about her hiding place. Margot
had needed Betty to spy for her—and she also needed Betty to
feed Joel clues, a crumb at a time.

Because Margot—who desperately wanted to hide—also desperately wanted to be found. It was called a compromise forma-
tion.

But that Margot would choose Betty—volatile, psychotic Betty—for such a job was more than disturbing: It was an indicator of just how frightened Margot was, how confused she must be. Maybe she was undergoing her own temporary psychosis.

"In the dream you're scaling a wall," he observed. His tone remained flat.

"It wasn't really the wall of a house, though. It was more like the wall of a castle. And . . . and there was something on top of the wall . . . broken glass." Pause. "I want this new job very badly. The fact is, it's been a long time since I've done a job like this, and I've just been living off my spousal support, and Al, that lousy louse, is always sending lawyers after me to find a way to cut it down."

Joel wondered if the broken glass referred to the windshield of the car that hit Robbie. He wanted to get into that, but it would have to be later. But what if there was no later? "In the dream, what is it you want on the other side of the wall?"

"It's not important. Do I have to tell you?"

Joel said nothing, but he had to keep his jaw very tight.

"All right. A doll. I guess there's nothing wrong with that, I just feel silly about it."

A doll—a baby. "You feel silly about wanting something you can't have."

"Well, of course," she snapped, "if I can't have it."

"You think that just because you can't have something, you should stop wanting it."

"Well, *yes.*" Long pause. "Otherwise you could go crazy from wanting it."

"Maybe you could just accept wanting it." Like all the fictitious decorating jobs. Like the relationship with Al, which was more in her head than anywhere else. Like pretending that her dead son received the letters she wrote. Because they never go away—all the things we want and can't have.

Like Margot?

"No," she said. "Never."

He smiled. An analytic *never* could actually mean never—or it could mean "eventually, when I feel safer." He looked at the clock. "We have to stop now," he said.

"We do? Are you sure?"

He hesitated. "Yes."

She sat up slowly. Her fingertips played with the ends of her hair. "I must look a fright," she muttered. Then: "Well, I guess I'll see you next week."

He followed her out. Is this what patients feel like when they terminate? He had long repressed his emotions about his own ambivalent termination. All he knew was that right then he did want to be with Betty, for *an analysis*, that long, long ride—all the excitement of a documentary on Finnish agriculture coupled with the safety of walking through the Tenderloin at night. The outcome as predictable as the weather in San Francisco.

"Well," she said at the door, "I'll see you next week." Her tote bag banged against the wall. "Oh, and wish me luck on that job."

After Betty left, Joel did something he had never done before: He lay down on his own couch.

It was an odd feeling. He had wanted to re-create the experience he had had sometimes on Dr. Schneider's couch, of being cared for and watched over—but to lie there with no one behind you was terribly lonely, the hollow feeling that follows masturbation, when there is no one to hold.

But if he lay on his couch, he would know what he needed to know from Betty's dream.

He closed his eyes. *Just let it come.* In the dream, Betty had pictured him as a dentist. That was a common dream representation among patients. In her case, it was especially appropriate—overdetermined—because Al was a gynecologist. Hands in mouth, displacement of genitals. He should have interpreted that to her—it would have released a new flow of associations. Now when would he get his chance?

Fixing a tooth. *Crowning* a tooth. Joel took off his glasses and reached behind himself for a piece of Kleenex to wipe them with. Crown. The decorating job she coveted would be a "crowning achievement." The Crown Garage? Wait, wait.

Joel sat up, quickly putting his glasses back on. Crowning a tooth . . . crowning achievement . . . and the insignia of Aurora Place was a crown over the cursive initials, AP.

Margot had gone back there. That's where she was now.

There was valet parking at Aurora Place, but predictably only for guests. Joel left his car in a garage in one of the big hotels on top of Nob Hill proper and walked down.

In the lobby, he headed straight for the assistant manager's office. But behind the marble-topped desk with the spindly legs and the cat's-paw feet, there sat, not Tami, but a dark, mustachioed man as thin and graceful as the table legs themselves. He had a great mane of curly black hair like a French poodle's, and he was examining his mustache in a hand mirror.

"Excuse me," Joel said, "there was a woman named Tami working here."

The young man slipped the mirror into a drawer and carefully placed the tips of his fingers together. "Tami is no longer on our staff, sir. How may I help you?"

Joel felt a stab of guilt. "What happened to her?"

The man stroked his mustache. "I'm sorry, but I can't give out any information regarding our staff. I'm sure you understand— *sir*."

Joel realized that it would be pointless to ask this man to use the men's room, let alone for an unofficial tour of a private suite. Better to come up with a more considered plan. If Margot heard that someone had been looking for her, she might move again, fearing that Ted or the police were closing in. "I'm an old friend of Tami's," Joel ad-libbed. He wanted to shift the focus of any suspicions the Mustache might have. "Um . . . I've been traveling and I guess we lost touch." He smiled, as a weary traveler might, and gave the assistant manager his card. "If you hear from her, will you tell her I stopped by?"

Who knew but that Margot might not be watching this whole scene on a closed-circuit TV? *Careful, careful, Joel.* Too much Betty-on-the-brain again.

Back at the top of the hill, he waited for an attendant to bring him his car. He wanted to talk to Denise. He *needed* to talk to Denise. There was no time to waste in analyzing that.

CHAPTER 14

REPETITION COMPULSION BLUES

Joel was out of breath by the time he got back to the office. He knocked on Denise's door, peeked in, and saw the room was empty.

He paced.

Then he saw Alex Forans coming out of the coffee room, carrying a pile of sugar packets which he no doubt planned to add to his paper recycling bag. "Have you seen Denise?" Joel asked, impulsively grabbing his arm. Alex pulled it away; Joel had forgotten how Alex hated to be touched.

"She said she was going for a *latte*," Alex told him, unconsciously rubbing his arm where Joel's hand had been.

Joel took off back down the stairs and ran down the street, his tie flapping over his shoulder. He saw her up ahead—recognized the shape of her rear end, and the blunt cut of her straight black hair. He recognized her walk, too, even from behind: the way she led slightly with her shoulders, and her determined pace.

"Denise!"

She turned around.

He was wheezing when he stopped beside her, though he ran a hundred times that distance every day.

"I found her," he gasped.

Denise blinked and looked at him as if he had just asked for spare change: that moment of deciding whether to say no and be a hardnosed citizen, or to say yes and contribute to his substance abuse. "Oh?"

"Yes. I mean, I think so." He didn't want to take the time to go back to the office. "Can we go somewhere for a minute?"

She tilted her head. "I was just going in here."

"Fine." He took her elbow, not paying much attention to where they were. On this block of Fillmore Street, there was one capuccino yuppiteria for every two pedestrians.

Denise swayed ahead of him, getting into the line. "She's back at Aurora Place," Joel whispered.

"Really? So what's the problem?" There was an edge to her voice.

"I can't get up to her suite. The security is tighter than a Middle Eastern airport." Joel only glanced at the designer pastries: the icing shaped into lemons and carrots; oatmeal cookies the size of Frisbees; the rows of perfect muffins. Jekyll-and-Hyde food: Women gushed over it, ate it with orgasmic sighs, and were suddenly transformed. *Why did I eat that? Why didn't you stop me?* Joel was still clutching Denise's elbow while she moved forward in the line; she puckered as she stared at those same pastries. He'd wanted to talk to her, for God's sake, not get a carbo high.

"So what do you want *me* to do about it?" she asked suddenly. Her finger squeaked along the glass of the display case, and she didn't look at him.

He let go of her elbow. What a bastard he was, really, asking her to help him again, when she'd helped him so much already. "Will you let me buy you something?" he offered.

"They're supposed to have authentic New York cheesecake here," she remarked sullenly.

"Whatever you want," Joel said quickly.

"Cheesecake," Denise told the teenager behind the counter, the one with the long pewter crucifix dangling from his ear. Then she looked at Joel, with unmistakable challenge. "Do you think I'm fat?"

"In what sense?"

"Do you?"

"I'm sorry. I don't think you're fat, no."

"*Zaftig?*"

He smiled. "Voluptuous."

A sign of relenting passed through her eyes. Joel knew that he could charm her into doing this, knew that he shouldn't. But he dutifully ordered a cup of coffee he didn't want, paid, and followed her with the appearance of docility to a table by the window.

He pulled out the chair for her. "What a nice blouse." It was peach silk—and he knew that when you consciously chose to give a woman a compliment, you'd better pick something you could genuinely compliment. Actually, Denise's style of dressing seemed to have changed, just in the past two weeks, from neo-hippie to Urban Feminine.

"It's the same one I wore to Beans," she said accusingly, and scooped a huge bite into her mouth.

This was like trying to get a woman to go to bed with you. The harder you worked at it, the guiltier you felt, and the more likely you were to fail. *To hell with this*, he thought. She'll either do it or she won't. "I want you to go back there with me."

She paused with another mound of cake in front of her already-chewing teeth. "Margot's probably holed up with enough chocolate-dipped fruit to last a month. I bet she sends Rosa out to do the laundry and to bring in videotapes. Sounds like a nice life to me."

"Will you?" Joel had a plan to get up to Margot's suite, but he couldn't do it alone. He needed someone's help, and he trusted Denise.

"You could at least be a little nicer about it." Denise plunged the fork into the creamy top of the cheesecake again. "But I'd say no, even if you were. I've realized that this whole thing is counterproductive for me. I thought you'd find her, and then you'd integrate the experience." She mimicked herself: "I wanted to be 'midwife to the birth of your anima.' But now I'm starting to think that you're just not going to individuate."

"I deserve that."

Mouth full: "You're afraid of your feelings."

"Which ones?"

She glared at him. "*About me.*"

"Ah." He humbly cast his gaze down into the oracle of black coffee.

Her fork clattered to the plate. "Why did you let me eat that?"

Joel smiled. "Because you wanted it. Because"— why not make a vice out of sincerity?—"you look terrific the way you are."

She leaned over the stump of cheesecake, putting her chin on her fists. But he pulled one of the fists toward him, unfolded it, wrapped it around his hand. "Denise, come help me just this one last time. You have every right to say no. But . . ." Denise might suspect that Margot had been involved in Melanie's death, but he wasn't going to tell her anything specific. That way she couldn't be implicated. *There ARE times when it's better not to know.*

"But *what?*"

"I need you now, and I don't have anyone else to ask."

Denise pulled her hand away. She picked up her fork, twirled it, gazed longingly at the cheesecake, then dropped it again. "I am such an idiot," she said. "But all right."

By 6:00 P.M., Joel and Denise were checking into Aurora Place for a second time. Once again, a bellman whose uniform out-ranked Prince Charles's escorted them to their room, which was on the third floor, as their last had been. This room was a mirror image of the other one: canopy bed, armoire, and fireplace all arranged in the same relation, only in reverse.

"Oooh," Denise crooned when they entered. As she scurried into the bathroom, and Joel tipped the bellman, he found himself wishing that she wasn't having quite such a good time. He could never understand her mood swings.

"It's funny," Denise observed, coming out a moment later, "how when I'm nervous, you're relaxed, and the other way around."

Joel was carefully arranging his socks in a drawer. He had overpacked his garment bag, out of a paranoid need to appear to be an actual guest planning an actual stay. After all, what if the Aurora Place Thought Police wanted to search his luggage? "We're not here to have fun."

"That's your problem, though." Denise flipped through the room-service menu. "You think that about everything." She tapped the menu. "I just made a choice. I decided that if I was going to come with you, I was going to have a good time. Whatever happens with you and little Miss Charity Ball, I'm staying here tonight—your treat—and I'm going to have dinner *sent up* to the room."

Joel reminded himself that he didn't want Denise to realize how serious this might be. Let her enjoy herself, for God's sake; she was helping him and he should be grateful. He hung his last shirt in the armoire. "Listen." He drew her away from the menu. "This is what we have to do first."

At the end of the hall there was a fire exit. With the obligatory glance over his shoulder, Joel went through it, into the stairwell, with Denise behind him. The walls and steps were concrete, the banister metal, painted green. Joel had almost expected thick carpeting and original artwork. So even Aurora Place had its grubby corners.

"This is creepy," Denise whispered.

Joel started climbing. Denise followed. They went up two flights, where Joel tried the door to the off-limits level, the way he might have stuck his finger into the coin-return slot of a pay phone. He knew it would be locked from the inside. The purpose of the fire stairs was to let people get out in an emergency, but once in the stairwell one could not reenter any floor without a key. Still, he rattled the doorknob one more time.

"If someone comes along and sees us snooping around here, he's going to be awfully suspicious," Denise pointed out.

"Who would come along? Unless there's a fire, in which case Margot will come along, too."

Denise sighed. "You know what this means, don't you? We have to walk all the way down to the street to get out."

"That's okay," he said trying to cheer her. "We're going shopping anyway."

They went down quietly. Joel thought he heard the faintest distant humming, and it reminded him of the noise he had heard just before he saw Melanie's corpse. He didn't want to think of her, or her parents, either. Even repression has its place.

It was five flights down to the lobby level, then an additional flight to a door which opened onto an alleyway that ran alongside the inn, perpendicular to Pine Street, which was busy and noisy at this time of day. Another wave of paranoia washed over him—what if Margot, or Rosa, saw them together? Even though Margot's suite was on the other side of the building, he pulled Denise a few feet closer to the wall. She frowned, resentful at being herded. "Tell me now if you don't want to do this," he said, stopping her.

"I do," she said. "I just want you to appreciate it."

"I do appreciate it," he promised. "I do."

Her face relaxed. "All right, then. Now what?"

"We have to buy flowers and masking tape."

"Masking tape?" Denise mouthed the words broadly; she looked fearful that he had finally signed up for one of his own joked-about excursions to Mars.

That made Joel laugh. Well, why not? "Pretend that we're going on 'Let's Make a Deal,' and the one thing that Monty Hall might want in exchange for a home entertainment center is a roll of masking tape."

They found masking tape at a corner grocery store, and flowers in the lobby of the Fairmont Hotel, where Joel bought a dozen roses.

"I have a feeling these aren't for me," Denise said, sitting on one of the red velveteen banquettes, near a sign welcoming a convention of dermatologists. The carpet was patterned with thick red-and-gold swirls. By contrast to Aurora Place, the Fairmont lobby looked like a bordello garage sale.

"These are for nobody," Joel said. "Nobody I know, anyway." He was noticing Denise's legs, in sheer black stockings. They were nicer than he remembered, not too long, but he liked the deep curves of them. He could not clearly picture what Margot's legs looked like. They must be shorter than Denise's, because Margot herself was a few inches shorter than Denise. He had always liked petite, dark women, perhaps because they were so containable, so easily held—or perhaps because his mother had looked that way when he was young, before she put on weight and let her hair go white. He wished he could make love with Denise just one last time. What if he told her that? She wouldn't like it, which made him sad. "You've got nice legs," he said. It seemed very important to say that, at least.

"Oh, shush," she said, looking pleased and irritated. "Let's get this over with, okay? Tell me what I'm supposed to do."

"I will, but—" He wanted to touch her, but it had to be on a part of her body where just-a-friend might touch her. And he wanted to say something definitive and profound, express his gratitude and—what? Say that whatever happened, he hoped they'd *stay* friends?

"And I don't want to talk about what's going to happen *after*, either," Denise snapped.

"Deal." *Ask her not to tell anyone what she knows, if I disappear after tonight. . . . No, no, leave her out of it.*

A tour bus had evidently arrived, because men and women who looked like dermatologists and their spouses were pouring in. White HELLO MY NAME IS tags floated past Joel's eyes, like the distant sails of a great regatta. He heard Denise: "You know, I hope you won't take this the wrong way, but I really don't want to see you hurt."

"Why should I—"

"Well, I don't know." She stroked the gold top of the flower box. It struck him that the box was coffin-shaped. "I mean, we don't know why she's been hiding out all this time, and—"

"That's okay." Joel put his hand on her wrist. That was a neutral enough place. He remembered how she had told him that "intuition was her dominant function." So maybe she *had* figured out what had happened. Of course, he'd told her about finding Melanie's purse, and Margot's ring.

He himself was still hoping for Margot's perfectly logical explanation. But if Margot was guilty, would he take her away, hide her? He didn't know. At least he could hope that he might see her soon, that she *might* be innocent, that she *might* leave Ted, that he might even get what he had thought he wanted— Margot herself. And that left him feeling blank, overcome by a sickening nothingness that could have been either fear or ecstasy.

The dermatologists were swarming past their banquette on either side, breaking into two columns like ants.

"Well, quit stalling, then," Denise said. "You've got to face her eventually."

Joel asked Denise to wait in the Fairmont lobby, while he got a head start down the hill. He didn't want them to be seen coming back together.

On his way up to the third floor, Joel surreptitiously tried to analyze the elevator operator. It was the same young man who had been there before: No more than twenty-two, he was blond, pudgy, and ruddy-complected. There were no braids dangling from his epaulettes. He at least *looked* like someone who'd be willing to enter into an Oedipal conspiracy with Denise against the hotel as displacement of Father.

There was a couple in the hallway (an older man with a svelte, much younger woman), so Joel stopped off at his and Denise's room, where he spent a couple of minutes pacing, looking in drawers, and rearranging socks. He noticed that the bedspread was wrinkled where he and Denise had sat. And Margot was just a couple of floors above him—he was sure of it. He imagined the smell of her perfume and felt queasy.

After checking to make sure that the hall was clear, he hurried back to the fire exit, hoping no one would see him. A fortunate by-product of Aurora Place's exclusivity was that there was usually no one around.

He remembered from his first visit with Tami that there seemed to be only the two suites on the fifth floor. The inn's floor plan was an L, with the elevator at the base. So the other suite, the not-Margot one, would have to be right next to the fire exit, out of the elevator's line of sight.

Denise was to come back to the hotel with the flowers and tell the elevator operator that she wanted to deliver them to that other suite. If he said no, or wanted her to go to the assistant manager, she would do the Woman Thing, nothing sexual, just some harmless wheedling: say, for example, that she really wanted the flowers to be a surprise, and point out that the elevator operator could even *watch* her as she left the box in front of the door and returned to the elevator. Joel wasn't particularly thrilled with this ploy, but if this was sleaze, he figured he had better make the most of it. And if it just didn't work, well—Joel would go back down to the alley and try to think of something else.

But if it did work, all Denise had to do was find an excuse to turn the knob of the fire-exit door—maybe when the elevator operator wasn't watching—just enough so that Joel could open it once she was gone.

Joel climbed the stairs slowly, counting the steps on his way up the last flight. Eight. A good number. A lucky number, he was convinced, though he wasn't sure why. Eight steps. Two flights per floor, times five floors, was eighty steps, but wait, wasn't there an extra flight between the lobby level and the exit to the alley? Ninety-six, then; he didn't like that number. He waited at the top, listening for the sound of Denise approaching. His hearing, at least, was excellent—genetic compensation for his eyesight. Did he get here too soon? Just his luck, the management would probably choose this as the night to have the first fire drill in ten years.

Another two minutes passed, according to his lethargic digital watch. Joel tried to remember when he had last taken his watch off. It was waterproof, so he even wore it in the shower. He sometimes took it off to have sex, but even then he felt nervous without it. Not as nervous as he felt now.

Finally—finally!—Denise's voice, very faint. "Just a second," he heard her say. She must be talking to the elevator operator. *Scritch-scritch.* She was coming closer.

"Ooops!" he heard her squeal. A thud against the door. She'd pretended to trip! Oh, clever, clever, smart girl. He wanted very badly to hug her. He had his hand on the doorknob, and when he felt it turn, he pulled it toward him, just enough to dislodge the clicker.

"Oh, God, I'm so clumsy." Faint *thwack* (the box of flowers on the carpet), then the fading *scritch-scritch* of her retreating footsteps. He heard another voice say something that could have been "All set?"

"Yeah, thanks!" Denise replied, a bit too loudly.

He waited another agonizingly slow thirty seconds. Then he opened the door. The gold-topped box of roses lay on the carpet in front of the door to the second suite. The hall was empty. Joel thanked God, just in case, adding a request for a few more seconds by himself there.

He held the door open with his knee, bit the masking tape off with his teeth, and taped the clicker down so that the door would not relock. If Margot *wasn't* there now, he'd be able to get back later, without having to come up with more of these stupid scams; he wasn't sure he was good for more of them.

He moved quickly, past the green-striped wallpaper and green parson's benches. And there he was, at the carved wooden door to 501. He used the knocker.

Nothing.

I know you're in there.

He knocked again. Should he pretend to be room service? "Margot," he said. It was as if someone else, standing behind him, had said it. "Margot, it's me. Joel." He pressed the side of his face against the wood. His arms seemed to embrace the door. His love would turn to fury in just a moment, he would kick the door, pound it until it collapsed, stand over it like a B-movie hero.

. . . And then the door swung open, so fast that he started to lose his balance. He saw Margot—she loomed in front of him, petite as she was—he registered the cloche hat and the blue lace dress before she snatched his glasses off his nose and pushed past him—before he could grab her—and ran down the hall back in the direction of the fire exit.

He sprinted after her. She was a bluish smear, and the walls on either side of him waved like long, green-striped sheets of water, but he could run faster than she could, even if he couldn't see.

The bluish thing turned the corner of the hall—it passed through the white patch, under the skylight, and resumed human form, only to dissolve again. She was pushing open the fire door. The EXIT sign above it was only a few green squiggles, like spinach noodles.

He felt the door hard under him as he pushed it open, but the stairwell was such cold empty space—and he couldn't see! He heard the clicking of her heels below him—the heels would slow her down—but the stairs were something from a fun house, soft as gray butter, melting under his weight. The green metal banister was just clear enough for him to grab. Over the edge, the stairs spiraled into nothingness. He clung to the banister and found the rhythm with his feet, counting the stairs on the first flight down—one, three, five, seven—*click, click*, he heard her heels, he even thought he heard her breathing, her heartbeat, but no, it was his—two, four, six, eight—at the landing he caught sight of the blue thing again, just half a flight below him—he still clung to the banister, but—*don't look over the edge!*—five, six, seven, eight—he was closer, and when she looked back up at him he could even tell that there was a face on top of the blue thing.

She must have seen him catching up to her, because she let out a little cry. There was something funny about the sound. She stopped for just a second before she started down the next flight—but that second was all he needed. He grabbed hold of something he hoped was her arm—it was—and held it tight. "Let me go!" she spat, and it wasn't Margot's voice.

Now a *clack*. She had dropped his glasses. Without letting go of her wrist, he groped for them with his free hand, and finally got them on.

Rosa. She pulled on her arm, but he didn't let it go. Now he used his free hand to pull off her cloche hat, and her thin black hair unwound itself, spiraling down, reaching her waist.

"Asshole," she spat at him. She raised her upper lip, and her braces glinted. "Why couldn't you leave us alone?"

Joel gave her arm a tug. "Where is she?" He had to move fast before someone heard them. It was lucky that they were so obsessed with privacy here—the soundproofing was as good as in his own office.

"Just let me *go*." Rosa tried to pull away. Then she tried to slap him, but he blocked her arm, and held her other wrist. "I'm going to scream."

"Scream that you told your brother to strangle her," Joel hissed. "Scream that you told him you'd do it if he didn't."

"You cocksucking bastard."

"Where is she?"

"She doesn't need *you*—asshole!"

Suddenly Joel knew. He let go of Rosa and bolted back up the stairs. He felt Rosa clutching at the back of his suit but he was too fast and the click of her heels quickly faded behind him. *Thud, thud, wheeze.* He was finally back at the fifth floor and—thank God for the masking tape!—the door had closed but he could still get in. He ran back down the hall.

The door to Margot's suite was slightly ajar. He stopped; his breathing a tidal wave in his ears. The door creaked as he slowly pushed it open the rest of the way.

Empty.

The room was empty.

The suite was as torn apart as Margot's bedroom had been. Joel took in the open drawers, the frilly pastel clothes strewn on the sofa and chairs. Even the drapes had been half-pulled down from under the valance. He turned around slowly, feeling as though his midsection had been cut out and his shoulders had sunk to his knees. Then he put his hand on the banister of the spiral stairway that Tami had said led to the roof garden. He knew—but he had wanted to be wrong, and there was a second, one entire, voluptuous second, when he simply refused to know.

And then he hit the stairs, climbing as fast as he could—there was a door at the top—he had it open, and ascended into sky. He saw a translucent, almost full moon risen against the deep blue, and the wind hit him so hard that his eyes watered, even under his glasses.

Margot had her back to him. She was about fifteen feet away, standing at a pink cross-hatch fence which was only about waist-high. She wore a thick white terry-cloth bathrobe that didn't cover her knees. Her legs were small, white, and pudgy, like a twelve-year-old's. She must be freezing. He remembered the night she had sat in the backyard in her halter top, how he had thought then that she must be cold.

He glanced around quickly. The "roof garden" was more roof than garden—just a few long planters among the lawn furniture, on green outdoor carpeting. The fence that surrounded the carpeting separated it from the tar and gravel part of the roof, but at the place where Margot was standing, the fence ran right along the edge of the building, so all she had to do . . .

She must know that someone was there. Why didn't she turn around? This was worse than he expected. He mustn't let himself get distracted. Everything must focus on this one thing. He would approach her very quietly, very slowly.

The wind slammed the door shut behind him.

She whirled. And when he saw her face, he couldn't quite believe that it was really her—she looked both more and less like what he remembered. His heart pumped blood to his brain until there were red spots within the borders of his peripheral vision.

She stared at him, her tiny mouth open. *"There* you are," she said finally. "Where have you *been?"*

"Looking for you." In the last few days, he had begun to think that he wasn't in love with her—but now he was, all over again. He ached with it. "Margot." In a moment she might disappear, the way she always did when he woke up. "I've missed you. Oh, God, I missed you. I'm so glad you're all right."

She covered her face with her hands, those small white hands. "All right?" she protested. "This is all right?"

Be real casual. "You're cold. Come inside."

She shook her head slowly. "No."

He started to move toward her. Goddamn this fucking wind! It was like someone shoving against him, over and over.

"Don't come any closer," she said quickly, uncovering her face. The wind made her short, curly hair dance on her forehead. "I just want you to help me work up the nerve—to just *do* it."

"Things aren't as bad as you think," Joel said, though he was thinking that they might be worse.

"Doctor, Ah am the best at *everything.*" She was doing her Southern Belle; she leaned with mock seductiveness against the fence, and even smoothed her hair with hands that showed signs of their old fluttering life. "Including getting myself in such a mess that theah is nothin' else Ah can do."

He gestured. *Like none of this is any big deal.* "C'mon, we'll talk about it."

She laughed. The sound made him shiver. "I can't stand that *room* anymore! I can't stand being cooped up. And you should *see* some of the places we've been. I just want to go home! It's not fair."

The buildings right across the street were about level with them. But if anyone looked over, they would only see two people having a conversation. Somebody might wonder why Margot was in her bathrobe, that was all. The one-way traffic on Pine Street was steady and very fast. Between the traffic and the wind, no one would hear them talking. *Oh, God*, Joel thought. *I need help.*

"I wish I could just *do* it," she said. "If I could just do it then it would all be over." She wrung her hands and he saw that they were ringless. Her engagement ring—*she* had stuck it in Melanie's purse. Danny had brought Melanie's purse back to Margot and Rosa, the first time they hid out at Aurora Place, right after killing her. Strangling her. Joel's throat tightened. He felt for his tie, to loosen it. What if he shouted *Help me, somebody*? But that would scare her. He had to stay calm. If only it wasn't so fucking windy. Where was Denise, for God's sake? Where was Rosa, the one fucking time he ever wanted her?

"I thought if you got here it would be easy," Margot said. "I'd see you and I'd know even you couldn't help me and then one quick jump and it's *over*. Melanie's dead, so it's like—it's like it can really happen, it can't be that bad."

"Did you know I was looking for you?" *A conversation, yes, get her interested in a conversation.* He took his glasses off and started cleaning them with his handkerchief. Casually. But quickly.

"Betty chatters about you all the time. Ted was right. She *is* Looney Tunes. I figured she would have let enough slip by now that you'd have found me. It took you longer than I thought it would, though."

Joel put his glasses back on, and saw her for the first time all over again. And knew he didn't love her. The loss hit him like the next gust of wind, and then there was a fainter gust of relief. *Stop her, damn it!* He couldn't let himself think of anything else. "I'm not as clever as you are."

"I'm fucked up, is what I am."

If he edged just so slowly forward, would she notice? She didn't *want* to do it. For one thing, it would be so messy. Men didn't mind that—they'd splatter their brains like so much spaghetti sauce across the walls of bathrooms. Women liked pills and clean nightgowns. No, she'd *never* go through with it. She was just frightened. He could probably pick her up and carry her in.

But what if he was wrong? What if, when he moved closer . . . *It couldn't happen. But it could.*

"I bet you think I didn't want to kill her. Well, I did. I thought we could get away with it. We had a whole plan, Rosa and I, and it was going to look as if she gassed herself in the Jaguar, in the garage. We had a note written out for the police to find. But she got away. She got away in my car—*my car*, the—the scummy bitch."

"But it was Rosa's idea." He stated it as fact. He wanted it to be true, and if it wasn't—well, he'd make *Margot* think it was true, just so she'd come inside.

"What?" Margot flattened her hand against her chest, feigning surprise. "Don't you think I could think of something like that? Give me some credit! All right now, I admit it—*Rosa* planned the part about the note. But I told Melanie to come over. I told her—you'll like this, Doctor—that we were going to talk about Ted woman-to-woman. And she believed me!"

"You're taking more blame than you should." He was trying to convince them both. "Because you feel guilty."

"No, Doctor. Rosa and I had it all set up. Danny was going to help us. See, I thought up the part about the car and turning on the engine and everything. I even *got* her in the car." Margot's hands fluttered, somehow capturing the motion of all of them moving into the garage. "I told her we were going to take a drive. It's just that she figured out what we were up to, and she *got away.*" Margot laughed her delighted party laugh, then gulped down a moan, and her hands fell, like sparrows shot from the sky.

"So you sent Danny after her." Joel spoke the thought aloud.

Her head drooped. "That's right." Then she raised her chin. "He brought back her purse." Suddenly she raised her voice at him, "Nobody ever cheated on you. You can't imagine how it feels."

"Margot," he tried, "I know you're hurting more than I could ever imagine."

"She came to see you, didn't she? Did you think she was prettier than I am?"

"Not half as pretty as you. Not a twentieth." He meant it. "Margot, come inside for my sake."

"Your sake?" She laughed. "You have an ego the size of Kansas, did you know that? None of this would have happened if it hadn't been for you! It's your fault!" And she started to cry, as if finally settling down to a long-overdue chore.

How can you say that? You used me! Don't think of that. It would be so natural to just put his arms around her now, surely she wanted him to hold her.

But as his foot slid forward she raised her head and glared at him. "Just stop right there! You always had such a crush on me, didn't you? Always acted as though you'd do anything for me. Fat fucking lot of good it did me!"

Joel heard a siren, just a few blocks away. Fire truck? Ambulance? Who needed help more than he did right now? *Over here, folks!* How had he gotten Betty to come inside? He couldn't remember.

"Then I wanted you to go to Carmel and you wouldn't." Choking sobs now.

"But I—I didn't know. If you had told me—" If she had told him what? What would that have changed? Forget that now—just get her to come inside! Margot's mother—the suicide in the car— Margot had wanted to kill Melanie the same way Margot's mother—oh shit, he said to the analyst inside his head, shut the hell up!

"If you'd—gone with me—that afternoon, I would have let Ted have—the stupid twat," she wept. "Then no one would have felt sorry for me. They wouldn't have been able to tell whether I left him or he left me."

"I wanted to go with you!" Joel protested. "I told you I did. We could have gone the very next day!"

"And I l-l-loved you." Whimpering now. "I realized I loved you when I found out that Ted was—that bastard. Then you rejected me, too." Suddenly the tears were all gone. She looked at him. "So of course I got a little carried away, I mean, I just went crazy. You understand, don't you?"

Goddamn Denise—she was probably in bed eating *rémoulade!*

"Yes, of course I understand." His tongue stuck to the roof of his mouth when he spoke.

"It's really okay, then, if you understand." Margot leaned back, placing her hands on the fence. "If you understand, you can explain to everyone."

"That's right," he agreed soothingly. "We'll just explain."

"We'll go to the police together." She sounded eager, the way she did when she was scheming to hit up some young investment banker for a contribution to Playground. "You'll help me explain. *You're* good at that. I heard that Melanie's parents were in town. They're probably relieved to be rid of her—she was such a stupid bitch. She was nobody, and I'm—I'm . . . I wish my daddy were here, *he'd* get me out of this. . . ."

Joel was afraid that if he had to run to catch her he wouldn't be able to, because his thighs and knees and calves felt so heavy.

"And I can always give them money." Margot was rubbing her hands on the sides of her terry-cloth robe. "Yes. Yes." She nodded. "I'll just give them a lot of money, and they'll be happy."

"I'm sure we can work something out," Joel said.

"Melanie went to see you once, didn't she?" Margot rubbed her hands together. "Did you think she was pretty?"

"No," Joel said.

"Everyone will understand once we explain." Suddenly Margot clutched handfuls of her hair. Her eyes were wide. "Oh, God, what am I thinking? *They're going to put me away.*" It was said in a whisper. He could barely hear it over the cars below them. Behind her, the moon looked whiter against the darkening sky. "It doesn't matter how rich I am. I can't get out of this." She looked over her shoulder. "I wish I could just *do* it! I could do it and it wouldn't last that long and then it would all be over. I ran up here when I knew you were coming. I told them to tell me if you checked in. I knew you'd come." A look of triumph passed over her face but vanished quickly.

"So many people love you, Margot. Think what you'd do to them."

"Hah. Do you love me? Do you—*Doctor?*"

"Yes," he lied. If she hadn't disappeared when she had, if he had gone to Carmel with her, it wouldn't have taken him more than a few days to find out that he didn't. Wait a second. "Margot—we can still go to Carmel. We can go tonight. Nobody knows yet. Nobody knows I'm here. Nobody knows what happened to Melanie but me and you—and Rosa." Rosa must have seen her last chance to get away and taken it. He had been right about her, anyway—her devotion to Margot had reached its limit. "Come on," he said. "We'll sneak out now. We'll go to Carmel."

She moistened her lips with her tongue. "No," she said. "They'll find us there."

Whoooosh. Another gust of wind. He had no strength left. The next one would knock him over. He would have to chance it, rush toward her, grab her, drag her in, or it would be too late.

He must have started moving closer to her unconsciously, because she flattened herself against the fence. "I mean it—don't come near me! You think I want to be the laughingstock of San Francisco?" She did Scarlett again: "Ah do declare, Margot Harvey's back, even after her husband ran off with that white trash nobody!" Furious now: "I wish she were here so I could kill her again! Do you know what she said when she was at my house? She said that Ted was going to give her *my* jewelry. She tried to take my ring." Margot shrieked, stabbing at her chest with her fingers, "*My* ring! I couldn't stand to *touch* it after that! I let her have the ring, all right." Cold now: "So don't come near me. I'm not that lunatic Betty. *She* thinks you're wonderful. Everyone thinks you're wonderful. Well, I don't. You probably wanted to fuck Melanie, too."

"Margot, you know that's not true." *Why didn't I have Denise call the police? She probably thinks that Margot and I are up here having sex! Help me, somebody—God, Mommy, Daddy, Dr. Schneider!*

Margot looked at her hands. "She was ugly. Her hair was bleached. She needed orthodontia. She had big, thick fingers."

"I loved *you*," Joel begged.

Margot pressed her palms against her temples and tilted back her head. Now there was moonlight enough to fall on her face, but it was getting harder for Joel to see. "She *was* prettier than I am."

"Margot, you still have so much to live for."

"Like *what*?"

"Like . . ." Oh, God, Joel, think fast. Invent the meaning of life! Like what? She couldn't go back to Ted—Mrs. Stone had already taken the snapshots down at Playground—Playground . . . the kids . . . wait! "Margot—what about a baby? You can still have a baby. I know you want that."

Her lips parted quickly, as if he had sliced them open.

"Melanie wasn't pregnant," Joel said. "She just told Ted she was. She lied. She wasn't pregnant."

Margot sucked in on her lower lip, then bit down hard. "You're just saying that."

"No, I'm not. It would have shown up on the autopsy, wouldn't it?" Another gust of wind; but he stood strong against it.

"Maybe they missed it." She spoke more softly; he could hardly hear her. "Maybe they covered it up."

"No—Melanie *told* me." A lie the size of an Excedrin headache. "She told me that she wasn't really pregnant."

"You swear?" she demanded.

He raised his right hand, brought out the same smile he had used on Chuck in his kitchen, on Denise in the café. "I swear." A lie, then. But a lie that might be close to the truth. He could live with that. He'd have to.

"Maybe I still can't . . ." She wanted to be reassured. She wanted him to promise. Then she'd *know* he was lying.

"But maybe you *can*," he insisted. "It still could be Ted's fault."

"I don't believe you." But her voice was different. It was almost . . . normal.

"Don't you want to find out?" He held his hand out to her. "Come on. You must be freezing."

She thoughtfully tightened the belt of her robe, then wrapped the ends around her hands. "It *is* sort of cold," she admitted. Then she took a few tottering steps in his direction.

EPILOGUE

WORKING THROUGH

Joel and Denise sat sideways on her porch, looking out toward the East Bay. The sun was just disappearing behind them. In the flashing, refracted light of its death, the waters of the bay shone turquoise and the windows of Berkeley glowed like tiny fires.

"Isn't this romantic?" Denise asked.

Joel winced. The word made him nervous; definitely a Pavlovian response. He wasn't against romance; it was just that he liked to think of it in a short-term way, as in: for the duration of this sunset. Denise, on the other hand, probably thought that fixed-rate, nonassumable mortgages were second only to life insurance policies on the Richter scale of romance.

"Will Margot go to prison, do you think?" Denise asked. "I suppose it could be a growth experience, but still, when you really *imagine* it . . ."

Three days had passed since Margot had come down from the Aurora Place roof garden with Joel. It had been her own idea to turn herself in. The police had caught up with Rosa at the airport just a few hours later, carrying two fake passports (one for herself and one intended for Margot), which Chuck had apparently obtained for her. Danny was finally located the following morning: wandering, lost, in the Tenderloin, where Rosa had abandoned him.

"My guess," Joel said to Denise now, "is that Margot will plead temporarily insane-with-jealousy and spend some time at the Silverado Lake Women's Correctional Facility and Tennis Club."

Easier to joke about it than, as Denise had said, to really imagine it. Most of the time Joel just wanted to forget, but all the media coverage wasn't helping. Cousin Frank had let Margot know that she had to give the *Courier* exclusive interviews or he would publish a few things that even the *Deliverer* hadn't dug up. The *Deliverer* had already interviewed many of the Harveys' inner circle, most of whom were eager to pass on dubious gossip. Merlin Davis, the former houseboy, actually had one of the more plausible tales, about how Ted liked to get drunk and run through the house naked except for a Richard Nixon mask.

Two AM radio stations had devoted call-in shows to the scandal, during which listeners aired their views on adultery, murder, and the corrupting power of money. One program had been hosted by a psychologist.

Joel sometimes overheard people discussing Ted and Margot on the street, referring to them by their first names only. But this was everyone's story, the way the Giants were everyone's team when they went to the playoffs.

Joel had been lucky: His name had slipped by, mentioned only in the middle of a paragraph somewhere, as the family friend to whom Margot had come when she was ready to go to the police. Nothing was said about the roof. Joel didn't return reporters' phone calls, and he had also avoided them by changing his running routes and by sleeping at Denise's.

Otherwise he'd gone back to his daily routines. He had seen Betty, who was sorry to lose her decorating assignment, but delighted to fill Joel in on the series of secret meetings Margot had arranged for them during her period of hiding. Betty kept her voice to a whisper as she described how Margot had first contacted her, leaving brief messages on her machine—and then went on to tell how Rosa had chauffeured her at midnight, in different rented cars, to Guerrero Street or to Aurora Place. Spying is what paranoids do best, after all.

And, Betty being Betty, if she had revealed Margot's hiding place, who would have believed her?

"But I'm glad it's over," Betty had sighed, then observed of Margot, "She's a troubled woman."

Andrea had sullenly reported to Joel that her father was letting it be known in the right circles that he would be willing to defend Margot. Grisly Griswald rarely did criminal work, but he made exceptions for trials that would get enough publicity. "You might even get a call from the old ambulance-chaser," she warned. "He'll be sucking up to you now, if he thinks you can get him in with her."

She grumbled on, "I can't believe he's doing this to me! Just when I was starting to come to terms with the accident, and with you knowing Margot and everything."

She only briefly mentioned that her first exam grades were back and that they were good. Joel had not commented, but tucked the information away carefully, like a cryptic note, for later study.

"You know," Denise said now, "good things *have* come out of this."

"H'm." Joel was still thinking of Andrea; feeling optimistic about her.

"Ted's stopped drinking, hasn't he?"

"It's only been two days," Joel pointed out. "That's not exactly a world's record."

Margot, free on her own recognizance, had returned to the Seacliff house and promptly evicted Ted. Then she held a press conference at the St. Francis Hotel, during which she announced her intention to start raising money to build an orphans' home in San Salvador. "The best way to take your mind off your troubles is by helping others," she had said, "and who needs our help more than the children of the world?"

At a separate press conference, at the Parc 55 Hotel, Ted had rebutted Merlin's charges and announced that he was now a *recovering* alcoholic, "through the help of God."

It was part of Joel's job to believe that people changed. Perhaps Margot's return, perhaps her finally kicking him out, or perhaps the fact that Margot needed *Ted* for a change, had been the inspiration that Ted had needed. But the announcement sounded phony to Joel; he suspected Ted's new lawyer had staged it, as a hedge against any unwelcome facts that might surface in the future.

And Joel suspected, too, that Ted would find his way back, one way or another, both to Seacliff and down the long neck of a bottle of Stolichnaya.

Denise sighed. "My place is *so* cramped." She drew her knees up and hugged them. "It's big enough for me, but—I mean, I've been thinking of looking for another place. Larger."

Fuh-lump went Joel's heart. But in spite of the anxiety army performing maneuvers in his intestinal tract, he put his arm around her. She immediately snuggled up to him, wrapping her own arms around his chest. "You don't love her anymore," she said. "I know you don't."

"No, I don't." Joel watched the little fires in the windows of Berkeley winking off, like birthday candles blown out one by one. He jostled her shoulder and teased, "But don't get any ideas."

"Who, me?" Mock innocence. "Ideas?" Then she chuckled. "I just want you to know that you'll never get away now."

"Let's not rush into anything," he said, but he noticed that he could still breathe while he said it.

"Mmmm." She leaned closer against him. How neat and perfect she felt under his arm! He was aware of the contours of her body, and surprised by how they seemed to mold to his, so that the curvy line that separated them resembled the border between two interlocking puzzle pieces. Joel looked up. The fading blue sky, in this hour cheated from night, was cloudless, and from where they sat it seemed that they could see all of it, and that he and Denise were the last two pieces stuck into the puzzle which comprised the whole of the earth.